PRAISE FOR
CAROLINE B. COONEY

PRAISE FOR *BEFORE SHE WAS HELEN*

"[M]ore Columbo than Miss Marple… A fine mystery."

—*Booklist*

"Caroline B. Cooney is a master of taking a small, common moment—seeing a face on a milk carton, posting a harmless photo—and turning that moment into a thrilling story. In this mystery, Cooney gives us Clemmie, a senior citizen living a long deception, who fights back with intelligence and courage against dangerous foes, both present and past. *Before She Was Helen* is an emotionally rich page-turner about the lives we want—and the lives we make."

—Jeff Abbott, *New York Times* bestselling author of *Never Ask Me*

"As *Before She Was Helen* opens, readers are drawn into what appears to be a light, retirement-community caper. But author Caroline B. Cooney quickly flips expectations upside down in this deceptively dark mystery. Between old crimes and fresh murders, septuagenarian protagonist Clemmie faces an unspeakable fear that will keep readers hooked in this twisty whodunit."

—Julie Hyzy, *New York Times* bestselling author

"Caroline B. Cooney has a genius for skewering culture, crime, and society. As once she demonstrated to the world a pressing level of danger we needed to understand, now she whips millennial angst,

W9-AAA-966

recreational drug use, and one feisty, heroic retiree into a thrilling, toxic brew that will leave readers cheering by the end. Retirement villages never seemed so mysterious and exciting! Under Cooney's deft hand, hidden dangers emerge, and the ties that bind us, young and old, just may save us in the end."

—Jenny Milchman, *USA Today* bestselling author of *Cover of Snow* and *Wicked River*

"Caroline B. Cooney's *Before She Was Helen* is a clever whodunit featuring an immensely likable septuagenarian heroine with a tragic past. Cooney is deft at weaving together the mysteries of a fifty-year-old cold case murder and a still-warm body at a retirement community, slowly unveiling a slew of possible motives and suspects for both crimes. Loaded with action, fast-paced, and offering a series of emotional punches, this book will leave mystery lovers wanting more."

—Carter Wilson, *USA Today* bestselling author of *The Dead Girl in 2A* and *Mister Tender's Girl*

PRAISE FOR *THE FACE ON THE MILK CARTON*

"Absorbing and convincing. Strong characterizations and suspenseful, impeccably paced action add to this novel's appeal."

—*Publishers Weekly*

"A real page-turner."

—*Kirkus Reviews*

"It's a gripper. You can't put it down until you've gone through the whole trauma with Janie Johnson, from that first moment of horrified recognition to the thoroughly satisfying conclusion."

—*Entertainment Weekly*

PRAISE FOR *THE RANSOM OF MERCY CARTER*

"Gripping and thought provoking."

—*Publishers Weekly*

PRAISE FOR *WHATEVER HAPPENED TO JANIE?*

"The power and nature of love is wrenchingly illustrated throughout this provocative novel… The emotions of its characters remain excruciatingly real."

—*Publishers Weekly,* Starred Review

"The gut-wrenching circumstances in which the characters find themselves are honestly conveyed."

—*Booklist*

PRAISE FOR *THE VOICE ON THE RADIO*

"Cooney's outstanding command of emotional tension has taken this novel to extraordinary heights."

—*School Library Journal,* Starred Review

ALSO BY CAROLINE B. COONEY

BEFORE SHE WAS HELEN

CAROLINE B. COONEY

Poisoned Pen
PRESS

Published by Poisoned Pen Press, an imprint of Sourcebooks
P.O. Box 4410, Naperville, Illinois 60567-4410
(630) 961-3900
sourcebooks.com

The Library of Congress has catalogued the hardcover edition as follows:

Names: Cooney, Caroline B., author.
Title: Before she was Helen / Caroline B. Cooney.
Description: Naperville : Poisoned Pen Press, [2020] | Summary: "Clementine
    Lakefield leads a simple life in her retirement community in Sun City,
    South Carolina. But while she plays cards, substitute teaches, and has
    learned to text with her niece and nephew, Clemmie is not who she says
    she is. Behind her carefree facade, she is hiding a lifetime of secrets.
    When Clemmie's curmudgeonly neighbor goes missing, Clemmie suddenly
    finds herself at the center of a dangerous conspiracy."-- Provided by
    publisher.
Identifiers: LCCN 2019025516 | (hardcover)
Subjects: GSAFD: Mystery fiction.
Classification: LCC PS3553.O578 B44 2020 | DDC 813/.54--dc23
LC record available at https://lccn.loc.gov/2019025516

Printed and bound in Canada.
MBP 10 9 8 7 6 5 4 3 2 1

ONE

Before she did anything else today, Clemmie had to check up on her next-door neighbor, Dom.

Why Dom had moved to Sun City was not clear. He had never joined anything, attended anything, nor shown interest in anything. He just sat in his villa watching TV, playing video games, and smoking cigarettes. He owned the tiniest of the three attached villas, the one in the middle with no side windows and little sun.

Clemmie lived on the left, and a couple she hardly ever saw owned the right-hand villa, using it as a hotel when they visited grandchildren in the area. When they arrived, which was infrequently, they used their automatic garage-door opener, drove in, closed the garage door behind them, and that was that. Nobody ever spotted them again. Clemmie wasn't sure she'd even recognize them.

It was agreed that Clemmie had the least rewarding neighbors in Sun City.

Luckily, in her pod—the slightly creepy collective noun Sun City used instead of *neighborhood*—the little villas were tucked close together in heavily landscaped culs-de-sac, so Clemmie knew all her other neighbors—wonderful friendly people who hosted outdoor barbecues and took her bowling and carpooled when everybody went to a Panthers game. Clemmie knew nothing about football, but she was following the Panthers now because everybody else did, and Sun City was all about doing what everybody else did.

Dom lived alone, and when he'd fallen last year, it took him a day and a half to crawl to his cell phone and summon help, so now he texted Clemmie every morning to let her know he was fine. She'd text back something cheerful like "Have a good day then!" although she found it hard to believe that Dom ever had a good day, since his only friends were the hosts of hostile political talk shows.

But this morning, Dom had not texted, nor did he answer her text, and then he didn't answer her phone call either. In spite of his COPD and arthritis, swollen ankles and weird splotchy complexion, not to mention all the beer he drank, plus still smoking in spite of his lung problems, Dom was actually in fairly good health. Still. Something must have happened.

He'd given Clemmie a key to his villa for emergencies, after first extracting a promise not to tell anybody she had his key. It was not unusual for old people to get paranoid, so Clemmie did promise, but in fact, everybody would assume that Clemmie had a key, because you always gave your neighbor a key. Well, Clemmie certainly hadn't given Dom one. The last person she would want in her unit or checking on her health was Dominic Spesante. Her across-the-street neighbors, Joyce and Johnny, had her key.

Clemmie so didn't want to go next door and find Dom dead. Or what if he had the flu, and she ended up taking him to the doctor's and picking up his prescriptions and buying his groceries and probably catching the flu herself? Although, of course, she had had her flu shot, and it wasn't flu season anymore anyway, but it would be just like Dom to have a bug not warded off by last fall's injection.

It wasn't that Clemmie was ungenerous. She loved to do things for other people—just not for Dom, who had no personality unless he was swearing, and then he had a regrettable personality.

Clemmie sighed, opened her front door, gasped at the South Carolina heat even at nine in the morning, crossed her tiny front lawn to Dom's, and rang his bell.

There was no answer.

She knocked hard on the glass part of the door. She couldn't peek in because Dom had installed blinds over the glass. Still no answer.

Clemmie considered crossing the street and getting Joyce or Johnny to go into Dom's with her. Joyce and Johnny were in their seventies and not married but living together. They loved to say that. "We're shacking up," they would whisper, giggling.

Joyce's children were not okay with her decision to have a live-in boyfriend. The Oregon daughter thought Joyce should have moved to Oregon, and the New Hampshire son thought Joyce should have moved to New Hampshire. Joyce said her children just wanted free babysitters, and that was not what she was doing this decade.

Johnny believed that his children didn't even know about Joyce because he had kept his own Sun City house, which was half a mile away, and even kept the cleaning lady who still came every other Tuesday afternoon, and when anybody in his family visited, he just moved back in. Deception was easier than dealing with children still furious that Johnny had divorced their mother after forty-nine years of marriage, just prior to the big fiftieth anniversary party they had planned. Johnny's ex-wife in Maryland was not doing well, still shocked at what had happened to her, and the children rightly held Johnny responsible. He wasn't about to tell them that the move to Sun City and acquiring a new woman were the best things that had ever happened to him.

But Joyce would refuse to come if Clemmie asked her to go inside Dom's. He was too creepy for her, and anyway, Joyce would be getting ready for their card game. She and Clemmie loved canasta, which they played twice a week at the clubhouse. The clubhouse was what turned Sun City into a magic kingdom; you just walked in and joined anything you felt like: poker, mah-jongg, pottery, table tennis, acoustic guitar jams, wine-tasting groups, Ohio State fans. Right now, Joyce would be choosing a complex outfit and accessories and fixing her face, having already blown dry and curled her hair. As for Johnny, he played pickleball today and was probably already gone.

Reluctantly, Clemmie inserted the key into Dom Spesante's front door. Don't be dead, she warned Dom silently.

Her own unit was sunny and delightful, but Dom's, having no side windows, was dark and unwelcoming. She poked her head in the door, sniffed the odd musty odor, and called, "Dominic! It's me, Helen. Are you okay?"

There was no answer.

Clemmie took a single step forward. She had never been inside Dom's, since she wholly agreed with Joyce that he was a creep, but she'd been in plenty of other middle units, so she knew exactly what the layout was. The miniature front hall was adjacent to the kitchen, dark in spite of the street-facing window in its tiny breakfast area because it did not get the morning sun. It featured white cabinets, a white counter, and white appliances, because Dom had not opted for the upgrades of granite and stainless steel.

"Dom!"

No answer. She peeked in the kitchen to see if Dom had fallen on the floor.

Dom's counter held a Keurig coffee maker, boxes of coffee pods, picnic-style cardboard salt and pepper shakers, and paper napkins still in their cellophane wrap. The dishwasher door hung open, revealing a few plates and glasses.

Dom had not bothered to buy a table for the breakfast nook,

opting for a stool tucked under the tiny counter, although Clemmie was pretty sure that he actually ate every meal in front of his television, with his plate or his takeout in his lap.

He had no car, because the severe arthritis in his knees and ankles made it hard to accelerate or brake, but he did have a golf cart. A large, spiffy grocery store sat conveniently in the strip mall adjacent to Sun City, and since it could be reached by interior paved paths, golf carts never had to use a regular road and fight the cars. There were also a pharmacy, a bank, and a cut-rate hair salon in the strip. Clemmie doubted if Dom ever went to the library branch or the expensive gift shop, but there were four fast-food restaurants, so he could rotate Asian food, hamburgers, pizza, and barbecue. He tootled over once or twice a day and, no matter how hot it might be, kept the plastic sides of his golf-cart cover zipped, so he could be seen only in a blurry sort of way. It was a wonder he hadn't cooked in there.

Dom never accepted invitations to neighborhood cookouts and card parties. Friday evenings in their pod meant a cocktail party in somebody's driveway—to which you brought your own folding chair and drink, and Clemmie loved how convivial and easy it was—but Dom didn't participate.

She breathed through her mouth to avoid the smell, which was probably just the odor of musty old man but seemed more pervasive, more pungent.

The kitchen and hall opened into the living-dining room, very dark because Dom kept the heavy drapes closed. Clemmie almost never covered her own sliding glass doors because she loved to look out on her tiny screened porch and the trees beyond. She turned on Dom's ceiling light, and the ceiling fan also came on, slowly rotating, the only thing alive in the whole place.

A brown recliner and a tan sofa faced a huge television fastened above the gas fireplace, where the pilot light provided a blue flicker. A floor lamp stood next to a substantial coffee table, on which lay empty pizza boxes, a charger but no device, the TV remote, and an old-fashioned heavy, glass triangle ashtray, half full. There was no body sprawled on the floor, however, which was good.

"Dom! It's me, Helen!"

No answer.

The guest room was closest, so she poked her head in. It was a tiny space with a twin bed, made up as if somebody actually stayed overnight now and then. The poor guest had no bedside table, no lamp, and no dresser. It couldn't be for Wilson, the only relative and, in fact, the only visitor Clemmie had met, because Wilson didn't usually stay more than an hour. Clemmie gave him full credit for that hour, however, because she could hardly be around Dom for five minutes.

Clemmie forced herself into the master bedroom and found the king-size bed unmade, wrinkled, and empty. The print of Dom's curled-up body was overly intimate. The size of the bed was overly intimate too, because it implied that Dom sometimes shared it.

Dom was also not unconscious on the floor of his walk-in closet or bathroom.

It dawned on Clemmie that he had simply gone out on his golf cart and forgotten to text her, though why he wouldn't answer his cell phone, she didn't know. Perhaps he couldn't hear it. Perhaps he was going deaf and didn't even know because he so rarely spoke to or listened to other people. With his friend the television, he could just keep upping the volume.

She walked through the back hall, exactly large enough to hold a washer and a dryer and be called a laundry room, and opened the door to the windowless garage. She flicked on the overhead light.

All garages in Sun City held two cars, but Dom had only his golf cart. Even his doctors were in the medical building between the library and the grocery. If he needed to go farther afield, he waited for Wilson.

Wilson was part of that crowd of young people with last names for first names, like her own grandnephew and grandniece, Bentley and Harper, which sounded like a law firm. Whatever happened to the sweet girl names? The cuddly ones ending in *y* or *ie*? Nobody nowadays was named Connie or Nancy or Janie.

She wasn't sure how Wilson was related to Dom. Not a son, certainly, because he didn't call Dom "Dad." Wilson was not particularly attentive. Not that Clemmie's young relatives were attentive. She texted them every week or two so they'd remember she was alive.

To her relief, Dom's garage was empty, which meant he was okay; he'd just gone shopping.

In fact, his garage was remarkably empty.

Most people moved here with tons of stuff from previously acquisitive lives and then installed garage storage shelves on which dozens of cardboard boxes and plastic containers rested, full of memorabilia, Christmas decorations, extra china, former hobbies, seasonal clothing, and the million other things they refused to part with. Some men packed their garages with tools for woodworking or plumbing. Many garages were so full of stuff the owners couldn't fit in one car, let alone two, and had to rent storage units in one of the massive facilities along the highway.

Dom's garage held his garbage wheelie, his recycling container, a broom, and to her amazement, an interior door. Not the door in which she now stood, which connected Dom's garage to his house, but a door cut through the far side of his garage, which could only open into the adjoining garage of the third unit—the one belonging to the couple she never saw.

All these times she'd thought Dom sat home alone… Had he actually zipped through his secret door and hustled over to eat with that couple, and they all hid behind closed drapes so nobody would know that Dom actually had friends?

A thousand things were prohibited in Sun City. Sheds. Excess front-garden decorations. Doors painted colors other than black. Fences not approved by the landscape committee. More than two bird feeders. It was surely prohibited to cut a door between yourself and your neighbor. The door was oddly placed, because the bottom of the door was not level with the floor, but up six or eight inches, probably to avoid damaging interior wires or pipes, although what wires and pipes might be channeled along the garage floor she didn't know. Normal, non–Sun City garages often had side doors, but there was no such variation on the Sun City housing and garage scheme. And yet she had never noticed this. A door in a garage is so acceptable that the eye does not analyze its presence.

Clemmie went carefully down the two steps from Dom's utility room (carefully because of her fear of falling) and into his garage, walked over to the peculiar door, and tested the knob.

It wasn't locked. Paranoid Dom didn't lock his custom-made exit?

She didn't think the people on the other side were here, but if they were, perhaps Dom was visiting them right now. But no, since his golf cart was gone, he was also gone.

She couldn't think of their name. It was probably a year since she'd even waved at them. Forgetting names was a constant in Sun City, a precursor to senility, and everybody was quick to comfort each other: *Oh, I always forget names!* friends would cry.

Clemmie went back into Dom's house, out his front door, across his tiny strip of grass, and under the little front door overhang of the third unit. Marcia and Roy Cogland, she remembered, relieved. People hadn't named their children Marcia or Roy in decades. It dated them. Nobody had *ever* named a daughter Clementine, so Clemmie's name was both rare and dated. She rang the bell.

If they came to the door, she'd ask if they'd seen Dom today.

But nothing and no one inside stirred.

She rang again, and then a third time, and if they did come to the door after all and asked why she was so persistent, she'd say, *I thought Dom was here, and he's very deaf, you know.*

Since the living rooms of Sun City houses opened onto backyards, not front yards, any residents who were up and about were almost certainly not facing the street. And because everybody here had invested heavily in drapes, plantation shutters, shades, and curtains, the three units across Blue Lilac, which were oriented to the east, kept their single front window covered in the morning. It was highly unlikely that anybody had spotted Clemmie's perfectly ordinary activity of ringing a neighbor's front doorbell.

Clemmie went back into Dom's, surprised and embarrassed by how much she wanted to open that connecting door.

It would be breaking and entering, she thought. Well, no, it isn't breaking, because the door is unlocked. It's just entering. And I have a reason. I'm checking on Dom. And if they say, "But you knew his golf cart wasn't there, so you also knew he was out," I say, "Oh goodness, I just didn't add that up."

You never commit crimes or misdemeanors, she told herself. You never even think of them. Do not trespass. Besides, the only thing on the other side of that door is another garage.

Which would be less of a trespass: she wasn't going into Marcia and Roy's actual house.

What if Dom came back on his golf cart just as she was peeking through his illegal door? She decided that she would hear him in time to skitter back to his house, although golf carts were very quiet and she probably wouldn't, plus she was a little too rickety for skittering anyhow.

She told herself she would just peek, not put a foot on the other side of the high and somewhat dangerous threshold, if you forgot it was there and tripped.

She opened the unexpected door.

The light from Dom's garage illuminated very little in the Cogland garage, but Clemmie was never without her cell phone. Really, it was quite amazing that her first six decades had been accomplished without one: that she had once done library research instead of Googling, had owned a camera, had kept up with correspondence on carefully chosen letter paper. Who knew that a more satisfying telephone life—in fact, a more satisfying life in general— lay waiting inside a flat, slim rectangle of technology?

Clemmie turned on the flashlight of her iPhone.

The Cogland garage, its single exterior window covered by closed blinds, was literally empty. It didn't even have the required garbage wheelie and recycle container. But that meant nothing, because the Coglands were here so rarely. They probably carried their garbage out with them, since garbage was picked up only once a week, and they wouldn't be here to bring the containers back inside, and it was a definite Sun City no-no to allow your trash container to linger at the curb.

A dozen steps across the garage was the door that would open into the Coglands' utility room which, like the entire unit, would be the same as her own villa, just reversed.

Since most people left home through their garage, not through their front door, they generally locked their house by lowering the garage door, and as a rule, they didn't bother to lock the interior door. Clemmie stepped over the raised threshold of the illegal connector door, tiptoed across the garage as if somebody might hear her, and fingered the knob of the Coglands' utility-room door.

It turned.

Go home, she ordered herself, and instead, she stepped into the Coglands' house.

Two

The Cogland utility room was as empty as the garage: every cabinet door closed, no clothes basket near the washer and dryer, not even a jug of detergent on the shelf.

A dozen more steps, and Clemmie stood in an utterly bare kitchen. No coffee maker, blender, or toaster sat on the counter. No salt and pepper shakers. The stove gleamed as if it had never seen a pot or pan.

It was hot in the villa, but not humid. They must have had their air-conditioning set to come on now and then to keep mold from developing, but not really cool the house.

In the living area, the sparse, bland furniture looked rented. There were no books, magazines, bowls, vases, or throw pillows. The flat-white walls were not disturbed by a single picture. There was not a television.

They really did use this place as a motel. They didn't fix meals and they didn't hang out, which made the connecting door even more puzzling. What were the Coglands and Dom getting together for?

And then perhaps the sun outside emerged from behind a cloud, because a prism of color suddenly danced on one bare white wall.

Clemmie moved into the living area to see what had caused the rainbow, and there, sitting on a tiny round table in front of the sliding doors, was a glass sculpture like nothing she had ever seen. It was both a tree and a dragon, its tail curving like a powerful whip, its spine and claws also tree leaves on fire. It was a fabulous piece, organic and elegant, emerald green with spurts of gleaming red and gold. It was complex, with an arch of glass that could be a handle and another that could be a spout as well as the dragon's head.

She was dazzled by the tree dragon's beauty. She stared at it, circling, seeing it at every angle, and then, reminded by the weight of her cell phone in her hand, took a photograph before she headed back into the Coglands' garage. Stepping carefully over the illegal door's threshold, she turned to snap a picture of that too, so she could share this weird story with Joyce and Johnny. Then she went back into Dom's house, leaving all doors unlocked, just as they had been, left by his front door, and locked that behind her with the key he'd given her.

Clemmie was exhilarated. Snooping in a neighbor's garage was, sadly, probably the definition of adventure for a semiretired Latin teacher. It was also sleazy. Perhaps she would not tell Joyce and Johnny after all.

She puzzled over the connecting door. If Dom didn't want to be seen going to the Coglands', why not go out his sliders? The three attached villas backed onto a deep woods (well, deep for a highly developed area; probably fifty feet) so there was no one from that direction to see. Hollies had been planted between each tiny patio, now grown so tall and dense that even if Clemmie were sitting outside, she would not see her neighbors' movements. But Clemmie never sat outside, because her unit had a small, rectangular screened porch set into the building, and if she wanted fresh air, she sat there, and had no view of anything ever at Dom's.

Perhaps Dom was having an affair with Marcia. Perhaps Roy didn't come most of the time and only Marcia came, and she and Dom had become a hot ticket. Fat, grubby, whiny, smelly, lurching Dom? Surely Marcia could do better. Besides, what kind of affair was only two or three times a year?

Clemmie giggled to herself, looked down at her cell phone, and admired her snapshot of the amazing glass tree dragon.

It was crucial to stay connected to her grandnephew and grandniece, or Clemmie would be stranded in old age with absolutely no one. Bentley and Harper were uninterested in her life, which was not surprising, because how excited could people in their twenties be about some old gal's card games? How delightful to have such a cool image to send.

She forwarded the photograph to her other cell phone—her family phone—and from that phone, she sent a group text to the two grands. Attaching the photograph, she wrote, Look at my neighbor's glass sculpture!

Then she studied her to-do list. Every day, she took a fresh page from her Hallmark card shopping pad and wrote down her chores, club meetings, card games, commitments, errands, and grocery list.

Clemmie was still teaching Latin part time at a county high school, so from late August to mid-May, life was satisfying, but over the summer, she could get frightened that her existence had dwindled to card games with strangers. The list gave her something to hang onto.

Of course, her card partners weren't strangers anymore; they were her best friends. But the fact was, people arrived in Sun City without a past and without acquaintances. They set about joining groups and making those friends, but in many cases—certainly in Clemmie's—they never recited a history. "Oh please, too boring," someone might say, and later you'd find out he was a famous cardiologist. "That's so last year," someone else might reply, and then you'd be told that she had been vice president of international affairs for some conglomerate, or else a drugstore clerk.

Clemmie set her mug on the coaster on her coffee table and leaned back on her sofa, both cell phones in hand. Like everyone these days, she used the phone as a pacifier. One stroked one's phone, opening the comforting apps of word games and weather, headline news, and Instagram. It was quite similar to sucking one's thumb.

Her family cell phone sang out the crazy cascade of notes Bentley had installed for her, and indeed it was Bentley, having received her snapshot of the tree dragon. Clemmie was thrilled to hear from him, because Bent had little use for his elderly aunt. If she ever ended up in assisted living or, God forbid, an Alzheimer's ward, Bent was not likely to visit. Cool! he texted. But it isn't a sculpture. It's a rig for smoking pot.

Clemmie's jaw dropped. You smoked a drug out of that gorgeous glass? How? Where did you put your mouth?

Harper texted seconds later. It's beautiful, all right. Your neighbors are serious stoners.

RICH serious stoners, added Bentley.

The one and only piece of decor in Marcia and Roy's entire home was a marijuana rig? She wondered now about the scent in Dom's place. Was it in fact the scent of marijuana?

Clemmie had not led a sheltered life, but pot was not among her experiences. She had read somewhere—she took three newspapers and glanced at headlines from three more on her smartphone—that aging baby boomers had returned to using weed, and it was commonplace all over again.

Clemmie ran her mind over all the men and women she knew from pinochle, euchre, canasta, dominoes, line dancing, water aerobics, book club, pottery, beading, and pickleball, although she no longer played pickleball, having fallen once and twisted an ankle. She considered everybody she knew from Monday-night lectures and Tuesday-morning Bible study. She visualized every other couple and single in her own pod of twenty-one villas. All those people were smoking weed?

Impossible.

And if Dom and the Coglands were using pot, they didn't need a door linking their garages to accomplish it.

Bentley texted again—Bentley, who never sent a birthday or Christmas card or thank-you note. Which neighbor? he asked. The guy with arthritis? It probably helps him feel better.

The guy with arthritis was Dom. She must have bored the grands with a list of Dom's ailments at some point. She wondered if Bent remembered any of *her* complaints, and whether marijuana would actually help Dom's arthritis or just cast a fog over the pain.

She was fixing herself a piece of toast when yet another text arrived. She had never excited her grands this much.

I did an image search on that glass, Bentley wrote. It's stolen. It was made by a lampworker called Borobasq. Go to Instagram and read his posts.

Clemmie's mouth went dry, which happened now and then due to medications, but this time it was horror. The third unit's sole accessory was stolen goods? She had been tiptoeing around leaving fingerprints in a place where neighbors completely unknown to her stored stolen drug paraphernalia?

She had never heard of an image search. Was there an app where you plugged in your snapshot and the app ran around the virtual universe and located identical photographs?

Clemmie tapped her Instagram icon, carefully entered the oddly spelled Borobasq, and sure enough, up popped a picture of the very glass she had seen while trespassing.

This fellow Borobasq, who had an astonishing eighty thousand followers, was in a rage, using many WTF's to describe his predicament. It wasn't clear how the piece had been stolen. Perhaps he had outlined that in an earlier post.

What was clear was that Clemmie's grandnephew, Bentley, had already posted on Borobasq's site: Your rig is sitting on a table in the house next door to my aunt. He had included her photograph of the tree dragon in the shaft of sunlight.

Bentley had involved her in a theft.

Borobasq of the filthy vocabulary now knew that he could find his stolen drug paraphernalia by coming to Clemmie's. The police would be summoned to arrest the thieves. Dom would find out that she had crept through his unit, found his cut-through door, and used it. The Coglands, owners of stolen goods, would find out that she had trespassed in *their* unit, photographed their possessions, and ratted them out.

Dominic Spesante had always sounded to Clemmie like a mob name. A name for somebody who offed people and abandoned their bodies in Jersey swamps. Did she want Dom for an enemy? On the other hand, would mob people name their son Wilson?

But Clemmie was in possession of some strange knowledge. Last year she'd been standing in front of her little villa, wondering whether to grub out a particularly boring foundation shrub and replace it with her favorite bridal wreath spirea, when Dom's garage door opened and out came his golf cart with its harsh backing-up beep. Dom always started lowering his garage door before he was wholly out, so that you always worried that the cart would get caught by the descending door. It occurred to her now that he didn't want anybody to spot his connecting door.

On that particular day, he had not zipped the cart walls up. A gust of wind blew a piece of paper from Dom's hand, or from the seat next to him, into Clemmie's yard.

She reached for it, but it blew further away. She pounced; it eluded her. On the third try, she stepped on it, picked it up, and because she was a compulsive reader, read the address on the envelope.

It was addressed to somebody named Sal Pesante. Very similar to Dom's name, which was Spesante.

S. Pesante.

Was it possible that the name Spesante didn't exist? That it was a condensed initial and real surname? She had been laughing when she handed the envelope back, not because of her uncoordinated leaps over the grass, but because—perhaps—both she and Dom were faking their identities here in quiet, bland Sun City.

"What's so funny?" Dom had snapped.

"Life," she had said.

He glared, gripped the envelope and the wheel at the same time, and drove away. Of course she hadn't told anybody about Dom's possible other name and never would, because she was filled with admiration for anybody who could pull off the trick of living under a false name. She well knew how hard it was.

Her family cell phone rang. An actual call, not a text. The only people with whom she used this phone were her niece, Peggy, who called monthly, and Peggy's children, Harper and Bentley, who never committed actual live conversation.

Clemmie did not recognize the number or area code on the caller ID. But then she didn't know the grands' phone numbers by heart, because she just tapped the little conversation balloon next to their names and typed a text without glancing at the number. And here in Sun City, where people came from all over the country and kept their original cell numbers, any area code could actually be somebody in her own pod. Except nobody down the street possessed the number of her family phone; she gave them her local cell number. The landline was for when she had to give out a number and didn't want to: the newspaper subscription, the plumber. She thought of it as another line of defense.

"Mrs. Lakefield?" asked a male voice she didn't know.

There was no Mrs. Lakefield, so this had to be somebody selling cruises or gutter guards. She used her stock answer, courteous but firm. "I don't purchase anything over the phone, thank you. Please take my name off your calling list."

"I'm not selling anything," said the man quickly. "It's my glass you located, and I'm grateful. Can we talk about how I'm going to get it back?"

Clemmie's eyes felt hollow, as if something had drained away her mind. Bentley had not only posted her photograph; he'd given out her phone number to a total stranger? To a man he knew in advance had, to say the least, a questionable career? Clementine Lakefield never told anybody where she lived, let alone self-proclaimed drug dealers. "I didn't post anything," she told him. "My grandnephew did that."

"And I can't tell you how thankful I am." He had good diction, which mattered to Clemmie. And he knew better than to use a WTF out loud, so he wasn't completely basement quality. "Where are you?" he asked.

"You're a total stranger. I can't tell you anything."

The man's voice became warm and comforting. "You are so right to be careful. I wouldn't want my aunt or grandmother handing out her address to just anybody either."

Makers of drug paraphernalia had grandmothers? Clemmie would never have pictured that.

He said, "I'd like to come and pick up the rig."

Clemmie had not felt this degree of panic in years. She side-stepped. "Why is it called a rig?"

"Well, in this case, because it's used for smoking oil. Marijuana oil. So it is an oil rig, just not petroleum-in-Saudi-Arabia-type oil."

Clemmie had never heard of marijuana being oil. She pictured it as dusty little dried-up mounds. She said faintly, "I thought the glass was just a pretty sculpture. A tree dragon prism. I cannot be involved in this. Please don't call back."

He didn't raise his voice or sound upset but said nicely, "I can see how this is a problem for you, Mrs. Lakefield. Tell you what. I'll call your nephew back, and we'll work something out. Don't you worry about a thing, okay?"

Not worry? When the only way to get the man's glass was to trespass again through a villa that would shortly contain Dom?

She disconnected without saying goodbye, rudeness very rare for Clemmie, and stared at her snapshot. The gleaming tree dragon gave no clue as to how one smoked it, or where you put the oil, or how it was lit, because you couldn't smoke without fire, could you?

Her Sun City cell phone rang with the imperious *rat-a-tat-tat* drum roll she kept meaning to change. Somebody's grandson at the clubhouse had set it up for her, and she hadn't wanted to be rude and tell him she hated his choice.

"Five-minute warning, Helen!" caroled Joyce, who often half sang instead of speaking. Joyce was almost always the driver when they went to the clubhouse for cards. Clemmie gave her usual answer, the one they both understood all too well. "Just let me powder my nose."

There were those who could speak quite graphically about the need to pee frequently, but Clemmie was not among them. She went into the bathroom for her final, never-skipped checkup and found that she was so anxious about the Borobasq call that it was affecting her nether regions. She considered not playing cards after all so she could think about Borobasq and Bentley, but she needed to get out of the house and get fresh air, and since Joyce drove very fast, being her passenger meant serious fresh air.

After some difficulty, Clemmie finished in the bathroom, tidied her wig and reapplied lipstick, located her purse, which sometimes got lost between the door and the kitchen counter where she liked it to live, stepped out her front door, and locked it carefully behind her. They lived in the safest zip code in America, and if anybody wanted to rob a house in Sun City, they wouldn't creep among the tiny villas; they'd hit the streets with four-thousand-square-foot mansions on three levels, but nevertheless, Clemmie exercised care.

But if the Coglands exercised such care to stay invisible that they created an inner passage, why did they not lock it? Perhaps they were so sure of their exterior locks that they shrugged about their interior locks.

Joyce and Johnny were ardent Panthers fans, and Joyce had stitched Panthers boxer shorts together to make a skirt around the roof of the golf cart. She was just now backing out of her garage, so she had thoughtfully waited ten whole minutes for Clemmie to have her checkup. Like most people, Joyce had had the automatic backup beeper silenced. Otherwise the only sound you'd hear all across Sun City would be that annoying high-pitched repeat.

The golf cart's top speed was twelve miles an hour, but Joyce hunched excitedly over the wheel as if she were going ninety. Clemmie had never gotten a golf cart. Every year she considered it, and every year, she passed. It was more fun to hitch rides with friends than to go alone, and with her villa so close to the shopping strip, it was a pleasant walk to return a library book or pick up a prescription.

Joyce had her usual massive handbag. She liked to tote her entire life around. The handbag took up so much floor space in the golf cart that Clemmie barely had room for her feet.

Joyce launched into a detailed story of how her pinochle group, with whom Clemmie was only a sub, had met at Myra's house last week, and Myra had refused to follow the new rule on refreshments, which required the hostess not to tempt women on diets, and nevertheless Myra had gone and offered seven fattening desserts instead of carrot strips and hummus. Furthermore, she cut the desserts into large slabs instead of narrow slices. The whole thing was unforgivable, especially since Joyce had eaten some of each.

They went into the clubhouse, Joyce showing her pass on her cell phone while Clemmie located the little laminated card in her wallet. She realized with a start that she had both cell phones with her, although it was her never-broken rule to leave the family cell phone at home. She silenced each phone and followed Joyce into the card room.

After everybody had hugged and asked after physical woes and updated one another on the betrayals or successes of a child or grandchild, and when it was ascertained that the cards had been adequately shuffled, the game went with amazing speed and Clemmie was so anxious she could hardly keep up. It always seemed to be her turn, and she thought, Maybe I'm having a stroke.

"It's your go, Helen!" yelled her partner, Evelyn. "Pay attention!"

Clemmie looked down at the cards lying on the table and the cards in her hand and could draw no conclusions. "I'm having a senior moment," she said, which was completely true because until Evelyn had shouted her name, she had lost track of whether she was Clemmie or Helen right now. "What game are we playing anyhow?"

Everybody was giggling. Senior moments were a constant, and the only way to deal with them was to laugh it off, or you'd be awake all night wondering if it was time to take anti-Alzheimer's medication. Aricept, the usual drug, not only gave you insomnia, lethargy, and a tendency to stumble, but its only promise was that it *might* slow the rate of memory loss. And you wouldn't even know whether it worked; somebody else would have to tell you. "Hand and foot canasta! You and Evelyn need another pure."

The game hurtled on.

Clemmie thought, The only decor in that villa is a stolen marijuana rig. When a stolen object is found, the police are called. My fingerprints are on two doorknobs. No, they're on four. Each side of two doors. No, six. Each side of three doors! Dom's garage, the illegal door, and the Coglands' inside door.

She had spent decades protecting herself. In one stupid,

self-indulgent moment of curiosity, had she become the agent of her own destruction?

By now Dom would be home. Clemmie couldn't get through his garage again.

When the police come, I could play the senility card, she thought. Say that Dom asked me to watch out for him and I sensibly checked every door.

She might be able to pull that off. God knew there were enough examples of senility around here.

But what would happen when they identified the fingerprints?

THREE

Several texts later, Harper McKeithen phoned Bentley, which the brother and sister rarely did, preferring communications more easily ignored or postponed. "This Borobasq?" she said. "I've read a bunch of his Instagram posts. He never reported that theft to the police. He just ranted."

"He probably doesn't live in a state where it's legal to sell marijuana, so he has to be careful. It's probably not safe for him to involve cops." Bentley was attracted to this concept: a man who had to be careful of cops. Bentley himself was careful of carbs.

"You go back enough posts," said Harper, "it gives the name of his studio, Boro Basking, and it's in Colorado, where marijuana is legal. I think the name is from borosilicate, the glass they use to make rigs and pipes. Whatever. People are wondering how come the thief took just one rig. Apparently, the studio is packed with fabulous stuff that costs unbelievable amounts of money—two thousand dollars here and eight thousand dollars there, and one for twenty-five thousand! Glass, Bent! People are paying that much for glass! But the posts say if you're in a position to steal one great piece of glass, why aren't you in a position to steal several?"

"Carrying them, maybe," said Bentley. "Glass breaks. You can't just throw it in a pillowcase and run down the street."

"True. They use gun cases to carry expensive glass pipes. Pelican brand."

"How come you know this and I don't?"

"You're very middle class, Bentley. What did our parents expect, giving you a name like that?"

"Speaking of names, Harp, I'm looking in my contacts, and I don't have Aunt Clemmie's street address. She uses a Charlotte PO box for mail, not that I've ever written to her, but for some reason I have that PO box number. I people-searched to get her address, and guess what? Not only is there no Sun City in Charlotte, North Carolina, but no Clementine Lakefield shows up."

"Doesn't show up where?"

"In the United States."

Harper giggled. "Maybe she calls herself by her middle name now, so she's Eleanor, instead of Clementine. Maybe she secretly married. Maybe you misspelled it. You probably have to use the kind of search where you pay for it. Why do you care?"

Bentley chose not to admit to Harp that he had had both text and phone exchanges with Borobasq. Bentley had launched a pleasing career. He wore expensive suits, had a collection of silk ties, ate at trendy restaurants, and drank trendy drinks. And now without thinking, he had put himself within range of a drug dealer.

Lampworker, he told himself firmly. The guy sells glass, not drugs.

He couldn't get over that steady, solid, boring old Aunt Clemmie lived next door to a stoner and a thief in a retirement village. Bentley himself had never tried weed because he had asthma and feared anything with smoke. Borobasq had said he wanted to go to Aunt Clemmie's and pick up his rig next door. And how would that work, exactly? Would Borobasq knock, crying, "Hand over your stolen goods"?

"I think originally those searches were built around landlines," said Harp. "So if you don't have one, and you don't have a mortgage or you're renting and somebody else pays the utility bills, I don't know how readily you appear. Okay, now I'm Googling 'Sun City,' and there's not one in Charlotte, but there is one a few miles away in South Carolina in a town called Fort Mill, which is silly, you shouldn't be both a fort and a mill. You should be one or the other. Anyway, I bet Aunt Clemmie was just rounding up when she told us Charlotte. Geographically up. I feel a little sad that we don't actually know where she lives. We see her at Thanksgiving or Christmas, and I never really think about her between times."

His phone let Bentley know that Borobasq was calling again. He had a trapped sensation, as if he were caught in an elevator with the guy. For a tiny moment he thought of telling his sister what their great-aunt had texted back when he texted to ask for her address. It's bad enough you gave out my phone number. I'm certainly not entrusting you with a house number. Call that man back and get me out of this.

But his sister had changed the subject. "Listen, are you going to the wedding or not?"

"Not."

"Mom is getting all depressed that you and I aren't going to be there," said Harp.

"Nothing would get Mom depressed."

"There's that," agreed Harper. "And another thing, did you submit to ancestry.com yet?" This had been her birthday present to her brother because tracing families had gotten so trendy that Bent wanted to be on board.

"Done," he said. "Waiting for saliva results." Mom, he thought, would definitely know where Aunt Clemmie lived.

———————

Bentley McKeithen liked his mother, who was a riot and had more going on in her life than anybody. She was about to marry her fourth husband, but Bentley had been to her last two weddings and that was enough for him.

"Hello, darling," said his mother, who never used his name. Had she chosen Bentley and then regretted it? "It's so busy here!" she cried joyfully. "We're getting ready to leave, and we're packing like mad. Won't you rethink your plans and come?"

"Really, Mom, I can't. I'm working. Now listen, I need Aunt Clemmie's actual address." What do I think I'm going do with it? he asked himself. I can't give it to Borobasq. I can't go down there myself. There's no point. I don't know how to demand stolen goods from neighbors.

"Oh, darling, she never gives that out. I've always thought that your aunt Clementine was in the CIA or else witness protection, because she uses only post office boxes and we are not allowed to visit her; she always visits us."

"I thought she was a Latin teacher."

"It's a cover. Nobody studies Latin anymore. But she's retired now and lives in Sun City and plays dominoes. Do you know, darling, Harp isn't coming to my wedding either? I'm a little hurt."

"Harp can't afford it," said Bentley. "It's your own fault for going so far away."

"Arch has his heart set on it."

"I thought his name was Morgan."

"Yes, but he loves McDonald's and his whole career was with McDonald's and he used to be called Arches, as in Golden, but I shortened it to Arch. He loves that. It makes him laugh. You know, if I have one skill, it's making people laugh."

"Yes, but Mom, if you had to get in touch with Aunt Clemmie, how would you do it?"

"Phone her, for heaven's sake. I was being silly when I said the CIA. She really was a Latin teacher. I think she might still be, actually. She used to correct millions of papers when she visited, and do you know what, darling? Even though I think she's retired, I somehow feel she's still correcting papers, which means she isn't retired. Could she be subbing? Would a sane person in her seventies agree to be a substitute teacher? Or even a sane person in her twenties? I have to run, darling. I'm sorry I can't help. We're such a tiny family. And we're not as close as we should be. It breaks my heart," she said cheerfully. "Kisses!"

———————

Cards ran about two and a half hours, and of course there was after-game chat, and rounding up sweaters (the clubhouse was drafty), and saying hello to people in the parking lot (which was blazing hot, so now the sweaters had to come off), and then Joyce had to stop on the way home at the grocery for a quart of milk, and when Clemmie was finally home alone, she was tired in that exasperating age-seventy-plus way. She wanted to put her feet up, read a chapter in her mystery, and play Words with Friends.

What she should do was deal with the tree dragon situation, but that seemed impossible, so she read her emails.

Clemmie's mother had loved correspondence, an endeavor in life now completely vanished. When Mama died, Clemmie's sister-in-law, Jeannie, took over writing the weekly letter, letters being the obligation of the women, not the men; Clemmie's brother, Pete, would never have dreamed of writing to his sister. Jeannie wrote mainly about their darling daughter, Peggy, but always enclosed clippings from the local newspaper. High school teams: their triumphs and failures. Church news. Obituaries. Engagements and weddings. There were many of these, because back then, everybody got married, except Clemmie.

Over the years, two new topics had crept into the news: crime and scandal. For a few years, Jeannie was shocked, but eventually she enjoyed crime and scandal as much as anybody else. Then Jeannie became a real estate agent and turned letter writing over to Peggy, who by now was out of college and married.

In those days, you loved mail, and if you were to receive mail, you had to send it, so you kept a good stock of fine writing paper: thank-you notes, card sets, condolence notes, and a supply of high-quality blank paper, perhaps with one engraved initial or a tiny Greek key design along the top edge. When email was invented, Peggy was on board in a minute. It was so much easier, and no stamp to buy. Clemmie was a teacher, and since school systems moved so quickly to digital communication, Clemmie was the first of Peggy's letter recipients also to go to email.

Clemmie, Peggy had written today, Costa Rica! Remember? Are you coming? Book the flight, forward the bill, we'll cover it. I want you there. What's a wedding without my only aunt?

I love you, Peggy, she thought. I'm willing to go to as many weddings as you're willing to have. But why does it have to be Costa Rica? It'll be even hotter there than it is here. My wig will feel awful. You've never seen me without a wig.

Peggy had appended a YouTube video, a name on Facebook, and a link to a newspaper article.

Clemmie almost never opened the YouTube nonsense, nor did she recognize the Facebook name. But Peggy not only cited the newspaper article, she added Dad was always upset by this, meaning Clemmie's brother, Pete, who had died long ago. Clemmie clicked on the link.

COLD CASE REOPENED, said the header. LONG AGO MURDER OF HIGH SCHOOL COACH TO BE EXAMINED.

Clemmie gasped.

The murdered man had been Pete's high-school basketball coach.

She had known all the players and all the places. She was fairly sure she knew all the secrets. No one would connect her. No one would question her or even remember her. But the police would not expect to learn anything five decades later by questioning people. Cold cases were solved by DNA and fingerprints.

Her fingerprints.

Which were now on the doors and knobs at Dom's and the Coglands'. Where police would shortly be summoned to reunite a rig with its owner.

FOUR

When Clemmie thought of high school, she tried to remember only her wonderful freshman year, full of friends and the excitement of being so grown up, so pretty and popular. She was very small and very curvy, and because of her tight, dark curls and the dark-red lipstick that was popular then, someone gave her the nickname Betty Boop. Betty Boop—although Clemmie's innocence was so complete that she did not analyze this—was a sexualized cartoon character, with well-defined breasts, a sassy protruding rear end, long legs below a short skirt, and a tiny ready-to-kiss mouth.

Clemmie didn't wear short skirts; nobody in the '50s even owned a short skirt—even the cheerleaders didn't have short skirts. A young lady didn't expose her thighs in high school; she kept her ankles close and her knees together. If she did cross her knees, she carefully rearranged her skirt. No girl wore shorts or pants to school. Even on the coldest winter days, a girl's legs were protected only by ankle socks or stockings secured on a garter belt.

But gym required uniforms: ill-fitting leaf-green, one-piece shorts and short-sleeved top, with silly, pointless pockets and a cute little belt. Most girls looked ridiculous, but Clemmie looked delightful.

There was a girls' gym and a boys' gym, but for field hockey, a ghastly sport required of all the girls, they had to trot past the boys, who whistled and cheered. The basketball coach, Coach Creek, was often there, standing in the big, open doors to the boys' gym, legs spread, hands on waist, elbows out, looking like a Greek god. Men cut their hair very short then, but even so, you could see how thick and curly his hair was. You could see that the hair on his chest was also thick and curly, because the tank top the men and boys wore for gym was loose and low. It was fashionable to have a crush on Rudyard Creek, with his wonderful grin and perfect teeth. Kids didn't get braces all that often, and perfect teeth were uncommon. But really, everything about Rudyard Creek was perfect. It helped, of course, that his team had an outstanding record.

The boys admired Coach as much as the girls did. Maybe more. His was the physique they wanted. The popularity. The style. The victories.

By sophomore year, Clemmie was aware that when she went down the hall in the gym wing, Coach had stationed himself just to look at her. She pretended not to notice, but all the other girls certainly did. "He thinks you're adorable," whispered one of the girls, and they all giggled, because the coach's admiration was well placed. Clemmie blushed furiously and wondered how old the coach was, anyway.

When Pete had been on the team, having the bachelor coach over for dinner had seemed a fine way to cement a friendship among the adults, and maybe even get Pete more playing time, so Clemmie knew the coach slightly from serving him a meal. Her parents had thought the world of Rudyard Creek. But Pete was in college now, not good enough to play at that level. If he came home for a weekend during basketball season, he always went to a game at his old high school, sitting as close as possible to the team, waiting for, and always receiving, the coach's special smile of acknowledgment: Yes. You're one of mine. I remember you well.

Sometimes their dad went to the game too, and then he too received that special smile.

That semester, Clemmie had been deep in a lovely, rewarding crush. She still thought of Bobby sometimes, of how warm and splendid he had been, what their lives might have been. Her girlfriends had nudged her, smiled knowingly, whispering, "You're in love," and she knew that the boys teased Bobby about her, and she knew that he didn't care.

When Bobby asked her to go steady, it was the most wonderful event of her life. She and Bobby even kissed, more than once, and she lay awake at night dreaming of him. She did not dream about sex because she hardly knew what it was. Children today knew what it was when they were in kindergarten; they even knew about erectile dysfunction. But when Clemmie Lakefield was sixteen, she dreamed about "making out," which consisted of hugs and kisses, and perhaps, although Clemmie did not feel ready, getting to know each other above the waist.

Promiscuity in the 1950s and early '60s was rare. The price to be paid was too high. Your only true goal was marriage to a good man, so you had to be good too, and that meant being a virgin until your wedding night. If you fooled around (a phrase that was so appropriate, because only fools did it), you could get pregnant. There was birth control in the form of condoms, but few girls could picture how that worked, let alone acquire such an item. The pill had not yet been invented. The only way to avoid pregnancy was not to have sex, and Clemmie, as far as she knew, was not acquainted with any girl who had actually "done it."

That day, Bobby had passed her a note during biology class. It didn't actually say anything. It just had a row of Xs and a row of Os. Sort of a nonliterate love letter, she thought, far more pleased with Xs and Os than any words would have made her. She tucked the note deep in her purse and planned where she would keep it so she would have it forever.

Which was when Coach gave her a ride home. She sat in the front seat, of course, on the wide bench. Seat belts were not yet common, and Clemmie had never used one. Coach asked her about Bobby, her favorite topic, so she beamed and listed Bobby's great virtues and strengths. Coach made a peculiar remark. "I have more," he said, in a husky voice that made her oddly anxious, and he drove down a street that would not take them to her house.

It was puzzling that he would not know the way. "Shouldn't you turn right at this corner?" she said, feeling a little uncomfortable to correct a grown-up.

"We're going to turn a different direction, you and I," said Rudyard Creek, and suddenly the fine smile became an ugly smirk. Clemmie didn't say, *You're frightening me.* She didn't say, *Let me out now, right here.* She had been raised, like all her friends, to believe that if you couldn't say something nice, you should say nothing at all.

She would never have gone into Coach's house, but he took her hand and insisted, and she did not know how to refuse any adult, let alone a man so respected in her family and school. A man she liked. A man whose admiration had increased her worth in school.

What happened next was short and brutal. Coach looked down at her with a terrible hatred while he was doing it and wild laughter when he was done, beaming down at where she was bleeding. He pointed to the bathroom, where she cleaned herself up, and then she had to accept a ride home with him. He let her out of the car a few blocks away, and she had to walk, and it hurt; it hurt all over.

Even after all these years, Clemmie could not bring herself to visualize the actual event. She had been so frightened, so shocked, humiliated, and appalled. What happened between her legs could not be whatever it was that married people did. The violence of Rudyard Creek, the hot, panting loathing of her at the very same time he was grinning, still frightened Clemmie in nightmares.

Clemmie did not tell her parents. There was no vocabulary. There was no appropriate time. Besides, in the 1950s, and right up into the '60s, there was not usually such a thing as rape. A girl had agreed, or had encouraged the man, or been passively accepting. In any event, it was her fault. Had Clemmie used the word *attacker*, even her mother and father would have corrected her. Maybe *especially* her mother and father, who would be so ashamed of her behavior.

The second horror was that Rudyard Creek continued to show up in her life because she encountered him so often in the halls at the high school. In her memory, Rudyard Creek loomed over her short, little frame like a grizzly bear on a trail, his smile worming up and down her figure.

But the third horror, the one that changed and darkened all the years to come, was that when Bobby touched her, she flinched. She knew things she shouldn't and had done things she shouldn't, while Bobby was still a good person. Bobby, confused by her sudden coolness, moved on. His heart wasn't broken; he just found another girlfriend.

She didn't know what had happened to her own heart, but it didn't beat the same, cherish the same, or hope the same. And the word *innocent* no longer belonged to Clemmie.

She didn't know the word *victim*. In those days, whatever happened to you, you had asked for it.

And whatever happened to Clemmie today, in Sun City, she had asked for it. She had trespassed, taken the photograph, forwarded it.

———————

Boro was seething. Bentley McKeithen's phone kept going to voicemail. Boro had been seething for days anyway, but now rage was coming out his pores, and he was actually panting when he finally reached the guy. Now he was forced to listen to a long, lame story about how nobody in the McKeithen family really knew where their aunt lived. Boro needed to find that rig and he needed to find it now and this loser was babbling. It took all the self-discipline Boro had not to lash out. He forced himself to chat with the imbecile nephew in a friendly way, digging for any information he could Google. "Was she always a nurse or what?" he asked, apropos of nothing.

"No, no. Latin teacher," said the idiot, whose job clearly required nothing of him, because he was so willing to sit at his desk and chatter pointlessly with a total stranger.

"English as a second language?" asked Boro, misunderstanding *Latin* to mean *Latino*.

"No, you know, like Julius Caesar and Cicero. Latin. Ancient Rome."

"I didn't know they still taught that. And she used to teach in Pittsburgh, right?"

"Pittsburgh! Where did you get that from? No, she used to teach in Ohio. Then I don't know, other places, and then a few years ago, she moved to Sun City. She's into card games and pottery and, you know, all the stuff they do in those places."

Sun City? thought Boro. Isn't that where fat, illiterate white people in Arizona go to play rummy? How could my rig end up in a retirement center? Who brought it there? "Wow, Sun City," he said. "What a crack-up. My grandmother lives in Arizona. I could get my glass and visit my grandmother in one trip."

"Except there are lots of Sun Cities. My aunt's Sun City is in Charlotte."

"Then you do know where she lives," said Boro, chuckling, which did not come naturally, so he sounded like a duck on drugs, but it must have sounded like laughter to the idiot because Bentley said, "Well, kind of, but we don't have the street. We just have the post office box. I think she's probably renting, so her name doesn't show up in a people search."

Or she's married and didn't tell her family, thought Boro, or she's living with a boyfriend and didn't tell them, or living with a girlfriend and didn't tell them. While Bentley talked, Boro checked Facebook, which had nobody named Lakefield. It asked if he meant Wakefield, of whom there were about twenty. Cool. Change one letter and vanish.

So Facebook was useless. He brought up the Charlotte Sun City website, found out it was actually over the state line in South

Carolina, and its resident directory open only to members, so he couldn't access it. "But she's retired now?" said Boro, staying warm and friendly.

"I think maybe still teaching."

"Wow," said Boro. "In her eighties and still teaching? You must be so proud of her."

"I don't think she's that old," said Bentley. "Early seventies, maybe."

"You know what, Bentley? I think we just have to shrug about the stolen glass," said Boro, trying to sound considerate and gentle, two qualities not in his personality. "I mean, these things happen. I can make another rig. What I don't want to do is upset your poor aunt any more. I'll just swallow the loss."

"Gosh, that's really great of you," said the idiot. "I'll call her and let her know she can stop worrying."

"No, no, you let me do it," said Boro graciously. "I have great-aunts, and a grandmother too, and I'm very close to them. I'll enjoy talking to Mrs. Lakefield a second time and bringing her peace of mind."

———

Clemmie fixed herself a cheese sandwich, telephoned Dom once more, and still he didn't answer. She couldn't imagine where he might be for so long. Had he gone on a vacation with Wilson? She couldn't picture that. A vacation with the Coglands? She couldn't picture that either. And there was the problem of the golf cart. If either Wilson or the Coglands had taken Dom away, his golf cart would be sitting silently in his garage, plugged into its charger.

Leaving the sandwich for later, she opened her sliders and went through the screened porch onto the little concrete slab the builders referred to as a patio. The sun attacked in the thick, humid way of a Carolina July. It was like getting hit with a skillet. She set down a tote bag in which she had placed Windex and rags and walked back through the house and out her front door. She leaned on Dom's bell, ready to go back in, retrieve her cleaning supplies, and scrub up her finger-prints, and Johnny yelled from across the street, "What's up, Helen?"

It was Clemmie's rule to like everybody, especially everybody she saw frequently. Liking Dom was beyond her, although she could be civil, but liking Johnny was also a bit of a challenge. He was dicta-torial in a way that Joyce seemed to enjoy, but Clemmie found hard to tolerate. Sometimes when the three of them ate out, he would order without asking what the girls wanted. If they agreed to see Movie A, Johnny might well drive to a theater where it wasn't play-ing, laugh, elbow Joyce, and remind her that he had wanted to see Movie B. Joyce would giggle as if she liked his masterful behavior. Clemmie would be subjected to a movie with a level of violence that meant she sat with her eyes closed.

Clemmie waved and called across the street. The front yards being so tiny and Blue Lilac Lane so narrow, she hardly needed to raise her voice. "Hi, Johnny. I'm just checking on Dom. He texts me every day to say he's fine, but today he didn't, and he hasn't answered his phone either, so I'm going in." She didn't imply that she'd already gone in and Johnny didn't correct her, so he hadn't witnessed her first foray, because if he had, he'd make a sly remark about hanky-panky.

To her dismay, Johnny loped over to join her, because although everybody at Sun City was extremely busy, nobody at Sun City actually had anything to do, and poking around the neighbor's house was a pleasant interruption to an otherwise repetitive existence. "I'll go in with you, Helen," he said in his paternal voice, the one that meant *Because otherwise you won't know how to do it.* "Just in case there's anything wrong."

"Thank you so much," she said falsely. Johnny held out his hand for the key, but she put the key in the lock herself, stepped back so Johnny had to go in first, and pocketed the key. Johnny didn't pause on the threshold but strode right into the living room, bellowing, "Hey! Dominic!"

No answer.

Johnny looked in the kitchen, the little guest room, the living room, the powder room, the bedroom and its bathroom, moving so fast he was like a cartoon. "He's not dead on the floor, he's just gone out," said Johnny. "I'll check for the golf cart."

"What a good idea," said Clemmie, her mind on the cold case in her hometown. Why were they even trying? What evidence could possibly have surfaced? And who was left to care, really?

With the middle villa barely a thousand square feet, it would take Johnny only a few seconds to walk over to the garage door. Clemmie hurried over Dom's carpet, felt around the heavy drapes for the slit, put her hand through, unlocked his sliding glass door, and made it back to her original position.

Johnny came back. "Dom must be away doing whatever. Nothing to worry about." He didn't even break his stride but headed for the front door and held it open for her.

So either Johnny's eye had not landed on the interior door, or he had seen it but not registered the fact that no unit came with such a door. Joyce and Johnny's villa was almost directly across the street, so they would watch Dom's garage door go up and down all the time, but perhaps they were not watchers, the way Clemmie was. Perhaps they just had a vague awareness of Dom coming and going and didn't waste their time examining interiors of other people's garages. Or more likely, the way in which Dom departed, starting the door closure before he was fully out, kept their eyes on Dom instead of the back-right corner of his garage. "Thank you for coming with me. I'm uncomfortable being here alone."

"He's an uncomfortable guy. I'm surprised he gave you a key."

"I was supposed to keep it a secret," she admitted.

Johnny chuckled. "Have a good day. Glad I could help."

Clemmie carefully locked Dom's front door again and lowered the key into her pocket. She made it into her own little villa, her beloved safe home, with its explosions of color and its shelves of books, and the old tears came back in a flood.

FIVE

The weeks had turned into months, and first semester final exams were over before Clemmie accepted that she was pregnant—a hideous word; a word that could not, must not, apply to her. She could not even use the word with her own mother, but finally managed to explain her predicament by talking around it and crying.

"We raised you right, and you let us down," said her mother, weeping and calling Clemmie's father into the room, breaking the awful news.

They didn't hug her. They didn't say they loved her anyway. Her father said grimly, "Was it Bobby?"

"No," Clemmie said. "He never did anything. We kissed once."

"You were running around with another boy at the same time?" cried her horrified mother.

"Who is this other boy?" demanded her father fiercely.

She thought of saying Coach's name, but they would not believe her. And if they believed and had the nerve to approach Rudyard Creek, Coach would act shocked. Perhaps he would be quietly sad for this pathetic girl as he denied her ugly accusation. They would believe him, not her, and loathe their wayward daughter even more for attempting to damage an upstanding man like Rudyard Creek.

"Who is it?" repeated her father, his voice rising.

Clemmie had heard of shotgun weddings, and she imagined a caricature of a bridal day, in which she was shoved down the aisle to live forever with Coach or some railroaded boy. She could not answer, so she shrugged, a motion of the shoulders that a girl simply did not make in those days, and certainly not to her parents. Clemmie's father despised tears. If she cried over anything at all, from a scraped knee to another child's snub, her father would yell, "You keep crying, and I'll give you something to cry about!" Her father had huge hands. A spanking from him was very painful, and all these decades later, Clemmie remembered separately all three times in her childhood that she had been thrashed.

He had wanted to thrash her when she admitted that she was going to have a baby, but clenched his fists instead and ordered her to be removed from the family for the duration, so that he himself would never see her in that condition nor be shamed in his town in front of his friends.

That was what you did then, and it certainly held down casual high school sex. Young people today thought that kids had always slept around, but that was not the case. Before birth control pills, girls were far more careful and boys far less likely to push. Society then was the opposite of society today: clothing was designed to soften sexuality, not thrust it forward. In Clemmie's high school, a girl hoped to be described as "demure," not "hot." And when a married woman was going to have a child, she wore gathered dresses, overblouses, and cardigans to keep her increasing size from view. Never would a woman have allowed her swollen self to be photographed. Never would she have worn a tight top that clung to her belly and outlined her. For that matter, she would never have used the word *belly*. The phrase *baby bump* was two generations in the future.

Clemmie's parents located an institution that up until the previous year had been called the Mountain School for Wayward Girls. Now it was simply the Mountain School, but inside the building, engraved in stone over the entrance to the office, the old name stood as a reminder.

The way in which the girls were wayward was that they were all going to have babies and none of them were married, a condition utterly scorned.

At the school, when the girls got really big, they shared a wardrobe of muumuus: great, big waistless cotton dresses. Since they didn't leave the institution, the weather outside didn't matter, and they didn't need coats or jackets. They were just waiting.

Like most of the girls, Clemmie had no visitors. None of her friends back home knew where she was, and her parents did not want to see their little girl all swollen and pregnant.

No teenage girl kept her baby. No parent would allow a wayward daughter to bring home the proof of her bad behavior. There was no such thing as day care—since a mother stayed home with her children—so a young mother could never earn a living or find housing because she had nowhere to leave the child. And a bad girl would not make a marriage with anybody, let alone a good man, if she had a bastard in tow.

Adoptions arranged by the Mountain School were anonymous. The adoptive parents never saw, met, or even knew anything about the birth mother. But the wayward girls were never referred to as mothers anyway, and the babies they bore were referred to as "the infant."

Clemmie found pregnancy horrifying, not simply because of the evil way in which it had happened, not just because she had been thrown out of her house, but also because of her body: the vomiting, weight gain, backache, splotchy complexion.

The procedure was that when labor pains began, you went to the hospital, you had anesthesia, and when you woke up, you weren't pregnant anymore. You didn't see or hold "the infant."

Clemmie had always loved babies. In church she often volunteered in the nursery, because what was better than cuddling a baby?

I'm going through all this, thought Clemmie, and I don't even get to see her? Or him? I don't get to hug my baby? Kiss its little cheek and count its little toes?

Her best friend at the Mountain School, Veronica, was a seriously tough cookie, the kind Clemmie would have been afraid of if they'd been on opposing field hockey teams, expecting the use of the hockey stick as a weapon. Ronnie said bluntly, "It's my kid, and I'm keeping it."

"Nonsense," said the matron. "Your parents won't even let you in the door. You'll have no place to live and no income. You can't get a job because there is no job where you can take a baby along. No decent married woman will associate with you, and the infant will starve."

These things were true. Jobs for women were scarce anyway: basic manufacturing, basic clerical. Teaching. Nursing. That was pretty much it.

Ronnie had temper tantrums, but even she came to realize that wayward girls had to go back home with their heads hanging down, pretending they had never been wayward.

I wasn't wayward, Clemmie used to think. *He* was.

Half a century later, Clementine Lakefield was still glad that Rudyard Creek had died young.

Bentley was majorly relieved after Boro's phone call. He didn't need to get involved, drive down to a place when he didn't even know where it was, or even worry.

He spent a minute on Boro's website, stunned by the amount of money Borobasq seemed to be earning from glass. The weirdest object was a glass Q-tip holder, which had just sold for $1,500, with fifty-two posts telling Borobasq what a killer piece it was. It was pretty enough, but $1,500?

Bentley went to Facebook and opened the page of an old college buddy who was a second-generation maker of pipes; his dad was, like, famous in lampworking circles. The whole family were serious stoners. They could tell him what the Q-tip container was for.

Bent was a little taken aback to find an ongoing discussion of *his* post. He knew Borobasq had eighty thousand followers, but somehow he hadn't perceived that therefore eighty thousand people might well read Bentley's own post and comment on it.

That aunt? She's toast.

Boro probably funnels a million a month through his studio. Probably a lot in cash and easy to steal. Best guess, somebody stole his cash and took the rig as a souvenir. The aunt's standing between Boro and his money.

You mean a million a year, don't you?

Come on. Colorado alone had $900 million in weed sales last

year. Boro isn't even a major player and he could be doing a million a month.

Bentley rounded up. Colorado was doing close to a billion dollars a year in weed sales? Was that possible?

Las Vegas pipe show? You'll find guys carrying money in shoeboxes they have so much cash. All hundred-dollar bills.

Bentley dismissed this idea. Maybe in Saturday-morning cartoons, the bad guys carried cash in shoeboxes. Or maybe a century ago when payrolls were still cash. But he was skeptical that glassblowers couldn't use a bank account. They'd figure how to launder their money, or deposit it bit by bit, or send it to some island in the Caribbean or whatever. They weren't using shoeboxes, okay?

He glanced at the photos and videos on the page. His buddy's glass pipe collection was sick in both meanings of the word: fabulous and also disgusting, especially the Mickey Mouse shooting up heroin. Bentley didn't approve of that. Some things were sacred.

That aunt is about to have a serious visit from a serious guy. If you're reading this, Auntie, start running.

But if you don't run fast enough? Oh well. Stuff happens.

But I want to know, why take the rig?

It's spectacular. Who wouldn't want it?

What I don't get, how could it be easy to steal the cash? Wouldn't Boro have his whole shop booby-trapped?

Depends if it's a shop meaning customers or a shop meaning studio.

Borobasq has a got a busy week ahead. Image to maintain, cash to get back, rig to retrieve, and a guy to kill.

Sounds like fun. Let's all go.

Bentley could not reconcile this melodrama and hysteria with the well-spoken, courteous man on the phone. It was a typical social media avalanche. Start with a pebble, and end up with a squashed village on a Swiss mountain.

Still, he kind of wanted a second opinion on the idea of his aunt as toast. Especially since he was the toaster. He called Harper, who said, "Bentley, get a life. If we don't know where Aunt Clemmie lives, how could some glassblower who's high as a kite figure it out? Are you picturing some druggie wandering around a retirement village hoping to spot an old lady carrying a big, green glass rig?"

"So you don't think I need to do anything."

"Aunt Clemmie texted you not to worry, didn't she? She's got it under control, Bent," said Harper. "Her life's a little weird, but hey. You teach a dead language and never have a boyfriend and hide out from your own relatives, of course your life is a little weird."

———————————

Still teaching, thought Boro.

He studied the map of the greater Charlotte area. A million people lived there. His best hope was that the old lady was a Latin teacher on a faculty somewhere, but his second hope was the pool of Latin teachers would be so small that retired and still-teaching Latin teachers had some little club, went out for lunch and discussed syntax. All he needed was one name. He didn't know what he'd say to that Latin teacher, but he'd come up with something, find Clementine Lakefield, and zero in on her next-door neighbor.

Sun City was in Lancaster County, which was adjacent to two other South Carolina counties and bordered by two North Carolina counties. That was a lot of school systems.

He started with the Charlotte-Mecklenburg Schools, a massive system whose website proclaimed that a few middle and high schools taught Latin. He called the main number, explaining to whoever answered that he and his wife were thinking of moving to Charlotte and wanted their daughters to study Latin. Which high schools should they consider?

The clerk gave him a list of schools but wouldn't give him teachers' names.

"We really want to talk with the teachers so we know what textbooks are being used," said Boro.

"My hands are tied. Privacy rules. Probably you could call the principal at each of those schools."

He went to each Latin-offering school website but couldn't get into the lists of staff members. Maybe he'd call the principals after all. "My wife and I are hoping that Mrs. Lakefield is your Latin teacher," he'd say, "because we've heard such good things about her."

People were idiots, so the principal might say, "No, Mrs. X is our Latin teacher," which would be fine, because then Boro would have a toehold.

———

Clemmie checked her family phone. There were no new texts, but there was a voice message from Harper. "Hi, Aunt Clemmie. Bent is worried that he sicced a drug dealer on you. What's the actual situation? Do you need me to call your police station? I looked you up. Lancaster County has a sheriff, which sounds very Wild West. Of course they probably don't know what they're doing. Call me back. Let's plan. Love you."

Clemmie's heart was pierced. Bentley had filled his sister in, so he understood the enormity of what he'd done, and it was lovely that Harper was worried, which meant she was not entirely thoughtless.

She texted back: How dear of you to check on me, Harper. But all is fine here and under control. No need to call the police—although in fact the sheriff was a speaker in a lecture series, and he is adorable and may visit me anytime. Hope you are well and that I will see you one of these days. Affectionately, your aunt Clemmie.

This is the definition of my life, she thought. *Pushing away the people I love.* She brushed away useless, stupid tears and texted Dom yet again, just to be sure. Are you okay? Are you home?

No response.

All evening, she sat in the dark on the puffy cushion of her breakfast-table chair, staring through the open gingham curtains at the little street and what she could glimpse of Pink Camellia, the next cul-de-sac over. People stayed up late. Joyce and Johnny always watched the news after their final TV show, and it looked as if Joan and Ed Schwartz did too. Betty Anne and Ralph spent a lot of time in their bathroom. (You always knew which window of a Sun City house was over the toilet, because it was a small, high rectangle of glass block.) Linda and Frank sat on their little front porch, having a last cigarette.

One by one, lights went off up and down her cul-de-sac and the lane behind it.

Dom never came home.

He couldn't have gone anywhere with Wilson, because either they'd go in Wilson's car, in which case, Dom's golf cart would still be here, or they'd go in the golf cart, in which case Wilson's car would be here.

Could Dom have parked somewhere and had a heart attack while sitting in his golf cart? Dom had those zip-up plastic sides on his golf cart, and although you could see through the clear vinyl, it was wavy and obscured your view. He could have fallen against the steering wheel and still look normal enough for somebody driving by not to wonder. Or he could have fallen across the passenger seat and be invisible, and he was lying there trying to breathe and signal from the floor of a golf cart, as hours and even days went by.

A good neighbor would report Dom missing. Clemmie certainly categorized herself as a good neighbor.

The police department here was indeed run by a sheriff, Bay Bennett, a pleasant, articulate man who often gave talks on Monday nights when there were lectures on a wide variety of topics—a visiting professor of southern geology, a dermatologist with a weird specialty, or a historian of Revolutionary War battles in the Carolinas. Sheriff Bennett was a popular speaker because he had such great subjects—forensics and homicides—so he had high attendance to go along with his lush southern accent. She could listen to him talk all evening.

But Clementine Eleanor Lakefield was not going to initiate contact with the law.

At one thirty in the morning, Clemmie donned a pair of cleaning gloves, slipped out her sliders, picked up her canvas tote bag, and circled her holly bushes to Dom's patio. Using the flashlight on her cell phone, she found the handle of Dom's sliding door, pulled it gently open, and eased through the thick folds of the drapes. She was almost sobbing with anxiety. She knew nobody was home, but what if somebody *was*?

Lest the glow of her flashlight show through the distant kitchen window, Clemmie pointed it directly at her feet. The kitchen's half wall into the living room would block that little bit of light from street view. She skirted the coffee table and the chair and went carefully to the utility room and the garage door.

All the garages had motion sensors to turn on the overhead light, but they didn't trip until you were several steps into the garage—which was a bad arrangement, because if you needed a light at all, you needed it for every step, but it was useful now. If she clung to the back wall, it would stay dark. Not that it mattered. Sandwiched between two units, Dom's garage had no windows. But what she was doing seemed to require the dark.

Beset by the fear that she would trip and lie helpless on the floor of Dom's garage with a broken hip, she kept her flash trained on her feet. Dom's garbage was beginning to smell. She breathed through her mouth, stepped carefully up and over the illegal door's threshold, made it into the Cogland garage, opened their back door, and walked into their house. The shadows felt fat and occupied.

Moonlight glistened on the stolen glass, although too weakly to show color. The rig was just a ghostly presence. She settled the tree dragon carefully in the tote bag and walked back to the utility room, where she cleaned the knobs on both sides of the regular door and then the illegal door. She tucked the Windex and rags into the tote with the tree dragon and was heading across Dom's garage to clean the final door when the cell phone wavered in her hand. Its flash illuminated Dom's golf cart.

Clemmie almost screamed.

His golf cart?

He was here? He wasn't away? He was home?

Dom had probably watched her creep through his place. No, because Dom was the type that if he'd seen an intruder, he'd've shot her dead. So he had slept through her trespassing.

Why didn't I see the golf cart when I walked through a few minutes ago? Was I so obsessed with not tripping that I didn't ever flash my light across the garage space?

Maybe Dom had arrived just now while she was in the Coglands'. No, because she had left the connecting door open and would have heard Dom's garage door go up and down, and anyway, he would have seen the door ajar and investigated.

Dom must have arrived home at some point between when she and Johnny checked his place and one thirty in the morning. But she had texted him! She had been watching for him!

However, she had used the bathroom several times, and she always closed her bathroom door even though she was alone in the house. She had prepared dinner, she had paced, reading and rereading the cold-case article, and she'd started a load of laundry. The washing machine was noisy. She obviously hadn't heard him come in.

He must have shrugged about her anxious texts. What did Dom care if a neighbor worried?

Tears of panic leaked out, sapping what was left of her energy. Still gloved, she went back into the Coglands' villa. Don't drop the tote, she told herself. Don't trip. Don't even drip tears on the floor. Get out of here. It's almost over.

Unless it wasn't. Unless the Coglands were home too. They could have been passengers in Dom's golf cart and entered through their illegal door. They could be asleep in their bare bedroom. With no sheets.

No, they couldn't. Their car wasn't here. People couldn't be anywhere their cars weren't.

She opened the Coglands' slider, closed it behind her but had no way to lock it, and went home over the grass. Even if he was awake, Dom couldn't see her walking past, since his drapes were closed. Inside her villa, she locked her sliders, having left the sliders of Dom and the Coglands unlocked, threw out her disposable gloves, and put the glass in its tote bag in the back seat of her car.

There had to have been a more rational way to deal with this, but it was too late now. In the morning, she would call the Borobasq person on his cell phone, get his mailing address, and ship the stolen glass back to him. Whatever else had happened here, she had protected her address.

Dom might not discover that anybody had been in his unit. Since he didn't ever open his drapes (How could he stand that?

63

No sunshine, ever!), it might be a long time before he realized his sliders were unlocked. But Marcia and Roy would certainly know that somebody had been in their unit, because the glass tree dragon was gone.

Her heart skipped. People whose lives are built around stolen goods probably have video cams. They probably watched me stealing it back. *They know.*

But since the tree dragon was stolen, they can't call the police. They'll come after me. Or tell Dom to come after me, because they were clearly in cahoots about something. What is a cahoot, anyway? Do people still have cahoots?

She was definitely going to Peggy's wedding. Now Costa Rica sounded nicely distant. Tomorrow, after she shipped the tree dragon, she would fly out on the next plane.

———

Boro got a ticket for the last flight out of Denver. Waiting at the gate, he worked on his laptop, searching for Latin teacher names.

Having struck out with Charlotte-Mecklenburg, he had begun a search of every other area high school, radiating out from Sun City. Each school district had curriculum listings on its website, which, annoyingly, he usually had to download and then look to see if they offered Latin.

No, no, and no was the Latin situation so far.

The pool of Latin teachers was obviously very tiny, though, so his theory of find one and you find them all still seemed possible. He just hadn't found the one.

He rested from the school search, returning to Facebook, where he found eleven Latin language sites, most of which were closed, and the others told him nothing, so he went back to school systems, and the flight boarded. Four long hours in which he could do no research. He slept.

They landed too early to telephone a school or an old lady, so he staked out a white rocking chair in the huge food court, bought a breakfast burrito, and continued his school search. He opened the website for Dexter River High School in Union County, North Carolina.

The Dexter River website displayed a staff directory, in which he could enter a first or last name, or just the first letter of a name, so he entered A under Last Name and up came three names beginning with A. The column next to each name listed the subject that teacher taught, while the third column gave the .edu email address of that teacher. He worked his way through the alphabet. Under S for last name, Dexter River High had a Latin teacher named Helen Stephens.

Whoever had stolen from him knew Boro and his studio well, and therefore Boro knew the thief. He just hadn't figured out who it was. The thief not only had Boro's boxes of cash and the tree dragon, but the man or woman was out there laughing at him.

Not for long.

This Helen Stephens was his key.

He did a people search for Helen Stephens's phone number, because she could ignore an email or not get around to answering it for days, but Boro was good on the phone and knew he could tease information out of her. He just had to stay in control. He found her landline easily, and then her address. Helen Stephens lived on Blue Lilac Lane in Fort Mill, South Carolina.

Boro Google-Mapped that Blue Lilac Lane.

It was in Sun City.

Well, well. Bentley might have been right. Clementine Lakefield might just be rooming with another Latin teacher. For sure, they knew each other.

Boro rented a car, dreaming of inflicting pain and justice.

SIX

Early the following morning, when Joyce was starting a load of laundry, her gaze fell upon the utility-room floor, whose tiles were smeared. In a minute, she was scrubbing the grout. Johnny was preparing to set out, because the horseshoe pits would be scorching hot when the sun got high. After horseshoes, they'd play poker or euchre at the clubhouse. Then he and his buddies would go out for barbecue.

Normally, since the garage contained Joyce's car and golf cart, Johnny parked in the driveway, but even so, he was out of the habit of using the front door and came and went through the garage. He couldn't get past Joyce and her cleaning equipment. "You keep leaving scuff marks," she told him, not looking up.

"It's a utility room," said Johnny. "That's why we have it. To collect scuff marks." He kissed the top of her head and left by the front door.

Joyce struggled to her feet and hurried to the kitchen, whose window was her only view of the front. It gave her no view of neighbors to the left or the right. She couldn't even see most of her own driveway. The rear end of Johnny's car appeared as he backed out, not glancing at the house, probably already thinking horseshoe thoughts, and slowly he drove away. She put away the cleaning supplies, finished her hair and makeup, and was ready to roll when the locksmith arrived at eight thirty.

The yellow van sported tall, green block numbers and letters: 24-HOUR LOCK AND KEY. The neighbors might phone or text, asking how both she and Johnny could have lost their keys at the same time. But no one seemed to notice, not even Helen.

Joyce and Helen could talk about anything—clothes, cards, music, weather, digestion, arthritis, television shows, politicians—and be pleased and amazed by the other woman's brilliant remarks and funny comebacks. But Joyce rarely talked about her long-divorced ex-husband, just as Helen rarely talked about any men who might have been in her life during the previous seven decades.

You came to a retirement village as pure as a newborn. Nobody knew a thing about you. You could tell what you felt like telling. And the fact was, your new friends did not care in the slightest what your career had been, how brilliant or dim your star. They did not care if you'd had a long and satisfying marriage ending in widowhood or three divorces and lots of anger. What mattered was, could you play cards and games? Drive the carpool for the weekly neighborhood girls' lunch out? Listen to every detail of somebody else's cruise or surgery?

While the locksmith worked on the front door, Joyce loaded all Johnny's clothing and possessions into the back seat and trunk of her car. Considering that he'd been sharing her house several nights a week for two years, she was surprised that only one trip would remove him, but then, at her house, he used her stuff, leaving his own home intact. If his children visited, which they didn't, they wouldn't guess he really lived with a woman down the road.

She eyed the shelves loaded with tools, paint cans, jars of screws, boxes of nails, garden equipment, picnic coolers, extension cords, Christmas tree stand, and rows of sealed cardboard and plastic boxes. Some of it was Johnny's, but for now she had to shrug. She paid the locksmith. The moment his truck was out of the driveway, she backed her car out and sat idling on the driveway while she reprogrammed the code of the garage door opener. Now the door opener clipped to Johnny's visor would not work, nor could he open the front door. The rear sliders were not keyed, but she had locked them from the inside, and the house was now inaccessible to anyone but her.

She drove to his place on the other side of Sun City via a seemingly endless tangle of curving roads lined with culs-de-sac contrived to fit as many houses as possible on the acreage and, at the same time, create cozy little neighborhoods. Using the garage door opener for *his* place, she drove right in. He had a freestanding house, only a little larger than her own attached villa. In his neighborhood, every garage protruded while every front door was recessed, which meant that residents here had even less view of the street than on Blue Lilac.

Johnny's immediate neighbors were among the unfathomable population that paid extra to buy in Sun City and then never used a single amenity or joined a single club. They just sat home and watched television, which they could do less expensively anywhere else. But what they couldn't do was watch Johnny's house.

Joyce was a very neat person and had planned to carry all his clothing into his bedroom and set it carefully on his bed so it wouldn't wrinkle. In the garage, she said to herself, "Really?" then tossed it all onto the concrete and drove home.

She had admitted to no one, not even Helen, that Johnny had figured out how to raid her checking account, in which she kept far too much, currently about $40,000, because she liked the accessibility of it, the comfort.

He apparently assumed that she wouldn't notice $200 here or $100 there, and since she never bothered to balance the account, figuring if she just kept enough in there everything would be fine, his assumption had been correct for many months. When she finally grasped that Johnny was using her ATM card and her PIN without her permission, Joyce cried secretly for days. She not only loved him, but she also had happily imagined their wedding. Now she could think only of how often he would beg her to bake his favorite dessert and how she'd leap to do it, beaming with pleasure at his pleasure, all on the same day he'd stolen from her. And there was no reason to steal. He was fine financially. She rather thought that Johnny was doing it for entertainment. Bocce, horseshoes, poker, theft.

But although Joyce wanted to kick him out, she did not want a showdown.

Once when Johnny had been replacing the garbage disposal in Joyce's kitchen and couldn't get the new unit engaged on the mounting ring, he got angrier and angrier at the appliance until suddenly he was beating it to death with his big adjustable wrench, whacking it over and over as if killing a snake.

"Honey, it's okay," she'd said nervously. "Just let me call a repairman." He'd looked up at her with such loathing that her skin crawled.

She'd put it out of her mind because it was nicer to be a couple than a single, and she didn't want a silly garbage disposal incident to jeopardize that. But now that she'd locked Johnny out of her house without telling him it was going to happen, Joyce found that she was afraid of him.

Anxiety rose in her chest. She wasn't this kind of person; she truly wasn't, and her irrevocable steps made her almost sick.

Clemmie was also awake early.

In the heat of summer, the only hour during which she could take her daily walk was dawn. But today, with the sun beginning to rise, it was already seventy-eight degrees and muggy. She was still frightened from her excursion last night into the third villa, and coffee, which usually comforted her, gave her the shakes. She lacked the energy to take a single step outdoors and instead turned on the overhead fan in her little screened porch, lay down on her comfy chaise lounge, and watched the sun through the belt of trees.

She kept replaying the moment in which she'd texted the grands and appended the photograph, wishing she could take it back, but there was no do-over. There was no do-over for her trespass last night either.

Had Dom seen her? Did he have a video cam and would watch it today or tomorrow? Was Dom preparing to confront her? What would she say? The senility card would get her only so far.

Marcia and Roy had never invited a single person into their condo. They would certainly be wondering how somebody's aunt had gotten in there. If they had a video, they wouldn't recognize Clemmie, whom they had never met, but Dom would tell them. They would be on their way.

She couldn't help that. She'd pack the tree dragon. She had Borobasq's number in her cell phone. She'd call, get his address, and ship his glass.

She kept a gift-wrap box in her little study, with scissors, tape, and carefully folded bubble wrap saved from previous shipments. She told herself to get up, get it done. But she just lay there, limp and hot and anxious, and the minutes crept by.

Dom did not text that he was fine.

Did she have to check on him again, as if this were an ordinary day? He had to be home again. The golf cart was there. She texted. No response. She telephoned. No answer.

It became too hot for the porch. Back inside, she headed for the sink to pour her cold coffee down the drain and saw a locksmith's van pull into Joyce's driveway. How odd. If Joyce lost her key, why not just make a copy of Johnny's?

Clemmie was blessed to have Joyce. It was such fun having a girlfriend across the street, giggling and telling stories and playing cards in the carefree way Clemmie remembered from elementary school. But Joyce could be very interrogatory, and today Clemmie felt too frail to withstand that machine-gun style of questioning.

Her two cell phones, plugged into their chargers, felt like grenades. She picked up the family phone to see if a grand had perpetrated another offense.

But no. She was the one perpetrating.

———————

Sun City turned out to be a forty-five-minute drive southeast of the airport. Piece of cake. Boro wanted to drive with his foot on the floor, but he didn't need police attention.

He was pleased to see a sign for a Cabela's outlet near the interstate. He purchased a Swiss Army knife, of which he now had quite a collection, because you couldn't carry them on a plane. He usually bought one wherever he needed it and mailed it home afterward.

He headed on to Sun City. At its entrance was a little gatehouse, but the cars ahead of him just slowed down and drove on through, so Boro did the same. Interesting. A fake gated community.

Very nicely landscaped. Green, pretty, symmetrical.

The GPS on his rental car sent Boro past the main clubhouse, half a mile into Sun City, left at the golf course clubhouse, and then right on Forsythia. The almost identical tan houses on Forsythia were large, with protruding two-car garages, two alternating styles of foundation landscaping, and sidewalk maple trees the exact same size between each driveway. No human activity was visible.

He'd pondered why his glass would end up in a retirement village, but now that he saw the weird anonymity of Sun City, he could sort of get it. Buying drugs was far less expensive in the West than in the East, and it was unlikely that a car driving carefully on interstates would be stopped by cops, so a good way to make an income was to buy in Colorado and sell in college towns on the opposite coast. You'd probably sell marijuana in its oil form, which was odorless and took little space, and not risk carrying the herb, with its telltale scent and bulk.

It made him laugh to think that there could be a trap house in Sun City. But he doubted if the actual customers would come here. A stream of crack, coke, or grass users would be pretty visible in this silent, motionless tan neighborhood. The house where Clementine Lakefield had taken her snapshot could be a way station.

Boro guessed that everybody on these curvy little streets knew one another by name and by sight, but people could choose to tell nobody anything. If some old dude or old lady was doing drug runs when they went out of town, they'd say they were leaving on a cruise. Who was to know they were picking up ganja oil? More likely, though, a grandson or granddaughter had taken Boro's tree dragon. Someone Boro's age. Say Grandma spent the summer in Maine and some of the winter in Florida. Her South Carolina place would be empty and easy to use for weeks or months at a stretch. Maybe Grandma knew what was going on, and maybe she didn't.

He turned onto Marigold, where the houses were half the size of the Forsythia places and had gray siding instead of tan. This road was narrower. Street parking anywhere except in a driveway would be an obstacle. You wanted to break in around here, you'd need a repair truck with a logo, but it would be sketchy. You'd be an annoying and perhaps memorable detour for every driver.

Two tiny culs-de-sac, White Lily and Pink Camellia, branched off, and then at last he reached the very short Blue Lilac. Here there were little attached one-floor homes in groups of three, each unit with its own two-car garage wider than the front part of the house. Their front yards were handkerchiefs, and their small backyards ran into each other with little landscaping to provide privacy. These streets had the aura of people who saved hard and carefully to get here. Why would anybody making a buck in pot tolerate such a tiny, literally dead-end place?

Blue Lilac had one three-villa set on the left, and two on the right. The lane ended in a tight circle with a tiny landscaped island. Behind the two-set side, the backyards would always be under observation by Pink Camellia neighbors, but on the Latin teacher's side of the street, the single unit of three homes backed onto a strip of trees.

At the sharp turn from Marigold onto Blue Lilac, a wide paved path went up a berm and through the trees. A little sign read: "Golf carts and pedestrians only." At the top of the berm was an automatic gate in a green chain-link fence, and beyond that was the brick back of the shopping strip that faced the highway where he'd come in.

Okay, it was beginning to make sense. A nice location for dealing. Just scoot through your own private gate at the hour of your choice—dawn, dusk, or high noon—and your customer would be parked in the middle of hundreds of other cars, every single shopper with plastic and paper bags, in a hurry, and not looking while you exchanged a plastic bag or two yourself.

The little woods curved around the cul-de-sac enclosure on the other side of the green chain-link fence, became deeper, and looked as if they might go all the way back to the golf course. At first, the chain-link appeared to be a real barrier, but when he circled the cul-de-sac, he saw that it ran only between the villas and the parking areas and then just stopped among the trees. So the woods and parking lots were accessible by foot. A dealer here had a variety of routes out.

What the dealer didn't have was street parking.

But none of this applied, because this was Helen Stephens's villa, not Clementine Lakefield's.

Boro decided not to park in Helen Stephens's driveway. He didn't want his rental car recognized later. He wasn't sure Helen Stephens would tell him where Clementine lived. If he had to use force, okay, that's why he had the knife, but ideally, he could get what he needed with charm. Boro had been born with charm, and he used it liberally.

There were problems. If he parked at the golf club and walked back here, he'd be obvious and vulnerable. And although he could cow an old lady into showing him the right place by twirling a knife blade, there was no such thing as a drug dealer without a gun. The dealer would recognize Boro, because that was the root of this: the thief had to be somebody Boro knew.

A trap house would have surveillance video and serious locks. Probably booby traps. Probably not a typical alarm system because they'd never want cops showing up to check out the property.

Wherever the aunt lived, he hoped it featured better parking.

He drove slowly away from Blue Lilac, glanced down the other culs-de-sac, and this time saw three people separately walking tiny dogs and carrying plastic poop bags. He parked at the golf clubhouse among fifty other cars and called the cell phone number Bentley had given him yesterday, the one that belonged to the great-aunt.

"Good morning," said Clementine Lakefield's ladylike voice.

"Good morning to you too, Mrs. Lakefield," said the man who had called yesterday.

Clemmie hadn't had to call him. He'd called her. She would insure the glass for whatever he wanted, drive her package to UPS, and in half an hour, this nightmare would be solved and she could think more deeply about the other one. The mere words *cold case* gave her the chills, as if she were coming down with the flu or facing prison.

"It's me, Boro, come to pick up my glass," he said, sounding very cheerful. "I'm right here in Sun City. I'm parked at the golf clubhouse."

Right here in Sun City?

Clemmie went damp and prickly under her wig. Her hands began to shake, and it became harder to fill her lungs.

How could he possibly be here? How could he possibly know where she lived? *Bentley* didn't know where she lived, and Bentley was this man's source. Could Bentley have informed a drug dealer than his aunt lived in Sun City? How could he betray her like that?

Her impression that Borobasq lived out west somewhere must be wrong. Or was getting his tree dragon so urgent that he'd leaped on a plane at dawn? Or even taken the red-eye? It doesn't matter, she told herself. He doesn't care about me. He wants his glass. I'll give it to him. It'll be over.

Panic had always been her enemy, and she felt it rising, looking for a way in.

"Now, I don't want you to worry about a thing, Mrs. Lakefield," he said. His voice oozed comfort, but Clemmie had been a teacher for fifty years and knew fake charm when she heard it. "I'm going to handle it all," he told her. "My thought is, you pick me up in the golf-club parking lot. The two of us will drive back to your place in your car. You'll park inside your garage, which means that nobody will realize you brought me into the situation. You'll point out the neighbors who stole my glass, and I'll just head on over."

His plan didn't sound workable, but that didn't matter, because Clemmie had a better one. When they met at the golf clubhouse, everybody preparing to golf or trotting into the restaurant for lunch, she'd be perfectly safe. She'd hand over the tree dragon, and they'd be done. "What are you driving?"

"A rental car. Four-door Toyota Corolla. Maroon."

———

Boro was laughing.

He had not only found her, but also coaxed her to meet him without actually stating anything. He hadn't had to mention Blue Lilac Lane, which was good, since Helen Stephens lived there, while he didn't know where Clementine Lakefield lived. He'd get the old bag to tell him everything she knew about those neighbors, and he knew he could get it out of her; he was outstanding with old women. And if for some reason she balked, there was the knife. Boro was not into killing. Maiming was more his style.

SEVEN

Clemmie stared at herself in the bathroom mirror. When her beautiful black hair first began to go gray, she'd dyed it, but when it got so sparse that her scalp showed, she'd started wearing a wig. Latin students were always the best kids, and classes were always small, so behavior was rarely a problem, but the fact was, you needed every weapon at your disposal when you were in charge of teenagers. Clemmie tried not to show weakness, even if the weakness was just thinning hair.

Wigs were so well done now, thanks to all those suffering chemo patients who went bald. But here in the South, where it was so hot for so long, a wig could be torture. Did she want to put on makeup, her black wig, and a nice blouse and look young and strong and unworried? Or should she skip makeup and exhibit her own sad, old hair?

Maybe instead the crisply short chestnut-brown hair she wore whenever she attended St. Saviour's, in the probably mistaken belief that nobody from church would recognize her if they crossed paths at a shopping mall. Maybe with those sparkly drugstore glasses? It was an excellent disguise. Although why she would need a disguise with Borobasq, she didn't know.

It was crucial to be calm. She knew from way too many encounters that panic was the deciding factor in failure. Looking her best would help her keep her poise. She decided on the black wig and a Sunday outfit. She dressed quickly, smearing on foundation, whisking on a little powder and color, outlining her lips in the bright red that suited her.

Just in case things went sour, she zipped her passport into a purse compartment. She was wearing a skirt with front pockets, mail-order because department-store skirts certainly didn't offer pockets. They hardly even offered fabric, skirts this season being the size of place mats. She decided to carry both phones. Left pocket, family phone, because I *left* my family behind, she told herself.

With the tote containing the glass in the back seat, she clicked her garage-door opener and backed out, grateful as always for her car's rearview camera system since she couldn't twist her neck as easily as she used to. She crept out of Blue Lilac, the shivers starting in her gut but not yet visible on her body. She turned on Marigold, passed Pink Camellia and then White Lily.

Some visitors to Sun City were horrified by the endless stretches of literally vanilla housing, but Clemmie relished the anonymity. Who could ever find you? All these little culs-de-sac and pods and nonsensical plot alignments, so that the builders could squish in every possible house? The insane numbering system so that a street with nine dwellings (Blue Lilac) began with 5244? When she was the hostess for rotating card games, she tied a bright-red scarf to her mailbox, because even after years of playing cards here once a month, somebody was bound to go to the wrong house.

The speed limit was 20 mph, and Clemmie, feeling a particular need to blend, drove the quarter mile to the golf course parking lot even slower than that. She saw Borobasq's maroon sedan parked at the end of a slanted row and drew alongside. She felt blind from anxiety. Gritting her teeth to steady herself, she put the car in Park and opened her door, an action that released the door locks. Before she even swung one leg out, a very handsome boy opened the passenger door and slid in next to her.

Fifty years of fear hit her in the heart. If she was in trouble, she couldn't move fast enough to escape. If anybody heard her scream, they wouldn't react quickly enough. She managed to look squarely at him as if she were at ease.

In Clemmie's day, a boy this good-looking would have been called a dreamboat. He wore jeans and a highly decorated black-and-white tee under a black denim jacket, looking both stylish and anonymous. His eyes had a hot, bright look, far too excited for meeting an elderly lady and picking up a piece of glass.

He grinned at her, slow and sly. She knew absolutely that he could see her fear, and like the worst kids in any high school, he would capitalize on it.

He doesn't care about me, she reminded herself. He cares about the glass.

Before glass, though, Clemmie needed the crucial details of how he had found her, because she had to solve that. There could be no cracks through which she could be found. "For heaven's sake," she said airily, a woman without a care. "How did you locate me?"

He was rightly proud of his technique and began with what Bentley had told him. It was sobering. Along with reciting her cell phone number, Bentley had casually revealed her last name (the one known to him, anyway), her occupation, and the particular Sun City in which she lived.

In this age, desperate to protect privacy (a need Clemmie certainly shared), she could hardly believe that a man of twenty-six—or whatever Bentley was, maybe it was Harper who was twenty-six— had so unthinkingly sold out his great-aunt.

Borobasq explained each step of his high-school staff searches, until he finally had located a Latin teacher named Helen Stephens.

If Clemmie had not had the steering wheel to hang onto, she would have fainted. *He knew her other name.* Now, with that ancient Connecticut murder moved to a front burner, somebody on this earth knew *both* her names. Somebody with a very questionable life.

But then, whose life was more questionable than her own, really?

"So I figured I'd drop in on old Helen Stephens," he said, leaning toward her. Her car was small, and he was now hideously close.

Clemmie clung to her plan. Reaching back between the front seats, she gripped the handle of the tote lying in the rear. "I have retrieved your glass for you," she said, hauling it through the gap.

He peered into the tote, saw his tree dragon resting in there, and laughed out loud. "You're a champ! I never took Latin, but if I had, I would have wanted you for a teacher."

She had to get rid of him and his knowledge; she had to close the door Bentley had opened. She had to get out of here before she fell apart. "In exchange for the glass," she said, without thinking it through, without analysis, just blurting it out, "kindly do not tell my grand-nephew my name."

He frowned slightly.

Oh, no, no, no, she thought.

She had made a huge error. The boy had not grasped that Clementine Lakefield and Helen Stephens were the same person. Instead of sitting in silence waiting to find out what he knew, Clemmie had leaped to solve his problems for him—stealing his glass back, driving here to meet him, telling him she was both women.

She had sold herself down the river.

It's because so many years have gone by, she thought. For decades, I was young and clever, but now I'm old and pathetic, just when I have to ward it off all over again. Oh, Connecticut. I can't face that all over again!

She could see the boy's thoughts spinning, slowing down, and stopping on the truth. Now he was grinning hugely. His parents had definitely supported an orthodontist. America had a rule: You could commit any number of terrible sins and crimes, but you must not present misaligned teeth. "I won't be talking to Bentley again," he said softly. "Or you either, for that matter. Drive us to your place. I have to get moving."

"There's no need to go to my house," she protested. "I got the glass for you."

"The glass doesn't matter. I need to get into your neighbor's house."

Clemmie had risked everything to get that tree dragon, and it didn't matter? How could it not matter? Wasn't it the point? "I can't let you into somebody else's house."

His face changed the way Rudyard Creek's face had changed, the real person staring out like a gargoyle. "*You* went in, lady. You stole it back. How did you do it? For that matter, why did you do it? Why didn't they stop you? They weren't home? You have a key to their place?"

She couldn't think.

"What's their name?" he said.

"You don't need their name. You have your glass back."

"The glass is nothing. Give me their name."

The glass was nothing? But what about all those posts lamenting its theft? What about all his searches online and his red-eye flight?

The boy opened the glove compartment, picked up the car regis-
tration that lay on top, and laughed silently. The car was registered to
Helen Stephens, although he had telephoned Clementine Lakefield.
He photographed the little document on his cell phone.

"What are you doing?" she whispered.

"You never know what information you might need. Drive, Mrs.
Lakefield. Or Helen Stephens. Whoever you are. I don't care about
you. Our destination," he said, holding up the registration, "is 5244
Blue Lilac."

"Please just take your glass and go."

"I told you, I don't care about the glass. And the people that stole
my stuff? They're not going to worry about you, Mrs. Lakefield.
They're going to worry about me. Get going." A little tic appeared
in his cheek, like a rogue dimple.

I could run into the clubhouse. But he'd grab me before I could
even get the car door open. And he knows my names. I can't let him
say anything. Or can I? Does it matter, after all these years? Perhaps
I can just laugh too. Except that right this very minute, the murder
of Rudyard Creek is being examined again.

She couldn't fathom that. How could it be a reasonable use of
police time?

When she didn't touch the ignition, the dreamboat's hand
flashed toward her. Was he going to hit her? Was he going to—? But
he gripped her black hair and yanked the wig off. "I thought that hair
was too perfect," he said, snickering.

It was like having her whole self ripped off—her Helen Stephens self, its lid gone, its bald spots exposed, its helplessness made clear. Her sad, thin gray locks would be sticking up in a pathetic tangle.

He tossed the wig into her lap, and now in his other hand she saw the distinctive red and silver oblong of a Swiss Army knife. The gleaming blade was pointed at her. "Drive," he said softly. "You're going to tell me everything I need to know about those neighbors, and everything about your two names, because you are no innocent bystander."

The knife changed everything.

She drove slowly out of the clubhouse lot, slowly turned onto Forsythia. The boy slumped down so that he was largely hidden by the doorframe and tinted windows. They passed dog walkers, who twinkled their fingers at Clemmie but did not really try to see who was in the passing car. Hers was just another white sedan among hundreds, and they were much more interested in the poop habits of their Yorkies.

At the stop sign for Marigold, she settled the wig back on her head, trying to tuck loose strands back in, but her hands were shaking and the wig felt ridiculous, like a bird perching.

She had left the Coglands' slider open. So he could go in, and nobody could get hurt because nobody was there. Nothing was there. She could get away from him before he realized that going into the Cogland villa would achieve nothing.

EIGHT

Joyce decided that a few hours from now, when Johnny was at cards, she would text him that it was over, that she knew about his thefts, had changed the locks and removed his belongings to his own house.

Johnny would be relieved that she wasn't going to the police, and no matter how mad he might also be, he wouldn't smash her front door just to show her a thing or two. It was all good timing, really. She'd visit her sister in Galveston to get away for a while.

Since she and Johnny both traipsed through the main clubhouse on and off all day, they would cross paths often in the future. She'd give Johnny plenty of time to cool off. Single men being a rare commodity in Sun City, Johnny would probably acquire another woman rather quickly, and his interests would be elsewhere by the time she returned from Galveston.

Her own carefully packed suitcases were waiting in the guest-room closet. Last night, she had changed the PINs on her accounts and stopped the mail. They'd still deliver today and tomorrow, but it wouldn't be enough for anybody to notice it lying in the box.

Joyce walked through her house, checking to be sure it was properly closed up. She raised the thermostat to eighty so that the AC would still run and keep mold from developing, but her bill wouldn't be too hideous. Uh-oh. She'd forgotten the refrigerator. A lot of food in there, because Johnny was a serious eater and she was a serious cook. Joyce couldn't bear the thought of wasting food or coming home to a house full of rotting food.

It was surprising how panicky she felt about the forgotten food. What else had she forgotten? Think! Think!

Her heart raced. She pressed her hand against her chest as if she could control things with a little pressure.

Through her kitchen window, she saw Helen's garage door go up, but the garage was empty, meaning that in a moment, Helen's car would appear in the slice of street Joyce could see. Sure enough, Helen drove seamlessly from Blue Lilac into her garage, and the door began to lower.

I'll run all the groceries over to her, thought Joyce, relieved to have something easily solved.

It was grass day on Blue Lilac. A dozen members of the landscape crew, variously armed with mowers, blowers, and edgers, were working their way up and down the lane. Clemmie cut off the engine, touched the garage-door device in her cup holder, and the door closed heavily, shutting off the racket from the blowers. Why couldn't they use rakes? Rakes were so comely, so quiet.

Borobasq was already out of her car, crossing the garage, opening her utility-room door, using the bottom of his T-shirt for gloves, and entering her house before she had unsnapped her seat belt. So what if his fingerprints aren't on the knob? she thought. They're on my car door and my glove box.

Perhaps Borobasq was also panicky. Why dart into the house? Why abandon his hostage?

She pressed the garage-door opener again, preparing to drive off while he reconnoitered her villa, but he was way too quick for her, already back and leaning across her to turn off the engine. When the door finished its journey up, he tapped the device and it began the journey down. "Get out," he said, not even looking at her. It took Clemmie three lurching tries to get herself out of the car and standing upright.

He waved her into her own living room, blessedly cool after the scorching garage, and looked around like a buyer. "Is the unit where you found the glass just like this? They all match?"

She was having a hard time breathing. Perhaps she was having a heart attack. Perhaps that would be best. Just collapse and die here on the floor.

"I'm not here to frighten you," he said softly, although a man who snatched off an old woman's wig definitely enjoyed frightening people. "I never tell anybody who I am either. You found my stuff for me. I'm not going to betray you."

If that were true, you wouldn't have photographed my registration, she thought. You have already made plans to betray me. My grandnephew betrayed me. I betrayed myself, and now I have to betray the Coglands. At least Marcia and Roy weren't home to get hurt. They didn't even have sheets on their beds. He could threaten all he wanted with his knife, but there were no people to hurt. "That unit is at the other end. It's the same as this but reversed. You can get in through the back. Their sliders are unlocked. And the middle occupant never opens his drapes, so just walk past his unit."

"You people always leave everything unlocked?"

"Not usually."

"How do you know those sliders aren't locked?"

"Because I was just there, getting the tree dragon."

"How did you know nobody was home?"

"I had previously knocked on the front door."

"Did you call them?"

"I don't have a phone number for them."

"Isn't there a neighborhood directory?"

"Yes, but they changed their number, which isn't unusual. People get new numbers all the time."

He leaned over her, a posture that even now, even all these

decades later, terrified her. Everyone else was always taller and stronger. She pretended he was a Latin student who had not studied his fourth conjugation.

"Why were you in their place to start with?" he demanded.

It occurred to her that once the boy was in the third unit, he would find the connecting door to the middle unit. To Dom, who was probably not home but might be.

She needed a plausible lie to keep Dom safe, and luckily she was a lie specialist from way back. "I was walking along the little woods, looking for leaves to use in pottery, because I do slab pottery—meaning you don't use a wheel, but you roll the clay out like pie dough, and impressions of leaves in clay are so attractive—and when I went by their sliders, I saw the most beautiful extraordinary thing!—a masterpiece!—I couldn't imagine what it was!—gleaming and casting prisms on the wall. It was a tree and a dragon and some sort of pitcher or container. I knew the people weren't home, they're never home, but I knocked on their sliders, and no one came, of course, and then I'm ashamed to say that I tried the sliders, and they weren't locked. Such carelessness, but anyway, I crept in to look at this whatever-it-was, this amazing thing. Did you create it? You are a brilliant artist."

He seemed to find it reasonable that Clemmie would be so mesmerized by his glass that she would walk straight into somebody's home. "And their name?"

"They're rarely here. Nobody actually knows them."

He was still holding the knife. The blade was short and narrow. If he stabbed her, it wouldn't go all the way through. But it could do serious damage. Probably deathly damage, if he wanted that. He took her hand and pressed the knife against the pad of her thumb. "I need their names."

She stared at the knife. "I met them only once or twice, not recently. Maybe a few years ago. They use their place as a hotel when they visit grandchildren. They don't care about the neighborhood or even Sun City itself."

"Who are the grandchildren?"

"I don't know. I never met them."

"Spell the last name."

She said, "You're scaring me. I can't think clearly."

They were next to the high breakfast bar that divided the living room from the kitchen. She never ate at the bar and had no stools. He glanced at her white refrigerator, on which many magnets held many pieces of paper. Residents with more expensive homes had stainless-steel appliances and couldn't use magnets. On the fridge door were business cards from handymen and house washers, doctors and physical therapists, a calendar, and a hand-drawn map of the pod, created by Eileen, who ran the Sunshine group sending birthday cards, get-well cards, condolence cards.

Borobasq ripped the map off. "So here you are. Stephens. And next door to you is Dominic Spesante." He pronounced it rhyming with *peasant*, but Dom pronounced it Speh-*sahn*-tay. "Marcia and

Roy Cogland," he read, smiling slightly. He tucked it into his jeans pocket. And pointed to her slider. They crossed the living room. She prayed she wouldn't be made to go with him. She released the catch and slid the heavy door back. The Carolina heat came in like a fist. He was overdressed in long sleeves and long pants, but he did not react to the heat and simply strode through the screened porch, onto the patio, and around the holly trees. Clemmie pulled her sliders shut. He certainly had faith that she would stay put.

Already hurrying to the garage, she phoned Dom and was asked by a robot to leave a message. "Dom, lock your doors. All of them. Now." She dropped the phone into its pocket and was crossing her little front hall where somebody waved through the glass and knocked very hard.

Joyce caroled, "Yoo-hoo, Helen!"

Harper McKeithen never used email herself, but you had to check Mom's emails, because this was the only way you'd find out that she was getting married again.

Harper scanned Mom's wedding news and opened the link about a cold-case murder in Mom's hometown in Connecticut, where none of the family lived anymore. Harper loved true crime—which was lucky, because television had so much of it—and she read the story greedily.

A guy in his thirties, once a basketball coach at Mom's and, before that, Granddad's old high school, had been killed at a highway picnic area in Old Lyme fifty years ago.

Her first detective question was: What's a highway picnic area? An old black-and-white photograph showed a two-lane road, presumably the "highway," and a grassy park with towering maple trees, picnic tables, and tiny charcoal grills on metal posts. A narrow, unpaved road wound through the trees, disappeared, and came back to rejoin the "highway." The man's body had been found at a picnic table hidden among the trees.

Harper found the original article rather touching. Fifty years ago, police figured the coach had been at this little park to grill a hamburger. Today's cops figured it was either a drug deal or a homosexual hookup, in those days equally low-life and dangerous events.

The dead man's widow, poor old thing, had been thrilled about the cold case opening up, expecting her husband to be proved brave, honorable, and true, but tragically overcome by the forces of evil. The cold-case police, however, seemed to believe he'd been complicit in his own death, because why would a man be back in a town where he no longer taught, hanging out alone in a picnic area when he had no picnic supplies, and then get himself murdered in the shade?

Now the widow wanted them to drop the cold case. "They're just trying to find dirt against my husband!" she said to the reporter.

Wow, thought Harper. Guy's been dead half a century, and she's still grieving. Harper could barely remember the boys she'd broken up with in high school.

The dead man was seriously handsome, in that neat, crew-cut way of men prior to the Summer of Love and people getting groovy. Six foot four, as befitted a basketball coach. It was one of the things that confused the police. This would not have been an easy man to overcome.

It wasn't clear to Harp how he had actually been killed because the police were "retaining crucial details." Well, yeah, that was pretty crucial. Gun? Knife? Vehicle? Crowbar?

She answered her mother, "Wedding sounds so exciting! So sorry I can't be there! Love you!"

———————

Bentley was reading the same attachment. He could actually remember Granddad talking about this crime. Coach Creek was a name that had stuck in Bent's mind because his mother liked Coach handbags, and because Creek sounded like a location, not a last name. Bent could still hear the pride in his grandfather's voice that the basketball coach had been a dinner guest in his home. Bent didn't know anybody who gave dinner parties or, for that matter, had guests; that was the whole point of restaurants.

Bentley couldn't see the point of the reopened investigation unless a small-town police force felt left out of the whole cold-case popularity thing and dragged this one up: the murder of a good man in a dark place. It might be about money, sex, jealousy, power, drugs—who knew? But more likely, the guy stopped to take a leak and encountered the wrong person. The wrong strong person, to be precise. But even if the police found that person, and went to trial, and proved the killer guilty, was a jury going to sentence some eighty- or ninety-year-old to life in prison?

The reporters were definitely more into it than the police, who kept saying, "No comment."

"No," he texted his mother, "still not going to the wedding. You have a great time though. Always on your team, Mom."

They had both forgotten their aunt Clemmie's glass. All that was so yesterday.

————————

The Latin teacher's little villa had been bright and warm, with hot colors and book-lined walls, but the third unit had its original flat-white paint and almost no furniture. The place was very clean, which bothered Boro. Drug dealers were not into housekeeping. Either these guys liked to Swiffer or they sensed trouble when they read Bentley's post, cleaned up, and moved on. But usually when drug dealers moved on, they skipped cleaning.

There was almost nothing in any drawer or cupboard. The closets held no clothing. The bathroom had no soap and no toilet paper roll. The refrigerator had a six-pack each of beer and sparkly lime-flavored water. The only condiments were a few tiny packets of mayo.

No TV, no dinnerware, no towels, no grandchildren's toys. They hadn't even been using this as a motel.

He examined the little table on which the tree dragon had sat, recognizing it from the photograph, but it was just Pier 1 mass production.

The mudroom was similar to the Latin teacher's but had a utility sink, which she did not. The only thing in the mudroom was a folding metal stool, which Boro used to check the top of every kitchen and mudroom cabinet. But although their facades went up higher than the actual cabinet, giving several inches of invisible storage room, nothing was stored there.

He circled again, looking for anything that could provide a hiding space. There had to be something because that had to be the purpose of the unit.

Only because he was checking out every tiny detail did he notice that one of the two side windows in the living room was unlocked and no longer had a screen. So not only could you come and go through the unlocked sliders, but you could pop in and out the window.

He would have expected booby traps, but this place was almost the reverse. Maybe the sleepy, old location had lulled them into sleepy, old behavior. He had their names now, but the names didn't matter because they wouldn't use their real names anyway. Given how the old lady said they came so rarely and vanished inside so completely, they weren't necessarily the same people each time either. In any event, the names Marcia and Roy Cogland meant nothing to him.

He opened every appliance, checking the washer, dryer, dishwasher, toilet tanks. Nothing.

There was no basement. He pulled down the attic stairs, but although the attic had a fairly high peak, it had no floor. He pulled up blankets of insulation, but there was nothing underneath the pink batts within reach, and you couldn't walk around up there.

He found two video cameras, one in a fake smoke alarm, the other in a fake light switch. Both used thumb drives, which were missing. It wasn't a system with live streaming, but motion activation, which meant somebody had to check it now and then. Like who?

He flicked the wall switch for the gas fireplace, but it didn't come on, no surprise, because why would they keep the pilot lit if they were never here? He stooped and peered in and saw nothing but the fake logs, but all the same, he felt around until he figured out how the glass front came off, removed it carefully, stuck his head inside the fake chimney, and found nothing.

He still didn't know who they were, and they still had his money.

It was a low-level operation, whatever it was, but then Boro had a pretty low-level operation, and he had netted over a million dollars in the last six months.

The attached garage was literally empty. Not one paint can. Not one yard tool. Not one trash can. The concrete floor had no trace of oil or water stains. The garage ceiling was almost entirely blocked by the automatic door system, so nothing could be added up there for storage.

A door in the sidewall stumped him. He pictured the exterior of the three villas. The garages of the second two villas were side by side in between their living spaces, while the old woman's garage was on her left. A side door in her garage would lead to her yard. A side door in this garage could only open into the adjacent garage.

These two villas were literally connected.

So assuming old Marcia and Roy were dealers, then so was the middle guy, because they didn't even go back and forth between their two units through the sheltered backyards; their access was inside their closed garages. And yet they left their back door and their side window open. You'd have to be a very stoned dealer to get that sloppy.

He wondered why they needed both the middle and the third units. Maybe it was just safer to own both units because the fewer neighbors keeping an eye on you, the better. Marcia and Roy's place had trees on two sides, not neighbors. In the two three-unit buildings across the street, every single front window had its shades and drapes closed because the morning sun was drilling the facade of their units, adding to the excellence of this position. It also meant that when the Latin teacher had tried to run a few minutes ago, nobody saw her garage door go up and down a second time.

Maybe the Latin teacher had taken the money as well as the photograph. No, because she was the type that couldn't change the battery in her smoke alarm, never mind find a cache he couldn't find. And she could hardly get out of her own car, so she certainly wasn't coming and going through a window. What he needed and who he needed was going to be in the middle unit.

Boro felt a satisfying blaze of triumph. He was going to get them, whoever they were.

He wasn't worried that the woman would call the cops. She was hiding serious stuff, using a second name that even her own family didn't know. But she could have called to warn the middle unit. He checked the name on his map. Spesante.

If anybody was going to be armed, it would be Spesante.

Standing back, Boro quietly opened the connecting door between the garages. Absolute silence. And complete dark. Using the flash on his phone, he looked in. No car, but there was a golf cart. The stench of old garbage was very strong. How often did they collect trash here?

He had to lift his foot quite high to go over the interior door threshold.

He thought about that. He thought about booby traps.

He walked in a complete circle around the golf cart, checking it out, and then eased himself silently into the utility room of the middle villa.

It was the home of a slob whose life centered on his massive television. Most kitchen drawers and cabinets were empty. There was no landline. A top kitchen drawer was full of paid bills. The usual: internet, electric, gas, cell phone... How come the guy didn't just pay online? Boro photographed the cell phone bill so he'd have the number.

He returned to the connecting door, knelt, and opened the

screwdriver on his knife, planning to remove the metal scuff strip and pry up the oak. But his money would not be here. People who could clean up as well as this wouldn't forget half a million dollars. What they might do is set it so he'd blow off his own hands if he unscrewed the strip and released a pressure point.

He breathed in the foul air and decided to gamble. The place didn't feel like anybody had ever bothered to put in real security. He removed the screws.

NINE

In her arms, Joyce carried a heavily packed brown-paper grocery bag, while the handles of three plastic bags of groceries were tangled in her huge fingers. Joyce had the largest hands of any woman Clemmie knew. Joyce beamed, air-kissed, trotted into the kitchen, and sprawled the bags across the counter. "I'm going to visit my sister," she said excitedly. "The Galveston sister. So much is happening, Helen, and I'm in such a huge hurry that I have to bolt. But who was that absolute doll you just brought home? Have you acquired a boy toy?" she teased.

Borobasq had been seen when Clemmie drove into her garage? The whole nightmare now had a witness. One of the more talkative witnesses, in fact, in all Sun City. "Galveston," repeated Clemmie. She shut the front door, and the roar of lawn mowers and blowers was silenced.

"Is it your grandnephew?" asked Joyce. "I've always wanted to meet a boy named Bent—or maybe his parents, so I can see what kind of mother and father would saddle their innocent child with that. Although it's not as bad as Eileen's granddaughter, who is named Custer. A girl, Helen. Named Custer. It's true. Anyway, here's everything that could spoil, since I'll be gone so long."

When could Clemmie possibly have told Joyce that she had a nephew named Bentley? Clemmie never mentioned her tiny family. She spoke only of herself, Helen Stephens, who had no family, just old friends scattered over the country.

I'm old and failing, thought Clemmie. I've mixed my fake and real lives and handed pieces of them to Joyce.

Joyce's departure for Texas was a good thing, because she wouldn't be here to mention Borobasq to anybody, and yet awful, because she was Clemmie's sidekick, and now Clemmie would have to go alone to every card game and activity. It took such energy to do things alone. Assuming, of course, that Borobasq let Helen Stephens go anywhere.

She wasn't afraid for her life. She was afraid he'd end Helen Stephens.

Joyce always talked at top speed, but now she sounded beyond giddy and into hysterical. Or perhaps it was Clemmie herself in that condition. "Listen, if Johnny comes around, avoid him," said Joyce. "I've changed the locks. He's out of my life."

That was the purpose of the locksmith? Keeping Johnny out of the house? What had gone wrong? Johnny had been cheerful and helpful at Dom's yesterday, no mention of distress at home. Of course, men were often clueless, and Johnny wasn't observant of emotional response. Joyce could have been dropping hints for weeks, and Johnny would just ask her to pass the hot sauce.

"Let me fix your wig. It's practically sideways," said Joyce, tucking and adjusting.

Clemmie found the fussing fingers unbearable, especially Joyce's fingers, huge and thick, with massive nails, as if they belonged on the wrists of a football player. Joyce was proud of her hands and was always heading off for a manicure.

Clemmie took the wig off entirely and held it in her hand. She'd deal with her horrible balding head later.

"Where is he right now?" asked Joyce.

Since the antecedent to that pronoun was Johnny, it took Clemmie a moment to grasp that Joyce was referring to Borobasq.

The family phone twinkled to let her know she had a message. *Twinkle* wasn't the right verb, but Clemmie had never settled on a better one for the restless collision of high-pitched bells. The grands don't message for weeks, she thought, and then they drown me.

She could think of no safe answer to give Joyce, because any lie would require her to produce more lies. I have to get Joyce out of here before Borobasq comes back, she thought. Unless perhaps a second person in my kitchen is protection for me, and Borobasq will just leave. But he can't leave. I have to drive him.

She swiped and read the first message in spite of the fact that her best friend was standing right there. There was something so doglike about relationships with cell phones, the whole world on a leash. Or perhaps she was on the leash, and the phone was her owner.

Did you read that cold-case article? Harper had written. I'm forwarding it to you in case Mom skipped you. You must have met the dead guy! Talk with the cold-case detectives. Bent remembers Granddad talking about it. Maybe they'll solve the case, and it'll be a TV show! You'll be on television!

The next text was from Bentley. You must have gone to all those games since your brother, Pete, our granddad, played on the guy's team. They don't seem to have a hotline, but the reporter's email is at the bottom of this next article.

To think that Clemmie had prayed to the Lord that Harper and Bentley would want to be part of her existence. She had not grasped how much this generation venerated fame or, if not fame, at least being noticed. Any possible window to importance—a cameo on some TV re-creation, a chance to talk to real detectives in a real case—must be seized, even if the experience is two generations removed.

Would you have a hotline for a cold case? The whole point was, nothing had been hot for fifty years.

Clemmie reminded herself to practice senility and confusion. Which Bent obviously believed she already possessed, since he had felt it necessary to remind her that her brother, Pete, was also Bent's grandfather.

Joyce, who was as tough as the weapon-like nails on her fingers, started to cry. "Johnny's a thief, Helen. Can you believe that? He's been rifling my checking account."

Johnny? Taking money from Joyce's account? Clemmie did not believe it. Joyce added so badly they didn't let her keep score at card games. If there were errors in Joyce's checking account, Johnny was unlikely to be responsible. But if Johnny *had* dipped into the petty cash, so to speak, how could the risk be worth it? Johnny was well-to-do. He was always leaping on a plane, taking Joyce on some wonderful vacation he was careful not to let his daughter know about, or she'd shriek, "You never took Mom to Bermuda!"

"How awful, Joyce."

"I dumped Johnny's clothes and his stuff in his garage because he's at horseshoes, so I have a little time, although now and then he comes back to the house between horseshoes and his card game, which is why I'm rushing. I have to hit the road as quickly as possible. I brought over all my perishables. Finish the casserole today, Helen. And the milk you should use by the end of the week."

"But, Joyce, if Johnny's the bad guy, why are *you* going to Texas? Shouldn't you call the police on him? Or at least confront Johnny?" Clemmie couldn't believe she'd said that. No reasonable person should call police into her life, let alone confront someone physically stronger. Or was Johnny stronger? Joyce was not a small woman.

But why was she thinking of physical confrontation at all? Civilized people didn't go after each other. She had been thrown by

Borobasq snatching her wig and waving his sharp blade. Why rip off her wig? Shouldn't he have assumed that she was a sweet old lady helping him out? What was so compelling in the third unit?

I'll just leave with Joyce, she thought. But no, Joyce is leaving for Texas.

"He has a temper," said Joyce, meaning Johnny, although Clemmie was thinking of Borobasq. "I'll be out of state, he'll cool off, he'll vanish from my life. I'll come back, pick up my activities where I left off, and that'll be that."

"You're handling it so well, Joyce. You're so right to avoid a scene. Let's get you into your car." She put her hand on Joyce's waist, lightly propelling her toward the front door. Behind her, the cell phone twinkled again. It was like a crowd of nagging pixies.

Outside by the little porch, her Knock Out roses lapped up the heat, roses of strong character, never giving in. Clemmie moved Joyce on down the sidewalk like an usher. "Given the circumstances, Joyce, you need to hit the road. You don't want to run into Johnny."

The mower started its path across the Cogland front yard, its roar startling both women. Next, the crew would do Dom's, and then Clemmie's, and then circle out back where they'd mow in long strips behind all three at one pass, because no sidewalks or driveways interrupted the flow of grass. The laborer with the blower was still on Joyce's side of the street, removing grass clippings. Clemmie hoped Borobasq was clever enough to avoid the crew's notice when he came back, or there would be even more witnesses. Not that the landscapers cared. As far as she could tell, they accepted the Sun City population as a couple thousand identical huts with twice that many identical residents, all obsessed with grass height.

Joyce bent over Clemmie to give her a farewell hug, scurried across the street, got into her car, and slammed the door, having forgotten, Clemmie hoped, about the dreamboat. Clemmie waved goodbye, turned to go back inside, and glimpsed Borobasq in Dom's breakfast area window.

If Borobasq can saunter around in Dom's, Dom can't be home. Where *is* Dom? Who brought the golf cart back, if not Dom?

Or was Dom right there, as trapped and afraid in his home as Clemmie was in hers?

She could not imagine Dom being afraid. In his past, in his prime, Dom had surely been the type to inspire fear.

Joyce exited Blue Lilac Lane, and Clemmie hurried back into her air-conditioning just as Borobasq opened her sliders and stepped in. "I had to wait until the lawn mower headed the other way," he said. "Who was that woman?" He didn't close the sliders behind him. The heat sucked her expensive, precious cool air outside. Clemmie turned into an irritated utility-bill payer and closed the sliders herself.

"My neighbor's leaving on vacation, and she brought me everything in her refrigerator that might spoil."

Borobasq saw the CorningWare casserole dish with its clear lid, the Tupperware containers of unknown leftovers, the half gallon of milk, the lettuce and peppers and peaches sprawling over the granite countertop, and he nodded and the doorbell rang again, followed immediately by sharp knocks.

She and Borobasq were equally startled.

Could Joyce be back? Had she forgotten something? Clemmie took the single step required to reach her little front hall and saw Johnny through the glass, waving and smiling where Joyce had been ten minutes ago.

"Who is it?" whispered Borobasq, safely out of view.

"Another neighbor."

Johnny had never seen her without a wig, and she had no time to primp. How vain I am, she thought. How desperate to impress. After all these years. And I don't even like Johnny very much.

"Get rid of him," said Borobasq.

He's confident I won't give him up, she thought. Because of my two names? Because he photographed my car registration? I could walk outside right now and stay with Johnny. He's bigger than Borobasq. We'd call the police. But if I explain Borobasq's presence, I have to explain my own. No. In a moment I'll drive him away, and it will be over. I just have to hang on. Wig or no wig.

She opened her front door, standing squarely in the center so Johnny couldn't come in. He towered over her, and Clemmie was assaulted by the familiar fear of men far bigger than she was. Fear of Johnny was ridiculous. He was a kind neighbor and had helped her with chores like renting a power sprayer to clean her patio and showing her how to change the water filter in her refrigerator. Skimming

Joyce's checking account was unlikely. Johnny was overbearing, but not stupid.

"Hey, Helen," he said, smiling. "Need the spare key. I can't get the garage door to go up, and my door key won't work. Totally weird. I spotted Joyce driving out of Sun City, but she must have her phone off, because I can't reach her. I gotta get in."

The grass-edging guy roared around Dom's, shortly to be in her own front yard. "Goodness," shouted Clemmie. "You know, I don't have a spare key anymore."

"Sure you do. Joyce and I put it on a red ribbon, and you hung it under your kitchen counter by the chargers."

"Goodness," she repeated, smiling. "You've forgotten. You and Joyce had the locks changed."

"Huh?"

"The locksmith just left!" She had to yell as the landscape guy began edging her driveway.

"Huh?"

She managed a facsimile of a smile. "You had the locks changed this morning because both of you lost your keys."

"No, we didn't. Listen, I gotta get in. Grab me the key, okay?"

"I wish I could help, but I don't have a copy of the new key. I'm so sorry, Johnny, but I have to get going. I'm sure when you reach Joyce, she'll tell you how to handle it."

Johnny could shove his way into her house and get the key himself, but of course he didn't. He was a perfectly pleasant, well-behaved man who kindly didn't remark on her ghastly appearance but just shook his head. "What a mix-up. Well, thanks anyway, Helen. See you later." He headed back to his car. The lawn guy paused the engine for Johnny to walk by.

She hadn't yet closed the front door when Johnny looked back. "You hear from Dom yet?"

She shook her head. "I haven't. I have no explanation, Johnny."

"Huh," he said, and instead of getting into his Avalon, he walked around Joyce's unit, perhaps hoping the back sliders were unlocked.

Well, everybody else's were. Maybe Joyce had messed up.

———

Borobasq microwaved himself a portion of Joyce's macaroni casserole, pawed through the drawers, found a fork, took a bite, looked pleased, and said to Clemmie, "Tell me about the guy who lives in the middle."

"I don't think you need to know about him," she said in her sharp spinster-teacher voice. "The glass was not in that unit."

"They're connected. Literally. They cut their own door. Where is he right now?" Borobasq had another forkful of Joyce's mac and cheese, which had bacon and spinach in it and was probably wonderful, especially since Borobasq didn't seem like the kind of person who home-cooked.

A huge roar came from the back patio. Borobasq dropped to his knees behind the kitchen bar as if he thought it was machine guns.

"It's the Weedwacker," she told him.

"How long does this grass insanity last?"

"A while. There are three steps. Mow, edge, and blow. It's choreographed so that they complete the whole cul-de-sac in a particular order."

"I have to leave," Boro said abruptly. "You have to drive me. Anyone at your door right now? Front or back?"

Clemmie was hugely relieved. She looked back and forth. "It's clear. I'll just get my purse, and we'll head out. If you keep low in the back seat, nobody can see you." No point in letting him know that Joyce had seen him just fine.

He retreated across the front hall into the little space onto which the bedroom, powder-room, and utility-room doors opened, bringing his mac and cheese.

Her doorbell rang again.

It was like the text messages. You don't hear a doorbell ring for months, and then it happens twice in five minutes. All Sun City front doors had glass on the top half, so she was completely visible to the men on her porch. She hoped Borobasq had not been seen darting across. "It's the yard crew," she told him. "I can't imagine what they want. Perhaps they need a drink of cold water. They can see me standing here. I have to talk to them."

He stepped back a few paces and nodded.

She opened her front door.

The man on her steps was Hispanic, like most of the workers, and in spite of the heat, wore long sleeves and a billed cap with a neck drape to protect his skin from sun.

Clemmie especially liked the Mexican crew because the men were short. Not as short as she was, but they didn't tower over her. They were just right. She was a little surprised because the man did not smile. Usually they were so friendly. "Next door? House?" he said urgently, pointing at Dom's. There was a rush of Spanish at which she could only shake her head. Maybe he saw Borobasq in there, she thought. But he couldn't know who ought to be in that unit to start with.

The man gestured with his hands, forming a sort of large box, and repeated, "Next door? *Door*."

"I'm sorry, I don't know what you need."

The man held up a finger, signaling her to wait, and trotted across the street for his foreman.

———

At the school for wayward girls, only Maureen had been brave enough to say out loud that she had been raped and that none of this was her fault.

"Nonsense," said the matron. "You encouraged some man, and you cooperated."

Clemmie had not encouraged Rudyard Creek. She had been afraid of him from the start. He had trapped her. As for cooperating, Clemmie was no match for a basketball coach more than a foot taller and much more than a hundred pounds heavier than she was. Was it called cooperating when you gave up and let it happen? It probably was. She was probably guilty as charged.

The matron wouldn't listen to Maureen's nonsense, and she *really* wouldn't listen to Clemmie, who asked to hold her baby when it was born and have a photograph. Matron marched off, having given orders that the girls were to behave themselves.

Maureen buried her face in her pillow.

Clemmie said to Ronnie, "I know we have to give up our babies, but I want to hold mine."

"They don't let you," said Ronnie sadly.

But Clementine Eleanor Lakefield won. She was the smallest wayward girl at the Mountain School, and the most likely to have trouble during delivery, but when labor began one evening, Clemmie said nothing to anybody. She gritted her teeth, gripped the iron rods of the headboard of her cot, and silently gave birth in her bed. By the time labor was seriously underway, all five other girls in her room were by her side. They had to guess about how to deal with the cord, but luckily they guessed right, and neither mother nor child bled to death or got infected.

In the morning, when six waywards failed to appear for breakfast, a staff member went to check on them. In those days, there were very few staff because girls were obedient, counseling was nonexistent, and the girls did their own housekeeping. The staff member had no idea what to do about the sleeping young mother with the baby cradled on her breast. Five girls stood protecting Clemmie while she slept, and troublemaker Veronica was the spokesman.

"Clemmie knows she has to give the baby up," said Ronnie. "She knows there's a family waiting. You call that family up and make them come here now, in person, because Clemmie needs to look at them and know that they are good people. Then she'll give them her son."

In those days, you pretended that an adoption had not happened. The child itself would never be told. Even relatives might not be told, because the adopting couple would manage to be transferred to a distant city and "have a baby" without doting grandparents, aunts, uncles, or friends around to realize that the little one was not a blood relative.

Matron stormed into the room and threatened to call the police. "All right," said Clemmie, knowing full well that the woman would not risk the good name of her school by summoning police. "But I'm not giving up the baby except to the mother and father who are adopting my little boy. I want to meet them."

Clemmie's perfect, beautiful, plump little boy made all the girls weep. His sweet tiny hands, his little Cheerio lips, his wide, slow-blinking blue eyes. They too would go through this, but not as bravely as Clemmie had, silencing her screams, arching her back, wiping her tears and snot against the pillow. They would never see whether their children were perfect, beautiful, and plump.

A Mr. and Mrs. Smith drove up to the Mountain School the next day and came right to Clemmie's dorm room. Mr. and Mrs. Smith were about the same age as Rudyard Creek. Thirty or so. Clemmie could not imagine getting that old.

Ronnie was a skeptic, a take on life Clemmie had never come across. Ronnie did not believe that Mr. and Mrs. Smith were actually named Smith.

In those days, you felt safe about almost everything, and since everything was safe, Mrs. Smith set her handbag down, thinking only of how to coax this wayward girl to let go of the tiny, beautiful boy who was now her own son. While the other girls milled around, and Matron found herself in the unaccustomed humiliating position of ordering the girls to leave while they just shrugged, Ronnie opened Mrs. Smith's bag, found her driver's license, and memorized the facts. Then she walked around the bed, kissed Clemmie on the forehead, and said gently, "It's time, Clem. Say goodbye."

Silence fell.

Mr. and Mrs. Smith hardly breathed, praying the girl would obey.

The five pregnant girls absorbed the terrible grief that came off Clemmie in waves, and they knew now why the infant was taken before the mother was awake from anesthesia. Bad as that was, this was worse.

Clemmie drank in her baby's sweet scent, touched his sweet cheek, stroked his sweet tiny bit of hair, and let him go.

She had had her son for a day and a half. She had nursed him. But she had not gotten her photograph. None of them owned a camera.

In her seventies, she sometimes thought that the most wonderful thing in the world was the cell phone, with its ready camera and its storage forever.

———————

Clemmie stood in her open doorway. The heat coming through the front door was suffocating, thick as a down comforter, damp as a used beach towel. How could the men stand it, in their long sleeves and long pants?

The foreman jogged over to translate. "Your neighbor's back door sliders are wide open," he explained, "although inside the house, the drapes are still pulled, so you can't see in. Manny says those doors have never been open in the five years we've mowed here. I knocked on the glass and yelled, but nobody answered."

"Open?" repeated Clemmie. "My goodness." Did I do that? she wondered. Or did Borobasq?

Now when the yardman gestured, she understood. He was demonstrating how many inches the door had been left open. "Thank you for your concern," she said. "I'm sure everything's all right. I'll call, though, and see if he's home." She double-checked that it was her Sun City phone in her hand, and it was, so she tapped Dom's name. His cell phone rang, no one answered, and she left a message, speaking loudly so both the foreman on the porch and Borobasq in the hall could hear. "Dom? You're still not home? Listen, it's Helen. Did you mean to leave your sliders open? We're worried."

Wet, hot air clung to the insides of her lungs like adhesive. She could hardly bear to think what the hair on her head looked like, with perspiration in rivulets among the thin tangles.

"I think you should call the sheriff," said the foreman. "Could have been a break-in."

"Oh, I'm sure it wasn't," said Clemmie hastily. "As soon as I've tidied up, I'll use my key and go in and check."

The foreman shook his head. "I don't like the idea that it's *never* been open in five years but it's open now. And it's ninety-four degrees out. Nobody would open a slider in this heat. And what with everybody in this neighborhood being kind of vulnerable, I'm just calling the sheriff myself. Whoever opened that door might still be in there, and I don't want you messing with him. The AME Zion Church a few miles south? The one on top of the hill? They had break-ins just last week." He smiled reassuringly and tapped 911. "They never mind false alarms," he said. "Actually, they like false alarms better than real alarms. They'll thank us for being careful."

Betty Anne and her husband, Ralph, who always left by their front door—because their garage was entirely full of furniture and stuff that didn't fit into the house, so they couldn't park in it—now came out their front door, saw the entire landscape crew gathered in Clemmie's front yard, and headed over. Joan and Ed had just driven into Blue Lilac, and they saw the action and also hurried to join everybody. "You all right, Helen?" called Ed.

Clemmie moved from the doorway onto the porch and shut

the front door firmly behind her. She stood next to the pretty little canvas sling chair and the pretty little container of scarlet geraniums, while the foreman reached 911 and reported a possible break-in on Blue Lilac Lane.

TEN

The sheriff arrived in two minutes, which meant he had already been in Sun City. Although it was almost crime-free, there were lots of falls, accidents, and ambulance calls, and then too, the sheriff's office supplied off-duty officers who earned extra money sitting at the entrances at certain hours of the night and day.

Clemmie knew Bay Bennett by sight from the Monday-evening lecture series, when he got the largest crowd because of his great topics. Everybody loved unraveling mysteries.

She was also coming unraveled. Borobasq was alone inside her house, and doing what? Probably what he'd done at Dom's. Searching. Clemmie was still holding her purse, which was good; at least Borobasq couldn't get at her Helen Stephens credit cards, driver's license, or passport.

Betty Anne and Ralph took up good positions on Clemmie's shady porch, and Betty Anne texted Shirley, her best friend from Pink Camellia, the next cul-de-sac over. Since their backyards adjoined, Shirley could arrive swiftly by walking between the units, and sure enough, within seconds, Shirley was headed over to participate in the excitement.

Clemmie wanted to portray herself as a bystander, not too bright but trying to be helpful in her elderly way.

Normally, she would offer her neighbors sweet tea, but she could not risk anybody following her inside, and they would. Trooping in and out of one another's homes was considered a right in Sun City.

Before the sheriff was fully out of his car, the foreman was describing the open sliders and how Miz Stephens's phone call established that the homeowner wasn't there. A deputy, accompanied by several landscapers, walked around Clemmie's unit to examine Dom's wide-open sliders, while the sheriff courteously introduced himself. "Miz Stephens? I'm Sheriff Bay Bennett. How are you this fine day?"

It took no acting to appear shaky. "I'm hoping all is well," she said.

"What can you tell me about your neighbor?"

"My neighbor Dom Spesante lives alone, so he texts me every morning to let me know he's fine, but I didn't get a text the other day. A neighbor and I went over to check, but nobody was home. We assumed there was no problem, and he'd just gone out and forgotten to text me."

"What day was that, exactly?"

"I think yesterday," she said, remembering a bit late that she had planned to be vague and confused.

"And who was the neighbor?"

"Johnny Marsh." She pointed toward Joyce's.

"When you were inside, did you notice that the back door was open?"

"Dom never opens the drapes, so the glass isn't visible on the inside."

"Well, since you have his key," said the sheriff, "and since it's okay for you to go in and check, how about you get your key, and with your permission, I'll go in."

It seemed to Clemmie he could go through the sliders, but she nodded and opened her front door, saying over her shoulder, "I'll just keep the air-conditioning in," a phrase they all used, as if air-conditioning were a cat that could get out and run into traffic, but it was a solid excuse to close the door firmly behind her. She got the key back out of the kitchen drawer. Borobasq was standing in the tiny back hall, arms folded, nothing but sunglasses in the dark.

A man who didn't summon the police when his precious glass rig was stolen wasn't going to flag them down when he had just finished trespassing in two homes. But the glass wasn't precious, she remembered. Something else was.

She went back out, and then she and the sheriff went to Dom's front door. She opened it, but only the sheriff went in. She could tell from a moment of talk that the deputies were already in, but the sheriff closed the door and she could hear nothing else.

The landscape crew hung around, hoping to be in on the excitement of a burglary, but nothing seemed to happen. Minutes went by, and then more minutes. The police were obviously doing a very thorough search.

Betty Anne and Shirley discussed Dom, but they barely knew him because he so rarely emerged. Shirley called her husband to ask if Bob knew Dom, and he didn't, but he said he was on his way.

After a while, the foreman sent his men back to work, and the roar of their blowers and mowers filled the air.

Clemmie couldn't imagine what the sheriff was finding to do. There wasn't anything inside Dom's except the same discarded pizza boxes and remotes that had been on the coffee table when she'd gone in.

But she had larger difficulties: Bentley and Harp, who seemed to have forgotten that Bent had sold Clemmie out with the photo, were now riveted by the cold case. Such a clever phrase—*cold case*. So enticing to the public—the concept of truth out there waiting, needing only a word or a photo or a DNA test. But the truth of Rudyard Creek's death would not be known, no matter who was arrested.

When Clemmie did not email that cold-case reporter, would the children? Was it possible that Bent and Harp were so eager for family involvement in an ancient murder that they would give her up? What would she say if a detective phoned her with questions? "I sort of remember the man," she would say. "My brother played basketball then. Oh? People say Mr. Creek had dinner at our house? It's possible. Our parents entertained a lot."

The key would be to get off the phone without giving out any facts and without showing any emotion.

The same key she needed right now on her front porch. Without her wig. Surrounded by neighbors. In killer heat. And a drug dealer on the other side of the wall.

After her son was taken from her arms that terrible day at the wayward school, Clemmie could have gone back to high school. Her mother had spread an excuse for her missing several months of junior year. Dear Clemmie had been helping a very sick aunt, who had had a disease nobody ever spoke of by name, but it began with a capital *C*.

There was also the option of staying on at the Mountain School through June, and Clemmie chose that rather than walking down a hall and encountering Rudyard Creek.

It meant she had to witness Maureen giving up her baby, and Veronica giving up hers. It meant meeting a whole string of other girls, most arriving when it didn't show yet, girls in various states of grief and shame.

Clemmie worried about her baby boy. Were his new mommy and daddy good to him? Was he sleeping well? Did his new grandma love him? Did he get enough fresh air? Was he smiling yet? Did his little fingers curl around his daddy's thumb?

According to the information Veronica had gotten off that driver's license, Mrs. Smith was in fact Marjorie Boone, so Clemmie's little boy was now Somebody Boone. They lived in Columbus, Ohio, which might as well have been Vladivostok, because Clemmie could never get there.

Pete, off at college, never even knew that his sister was away half the school year because he was a senior, far too busy and having far too much fun to come home weekends or vacations. His parents did drive up to the campus a few times for a visit, and when he asked, "How's Clemmie?" they said, "She's fine," and he moved on to interesting topics.

Pete graduated from college that spring and, in the tradition of the day, was married the following Saturday in the campus chapel to his sweetheart since junior high: Jeanne.

Jeanne's younger sister Trudy had mentioned Clemmie's absence from school, and Jeanne drew the correct conclusion. Lest the shame of Clemmie's behavior infect her lovely new marriage, she said nothing to her parents and certainly not to Pete, her fiancé. This was not extraordinary. Nobody said anything out loud in those days; those pre-talk-show days, when displaying feelings and opinions in public had not yet begun. So Clemmie was in the wedding party, and the deep pit into which she had fallen sealed over. She was just another pretty bridesmaid, standing at the end of the line because she was the shortest.

All she could think of was that Pete and Jeannie would now have a baby, having followed the proper order of engagement, wedding, and wedding night, while her own baby was in another woman's arms. Forever.

When Clemmie's senior year at high school began, her parents talked of nothing but college. Clemmie's mother wanted her to attend Sweet Briar, as she had, or perhaps Wells, as Clemmie's godmother had. Clemmie was not interested in Virginia or northern New York State.

At school, she would linger at the junctions of halls until she had company to walk farther. She dropped band because she had to walk to the music rooms down the same hall that led to the boys' gym. On the days Rudyard Creek drew lunch duty, she sat it out in the girls' restroom. And still he managed to catch her eye, and wave, and grin, and people said, "It's so cute the way he keeps up with Pete's little sister." Senior year consisted of avoiding Rudyard Creek and studying college catalogs.

In those days, colleges sent out enticing, thick paperbacks which described the campus and the buildings and gave a paragraph about every course for every major. Fall of senior year, high school students were buried in those catalogs.

Clemmie read and reread the catalogs for Ohio colleges, of

which there were many. She was accepted at Ohio State—oh joy! because it was in Columbus, where she needed to be if she were ever to see her son again. But her parents decreed that Ohio State was far too large and there might be packs of undesirable girls and their daughter must have a better class of friend, since it was clear that she was easily led astray, or perhaps had even led others astray.

Clemmie loved her parents. It hurt to know that they had reservations about her morals.

They allowed her to apply at a few small church-related colleges in Ohio, all of which accepted her. Her parents were embarrassed because only losers with poor grades went to that kind of school, and when people asked where their daughter was going, they replied shamefacedly that Clemmie had wanted a small, undemanding rural campus and had chosen some little place in Ohio. Other parents always liked that answer because then they could brag about how *their* daughter was going to Pembroke or Vassar.

Rudyard Creek got married over Christmas break, and there was a fine photograph in the paper of the bride in her white velvet gown. His new wife of course came to all the basketball games that season and looked at her husband with pride, and they were a popular couple. He was an excellent coach, and after the high school won the Class M state basketball championship, Rudyard Creek was offered a coaching position at a much bigger school with many more fine athletes. It was up by Albany—probably a two- or three-hour drive northwest.

Clemmie literally counted the days until his departure. School ended June 19, and on that date he would vanish from her life. She felt that she would stand taller, laugh again, and have more friends.

Over Memorial Day weekend, her parents went to visit Pete and Jeanne, while Clemmie stayed home alone. Back then, you didn't worry about locking the house during the day. People knocked and you opened the door, whether they were Fuller Brush men selling brooms or a neighbor offering to split her overgrown daffodil bulbs.

There was no peephole in Clemmie's front door. There was no window overlooking those few square feet where somebody stood knocking. Clemmie heard a knock, came to the door, and opened it.

Rudyard Creek was inside and shutting the door behind him before she had even realized who it was.

There was no time to run or scream or kick. "I keep track of things," he whispered, grinning down, locking the door. "I heard your parents were up visiting old Pete." He gripped her slender shoulder in his huge, strong fingers. "Oh my darlin'," sang the coach, "oh my darlin', Clementine, thou art lost and gone forever, dreadful sorry, Clementine."

ELEVEN

A second police car turned into Blue Lilac Lane, presumably because the police, like the neighbors, wanted to be in on the action. What action? Clemmie wondered. The second police car left its strobe lights silently circling, which drew Frank and Linda from their house.

Clemmie wanted to collapse in her little sling chair, but if her neighbors got thirsty in this heat, they'd ask Clemmie for a bottle of water from her fridge. If she were seated, they'd just walk right in, saying, "No trouble. I'll get it," so she had to keep standing there, blocking her own front door.

And then an ambulance arrived, lights whirling, but no siren. They rarely used sirens in Sun City, either because they didn't want to frighten people or because there wasn't any traffic to push out of the way. Clemmie felt a tremor. An ambulance for whom?

"Poor old dude," said Ralph. "Probably had a heart attack and he's been lying there."

She was stricken. Her entire purpose as the neighbor with the spare key was to check on Dom and make sure he didn't die alone. But she—and later she and Johnny—had checked out the villa, and Dom hadn't been there. He had come in at some other point, though, on his golf cart. But he hadn't answered calls and texts, so Clemmie had wrongly assumed he'd left again. Had he fallen in his room? Or the kitchen? Had Borobasq seen him lying there and done nothing? Had Borobasq trotted back to her house to eat Joyce's macaroni and not bothered to mention Dom on the floor of some room?

That was sick and twisted, but sick and twisted was Borobasq's profession, wasn't it?

Dom's garage door went up, revealing four policemen huddled just inside. Clemmie's neighbors shifted position to see better. The ambulance crew joined the police, and yet another police car arrived, and there was no view now but the backs of uniforms. There was also nowhere left to park, and for Clemmie to back her car out with all these vehicles in the way would be a test of her skills.

"Oh my goodness, it's hot out here," said Shirley. "Helen, honey, do you mind if I get a little ice water?"

"Bring me some too, Shirley," said Betty Anne. "Or better yet, I'll come inside with you and carry a tray out. Who's thirsty?"

Sun City was like living in a dorm, with separate houses instead of separate rooms.

Clemmie had no alternative. She opened her front door and said loudly before she stepped in, "Does everybody want water? Or sweet tea? You stay there. I'll bring everything."

"No, no, don't be silly, we're coming in."

Clemmie managed to block the little back hall while she gestured the two women into her kitchen. She hoped Borobasq hadn't chosen the powder room to hide in because at their age, somebody always needed to go.

"You didn't get your groceries put away," said Shirley. "They'll go bad. Here. I'll help." She frowned at the open, half-eaten eight-serving casserole and the open, half-empty milk carton.

"Joyce went out of town," explained Clemmie. "She brought me everything in her refrigerator."

"But I played mah-jongg with her the other day," said Shirley. "She didn't say a word about going out of town for a long trip." Because you wouldn't empty your fridge for a short trip. "Has Johnny gone too? I guess not, because I saw him buzzing around the house a little while ago."

"I don't know," said Clemmie, which would have to be her stock answer. She removed a pack of water bottles from the fridge while Betty Anne rummaged in the little pantry, located large red plastic cups, filled them with ice cubes from the refrigerator dispenser, poured iced tea, and arranged the cups on the tray Clemmie kept on top of her fridge. Betty Anne and Shirley discussed trays and the art of tray decoupage, a hobby of decades ago they might just take up again.

At last they were all on their way out, and Clemmie could step outside and close her door, keeping her own personal trespasser safe.

What am I doing? I know who left the slider open. A mean, taunting creep who doesn't live in a hot climate and didn't realize that doors always have to stay closed. He probably got his glass stolen because he didn't lock his own place. He's stupid, not smart.

But he'd been smart enough to find her.

The sheriff walked the dozen paces from Dom's garage to Clemmie's porch and said in his gentle drawl, "I'm so sorry to tell you that there has been a death next door."

They had known that, since the ambulance had not loaded a sick person and driven swiftly away, but now it was a fact. They were silent with the certain knowledge of their own deaths—not that far away, because they were all looking eighty in the eye, and Frank and Linda, at least, had left eighty in the dust.

Clemmie didn't think that anybody had loved Dom, and nobody would care much that he had died. Certainly, Wilson never acted as if Dom was anything but a responsibility to tend to for an hour now and then. What a dreadful, dusty life Dom had led in that house, with his television and his closed drapes.

Does anybody love me? Will anybody really care when I die? Will the grands just text each other? Will Peggy just say to husband number four, "How sad," and go on with her life? Will my death even be a ripple for anybody?

The iced tea had been passed out. Clemmie's hands were shaking. She couldn't hold her cup and set it back down.

"Helen, honey, you've had a shock," said Ralph. "You're withering on the vine," he added, as if she were a wrinkled old raisin. "Listen, everybody, it's too hot out here for Helen. We're going inside, and I'm going to get you a nice, cold Co-Cola, Helen."

Everybody else in the neighborhood was from the Northeast or the Midwest. Only Ralph said Co-Cola, proving he was a southerner. She forgave him the raisin remark because Ralph had remembered from the neighborhood gatherings that there were few things Clemmie liked more than a Coke.

The sheriff said, "Good idea. Let's talk inside."

She touched her hair for reassurance and was appalled to find no hair. None of these people had ever seen her wigless, and now they knew she was just another old, balding hag. Oh Lord, they'd known anyway, but at least she had kept up appearances.

Ralph herded almost everybody into her living room. Linda and Frank stayed on the porch, probably hoping for a good look. Ralph got a cold Coke from Clemmie's refrigerator and opened it for her, and the sheriff perched right next to Clemmie on the arm of her sofa.

Clemmie's door was thrown open. The landscape foreman rushed in. "He was *murdered*? Somebody murdered the guy in that unit? Is that true?"

Clemmie just barely managed to set her Coke on the coffee

table before she spilled soda everywhere. She imagined Dom hearing Borobasq's intrusion and whipping out a gun. Dom probably slept with a gun under his pillow and transferred it to the recliner during the day. She imagined Borobasq reacting faster because he was young and trim and quick, while Dom was old and fat and slow. Boro would have used his knife. Or disarmed Dom with the knife and turned the gun on its owner. And she, Clemmie, was complicit.

When Clementine Lakefield had been in the third grade, Miss Heath divided the class into six sets of four children, their assignment to write each other's biographies. It was so exciting. None of the children had ever done a group project. Miss Heath described what should be in the biography: when and where you were born; who your mother and father were and also your grandparents; places you had lived; places you had traveled; things you had done; and of course, photographs if you had them. All these would be fastened in a book written by your partner, and the title of the book would be your very own name.

Many children were puzzled by these instructions. They had always lived in the same place, because in those days, there was far less upheaval. They had traveled only to visit relatives, although a few exciting families had gone to Florida for a week in the winter.

It gave nine-year-old Clemmie a sick shiver to realize that she was going to lie in her biography. Lying was a sin, and even the tiniest fib made Clemmie feel ill. But there was a terrible secret in her family. *Her parents were divorced.*

There were no divorces to speak of in the early 1950s. Certainly Clemmie had never met another child of divorce. The class telephone list (phone numbers the year Clemmie was in kindergarten had five digits; by third grade, they were up to seven. Understanding that nobody could readily memorize seven digits, the phone company made up names to go with the numbers. Clemmie's phone number was NEptune 7–0221) consisted exclusively of married couples and used only the husband's name. Mr. and Mrs. Charles Cook, for example, were the parents of Sarah, Mr. and Mrs. John Stephens were the parents of Helen, and Mr. and Mrs. Harrington Leftwich were the parents of Regina. According to the telephone list, Mr. and Mrs. Clarence Lakefield were the parents of Clementine.

But that was not so. Pete and Clemmie's father was another person entirely.

Clemmie would not name her real father in her biography because you were never to admit that a divorce had happened in your family. But he existed, and she got to see him now and then, and she loved him so much, loved all the adventures they had together, because he lived in New York City, and they took the train back and forth! And taxis! And ate at the Automat!

Sarah Cook raised her hand. "Can you describe the restaurants where you eat out?"

The class was awed. Few had "eaten out." Your mother cooked all the meals. At school, there were children (much to be envied) who bought hot lunch, but Clemmie and the majority of children carried bag lunches, so they didn't even "eat out" in the cafeteria.

Clemmie didn't see how she could describe the Automat without mentioning her real father.

"Sarah, that is an important distinction," said Miss Heath. "What you do during the day—for example, having dinner at a restaurant—is not part of a biography. That is simply an activity. A biography describes who you are. Your birth certificate, for example."

Clemmie had never heard of a birth certificate, but she knew immediately it would have the forbidden name on it. Her real daddy's name.

Miss Heath assigned Clemmie, Sarah Cook, Regina Leftwich, and Helen Stephens to the same group. She suggested that each group should meet at somebody's house and work together, an idea everybody loved. They were to bring paperwork and photographs to include in the biographies. Clemmie did not offer her house, because her pesky brother, Pete, would bother them and Mama would hang over them.

Luckily, Sarah Cook loved to have people come to her house. Once she even had a slumber party, the most thrilling event Clemmie had ever gone to.

So Regina and Clemmie and Helen went to Sarah's house.

Helen was the sorry member of the group. The words *loser* or *victim* weren't used yet, but there were children who didn't measure up, and the teacher carefully allocated one to each group. Helen used to be fun but had gotten boring, never saying much, just slumping around. She didn't play on the playground anymore, but just stood waiting for recess to end. In class, she'd answer when the teacher called on her, but after that, she would close her eyes and sigh.

In the 1950s, people paid little attention to the topic called medicine. There were no talk shows. Health issues were not covered in the newspaper. If your doctor told you something, it was true, so what was there to read about? Furthermore, people had lower expectations for their lives and bodies.

Clemmie had been sick a few times—mumps, measles, and chicken pox. But her acquaintance with illness was that it came, you suffered, and it ended. She had no idea that an illness could settle in and take hold, and you would be the one that ended.

Sarah quickly claimed Regina as her partner, and they got happily to work, while Clemmie and Helen watched. Regina produced a baby picture, a photograph of her house, a photograph of her parents, and a carefully hand-printed list of details, including something called a social security number. Clemmie had never heard of such a thing, because in the 1950s, you needed very few numbers. Phones might be up to seven digits, but house addresses were rarely more than two. Clemmie lived at 3 Park Lane. But here was Regina with three numbers and a dash, two more and a dash, and then four more.

Clemmie would ask Mama if she had a social security number.

Helen had brought a large manila envelope with paper buttons, around which a thin, waxed thread was wound to keep the envelope closed. Clemmie loved the envelope. Out of it, Helen took the same sort of things that Regina had. She possessed a birth certificate and a social security number, but she had one more paper. Well, not a paper, really, but a little green notebook. A United States passport.

"What is it for?" Clemmie wanted to know.

"It's for crossing borders of foreign countries," explained Helen. "I need it when I visit my grandmother in England."

Helen had been to England? The other three were awestruck. In the 1950s, you never went anywhere or did anything, so hardly anyone had a passport or went abroad.

"How did you get there?" asked Regina.

"Once we flew, and once we took the *Queen Elizabeth*." Helen produced a photograph of herself standing on the deck of a massive ship at a massive dock and another photograph of herself walking up to a big, fat airplane with propellers.

Quiet Helen had the most exciting life the girls had ever heard of. Sarah bristled and turned her back to work with Regina.

Clemmie had brought blank paper, sharp pencils, and cellophane tape. She and Helen began to arrange Helen's biography.

Helen Anne Stephens. Born in Bridgeport, Connecticut, to John and Coralie (Pitkethley) Stephens. Clemmie loved that name! Coralie Pitkethley. It was so romantic. Coralie Pitkethley had been born in England.

Clemmie affixed Helen's photographs to the blank pages and

wrote the captions Helen dictated. Helen's social security number was printed on a little cardboard rectangle, and Helen was worried about using tape, because the card might tear when they removed it, so Clemmie copied out the number on a separate biography page, labeled it, and slid the actual rectangle back into the button-twine envelope. They agreed that the passport with its strong, slick covers could safely be taped. Clemmie centered it carefully on its own page. She loved how the thickness of the passport made the biography thick too.

Helen fell asleep at the table.

Sarah's mother walked by and frowned. "Her parents don't supervise her bedtime properly," she said, and she left the room. In the 1950s, nobody helped with your homework; they didn't even ask if you had homework. That was your job.

Sarah and Regina giggled over their project, but Helen put her head back down. "Clemmie, I don't think I can write yours today. I'm so tired. Even my hair is tired. It won't curl or shine anymore."

Clemmie had never heard the word *symptom*, and it didn't occur to her to worry about Helen's tired hair. She worried about the biographies, which had to be done properly and handed in on time. So Helen's exhaustion worked out well, because of the lies that had to be dealt with. "I'll write my biography for you," Clemmie whispered, so Sarah and Regina wouldn't know. "I'll bring it to class all done, and nobody will know you didn't do it."

Helen smiled with gratitude, and neither little girl realized that this was not a fine gift from Clemmie, but yet another moment in which Helen's illness was not recognized. But even if it had been recognized, there was little to be done about pediatric leukemia in 1955. The new drug methotrexate might have helped, had Helen taken it earlier, but it was never administered.

After Sarah's mother passed out a plate of delicious square iced layer cakes hardly bigger than dice, the mothers came to get Helen and Regina, while Clemmie walked home, carrying the buttoned envelope with her biography of Helen inside. Over the weekend, she wrote the biography of herself.

CLEMENTINE ELEANOR LAKEFIELD, she wrote on the first page, centering the words and using capital letters, although of course that had not originally been her name.

She gave a whole page to describing Clementine Churchill, wife of the British prime minister, from whom she received her first name, and another whole page to Eleanor Roosevelt, from whom she received her middle name. She did not ask Mama for the birth certificate, but hoped that these extra pages would suffice.

She gave a two-page spread to photographs of her parents and Pete, and a page each for their spaniel, Butter, and their parakeet, Whistle. Then she went outside with Pete and played Spud with the neighborhood children.

As it happened, her true father came to visit on Sunday, but he had only a few hours and they couldn't take the train to New York. Instead they went in his car. Since he wanted to be called Daddy too, she felt blurry when she addressed him, her two daddies merging and separating. Daddy took Clemmie and Pete to a restaurant called the Clam Box, which was very exciting, even though Clemmie disliked fish, and then they went to Howard Johnson's for ice cream.

Clemmie didn't tell her true father about the biography because she hadn't put him in it. There was something terrible about sitting in the front seat next to this wonderful man, who so carefully put his arm out to catch her if he had to brake quickly. She was about to complete a project in which he didn't exist.

She thought of telling her father about the biography, but in the 1950s, you didn't confess you had a problem because it was wrong to burden others. Presenting your own problem was nothing but whining. Furthermore, in the 1950s, people just soldiered on. Nobody ever asked, "How do you feel about that?"

Monday morning, Clemmie and Pete walked to school, saying hello to the crossing guards and not stepping on the cracks of the sidewalk divisions.

Helen was absent that day, but that was all right; the biography assignment was not due for another week. Clemmie stowed the biographies in her desk, which had a slanted lid that lifted up for storage. The next day, Helen was also not in school. She was absent the whole week.

A strange thing happened. The desks in the third grade classroom were rearranged. There was no longer a place for Helen to sit. Nobody said anything about it. Nobody said anything all morning, and nobody said anything during lunch, and nobody said anything after lunch.

Clemmie raised her hand during arithmetic. "Miss Heath, where is Helen's desk?"

Miss Heath said, "We'll talk about it later, dear. You concentrate on your work."

This was how things were handled in the 1950s. You did not ever use the word *cancer*, not out loud and not in your mind, any more than you used the word *divorce*, and you certainly did not discuss death.

Clemmie found out that Helen was dead entirely by accident. It was raining out, and the neighborhood girls were roller-skating around and around the furnace on the concrete floor of the cellar of Clemmie's next-door neighbors, and Clemmie went upstairs to use the bathroom. The mothers were talking about how Helen Stephens had been taken to the emergency room last Saturday. In those days, nobody went to the emergency room unless they were smashed up in car accidents. They waited decently until the doctor's office opened on Monday.

"It was too late to do anything," said one of the mothers.

"At least she was never in pain," said another mother.

"My sister is a nurse. She says that Helen must have been in pain and was just brave about it."

"But her actual suffering was only three days," said another mother, as if this were a nice thing.

"When is the funeral?" somebody asked.

Clemmie ran home. "Mama. Is Helen Stephens dead?"

"Oh, darling. I'm so sorry you found out. Yes, she is. But she's in heaven now, and we won't worry about her."

In the 1950s, heaven was a good place to stash people you weren't going to worry about anymore.

Clemmie didn't know what a funeral was, so she didn't ask to go. She had never met Helen's parents, so she didn't ask to be driven over there to say how sad she was. It did not cross her mind that Helen's parents might want those photographs and papers back.

In school, she stared down into her desk where the two reports lay.

Helen's biography did not contain the important truth of her death, and Clemmie didn't want to add it, because then Helen's report would be like a gravestone, with a date at both ends.

As for her own biography, it did not contain the important truth of her true father's existence.

She knew what would happen when the class biographies were finished and graded. They would be displayed on Parents' Night. Her daddy would like the biography because it would list him. Her real daddy would not be invited and probably wouldn't even know there was a Parents' Night.

But Clemmie would know that she had officially left him out of her life.

Clemmie took the reports home and stored them beneath the

stamp album her stepfather had given her two Christmases ago (she had never touched it) and the photograph album (she never got to use the family camera because it was too expensive to develop the pictures) and her Bible, which was leather with a tiny zipper that kept the onionskin pages safe and her name stamped in gold. It had never occurred to Clemmie to unzip the Bible and read it. Its job was to sit there and spread protection around the room.

The day before the report was due, Clemmie waited for the rest of the class to leave for recess. Then she tiptoed over to Miss Heath and whispered, "The biographies? I was doing mine with Helen. They're both at Helen's house. Shall we just forget about them?" It was a huge lie. Clemmie was amazed at how easily her eyes filled with tears.

Miss Heath said, "Oh, my dear child. Yes. You and I will never mention it again."

Because that was also the 1950s. "Never mention it" could have been the slogan.

The Bible and the albums protected the two biographies for years, until Clementine Lakefield realized that it might be very useful to have a different name, a different social security number, and a different passport.

TWELVE

The neighbors in Clemmie's living room clutched each other. *"Murdered?"* they chorused. "What happened?"

Clemmie had taken a photograph of Borobasq in the car when he was peering down into the tote at his tree dragon. She prepared to tell the sheriff of Lancaster County about Borobasq, handing him the cell phone photo. But Boro was only a few feet away, armed and dangerous. The living room was packed with possible hostages. Practically everyone except the sheriff was weak and frail, or else fat and useless.

It was safer to write it out, pass the paper to the sheriff, and assume he knew how to deal with it.

Clemmie loved to take notes. She kept notebooks of various sizes around for various purposes—from Bible study to pottery studio rules—and lots of sharp pencils. She picked up nearest note-book and the nearest pencil.

"We don't know what happened," said the sheriff, "but he's been shot."

Shot? thought Clemmie. I didn't hear a shot! I know the units are very well soundproofed, but I wouldn't have said *that* well.

"Miz Stephens," asked the sheriff, "can you describe Mr. Spesante for me?"

It seemed an odd request, since the sheriff had been hanging out with the body for quite a while, but before she could rally, her family phone rang.

"You changed your ringtone," said Betty Anne, who of course didn't know there were two phones. Shortly, everybody would know. Everybody would know everything, because Clemmie would have to hand over the phones to give the sheriff her photos and texts.

The sheriff's smile was sweet and patient as he waited for her to answer the call. She had the odd thought that this was the kind of man she had hoped to meet when she was young, to marry and have children with. She ignored the rings, which would stop after four. "Dom is five foot four or five," said Clemmie, who was four foot ten. "Mostly bald, and his remaining hair is white and rather long. He doesn't shave very often. He has a mottled complexion." She didn't add that he smelled bad, a combination of not bathing enough and smoking so much. She gripped her pencil to write.

"When did it happen?" demanded the foreman. "It must have

been quite a while ago, because the stench is horrific. I don't know why we didn't smell the corpse when we were doing the yard. I guess the garage is really sealed. The guy's flesh just cooked in there. Was it like last week or something?"

Clemmie's pencil froze. Her neighbors gagged and cried out.

"I don't know when," said the sheriff. "Not in the last several hours, anyway, because of the degree of decay."

"It has to be after Clemmie and Johnny went inside to check on him," said Ralph, "or they'd have seen him. Smelled him."

The sheriff nodded. "He's still in the golf cart, kind of slumped over. In fact the zipped-up plastic wall of the cart is keeping him from falling out. I think somebody just glancing into the garage wouldn't notice him. And he wouldn't stink at first."

Dom had been dead inside his golf cart when she tiptoed through the garage last night with her eyes glued to her feet? When she'd finally noticed the cart, she never considered the possibility that Dom was still inside it. She'd fled out the Cogland sliders, darted over the black grass to her own place, and eventually fallen asleep at home, with dead Dom on the other side of their shared wall. Well, not exactly, because on the other side of their shared wall was his living room and kitchen, and *then* came his garage, but still.

Still: Borobasq had not killed Dom.

Borobasq hadn't gotten here until an hour ago.

Oh, thank you, God. I am not responsible for Dom's death.

But Borobasq had to have seen and smelled the body, because

he'd passed through that garage to reach the second unit. It took some cool nerve to shrug, saunter into Clemmie's kitchen, serve himself macaroni, nuke it, find a fork, and stand there snacking after that.

Shirley's husband, Bob, asked rather sternly, "Exactly how advanced is the decomposition?"

What had Bob done for a living? Clemmie hadn't the slightest idea. Doctors never gave up their titles, so he hadn't been, say, a pathologist. Perhaps he watched all those TV shows dealing with murder.

The sheriff skipped Bob's question. "Is there anybody on the street besides Miz Stephens who can identify the body? It's a necessary formality."

The neighbors exchanged glances. "He never came to a single neighborhood event," said Bob, who lived on Pink Camellia. "I wouldn't even recognize his golf cart."

This was huge, because they all knew each other's golf carts.

"Johnny could ID the body," offered Shirley. "He and Joyce live right across the street, and he went inside with Helen to check anyway. Helen, do you have Johnny's cell number?"

"Just Joyce's, and she's out of town."

The sheriff said, "Miz Stephens, for now I think we'll just use a photograph I took on my cell phone. Can you take a look at this?"

"Eeuh," said Betty Anne. "What he must look like. Maggots, I'm sure."

Everybody leaned in eagerly, as if Clemmie were holding a photograph of a new grandchild. It was a headshot, but there were no maggots and no blood. The head was tilted in a dead sort of way, and it had swollen and changed color.

Clemmie found herself whimpering in horror, turning the cell phone around as if she could adjust what she was seeing. "It's Wilson! Not Dom. It's Dom's only relative. Wilson's young. He's just a boy! I thought you were telling us Dom died! But it's *Wilson*."

Wilson. Killed by some other human being. Oh, poor, poor Wilson! He was so young. His life was over. His dreams, his plans.

Another horror thrust itself into her heart. The only possible killer was Dom. A good explanation for why Dom wasn't home and hadn't texted.

Clemmie began to weep. Oh, Dom, what went wrong? Wilson was all you had, I think. What could possibly have been said or done so that you shot him?

"When you say 'just a boy,' Miz Stephens," asked the sheriff, "how old do you actually mean?" because he knew that for the Sun City residents, *youthful* could be fifty and under.

"I don't think he was thirty yet. Maybe twenty-five. Oh, Wilson! Poor Wilson!" She accepted the tissue box that Shirley passed from its position on the kitchen counter and thought dimly, Wouldn't his name and date of birth be on his driver's license? Why ask me? Why not check his license?

"Do you know what kind of car Dom drives?" asked the sheriff. "And what kind of car Wilson drives? Do you have any idea where their cars are?"

"Dom doesn't have a car. When Wilson drives here, he parks in the driveway, not in the garage, so I've seen his car. But I don't know. It's just a car." She wasn't lying. She could not picture the car, only the big, slovenly, sagging body of a man much too young for such bad posture and so much extra weight.

Wilson. Murdered.

Any action in a golf cart would be awkward, because it was such a small space, and a zipped-up cart meant no maneuvering room whatsoever. If Dom had been sitting next to Wilson, he'd just press the gun against Wilson's head and fire. But whatever had been going wrong between them, Wilson had to know it was going wrong. Why would they sit together in the golf cart if things were that bad? The murder could not have been the decision of a split second, because one of them, or perhaps both of them, had brought along a loaded gun.

The killing of Wilson could not have happened outside the golf cart, because Dom could hardly lift a pizza delivery, never mind pick up huge, heavy dead Wilson and shovel him back into the cart.

The first time Clemmie went through, without a doubt the garage had been empty. Dom must have driven the golf cart back later, maybe after dark. Then the murder scene, as they called it on television, was somewhere else entirely. But if Wilson had been the driver, as he always was when he visited, Dom could not have shifted that big body an inch. He could not have squeezed himself behind the wheel to drive home either. So it was more likely that Wilson had been killed right there in the garage.

"What is Wilson's last name?" asked the sheriff.

"You didn't find his wallet?" asked Bob. "Was it stolen? It was a robbery gone wild?"

Clemmie thought that Dom wouldn't rob Wilson, but Wilson might have robbed Dom. Dom lived as if he hardly had a penny, but he was just the type to be a closet multimillionaire. Clemmie had known quite a few of those in the generation ahead of hers: Depression children, who scrimped long after it was necessary.

Clemmie's sorrow for Wilson and horror at Dom tangled with her own reality. She had to get these people out of her house, get Borobasq into her car and drive him back to the golf club. Except she should not do any of that. She ought to turn him in.

But what crime had he committed? So far, he had thrown a wig in the air and then trespassed, a trespass Clemmie had aided and abetted. Her only hope of keeping Helen Stephens safe from exposure was to get rid of Borobasq.

But even if Borobasq lay down on the floor of the back seat, a sheriff, a neighbor, a deputy—whoever—might very well see him. Would Borobasq have to stay in Clemmie's house for the duration? If a real-life murder was similar to a television murder, the police would be next door for hours. Maybe days. She could never get away with it.

Why would I *want* to get away with it? Borobasq has something to do with this murder, even if he didn't do it himself. Or maybe it's his other reason that's the reason for the murder, the reason that made the glass meaningless. The glass I still have, in my car, peeking out of the tote bag.

"Clemmie," said Shirley, jabbing her, "the sheriff needs Wilson's last name."

She jumped nervously, and the sheriff smiled at her.

"The same as Dom's," she said, trying not to cry.

"Could you spell Spesante for me?" asked the sheriff.

Spelling was not normally a trick question, and a Latin teacher was inevitably an excellent speller, but Clemmie was flustered. Borobasq doesn't know Dom's real name, she thought, and he's definitely listening to every word of this. Would things get even worse if Borobasq knew what name to search? But if she didn't tell the police, they'd search under *S* when she believed that Dom's last name actually came under *P*, and presumably so did Wilson's.

She had the craziest sense of loyalty to Dom. It had been extraordinary, that moment on the grass last year when she discovered that in this bland, vanilla place, she lived next door to another person hiding under a name not his own. She didn't like Dom, but she admired his guts. What had Wilson done so that Dom made such a violent decision? And how could Dom have done it? Wilson was young, big, and strong. Dom was old, small, and weak.

But then, no one knew better than Clementine Lakefield that size did not matter if the enemy failed to take precautions.

She was shocked to find that she wanted Dom to get away.

As she had.

"Spesante," she said. "*S-P-E-S-A-N-T-E*."

THIRTEEN

A few months after Clemmie learned to her cost never to open a door, and just before she departed for college, Rudyard Creek invited himself and his wife to dinner at the Lakefields'. "He said I'm one of the men he'll really miss," said Clemmie's father proudly. "And he's hoping for another bite of one of your wonderful pies," he told his wife.

Clemmie announced that she was spending the night at her girl-friend Beverly's place, which was not true. She hardly knew Bev—the name just came out—but her mother said, "Cancel it."

"I can't. I don't know when Bev and I will see each other again, because not only is she going to college in California, but her parents are moving there."

Her mother launched into the familiar lecture about how

Clementine had let her down so badly in the past year, and the least Clemmie could do was to help with a dinner party.

Clemmie's mother preferred a table of eight, so she invited a couple named Vincent, whose son Cal had also been on Pete's basketball team. Cal had not gone to college and still lived at home, so he would come for dinner too. Clemmie assumed this was matchmaking, which was wonderful, because she could arrange the place cards to put Cal between herself and Coach.

She armed herself with a tray of drinks so she could not be hugged or kissed by Coach or anyone else. Rudyard Creek's wife was also very small. Clemmie hoped the poor thing would never know what her husband was capable of. They had said grace but not yet begun to eat when Coach tilted his chair back and spoke to Clemmie behind Cal's back, "So where will you be going to college this fall?"

Clemmie said, "Cal, won't you have some green beans?"

"Oh sure, thanks, Clemmie," said Cal, taking the bowl.

Her mother said, "Clemmie's going to a sweet little Presbyterian college in Ohio. You've probably never heard of it. Muskingum."

———————

Clemmie loved college. It was joyful, like her first two years of high school: a pretty campus, wonderful new friends, fine professors. Many Ohio parents wanted the advantages of a small, rural Presbyterian college, and Clemmie searched out girls from Columbus.

Mr. and Mrs. Boone and Clemmie's precious son were a mere

seventy miles away. But how to cross that distance? In those days, hardly anybody had a car of her own. Maybe one of her new friends would invite her home for a weekend. Although exactly how she would get to the Boone house in the event of such a weekend, Clemmie did not know.

Her mother wrote long, interesting weekly letters packed with detail. Her father never wrote, because that was Mother's job, but he often signed the bottom of her letter.

You did that then. People set aside time each week, or even each day, to write their letters, rather like the characters in Jane Austen books. Clemmie's mother fattened the letter with articles cut from the local paper: wedding pictures (girls were wearing gowns of peau de soie with Chantilly lace) and engagement photographs (never with the future groom in the picture), club news, and one day an article about a man who had been accused of a rape that supposedly had taken place a few years ago.

It was unusual for the local paper to cover crime, but in this case the accused had had some standing in the community, and everybody was horrified that some lying, ugly woman was trying to hurt him. The word *alleged* was not yet in use, but it was strongly implied, because the accused was Rudyard Creek.

The article quoted him. "It's pitiful. Just another girl longing for a man, telling vicious lies to get attention."

The journalist, who did not have a byline, believed Rudyard Creek, not the girl.

I never accused him at all, thought Clemmie, because I knew I wouldn't be believed. And I was right, because this girl isn't believed either. Why did Mother send this to me? Is she letting me know that there are other girls as immoral as I am? Or more so? Because this girl is trying to bring an innocent man down?

Clemmie prayed for the unnamed girl.

It was many years before she understood that silence worked to the benefit of the criminal, that she had been a contributor to the ongoing evil of Rudyard Creek. All she thought at the time was how lucky to be so far away in Ohio, where people were good.

In those days, there weren't room phones in dorms. There was a sign-in sheet, protected by a solid, tough matron, while the girls themselves rotated desk duty. You stopped at the desk for your mail and went on up to your room, and if you had a visitor or a phone call, somebody trotted upstairs to get you.

Clemmie came back to her dorm that day windswept and happy. She was taking a wonderful Latin class. How beautiful were the mathematics of Latin conjugations and declensions; how intensely she enjoyed seeing how English words sprang from those antique syllables. Her professor suggested that she would also love Greek and handed her a beginner text for the Gospel of John, the easiest extant ancient Greek. She could hardly wait to practice the new alphabet.

"You have a visitor," said Judy, a girl on her floor with an astonishing wardrobe. Clemmie had never met anybody with so many nice clothes. Judy was giggling. "Your gentleman caller is very handsome," she whispered. Because Clemmie had a crush on a senior named Biff who was going on to law school after graduation—rare in those days, an indication of a scholar, a man consumed by respect for justice—Clemmie made a bad guess and thought the gentleman caller was Biff.

But it was Rudyard Creek.

Her legs wanted to run, and her mouth wanted to scream, but she had to be polite. She couldn't tell Coach to get lost. She couldn't spit on him. She couldn't turn around and march back to her room. Everybody was watching, and her behavior was judged.

And Clemmie did hold herself responsible. Her behavior, her figure, her bee-stung lips, or her curly black hair had enticed him. The shame of what had happened had not yet been replaced by rage. Not wanting the beloved dorm parlor infected by his presence, she said, "Let's sit on the porch."

The porch was sunny and pleasant, with creaky rockers and old wicker chairs. There was no furniture that allowed a boy and girl to sit thigh to thigh.

But once they were on the porch, Rudyard Creek's big fingers closed around her wrist and tightened, as if her bones were twigs and he might snap her for kindling. He was chortling to himself. "And now let's go for a walk," he said.

Clemmie still had physical memory of what he had done to her and now she felt again the pressure, the violence, saw again the grinning hatred on his face, experienced the pain and horror.

She should have stayed in the dorm parlor. Sat alone in one of the deep leather chairs, so that only by dragging her could he have gotten her up. Yet again, she had miscalculated. Fear crippled her. Once it got started, she couldn't peel it off. And now they were in public, in the middle of the campus, and Clemmie could not make a spectacle of herself. She thought of that over the years: that in the 1950s and well into the '60s, you protected your enemy because of your firm belief in courtesy and your need to retain your community standing.

He had parked rather far from her dorm, at the end of a gravel lot, beneath a towering tree. He swung her toward the passenger door, and she knew what would happen if they drove away, and she felt weaker and weaker.

But it was a small campus. Down the slightly tilted slate sidewalk came two boys she barely knew, but she certainly knew they would be polite. "Curtis!" she called. "Ronald! Hello there!"

"Hi, Clemmie!" they called back, walking on.

"Come meet a visitor of mine! An old high school coach dropped by!"

Curtis and Ronald came right over, smiling dutifully, holding out their right hands.

Since Rudyard Creek was gripping her wrist with his right hand, he had to let go to shake hands with Ronald and Curtis, because he, like Clemmie, had to follow etiquette. Clemmie moved behind Curtis and said, "How nice of you to come and say hello, Mr. Creek. Goodbye now!"

Over his shoulder, Ronald said, "Nice to meet you, Mr. Creek," and Curtis spoke to Clemmie. "We're headed to calculus. I can't remember. Are you in the other calculus section, Clemmie?"

They fell in step. "Actually, I haven't taken calculus yet, Curtis. Is it as difficult as they say?"

I love Muskingum, she thought, but I have to transfer. I want to be in Columbus anyway. He won't know I've switched schools. He can't possibly use his free days to drive all the way to Muskingum again. And even if he does find out that I'm at Ohio State, he'll never find me among all those thousands of students.

Safely inside a building with the boys, Clemmie wandered the halls until she found a window seat where she could pretend to study, mentally timing Rudyard Creek's drive back to New York. She visualized the road, which she had never taken. It had to be a very long drive, but Clemmie had done so little driving herself that she could not estimate the hours.

She needed to sign in at her dorm before curfew. A few minutes before ten, she crept down the stairs—darkened because the custodians had assumed the building was empty and had turned off most lights—and walked slowly to the glowing red exit sign.

Rudyard Creek had made an enormous effort to get here from Albany or wherever he lived. Would he just drive away, defeated? Or would her escape whet his appetite? He was a man who fought literally to the last second of any basketball game. That's why his teams won.

Was she a game? Would he have staked out her dorm?

She peered carefully out a window and realized for the first time how little light there was on campus. How many shadows where a man could lie in wait. How many towering trees that could shelter him.

What would happen if she didn't get in before curfew? Demerits? Or would her worried roommates call the police?

It never crossed her mind to call the police herself and ask for an escort. They would have laughed anyway. There was no such thing as campus crime.

She made her way down dark stairs to the pay phones on the lowest level of the building and called the dorm. Luck was with her; Judy answered. Judy thought it was marvelous fun that Clemmie was going to stay out all night and promised to let the roomies know.

"We need to find Dominic Spesante," said the sheriff. "I'll take his cell phone number, please, Miz Stephens, ma'am, and any other information you can give me."

You goofed up, Dom, thought Clemmie. You should have texted me that all was well. You could have gone on basically forever hiding the body in there. Maybe it would mummify. No, because there's too much humidity in South Carolina for mummies. Still, I'd never have gone into your house to start with, let alone explored the third unit and found the glass, if you'd just texted.

She took out the phone in the right pocket, clicked to Contacts, and read the number aloud.

"And the neighbors directly across the street from Mr. Spesante?" asked the sheriff. "Joyce and Johnny, you said. What's their last name?"

"Joyce Biggs and Johnny Marsh," said Shirley, wanting to participate. "They're out of town. Visiting Joyce's family."

I should correct that, thought Clemmie. But I won't. I'm in shock, you see. That's what I'll say later. I'll let Johnny tell the police about the house check we did together. I will have wall-to-wall senior moments. Not having my wig on is a good thing after all. It supports the pathetic-old-lady claim.

Next would come a crime team. Would they want to fingerprint Clemmie to eliminate her prints from suspicion? Could she say, "Oh no, I never went in"? No, she'd already told them she went in.

Maybe "I wore my gardening gloves." Or "I'm very keen on privacy. Fingerprinting might set me up for identity theft." Would they shove her poor hands down on the ink pad anyway?

Shirley said, "You must have known this man Wilson pretty well, Helen, because you're really upset. I wish Joyce were here. She'd be such a comfort for you."

"I'll just call Joyce myself," said Betty Anne, "and let her know what's happening." Betty Anne brought out her cell phone with the kind of affectionate pleasure everybody showed toward their phones, as if the phone were a well-behaved pet.

"No, no," said Clemmie. "Joyce is on her way to visit her sister. Let's not give her anything else to fret about." Shouldn't have said *else*, she thought. The sheriff might ask me what else I was referring to. I'm certainly not bringing up Johnny's possible embezzlement.

"It's a murder, Helen?" said Shirley, with the intonation people used these days, making a declarative sentence an interrogative. "You don't *fret* about murders? Especially one directly across the street? Joyce needs and deserves to know."

"She's right, Helen," said Betty Anne. "Joyce might even turn around so she can be part of it after all."

The girls went to their phones in a race to reach Joyce first. Betty Anne won. "I really don't want to leave a message, but I'll have to," said Betty Anne. "You must be on the road and can't pick up. I thought you had Bluetooth, Joyce. Is it the traffic? You might be near Atlanta. That always takes such concentration. Listen up. A terrible, terrible event has occurred," she said in a hot, pleased voice. "Dom Spenceray, Spentray—I hate these weird names—anyway, across the street from you, the one who never comes out, his young nephew or whatever, we don't know the relationship, Wilson, was *murdered*. It's *true*. *Murdered*, Joyce. Right here in Dom's garage. Clemmie is taking it very hard. Call me back. I'll tell you what's going on."

"Excuse me," Clemmie said delicately. "I must powder my nose." She stepped around the sheriff's knees and headed for her bedroom, praying Borobasq had stayed in the garage and was not crouching in her bathroom. Safely in the empty bathroom, she locked it, which she could not recall ever doing, ran cold tap water, and soaked a washcloth. When she had wrung it out, she pressed it to her forehead with one hand and checked messages on her family phone with the other.

"Aunt Clemmie," said Bentley's voice, "there's a lot of stuff online. This guy Borobasq? It's probably not about the glass. It's about money. The thief of the glass is probably also the thief of a huge amount of money. Hundreds of thousands of dollars in cash. And that cash is probably sitting next to the glass you photographed. So it's a crummy situation. I don't think Borobasq can locate you, and I'm not sure what I'd do when I got there, but I could come if you want."

Bentley cleared his throat. "There's an eight-oh-eight flight tonight out of LaGuardia. Want me to fly down and help?" His voice became diffident. "I won't get a plane ticket until you call," he said, clearly hoping she wouldn't ask him to come. There was another pause. "I love you, Aunt Clemmie," he said awkwardly.

It was the first time he had ever said such a thing, and she sort of believed it. At the same time, she hated him for getting her into this. But Bentley—who had never heard of Helen Stephens—here while the police were in the living room was the last thing she wanted. Well, no, the last thing she wanted was for Joyce to come back and mention the presence of a dreamboat in Clemmie's car.

Bentley's news, however, explained a good deal. If Borobasq was searching for hundreds of thousands of dollars in drug money, the tree dragon was a clue, not a concern. Definitely Borobasq hadn't found the money because he hadn't carried anything back from his exploration in the two villas. Had Dom taken it? Was that the reason he and Wilson had had a falling-out?

Who were Dom and Wilson to each other? All these visits from Wilson that she had attributed to kindness? Maybe in some horrible way Dom had been Wilson's prisoner, because nobody could *want* to live the way Dom lived. Maybe the stolen cash funded Dom's escape route.

She texted Bentley. Thank you for being so sweet and worrying about me. But all is well. And just in case it isn't, I've made arrangements to stay elsewhere. Don't get on a plane!!! But you are such a dear to suggest it. I love you too. Aunt Clemmie.

Fourteen

Clemmie coaxed her parents to let her transfer to Ohio State for sophomore year. She promised to be ladylike and not shame them in the future. They said sternly that there would be many temptations on a big campus. Clemmie promised not to be tempted and, if tempted, not to yield.

She did not fear that Rudyard Creek would show up at Ohio State. Even if he found out she was going there, he could never find her amid the tens of thousands of people. But how would he find out? He couldn't keep inviting himself for dinner in a town where he no longer lived.

And for a bonus, she loved Ohio State too. Maybe she could still have a happily ever after; still fall in love and end up with the life she wanted: a good husband, several children, a little house, and a big garden.

Her very first week, Clemmie purchased a used bike—the kind with no gears and fat tires that would shortly go out fashion, stay out of fashion for decades, and suddenly reappear as trendy. She biked everywhere, a scarf tied under her chin to keep her hair neat. Nobody had big hair yet, so they didn't worry about flattening it.

As soon as possible, she found time to pedal all the way to the address Ronnie had copied off the driver's license of Mrs. Boone. It was early fall, and the sky was beautiful, the trees bright with color, but it was cold. A station wagon sat in the Boone driveway. Clemmie memorized the plate number.

She was blessed, because she'd circled the block only twice when out came the mother holding Clemmie's son's hand, and down the sidewalk they went. They crossed two streets to a park. It was basic. A little duck pond and a little grass, some swings and a teeter-totter. There were stone benches, too cold to sit on, and a few trees turning color.

The little boy and his mother went straight to the swings, and the little boy joyfully cried out every time his mommy pushed him. His laughter was the loveliest sound Clemmie had ever heard. She tried to memorize it, the way she'd memorize any other music.

Cycling down a narrow tarred path, Clemmie passed a sand-box, curved around a war monument, and ended up alongside the Boones. Mrs. Boone could not possibly have guessed that this pretty, black-haired little athlete with the bright-red lips and the khaki trousers clipped at the bottom so the fabric wouldn't catch in the chain was the bedraggled, exhausted, sweat-stained teen mother of her little boy.

In later years, girls in Clementine Lakefield's position had abortions. Clemmie was so grateful that in her day, you didn't kill the victim. Two parents and one little boy were happy, and if Clemmie's heart was broken, then it was.

The mother waved at Clemmie, and she waved back and kept pedaling, although she yearned to leap off her bike and run over to hug and hold and kiss and caress.

"Sandbox!" shouted the little boy.

His mother stopped the swing, and the little boy slid down and ran.

It was cold for playing in damp sand. Clemmie didn't think this would last. She cycled around the entire park, her heart pounding, her prayers ringing, *Don't let them leave yet, please, God.* Once again, she risked the little tar path that went right alongside the sandbox, hoping the mother was too occupied to sense anything odd about the continually passing cyclist.

Clemmie had just passed them when Mrs. Boone said, "Time to go, Billy."

Billy. My son is Billy Boone.

———————————

Since bumping into Mrs. Boone and Billy in the park was a miracle unlikely to recur, Clemmie needed a regular way to see them, so she considered another possibility: church.

Most people went to church, so it was a good guess that the Boones regularly or semiregularly showed up in some congregation. Clemmie cycled to the Boone neighborhood every Sunday morning. She cycled through the parking lots of area churches looking for the station wagon. But there were many churches, and they all seemed to have two services. When that didn't work, she lurked near the Boones' around quarter to nine, when they'd leave if they went to the early service, and then again around ten thirty, in case they went to the eleven o'clock service.

She was well aware that she was going way overboard. But the yearning to see her little son again filled her heart. Finally, one Sunday morning at ten forty-five, the Boones appeared at the red light she was facing and drove down a main thoroughfare. Clemmie found their station wagon in the lot of a big Methodist church. The service had just begun when she slid into the back pew. Billy was not with his parents. After a moment of confusion and despair, she realized why, slipped out the back, and made her way to the Sunday School wing. At the nursery, she found a teacher and offered to help with the children. "Oh, wonderful timing!" cried the teacher. "We're short on helpers this morning."

In those days, nobody worried about creepy, perverted childcare workers; nobody wondered if a person was unqualified or fibbing or somebody else entirely. First names were simply not used by children or in front of children, so she was Miss Blake, a name that popped out of her mouth, and she never did know where it came from. She added the name Blake to her chart of lies. Over the weeks, she once had the privilege of holding Billy in her arms. Another time, when the Bible story was a little scary, he reached for her hand and held it tightly. She did not worry that the Boones would recognize her, or even notice her, and they didn't.

At Thanksgiving, she helped Billy make a turkey by tracing his fingers on construction paper for the big, feathery tail. The first Sunday in Advent, she helped Billy glue cotton balls to white oval construction-paper cutouts. "Sheep," he said proudly.

Clemmie brought a camera to Sunday School. In those days, they were bulky. No picture could be taken clandestinely. She photographed every child, so no one would guess that only Billy mattered.

It was strange and awful to know that if she had not taken that picture, Rudyard Creek would have lived.

"We'll need to talk to everyone in the neighborhood," said the sheriff. "See if they noticed anyone or anything unusual."

Ralph clearly wanted to get involved, but had no material, so he said, "Helen, I don't want you to stay home alone." It was the sort of paternal overseer voice that always made Clemmie glad she hadn't married after all. "This happened right next door to you, Helen," he said, in case she hadn't noticed. "There's a killer out here. You come stay in our guest room until they've solved this."

"I agree. I'll help you pack," said Betty Anne.

Clemmie tried to think. Was this best? Should she vacate the premises, leaving Borobasq to get out or not on his own?

"We are tiring Helen out," trumpeted Ralph, and he swept the whole gathering out of Clemmie's house again, including Clemmie, because Ralph didn't give a hoot if she were tired; he didn't want to miss the action. Everybody trucked onto the porch and down the steps to get as close as they could to Dom's garage. Nothing had changed except there were a lot more people around, half taking photographs and videos, and the other half drinking coffee from to-go cups some minion must have fetched.

The sheriff joined his people in Dom's garage.

Clemmie sat down in her canvas chair so that Ralph could not take her arm and lead her away, and Ralph said quietly, "Don't let the police into your house again, Helen, because then they have the right to search it."

"Search it?" she repeated. What was Ralph thinking? That *she* had killed Wilson? That there was some clue in *her* house? Or had he glimpsed Borobasq?

No. If Ralph had seen some man standing in Clemmie's hall, he'd have told the sheriff.

Clemmie could not organize her mind. Rudyard Creek and Bent, Joyce and Dom, Wilson and the police, photographs of glass rigs, a snapshot of a small boy—the whole collage of figures from the past, the present, and the imagined fluttered in her mind.

Joyce would call back as soon as she heard Betty Anne's message.

She really might turn around, skipping Galveston altogether, because it would kill Joyce to miss the biggest event ever to happen on Blue Lilac. Clemmie had to get Borobasq to his rental car right now. But aside from the fact that this was impossible, what difference would it make?

Things were converging. She would be found out. All these people would soon know that Helen Stephens not only didn't live here, she didn't live anywhere else. Did you go to prison for stealing an identity? Probably not, but you certainly lost your teaching job, your friends, and your easy camaraderie in pottery and at the pool.

At least the parents of the real Helen Stephens could not still be alive to know that their daughter's name had been stolen and used for all these years.

Long ago, Clemmie had bought a tiny Florida condo. It wasn't under the name Clementine Lakefield or the name Helen Stephens, but under the name on her birth certificate, before her parents divorced and her stepfather adopted her: Clementine Eleanor Murray, a person she had not been in seven decades.

It was possible that no one else on earth knew that she had not been born a Lakefield. The records knew, and the records, she presumed, were online. But not necessarily. Adoptions and divorces were kept very secret back then, and it was also possible that after so many decades, the physical records had been discarded or lost before anybody began transferring them to digital storage.

At some point in junior high, Clemmie had asked her real daddy to get her a passport because, she told him, someday the two of them would travel abroad. He was as delighted by this plan as she was and took the steps required for a passport using her birth name. Clemmie kept it safe, zipped in her little black Bible, but Daddy had a heart attack and they never went anywhere after all.

In the end, though, she had three passports: Clementine Lakefield, Helen Stephens, and Clementine Eleanor Murray. She had bought the Florida condo way back when security was non-existent, planning to use the ancient Clementine Eleanor Murray passport as her ID, but it was unnecessary because she didn't get a mortgage; she had inherited enough from her father to buy the place.

I've made so many mistakes in my life, she thought. I can't blame them all on Rudyard Creek. The mistakes of yesterday and today are my own.

The tears she had been fighting began to spill over.

"Ralph," said Betty Anne severely, "you stop it. He's not a criminal attorney or anything, Helen," she said, rolling her eyes. "He was a FedEx driver. But he loves to claim exciting occupations. He's always saying he's a cardiac surgeon or an Egyptologist."

Ralph was laughing. "Sometimes I get away with it for hours," he told her. "Now and then, I get away with stories for a lifetime. It's a kick."

Clemmie, who had indeed gotten away with a story for her lifetime, suddenly liked Ralph a lot. And he was right. She would not let the sheriff back in. This is a murder case, she thought. There are two such cases in my life today. I'm not telling anybody anything. They'll learn the facts on their own, or they won't.

"Wait," said Ed in his important voice. "Where's Dom? If he's been gone all this time, it doesn't look good. You can't help concluding that Dom has something to do with this."

There were gasps all around, although Clemmie felt sure everybody else had reached this conclusion long before Ed.

Dom must have taken Wilson's car to make his getaway. Perhaps Wilson's car had been in the mall behind them. Dom could have walked that far—he wasn't actually crippled—and he certainly would have been motivated.

She had read somewhere—probably the *Wall Street Journal*, one of the two real newspapers she still took; the rest she read online or, truthfully, skimmed the headlines—that hundred-dollar bills greatly contributed to the sinister side of society, because they were the basis of major drug transactions. She Googled. Two pounds was the approximate weight of $100,000 in $100 bills. So $500,000 would weigh ten pounds, or two bags of sugar. It didn't say how much space that took up, but it wasn't a mountain of cash. More like a cat carrier.

They say you can't disappear anymore, that the internet can always find you, she thought. Certainly Borobasq found me. But Dom has his other identity out there too, waiting for him. My guess is that he can be a Pesante and disappear. *Disappear* might not be the right word. He might just return to who he is anyway.

Was it time to go back to the name she had had at birth? That would mean giving up her little house. Leaving Sun City. Leaving her sweet, easy teaching job, with seven students in third-year Latin and six students in second year and eleven in first. She would never see them again and she loved them; she cared about their lives and their future. Would she be able to get in touch with the grands or Peggy?

"Helen, let's go in and get you packed," said Betty Anne briskly.

"Betty Anne, you're so kind and thoughtful, but I'll stay here. I'm not worried."

"Why not?" demanded Shirley. "*I'm* certainly worried. You had a murder next door! You were probably playing Words with Friends or scrambling an egg while that poor man was being shot!"

Never talk, Clemmie reminded herself. I can't explain why I'm not worried, so I was wrong to speak.

Ralph saved her. "Hey, that's weird. What's that door? Hey, Helen, look at that. You ever notice that? Those guys must have cut that door into the wall. Their units are connected! And the people in that last unit? They are never around. I met 'em once, and they said they just use their place when they're visiting their grandchildren, but when I asked where the grandkids live and what school system they're in and all—because my grandkids are here too, we got eleven of 'em, seven boys and four girls—you know what? They didn't tell me! Listen, nobody's out there who doesn't brag about grandkids. They didn't even have pictures! Who doesn't show off their grandkids' pictures? Hey, I'm telling the sheriff to check out that unit too. Maybe they're the murderers."

Maybe they are, thought Clemmie. They're the ones with the stolen glass.

Had the Coglands taken Dom with them? Somehow everything went wrong. Wilson was shot, they all drove away, and texting Helen Stephens was forgotten.

How much could Borobasq hear of the conversations in her living room and on her porch?

If he were really gutsy, he'd be creeping out her sliders right now, with everybody in the front and the police in Dom's garage.

In January the Boones were not in church.

"Billy's family moved away," said a teacher one Sunday. "It's a shame. They were so active. We really miss them."

Clemmie lived through the morning, which surprised her.

On Monday, she called the church secretary, remembering to identify herself with her church volunteer name. "Hello," she said, trying not to sound desperate or burst into tears, "it's Helen Blake. I help in the nursery. You know, I was so fond of Billy Boone and his parents, and I wonder if you can give me their forwarding address so I can send a card."

In those days, nobody worried that you were up to no good; it would never have occurred to anybody. "Let me look," said the secretary, and Clemmie could hear the shuffling of papers and the opening and closing of a metal file drawer and the drop of a manila folder against a desk surface. In later years, all this would be replaced by clicks.

"I'm so sorry, Miss Blake. I don't seem to have a forwarding address."

Because Billy was lost to her, Clemmie went home for spring break, hoping for comfort from her parents, and she was at her parents' house when Rudyard Creek drove by, saw the Lakefields sitting on their front porch to enjoy an unseasonably warm day, and parked at the curb.

Rudyard Creek loped across the grass and up the porch steps, and her parents beamed. Of course her mother asked him to stay for dinner.

Clemmie's entire body failed her. She was about to faint, gag, and have diarrhea.

"I'm amazed you have time to drive down here," said Clemmie's father. "Your high school's gotta be a hundred miles away."

"A hundred fifty," he said, laughing. "But basketball season is over. We didn't win the state championship, but we were in the final four. I'm taking a hard-earned break and visiting old friends." He smiled at Clemmie. "So what's OSU like?"

Clemmie held her trembling hands under the table and kept her spine straight. Had he looked for her again at Muskingum only to find her gone? Had he asked Pete where she was? Why was he doing this? He had a wife and a career and evening ball games and weekend games—and he was following her? Why?

The word *stalking* had not been used for people in the 1950s and '60s. A hunter stalked his prey, but the idea that one person might stalk another person for a hobby was decades away. And by the time Clemmie first heard the word used with that meaning, she had become a stalker herself.

"It's a big school," she said finally. "Quite different from Muskingum."

"She's majoring in Latin!" said her mother. "Isn't that dear? She wants to be a Latin teacher just like Miss Gardener, who taught her all four years in high school. And OSU has such a fine classics department!"

"I'm impressed," said Rudyard Creek. "Tell me about your dorm. It must be massive."

Clemmie's stomach churned. Her mother's silver gleamed, the crystal winked, and the heavily starched tablecloth lay flat and flawless under the china. It was a representation of what life ought to be: shiny and smooth.

"It's called the Towers," said her mother. "Clemmie is on the ninth floor! Can you imagine? She's practically in a skyscraper."

Her mother had told her rapist where she lived.

FIFTEEN

Clemmie had to move out of her high-rise dorm right away.

She knew a girl from the New England Club who was renting a tiny garage apartment off campus and whose roommate had decided not to finish out the semester. The following morning, when her parents were out of the house, Clemmie hurried to their only phone: a matte-black dial phone that sat on the phone table in the front hall. The single little drawer held the phone book, her mother's address book, scrap paper (mainly the backs of used envelopes), and pencil stubs.

"Clemmie!" Barbara Farmer cried. "Of course I want you for a roommate. This saves me from having to post an index card on the bulletin board outside the Housing Office, hoping for the best and dreading the worst. I might get a roommate who was messy or couldn't cook."

"I'm very tidy," Clemmie assured her, "and I'm quite a good cook. Wait until you taste my pie crust."

"You'll have to teach me! My crusts are always soggy."

The girls finally hung up, having giggled and gossiped and discussed color choices for the curtains they would sew.

Clemmie celebrated by going out for a bike ride.

There was something wonderful and free about a bike. Bikes were only for kids back then, and grown-ups rarely mounted one, but Clemmie was young enough to be unremarkable. She loved pedaling, the wind on her face, and the pleasure of using her muscles. She rode to the town park, a lovely long oval of grass and trees, gardens and ponds, with a stone pavilion built in the 1930s by the CCC on a little man-made island, everybody's favorite place for photographs and rendezvous.

Surprisingly for so early in the spring, it was a warm and lovely day.

Four small children and their mother were in the pavilion, the children climbing on the wide window-seat-type walls, chasing each other and screaming happily.

On the grass, two teenage boys played with a Frisbee, a rather new toy whose appeal Clemmie did not understand. Their Labrador retriever made dramatic leaps into the air, trying to catch the Frisbee in its jaws. It was such a pretty sight: boys and their dog.

She got off her bike and leaned it against the side of a stone pillar, and Rudyard Creek came up behind her.

She prayed that the boys and their dog and the mother and her four children would not go anywhere. There was a wooden bench in the sun, the slats painted glossy park green, and she sat down, partly because she was almost fainting, but also so she could hang onto the bench and he couldn't drag her to his car.

"Nice here, isn't it?" said Rudyard Creek loudly, for the mother to hear. And then, just for Clemmie, he said softly, "My wife hasn't been able to have children. I want a child. I know you and I had a baby. I know you gave our baby away."

Clemmie flinched. She was hot and cold at the same time.

He dared called Billy "our" baby? He used that pronoun as if they had done something shared? For the first time, Clemmie felt rage. She could have killed him.

"I have a fine house," he said, as if real estate mattered. "I have a beautiful wife, a boat, two cars. I need a kid. Our kid."

Clemmie had thought in terms of protecting herself and her body. Now she understood that she was a minor player. The one who counted was Billy, who from his birth had been safe and happy with good people. He must not be in the presence of this horrible man, let alone in the same house for the rest of his life. Having to call him Daddy. Sitting at a dining table with him, celebrating Christmas with him, practicing basketball with him. And the most chilling possible outcome: learning to be like him. Learning to attack the weak.

She would kill Rudyard Creek before she would let him near Billy.

"Where is it?" said the coach.

Clemmie did not know what the neuter pronoun referred to until she realized that while Rudyard Creek knew there had been a child, he did not know whether the baby had been a boy or a girl. So he had not acquired records from the Mountain School.

Farther away now, the boys and their dog and their Frisbee frolicked, so careless in that happiness, with no idea how quickly pleasure could be destroyed.

"You didn't go to some crummy little school in Ohio just for the privilege of going to a crummy little school in Ohio," said Rudyard Creek. "He's there, isn't he? What do you do—babysit for him? Spy on the family? Pretend to people you aren't loose and free with your favors?"

She pondered the pronoun change and decided he was just using proper grammar. He did not know there was a boy. Clemmie had to convince him there was no such child at all. "Don't be silly. Muskingum is a wonderful school."

"Then why did you transfer to OSU?"

"Because you showed up!"

One long, wild toss of the Frisbee, and the boys and their dog were racing to the far end of the meadow.

"What are their names?" said Rudyard Creek. "The people who have my child. Where do they live?"

Her mother had told him what her major was, so he could haunt the Classics Department, and she would have to be watchful, but the man would never know about nor find Barbara's three tiny rooms above a big garage.

"How do I know you had our baby?" he said, chortling as if it were a joke. "I had no idea you were pregnant. I actually fell for the line that you were out of school because you were helping your aunt with cancer. It was the kind of thing you'd do. But your brother, Pete, came clean with me. He admitted the family scandal."

Pete had betrayed her.

Clemmie's heart thundered. She could not hear her own thoughts.

The mother and her family crossed the little stone bridge, heading over a wide swale of lawn to the big, metal A-frame swing sets. "I love to swing!" cried Clemmie, and she leaped up and dashed after them.

"Me too," Rudyard Creek said, getting up. But he did not run. Running and jogging were not popularized until the 1970s. In the early '60s, a grown man didn't go for a walk, let alone run. He wasn't worried. She could not elude him for long because she had to come back for her bike.

But he was foiled. This was, after all, the town in whose high school he had coached, and a young man headed for the tennis courts recognized him. "Hey, Coach!" shouted the boy, delighted. He fell in step with Rudyard Creek, and Clemmie safely doubled back, got her bike, and rode home.

———

In her bedroom, Clemmie went into the top drawer of her dresser where her savings account passbook lay under the neatly ironed cotton and linen handkerchiefs she no longer used, having entirely switched to Kleenex. She was so proud of that little booklet with its tiny bank-posted entries and 4.25 percent interest. She had enough money of her own for several months of her half of the rent. She went through desk drawers, folders, boxes, spring and fall handbags, beaded clasp bags, and leather change purses in the faint hope that she had once squirreled away a dollar bill or two.

She had not. But what she did find was the paperwork of Helen Stephens, the elementary school biography still in its envelope, its thin, waxed string wrapped around the paper buttons. She took the envelope back to Ohio State. As a bonus, to her delight, the residence office returned the unused portion of her room and board.

Since another girl now occupied her dorm room, Clemmie could no longer get mail at her box at the big dorm, so she wrote to her parents, explaining that she had a marvelous opportunity for growth and experience and therefore was living independently with Barbara, whose address she gave them.

In those days, parents were not interested in a daughter getting growth or experience. They wanted their girls supervised in a dorm. Clemmie had already proved she was unreliable at best, and they felt she needed structure. They had not even met Barbara. What kind of girl was she? There was much writing to and fro, but there were no phone calls. Most people then were too frugal for long-distance calls and besides, a person could think each thought through and deliver it with precision and care in a letter.

Clemmie ignored their advice and their questions and wrote gaily about the joys of ancient languages.

She took certain precautions on the campus, but its vast size and the staggering number of students gave her a sense of safety.

———————

"I called Johnny," Bob announced, holding up his cell phone.

Sheriff Bennett nodded. He was talking to each neighbor, every conversation short because nobody knew a thing about Dom or Wilson, and was now questioning Eileen and Al, who had just hurried over from White Lily.

Eileen said breathlessly, "I wondered who was hurt! We spotted the ambulance and the police, and I said to Al, I said, 'Let's just see what's happened.'" Eileen was thrilled when the sheriff asked if she knew Marcia and Roy Cogland.

It's like the grands fascinated by the cold case, thought Clemmie. Oooh, this is fun! And I'm part of it!

"Well, of course, I came over a few years ago when I found out that we had new neighbors," said Eileen happily, "because I run the Sunshine Committee for our pod. We spoke in the street because they were headed out, and in fact, I actually had to wave them down to introduce myself. I had made a baked pineapple cheese casserole—it sounds strange, but it's a delicious dish; I always bring it to church suppers; you take two sixteen-ounce cans of diced pineapple, add brown sugar, a stick of butter, and a pack of shredded cheese, give it a topping of buttered crushed Ritz crackers, and serve it hot, and it's sort of a dessert and sort of a side dish—"

"Eileen," said her husband, "he doesn't want a recipe."

Eileen flushed.

"You took them your delicious casserole," encouraged the sheriff.

"And Marcia said how lovely of me, how thoughtful, but they were just leaving. They didn't even have furniture yet, she said. It would be delivered shortly. And they would be here only occasionally, using the villa as a home base for visiting the grandchildren until they retired, which would probably not be for several years."

"Did you get their year-round address or phone number?"

"No," said Eileen. "Marcia said she'd get back to me, but she never did. And they didn't even take the casserole, not that it went to waste, because Wanda Pruitt on Yellow Quince was ill, and she was very grateful, but Marcia told me they just wouldn't be home to eat it."

"Did you go back and visit?" he asked.

"I tried. But really, I never found them at home. From our house, we can see the far edge of their house, which means that at night, we'd know if they're home because we'd see the light shining out their windows. But we never did see a light. Not once!"

"That's no mystery," said her husband in the irritated voice Clemmie so often noted in spouses. "They just pulled the drapes."

Betty Anne nodded. "The Coglands keep their blinds closed all the time. Some people do that. They live like creatures in caves, without any sunlight, and you wonder why they even have windows, since they never look out or open them for fresh air."

This declaration was a little disturbing. Everybody would know if the front blinds were always closed, but you could only know about side and back windows if you routinely traipsed around the villas. Clemmie had a less-than-attractive vision of neighbors creeping in circles around the pod, keeping tabs on drapes and lights.

"Fresh air is overrated," said Ralph. "All it is around here is a truckload of yellow pollen coming in through the screen."

When the subject of pollen, filth, and allergic reactions had been used up, the sheriff said, "Actually, my people have already checked, and the third unit still belongs to its original owner, Dominic Spesante. It was never sold to anybody. We have no record of Marcia and Roy Cogland."

"They were renting from Dom?" said Ralph incredulously.

How extraordinary, thought Clemmie. Dom was the one in charge, not the one imprisoned. Dom ran the show. Whatever the show was. I mean is, because Dom is still alive.

Unless Marcia and Roy had killed Dom as well as Wilson, and his body was moldering in the woods.

"Did Dom ever discuss his rental property?" asked the sheriff, swinging his glance around the group.

"Dom never discussed anything with anybody," said Bob. "He never took part in anything or showed up anywhere."

The sheriff turned to Clemmie. "Do you remember how you met Wilson Spesante?"

Somebody had left a red plastic cup of water on the porch floor, so Clemmie drank from it. Possible other-people germs hardly mattered at this point. The water was already warm from the heat of the day. It gave her a moment to think. "I was sitting on a lawn chair inside my garage with the garage door open, so it must have been cold weather, because in winter, the garage is an afternoon sun trap since it faces west. I wrap up in an afghan and sit in the sun but out of the wind, and I read. This young man drove into Dom's driveway, which of course is only a few feet away, and looked over at me and probably thought, *What's that old lady doing sitting in her garage?* so I introduced myself."

It hit her again that Wilson was no longer alive.

Oh, Wilson! Your life is over. You had plans. Maybe you're married. You certainly have a mother and father. Maybe you were the good guy in the family, the only one kind enough to check on difficult, old uncle Dom. On the other hand, maybe you're a drug dealer, a thief, and the worst one in the whole family.

Dom, Dom! Did you actually kill him?

She didn't want it to be true.

If she really wanted to give Dom time to cover his tracks, she could give Borobasq up, which would completely derail the search for Dom and consume the first forty-eight hours that were supposed to be crucial in achieving homicide case success.

How sick is that? I'm thinking up ways to save Wilson's killer.

"That's what we do here," put in Eileen. "This whole place is about friendships. We arrive, drop the suitcases in our bedrooms, and trot out to make friends."

"Nice," said the sheriff, meaning it. Clemmie liked that. "So how did the young man introduce himself to you, Miz Stephens?"

The young man who would never introduce himself to anybody again. Nausea hit her, seeping down to her bowels and up into her throat. "I must have said, Good morning, I'm—"

There was a wavy, cloudy moment in which she did not know who she was. The gray-haired, thick-bodied neighbors standing so close seemed like swollen clothespin dolls. Clemmie could not come up with her own name. "'I'm the next-door neighbor,' I said to him. And he said, 'Hey, I'm visiting Dom,' and then Dom came out and—no, I must be wrong. We must have exchanged names because I always knew he was Wilson." She memorized her sentences. She might need them a second time.

Helen, she remembered with relief. *Helen*, she repeated to herself.

Another vehicle appeared on Blue Lilac Lane.

Johnny maneuvered his Avalon between the official vehicles with inches to spare, parked in Joyce's driveway, and walked straight over. He must have been told what was going on, because he was visibly shocked. Pale and shaking his head, he stared at the uniformed sheriff. "Wow," he said, and had to catch his breath from just that syllable. "I can't believe it. Dom killed Wilson? I can't picture that. Dom's old and half crippled. Wilson's young and big." His voice was not its usual booming bass, but thin and reedy, like a kid's.

"Poor old Dom. I mean, he was a difficult guy, but he wasn't *that* difficult. He was just living his own weird life. I can't believe he'd do anything to Wilson. Wilson was his only whatever. Grandson, maybe? Nephew? I don't know, but there wasn't anybody else. I cannot imagine Dom, like, you know, like, attacking him. I mean, *why?*" He was babbling, more Joyce's style than his own.

"So you met Wilson?" the sheriff asked.

"Yup. One day they couldn't get their golf cart going, so I came over and helped. Dom forgot to add water to the battery. People think a golf cart takes care of itself, but it doesn't."

The men made noises of agreement. Most of them liked doing the maintenance and thought poorly of people who skipped it or refused to learn how.

"I let them use my golf cart while Dom's was charging," said Johnny.

Clemmie wondered how Wilson had liked driving around under a swag of boxer shorts.

"Do you think you handled the golf cart any time after that?" the sheriff asked Johnny.

"Sure. Used to say hello to Dom now and then. I'm a grabber. I hang on to stuff. Probably grabbed the frame or patted the sides."

Dom kept the plastic zipped. Grabbing wouldn't be easy. But then, the day his mail skittered across her yard, he hadn't zipped himself in. So he hadn't always enclosed himself.

"We got an awful lot of prints on his golf cart," said the sheriff. "Would you mind if we fingerprinted you? Just to rule yours out."

"I don't mind," said Johnny, "and anyway, they're on file someplace because I was in the army."

"What can you tell me about Marcia and Roy Cogland?"

Johnny shook his head. "Them I don't think I ever met. Maybe Joyce did."

"Your wife isn't home?"

"Mmm," said Johnny, looking rueful. "She's my significant other, I guess. Went to visit her sister. I'll give you her cell number."

Clemmie could not tell from Johnny's face or voice if he knew that Joyce had left him and if he understood that he was no longer a significant other, just a guy locked out of a house.

"Have you ever been inside Dom's?" the sheriff asked.

"Just the once. I'm sure Helen told you that we checked on him yesterday. Was it yesterday, Helen? Or the day before?"

"I forget," she said, establishing forgetfulness.

The sheriff did not scold Clemmie for leaving this out of her own story. Perhaps she had already succeeded in creating her senile persona. "How thoroughly did you check the house, Mr. Marsh?" he asked.

"Not very. We didn't look in closets or anything, did we, Helen?

We were just making sure he hadn't fallen or something. And he hadn't."

"What time would this have been?'" asked the sheriff.

"I can't remember," said Johnny. "When was it, Helen?"

"I just remember how hot it was."

"Miz Stephens, do you have Wilson's address or phone number?"

Johnny said, "He's gotta have his cell phone on him."

"No. No phone. No wallet."

"He doesn't have a wallet?" exclaimed Betty Anne. "It was a robbery then? It wasn't Dom who killed him? It was some stranger after money? I bet that's it! I mean, here we are, right next to a gate that is right next to a mall that is right next to a highway that is not very far south of an interstate!"

"Robbed inside his own garage?" said Bob doubtfully.

"Probably the killer took the wallet and phone to prevent identification of the body," said Ralph.

That's ridiculous, thought Clemmie. How many bodies could there be in Dom's garage? It would only be Dom or Wilson.

"Miz Stephens, what do you think you touched in Dom's house? Or his golf cart?"

"I'm a little overboard on cleanliness," she told him. "I don't touch things if I'm not wearing gloves. Remember white gloves?" she said to the girls. "Remember how if you went into the city, you wore your white gloves?"

"Oh my goodness! And dancing lessons!" cried Eileen.

There, thought Clemmie. I can be just as casual about murder as my neighbors.

———————————

In the garage, Borobasq considered his options.

He didn't have any.

There was a sheriff between him and escape. He'd inched to the old lady's bedroom window and peered out to see a cop searching the shrubbery. For what, he didn't know, but there was no rear exit available.

He thought about the cache he'd found under the connecting door between the garages. The screws holding down the oak strip had been so tight, he'd thought he might snap the screwdriver off the knife. The old lady couldn't have used that space because her hands were knotted with arthritis, and she couldn't have tightened anything.

The space had been crammed with brick-sized packages heavily wrapped and taped. You didn't do that with hundred-dollar bills. You didn't do that with marijuana, and in any case, there was no accompanying scent. Could have been anything, from opiates to crack.

In the marijuana world, people liked to say they were all laid-back and nice and nonviolent. That was often true until you were talking about money, and then they were just as angry, vicious, and violent as any other gang. As for guys that dealt coke or oxycodone, Boro would never touch their world. He left the drugs where they were.

Without a doubt, the cops had found the cache, knew these two units were dealing, and assumed that the murder was a drug deal gone bad. Maybe so, but Borobasq considered it more likely that his own cash was at the heart of this.

The old lady with two names hadn't given him up. A murder next door, and she was protecting the home invader?

She had to be part of it.

And although it was a reasonable guess that his money had disappeared with the guy Dom or the couple Marcia and Roy, it was also a reasonable guess that his money had stayed right here and the old lady had it.

Sixteen

Barbara Farmer loved her little apartment. All her life, she had yearned to live on her own, a status not acceptable in her circle. Her parents having refused to let her rent an apartment unless she had a roommate, Barbara did not tell them that her roommate had quit college to become an airline stewardess. Clemmie Lakefield moving in was wonderful because Barbara hated lying to her parents. Clemmie was also very domestic and, like Barbara, loved to cook and clean and decorate. Having their own tiny kitchen made them both so happy. Amazingly, they even were the same size, although Barbara was not nearly as generously endowed, so they could swap many of their dresses and skirts, thus doubling their wardrobes.

The girls enjoyed the same books and movies, and they both loved the New England Club, not because they missed Connecticut, but because it was good to be in a small group on a huge campus. Barbara was treasurer, and Clemmie was secretary.

A classmate named Flossy, whose parents insisted she must major in home economics, had been forced to take advanced sewing classes. More than anything, Flossy hated tailoring. The same week Flossy dropped her nickname and required her friends to call her Florence, she dropped out of tailoring and said that next, she'd drop the sewing machine out the window.

"No, no!" cried Barbara. "May I have it?"

Flossy suddenly remembered that the sewing machine had monetary value, so she and Barbara struck a deal, and Barbara went home with a fine Singer machine. She had just finished a sweet deep ruffle on a gingham kitchen curtain when the doorbell rang. In those days, you opened the door. You smiled. Of course, you invited Clemmie's dear friend Rudyard inside and suggested that he wait until Clemmie got home, which would be probably an hour from now. No, probably not earlier, you explained, because this professor always ran over, and Clemmie never skipped class.

When Clemmie got back to the apartment, Barbara was lying on her twin bed, wrapped in a blanket, sobbing. She could not use the word *rape* out loud, but she managed to blurt out enough for Clemmie to understand.

Clemmie collapsed, sobbing even harder than Barbara. She lay down next to her, and they clung to each other, and neither could stop weeping.

The girls never considered going to the police. They didn't even consider going to a doctor. Barbara had invited a complete stranger into her apartment. *What had she expected?* the police would say. The police—and very possibly her own parents—might add, *What had she wanted?*

But how did Rudyard Creek find me? Clemmie thought. The apartment is in Barbara's name. My parents do know my address, but surely even they would not give out their nineteen-year-old daughter's private address to a thirty-year-old married man.

I can never use my actual address again, she thought. I'll have to use post office boxes.

Clemmie was responsible for this catastrophe. This cruel, wicked violence. She had to tell Barbara the whole sordid history, and Barbara would rightly require her to move out.

Once started on the confession she had never been able to make, Clemmie told Barbara everything. How she'd been the only girl at the Mountain School who actually held her infant. How Veronica had sneaked a peek into the adoptive mother's handbag, so Clemmie knew their name was Boone and they lived in Columbus. How she attended Muskingum to get closer to her son, because she absolutely had to see that precious child again. "I pulled it off," she said. "Look." She took the precious black-and-white photograph out from under her ironed hankies: Billy in Sunday School.

"What happened to you is my fault, Barbara. I moved in with you to hide from Rudyard Creek, and I didn't warn you. It never occurred to me he could find me here because the apartment is in your name. I'm so sorry. I was so wrong. I used you. I created this nightmare."

Barbara was stunned. Her innocent, sweet, dear little roommate had been raped and borne a child. She saw that Clemmie would give up everything in her life to have that little boy back, but had to settle for a photograph. Barbara thought that if she were to get pregnant by that same rapist, she'd get an abortion if she had to use a carving knife.

"You are not responsible, Clemmie. That man did this, not you. The whole thing is insane. From Albany, he could have taken interstates some of the way here, but at times he had to use regular two- or four-lane roads. Waiting at red lights, pausing for school buses, driving for hours and hours, leaving his wife and his job to come after you. Rudyard Creek is insane."

It occurred to Clemmie for the first time that yes, Rudyard Creek was insane. It did not lessen her guilt that Barbara had suffered at his hands. No one knew better than Clemmie what Barbara would continue to suffer: the slow pace—if there was a pace—of recovery.

She could not believe that Barbara forgave her. She certainly didn't forgive herself. Ways in which she could have acted differently coursed through her mind day and night, but there was never a way out. It was done; it had happened.

For the remainder of the semester, the girls slept on the floors of friends' dorm rooms, using as their excuse that they had run out of money and had to give the apartment up.

The week of final exams, Barbara said gently, "Literally the hour that my last exam is over, I'm going home and I'm never coming back. You didn't betray me. You don't have to keep apologizing. But I can't be anywhere that man has been or is likely to be." She looked intensely at her friend. "He'll come again, Clemmie. *You are his hobby.* You are what he does for fun. When you escaped him, it didn't deter him. I think it appealed to him. You turned out to be more exciting prey than he expected."

One of the last days, when they couldn't study another minute and were desperate for diversion, Barbara straightened Clemmie's hair using chemicals in a box. They laughed hysterically at the rectangle of hair that replaced her corkscrews. Barbara took out all the makeup she owned and painted Clemmie vividly, until looking out of the mirror was somebody neither girl recognized, especially when Barbara added gaudy sunglasses and glittering earrings.

Clemmie knew at last what she was going to do with Helen Stephens's paperwork.

Barbara headed to the library for a final round of study. Clemmie took out the passport and social security card of Helen Stephens. Did such things get canceled? Had Helen Stephens's parents notified somebody somewhere that there was no longer a Helen Stephens on earth to use them? If Clemmie used them, how might that backfire? Would some authority investigate and find that Helen Stephens had died years ago? She had no idea and no way to research it.

Clemmie removed layers of makeup, put away the jewelry, and walked to the nearest drugstore, where she purchased plain black-rimmed drugstore reading glasses and a hairband. Carrying the identification of Helen Stephens, she went to the Bureau of Motor Vehicles, filled out the right form, stood in the right line, and hoped no one would ask why she hadn't gotten her driver's license the day she turned sixteen, like any other teenager.

But in those days, you could still tremble a little, telling the nice man that your father had taught you to drive, but you had never had the courage to take the driving test, and now your father was insisting that you needed your license. And the nice man took you for a drive, and even let you skip parallel parking, and you passed.

The clerk made a photo ID for Helen Stephens, who turned out to be a plain girl with pitiful straight hair and bad eyes behind fat lenses. They didn't check her eyes, only checked a box that she needed corrective lenses.

Clemmie didn't remember Helen very well. Would Helen have gotten a kick out of this or turned Clemmie in? *Don't be mad, Helen. Please. I need you to save me. Please be okay with it.*

But the guilt of letting rape happen to Barbara was worse than any guilt she would ever have over Helen Stephens.

Helen's passport had expired. In her old photograph, the real Helen was just a little girl with dark hair. It was easy for Clemmie to be a bigger girl with dark hair. She went to the camera shop the next day, had passport photos taken, and then sent the photos, Helen's birth certificate, and the fee in to the passport office.

Would federal agents come for her? What would she say to Helen's poor parents about stealing Helen?

———————

So Barbara went home, and although her home was also Connecticut, her placid northwest corner was completely removed from Clemmie's southeastern shoreline. Connecticut's many north-south rock ridges made it surprisingly difficult to travel diagonally across the tiny state. Barbara was safe from the scourge of Rudyard Creek, but she could not feel safe in her heart.

Barbara's father loved hunting, and Barbara, who had been unwilling to touch a gun for her entire twenty years, told Daddy she wanted to learn after all. She was good from the get-go, and her dad was amazed and proud. Of course I'm good, thought Barbara, because every target is the heart of Rudyard Creek.

At the shooting range, she also learned how to use handguns. It took a while to find just the right purse to hold just the right protection. Barbara knew that she would never travel without this gun either in her purse or under the car seat. I never want to see Rudyard Creek again, she thought. On the other hand, I hope I do. I'll kill him.

Clemmie did not visit her family in Connecticut over the summer. The risk of Rudyard Creek showing up was too high.

In the school store, along with rings and sweatshirts and billed caps, were lockets: lovely delicate gold ovals, with no initials or crests because they were meant for a boy to engrave and give to his girl. Clemmie bought one. She cropped her precious photo of Billy and put it into the locket. Now it was always with her.

Her passport arrived, and the birth certificate of Helen Stephens was returned with it.

Clemmie had all the credits necessary for her Latin major. She just needed a few more credits in science and history, both of which she had put off. She took these in the summer session. Student teaching would start in the fall.

She and Barbara talked fairly often those hot July and August evenings, even though the calls were long distance and the toll rates were unthinkable. Barbara had decided to attend a school in Boston and live with a married cousin so there was a man in the house for protection. "Clemmie, you're my dear friend, but I'm not going to give you my cousin's name, address, or phone number. Write to me care of my parents. Your coach is a devil. He finds things out. He'll find you again, Clemmie, and somehow, he could find me again. So I can't give you my location. It's too risky."

SEVENTEEN

On Blue Lilac Lane, the mailman appeared. Because of all the emergency vehicles, there wasn't room to drive his little truck down the lane, so he hand-delivered to the villas on the cul-de-sac, whose occupants eagerly gave him all the details about the murder of Wilson Spesante. On his cell phone, the mailman called his nephew, whose wife worked at a television station in Charlotte.

Clemmie went inside once more, locking the door behind her.

Because the front door was half glass, she could not lean back against it and sob, which would have been her first choice. She had to walk into her home and turn a corner to be invisible. But since Clemmie loved light and disliked drapes, anybody could peer into her front kitchen-dining area window or into her back sliders, and right now, anybody might. The place was crawling with people. She flicked the kitchen curtains closed and pulled her living-room drapes, which she did so rarely the mechanism didn't want to move. Then she faced Borobasq, who was standing just inside the laundry room, leaning against the dryer.

She wasn't afraid of him because half a dozen officers and a whole lot of first responders were on the other side of the garage door, but she was certainly anxious about her plan to get rid of him. "You have to be in that rental car and driving away before the golf-club parking lot empties and the car is noticed. No doubt someone is calling the TV station, so there will shortly be even more people and vehicles here. What is all this about, anyway? What did you really come for? Was Wilson killed for it?"

To her surprise, he verified Bentley's phone message. "Whoever stole that rig? They stole my cash too."

Put that way, it sounded like twenty-five dollars, because who used cash anymore? Well, Clemmie did, but she was a rarity.

"So the dead guy?" said Borobasq. "He's my thief."

How did Borobasq know that Wilson was the thief? Had he recognized Wilson? Had he leaned over the golf cart and said to himself, "Huh. My old buddy Wilson got plugged. Yeah, whatever."

When she had crossed the garage during the night, Dom's garbage had started to smell. But it hadn't been garbage. It had been poor Wilson. Then Wilson was in there, dead, when Johnny went in to check, she thought. Did Johnny smell him, see him, and decide to ignore him? I want to say that's impossible. But nothing is impossible today.

"But the money isn't there," said Borobasq, tapping his knife against his palm. It was not the blade that was protruding this time, but a tiny Phillips head screwdriver. He had opened something and expected the cash to be in it. What on earth could that be? There was nothing to open.

"Maybe the group had a falling-out," said Borobasq.

"What group?"

"Your dead Wilson. Your missing Dom. Your unknown Coglands. They're drug dealers. Maybe somebody wanted more than his share. Maybe somebody else took more than his share." He smiled. "Like you, say."

Clemmie looked up at him. In her next life, she hoped to look down at people. "You saw the body when you were in Dom's garage."

"Yup."

"And you recognized him."

"Yup."

"But you just sauntered back in here and had a little macaroni and cheese?"

"I'm a cool customer," he said with an engaging grin. In high school, she would have been swept away. But after fifty years of teaching, not so much. And how cool was Johnny? Cool enough to take in the sight of a dead body and walk back without a tremor? Or was Johnny unobservant? Or lacking a sense of smell, which happened with some medications? Or had the golf cart been driven into the garage later in the day and Johnny had been truthful about the garage being empty?

"I'm going to freshen up," she told Borobasq. "Then I'll tell the sheriff I have a card game to attend, and will he please move the vehicles away from my driveway. You lie on the floor of the back seat of my car. I'll throw a blanket over you. If we have to pause for some reason, and somebody leans close, they'll just see a blanket, but if they do see you, I will claim that you have been holding me hostage."

"But then I'll give them your other name."

"That would be embarrassing. I don't wish to explain myself. But I will. The worst that can happen is that my nephew, Bentley, will be impressed by my exotic life."

"If that were the worst that could happen," said Boro, properly using the subjunctive, which Clemmie liked in a person, "you'd have shrugged about your two names long ago. So there is more, and you're bluffing."

"Nothing worse can happen to me," she said. "But a lot worse can happen to you. You do not want the sheriff pulling you out of my car. Now step out of my way so I can powder my nose." He moved back, and she walked through her bedroom and into her bathroom and locked the door. How flimsy the lock was! It merely kept one guest from accidentally walking in on another guest. It would not keep Borobasq out, should he choose to shove against it.

If all this had happened last week, before the news of the cold case in Connecticut, she would have been able to laugh a rueful, publicly embarrassed laugh. *Okay, the jig is up. I'm not Helen Stephens, and I never was.*

Would she have told the truth? *I was hiding from a rapist.*

Would she have fabricated reasons? *It was a lark. I had all that paperwork, and I was only twenty-one, and I acted on it.*

Or would she have pulled up a wild and dramatic piece of nonsense that nobody local could prove or disprove? Something to do with the CIA? Could she still try that? What was there to lose?

She was rather attracted to the CIA possibility. Could she establish herself as senile and confused today, but intelligent and daring in the past?

She chose the chestnut Sunday wig, with its carefully tended rolls of hair, the one that was quite obviously a wig, and since the neighbors and crime responders had just seen her half bald, they would be amused and perhaps even distracted, not thinking about what might be on the floor of her back seat. She applied more makeup than usual.

In the mudroom, the dreamboat blocked the way to the garage and examined her like a product. "Who are you, anyway?"

He was dependent on her now, which didn't make her taller, but did make her safer. She picked out a different lie. "I was in witness protection. It ends, you know. After you've testified, they bother with you for another decade or so, and then you're on your own. For the most part, I've stayed in my fabricated life. But I am in touch with my family under my original name."

He snorted. "A Latin teacher in witness protection?"

"Prior to becoming a Latin teacher, I paid my way through college working as a secretary. It happened to be for the mob, although at the time, I thought a mob was a gathering of rowdy people. I was a sheltered, sweet, stupid little girl. But we're not going there, Borobasq. It's too long ago. We have problems of our own."

"Boro," he said. "People call me Boro."

She moved her step stool in front of the dryer, balanced carefully, and from the cabinet overhead withdrew a light blanket from a stack of carefully folded linens. She put away the step stool, which otherwise she might trip over when she came home, led the way into the garage, opened the back door of her car, and gestured.

"It's got to be a hundred and twenty in there," he said irritably.

"It won't kill you. I'll be a few minutes talking to the sheriff, and then I'll put on the air-conditioning."

"Is there actually a card game for you to go to?"

"Hearts, which I rarely play. But if anybody asks, I'll say that since I missed my usual canasta game with Joyce, I'm going to hearts."

She thought how cold that sounded. Woman living next door to brutal shooting shrugs and plays cards. But here in Sun City, people took their card games seriously. None of her neighbors would think twice about her actions. Maybe the police would think twice, but she doubted it.

Borobasq got in the car and with difficulty lowered himself to the floor, curling his arms, knees, and head to fit. "What if one of those nosy women says she wants to come and play Hearts too?"

Clemmie flapped the blanket, covering him. He twitched it to give himself a breathing hole. "I'll say, 'Wonderful! See you there!' and drive on."

Because—to use the current phrase—this was not Clementine Lakefield's first rodeo.

———————

The day on which Clemmie's escape door opened was so vivid in her mind that all these decades later, she could still stand amazed at how everything fell into place.

It was August of that summer session at OSU. There was not yet air-conditioning in every building on campus, and she was fanning herself with a cardboard advertising fan on a Popsicle stick, the kind given out at concerts or in church. She was walking down the hallway to the last Latin class of the summer session, in which she was a teaching assistant, when she ran into one of her elderly professors, a dear old gentleman who had more or less married Latin and Greek. He taught only advanced courses and tutorials, loved his students and every bit of syntax, grammar, and vocabulary of his beautiful dead languages, and even ran a summer camp at which the adult campers spoke only Latin for a week, proving that a dead language could be alive again. Clemmie hoped to attend next summer. She smiled just thinking of it.

The professor was chatting with a somewhat younger man, who seemed downcast. "Aha!" cried the professor, taking Clemmie's elbow. "Here is one of my very best students! She just graduated!"

Clemmie was a year away from graduation, but she did not correct him because she adored him. He couldn't remember her name, because names were superfluous to him, and in those days, professors cultivated absentmindedness the way they would shortly cultivate being hip.

The depressed visitor smiled weakly at Clemmie. "My name is Ed Aldridge. I'm trying to find a Latin teacher for the fall." He sighed, knowing the impact of his next sentence. "My high school is in Akron, and I'm having a hard time filling the position." Akron had recently suffered a six-day race riot, and hundreds of National Guardsmen had been sent to stop it.

The professor shook his head. "Such a sad situation. It will be difficult to convince anyone to teach in Akron right now."

"The high school isn't in that neighborhood," said Mr. Aldridge. "It's a fine academic school with excellent students."

"I cannot recommend any Latin student more than this sweet little lady," said her old professor, beaming at her. "Now I must be on my way. My drama class begins in a moment." He was teaching Euripides. It was a class Clemmie had taken, one of the highlights of her college years. Clemmie and Mr. Aldridge watched him hunt for the right door. A student flagged him down.

Clementine Lakefield turned to the man who needed a Latin teacher. "My name is Helen Stephens, and I would love to teach in Akron."

They never checked.

They never asked for a transcript or proof of graduation. Clemmie had never claimed to be a college graduate anyway. She was offered a job, and she took it. She even had a social security number to go with it.

She found an apartment near her new high school and rented it in Helen Stephens's name, and then also rented a post office box for Clementine Lakefield several miles away.

She told her parents she was taking a year off college to be a secretary at a law firm and consider her future.

In those days, you didn't "find yourself." The whole concept was ludicrous, although in just a few years, everybody would agree that yes, of course, you must find yourself.

Her parents were horrified. "But you want to teach Latin!" they cried. "You can't be a typist!"

"I've already started. You and Dad don't need to pay my bills now. I'll be getting a paycheck."

"Skip the fall semester if you must, but it is imperative that you go back in the spring, and we'll pay the tuition. When are you coming home to visit, darling?"

"I'm not, Mama. I have a job."

"But you didn't come all summer! You're breaking my heart!"

"I miss you too, Mama. But I have to figure out how to be a grown-up."

"All you have to do is find a good man and get your MRS. Then *he* worries about being the grown-up while you have babies."

Clemmie agreed with this lovely vision of the future. Although Betty Friedan and Gloria Steinem were making waves, Clemmie had been reading Livy and Herodotus instead, and could think of nothing more wonderful than finding Mr. Right and living happily ever after. At OSU, there had been plenty of fine young men, but she was afraid of them, unable to erase the legacy of Rudyard Creek. She had not kissed a man since that first high-school crush on Bobby, couldn't relax in a man's arms, couldn't imagine a marriage bed as a place she would want to be.

It did not occur to Clemmie to "get counseling" because that too was in the future. Her generation was stoic. You accepted your lot in life and soldiered on. The idea of paying somebody to listen to your complaints was a decade away, and then almost overnight became a necessity.

"Maybe the law firm is a good idea," Clemmie's mother conceded. "A lawyer is an acceptable husband."

Clemmie reminded herself to tell law-firm lies in her letters.

In Akron, she learned how to teach (not as easy as it looked), how to get along with other faculty, how to correct papers and make lesson plans and find a good grocery and buy proper clothing and choose a church—and she had to do all this under the name Helen Stephens. It was marvelous, challenging, and a little creepy. She kept thinking she would be found out, but nobody ever showed the faintest interest in the background of Helen Stephens.

She picked up mail from the box once a week, because her

mother wrote once a week. She gave the post office address to Barbara and a few old high school friends and continued to chart the lies so they would match. Barbara mailed her letters where she lived, but wrote the return address of her parents in Connecticut in the upper-left corner.

Clemmie's parents, now used to their daughter's difficult ways, dutifully accepted the address change. Her father sent money to buy a used car, and she loved him for it, and she loved her car. It was a red-and-white Ford Falcon, which she proudly washed herself in the driveway. Gas was thirty-one cents a gallon.

———

The news that a town in Connecticut was opening up a fifty-year-old murder was sufficiently interesting to find a place in the brief semi- and non-news slots featured on so many online sites, every sentence interrupted by ads and arrows. The photograph of the victim—a handsome, young, blond, crew-cut high school coach—was appealing. Most sites also used the photograph of the roadside picnic area, which was oddly sinister in the way of still pictures of common objects set to creepy music.

Veronica read the article.

Barbara read it.

A woman named Carol-Lee Sherman read it.

Eighteen

Teaching was so demanding that Clemmie could not think about other things. It wasn't until the first three-day weekend that she realized there might be a way to find Billy again. She debated in her heart. Did she have the right to try? Nobody would know. Certainly Rudyard Creek couldn't find out.

She got in her beloved car, drove back to Columbus, and parked in front of the house where the Boones had previously lived. In those days, most women were still home, so the wife of the new family chatted easily with Clemmie, who said she had borrowed a silver serving tray from Mrs. Boone and needed to return it, even though it was months late, and did they have the Boones' new address?

They did not.

Clemmie walked to the next-door neighbors and the across-the-street neighbors, and in both cases, the wives were home but unable to help. "It's somewhere in Connecticut though," said the third neighbor. "They used to live there, and they wanted to move back near their families."

Of course, thought Clemmie. Because they used a Connecticut adoption agency. They established themselves in Columbus, announced the birth of their son, and now it's been years. They're safe from anybody's guess that there's been an adoption, and they've gone home.

The fourth neighbor said, "I have their address. Here it is."

Because that was another good thing about those years. Doors stayed unlocked, keys stayed in the ignition, and information was shared.

The neighbor handed Clemmie a Rolodex card, which was a small white paper rectangle with rounded corners and two holes in the bottom so it could be attached in alphabetical order, along with hundreds of other cards, on two metal hoops. To find the name you needed, you flipped your Rolodex cards, sort of like shuffling a deck, and there it was at the top.

The Connecticut address was only half an hour east of where Clemmie had grown up. When it was possible to visit her parents again, she'd drive from Ohio and—

Do what?

Spy on Billy's family? Increase a heartache nothing could solve?

"You can keep it," the woman said cheerfully. "I've got the new address in my Christmas card list."

Clemmie tucked the card in her wallet. She now had two precious pieces of Billy. A locket and a Rolodex card.

———————

Thursdays after school, Clemmie went to her post office box because her mother wrote every Monday and mailed every Tuesday, so a letter arrived every Thursday. That particular Thursday, Clemmie had stayed late to help the yearbook committee, so it was almost four thirty when she reached the suburb where she picked up her Connecticut mail. There was always a letter from her mother, and occasionally letters from others.

Clemmie was not a fine parallel parker, and only parallel parking slots were available that day, so she drove past the post office and ended up in a lot across from her favorite dress shop. She would have liked to duck in and browse, but it would no longer be open by the time she finished at the post office. In fact, she would just barely make it before the post office locked up.

She walked as quickly as she could manage on her high heels. She loved dressing well. In her dove-gray silk suit, with the simple ivory shell underneath, the pearls she had been given for high school graduation, and matching clip-on earrings, Clemmie felt like a million dollars. She wore her charcoal wool winter coat, but left it unbuttoned in spite of the cold wind because she wanted the suit to show. The weather called for a heavy wool scarf, but Clemmie instead had chosen a sophisticated, silky gray-and-white scarf which did not keep her the slightest bit warm. She was wearing her pale-gray leather gloves to protect her fingers from the raw chill and carrying a new patent leather purse, black and shiny with silver buttons and double handles that fit perfectly in her small palm. She loved changing purses, carefully sorting and switching all the contents.

She was humming as she went into the post office. Even in high heels she had to stand on tippy-toes to get the key into her little box in the top row. Rudyard Creek took her key out of her hand and said, "I'll get it for you."

She stared at him, sick with shock.

He was laughing silently. He gripped her wrist. Her little bones were helpless in that crunch. He towed her outside and marched her across the street to a little green park with two benches and made her sit next to him. He didn't let go of her wrist.

In later years, she would wonder why she hadn't just fallen to the floor in the post office and screamed for help. But it was so crucial to be well behaved and not draw attention to yourself.

"How I found you? I just checked your parents' mailbox whenever the red flag was up. And there was your mother's letter to you, with this box number."

How could he do that? He lived in Albany! He had a job! Had he spent vacation days on that project? And more vacation days to find her here?

He's insane, Barbara had said.

Clemmie felt it then—the thrum, the vibration of his madness.

"You live here because of my baby," said Rudyard Creek. "Who adopted it?"

She had not forgotten his demand to have Billy, but she had shelved it as idiocy, something criminal his wife would never agree to, something impossible. But here it was again, and in her purse was her wallet holding the Rolodex card with Billy Boone's Connecticut address and the driver's license of Helen Stephens.

"Don't be silly," she said, tugging at her gloves to occupy herself. "I'm here because my boyfriend lives here."

"I'll find your boyfriend and let him know that you are a very experienced woman, and if he's looking for a virgin, it isn't you. Or you can tell me where to find our kid."

So Pete had never been told where their parents had sent Clemmie, because if Pete knew, he'd have told Rudyard Creek, and if the coach knew the name of the Mountain School, he'd be there now, paying people off or hurting them or finding Veronica or buying the files or breaking in to steal them.

Of course, there was no way for him to prove he was the natural father of the Boones' son. If you could call what Rudyard Creek had done to her "natural." But people usually gave Rudyard Creek what he wanted, and he had no scruples. Just because Clemmie couldn't imagine how he'd get the Boones to give Billy up didn't mean he couldn't pull it off.

Clemmie gave the coach her most sparkling smile. She knew it was sparkling, because people were always telling her what a lovely smile she had and how she should smile more often. "My boyfriend and I are moving to California shortly. We're going to work at Disneyland! I already flew out for my interview!" Clemmie had never been on a plane. "I'm going to be Snow White," she added, and realized suddenly that she did look like Disney's Snow White, complete with porcelain complexion, thick dark hair, rosy cheeks, and rosebud lips.

"What about Latin?" he said suspiciously.

"I completed my student teaching, and it's less fun than I thought it would be."

In fact, teaching was immensely more fun than she'd thought it would be. She loved her kids, the camaraderie of the other teachers, and the high school performances and concerts and games, where all her students would shout affectionately, "Hi, Miss Stephens!"

The coach shifted his considerable weight, and Clemmie stood. She needed the protection of strangers. "I'm cold. Let's get a cup of coffee at that diner."

Perhaps because there were pedestrians, cars parking, people getting in and out of them, Rudyard Creek stood with her. Holding her wrist was abnormal, so he shifted to her hand instead. She was grateful for the glove that protected her from his actual skin. Inside the diner, he chose a booth by the window and stood blocking the exit. She slowly took off her coat, folded it neatly on the red leatherette bench, set down her hat, and peeled off her leather gloves one at a time.

And then she made a fatal error. She fingered her locket, the talisman that had to substitute for Billy.

"Let me help you," said Rudyard Creek, as the waitress arrived with menus. He took off her scarf. His fingers lingered on the back of her neck and she wanted to scream but instead said to the waitress, "I'll just have a coffee, please. Excuse me, I must powder my nose."

Rudyard Creek was folding her scarf. Dangling in his hand was her locket. He had undone the tiny closure.

Clemmie left her coat and gloves on the bench as collateral, taking only her handbag. *He has my picture of Billy*. Now she seriously thought of killing him. How would she do it? He was so much larger. So much stronger. It would have to be from a distance, with a bullet. She would have to learn.

But more important was to escape. Losing the beloved picture was terrible, but staying in his clutches was worse. The only identification in her purse was her Helen Stephens driver's license. The onslaught of credit cards had begun, but Clemmie did not yet have one, not in any name.

The ladies' room was near the kitchen toward the back of the diner, but as she was reaching for the handle of the ladies'-room door, thinking how she could hide her license in a toilet roll or something, she spotted the rear exit and walked through the crowded, greasy kitchen and out the back door. She took off her heels and raced down the alley in her stocking feet, going the wrong way on a one-way street to her car. She leaped in, her heart pounding, stockings shredded, feet torn.

She opened her purse, took out her wallet, and slid the license under the floor mat of the driver's seat. That way, she would always have it when she drove, but not if he grabbed her. Then she took out the Rolodex card, tore it in two, and had turned the card pieces to tear them a second time when Rudyard Creek parked his car against her front bumper. She could not drive out of her parking slot.

Keys in one hand, wallet in the other, she pressed the door lock down and slid desperately over the front seat bench to lock the passenger door, because in those days, every lock had to be closed manually and separately, but he had already raced over and grabbed the handle.

Why hadn't she put the Rolodex card under the mat too? Horrified, she stuffed the Rolodex card into her mouth.

He flung himself onto the front seat and didn't bother to look at Clemmie at all, but took the purse sitting on the bench between them.

She couldn't drive away, but she could leave. Keys and wallet still in hand, she was out of the car before he could reach her, running barefoot across the street and into the dress store. "We're just closing, ma'am," said a tired, beautifully dressed woman.

In Clemmie's mouth, the little white bits of paper disintegrated. "I know," she said, looking desperately behind her. "I'm so sorry. May I please go out the back?"

So many times in her life Clemmie had been grateful for the kindness of strangers. The clerk saw the looming figure of Rudyard Creek striding over the pavement, and she locked the shop door and turned off the lights. "Shall I call the police?" whispered the clerk.

Clemmie shook her head. She had an identity problem with which the police would probably not sympathize.

Police, police. Clemmie had never called them all those times she needed them in her youth, and here she was again, not calling them when she needed them in Sun City.

The police had put yellow crime tape around Dom's. Black capital letters read: SHERIFF'S LINE DO NOT CROSS and, without punctuation, repeated the same words endlessly down the tape. She went down her front steps and called across the grass, "Sheriff Bennett! I'm going to my card game! Would you please move the vehicles so I can get out of my driveway?"

"We still need to talk," he called back. "When will you be done?"

"Probably around five thirty."

He nodded and waved to a subordinate, who spoke to various drivers.

Clemmie went back into her house, locked the door behind her, darted into the garage, raised its door with her clicker, and said, "Okay, this is it. Sit tight."

The interior of the vehicle was very hot from being in the

enclosed garage, so she upped the air-conditioning fan, and its noisy *whoosh* filled her ears. A uniformed woman beckoned, helping her back into the street without hitting anything. Clemmie waved thanks and steered carefully between cars and onlookers.

Just as she turned onto Forsythia, a television van came around the corner. Everyone's attention turned to the TV logo, and nobody looked at Clemmie. Her heart hurt. Her head hurt. She was doing a mental countdown. Two more minutes, and Boro would be gone. She would have pulled it off.

She turned into the golf-course parking lot and drove into a space two down from the rental car. She put the car in Park and actually gasped to keep breathing. "I'll get out first," she told him, "and look around to make sure we're okay."

There wasn't a sound from the back seat.

She got out but did not shut the door behind her. The parking lot surface shimmered with heat. The sky was a motionless Carolina blue. From somewhere came canned music. A swearing golfer came in on his cart. She could not imagine golfing in this weather.

"You're good," she said. "It's safe."

Boro didn't stir. She had a vision of him suffocating from the blanket and the heat; Boro dead on the floor of her car, yet another body to get rid of.

She knelt on the driver's seat and looked over the headrest. The bulges under the blanket didn't move. There was no sign or sound of breathing.

For one hideous moment, she couldn't make herself pull up the blanket.

Then she did.

NINETEEN

Carol-Lee Sherman could think of nothing but the little online article she had read about that cold case in Connecticut. Every pulse beat hurled her into memories she had not suffered in decades. Eventually, when her husband had taken the car for an oil change and she was alone for a stretch, she felt calm enough to rehearse a statement to the police.

She closed herself in the master bathroom because she was less self-conscious talking out loud in a small space.

"In your investigation," she practiced, "you may have discovered that more than fifty years ago Rudyard Creek was accused of rape by an underage victim who was not named in newspaper articles." Even alone with nobody listening, she could hardly get the next sentence out. She found herself whispering, as if somebody were crouching on the other side of the door and taking notes. "I was that victim. I made the accusation."

Could she describe what had been done to her by the coach? What had been done to her by the disbelieving authorities, especially the disbelieving police? The utter contempt with which they had regarded her? No one considered for a moment that little Carol-Lee was telling the truth. She had had no use for any police department ever since, and now, staring at the white tiles of her scrubbed bathroom, she was surprised by the bitterness that swept over her. "I wasn't the only one," she said out loud. "Every year he picked a girl to go after. I want you know that he was an evil man. Handsome. Affable. Popular. A fine coach. But whoever killed him did the world a favor."

And if I tell the police all this, she thought, then what happens?

The officer would want her to name those other girls who were picked every year. If she said the wrong thing—or perhaps the right thing—some other damaged girl might be found all these decades later, be exposed and charged for a homicide that Carol-Lee would certainly have committed herself had she been in a position to fight back.

His murder was still puzzling, because no victim of Rudyard Creek could have bruised him, let alone killed him. He specialized in very small girls; girls whose two wrists he could hold in one hand while he laughed. She vividly remembered the way his huge fingers had wrapped both her wrists. Helplessness itself was terrifying.

But you did not have to be big and strong to pull a trigger. How had the man been killed? By a gun? She wanted to ask the detectives on the case, but that might establish some sort of quid pro quo: I told you how he was murdered, so you tell me who the other girls were.

Carol-Lee had the excellent alibi that her own family had lived in Tokyo the year Rudyard Creek was murdered. But who knew about the others?

If she called, the officer would wait, his pencil poised. Well, probably not. Probably his fingers would be poised to type on his keyboard the names of those who had been raped by Rudyard Creek half a century ago. Some victim whose DNA—an unknown acronym at the time—might establish the identity of the killer.

She would call anonymously, but caller ID had removed that choice.

She reread the little news squib on her cell phone app and felt terribly sad for that girl, whoever she was, who had taken Rudyard Creek's life. Unless it was a brother or father or boyfriend who had done it. Which opened up whole new worlds of worry.

So in the end, Carol-Lee did nothing.

———

Veronica had retired to Pompano Beach. Wet from her morning swim, she had been sitting at her outdoor bar inside the screen house that covered both lap pool and patio, sipping her morning coffee. Every day at this hour, she tucked up with her smartphone and scrolled through headlines of the *Stamford Advocate* and the *New London Day*, because Veronica had lived at both ends of the state. Once she had her fill of Connecticut, usually about five minutes, she'd move on to the *New York Post*, because when she lived in Stamford, she had commuted into the city by train and the *Post* was a much more fun read than the *Times*.

She did not normally bother with crime stories, because that would have taken up her whole morning, but as she scrolled down the *New London Day*, she came across a reference to a fifty-year-old cold case being resurrected in Old Lyme. Fifty years ago! That was crazy. It was even comical. Like they were going to find alibis or lack of them after all those years. Even if they found DNA or fingerprints, Veronica couldn't imagine they'd be much use. The owner of the DNA and fingerprints would be dead or have Alzheimer's by now.

The murder victim was a high school coach named Rudyard Creek. In the photograph, he was a good-looking man, all crew cut and big jaw and wide shoulders. The article didn't say how he'd been killed—in fact, the article didn't say much of anything—but Veronica thought he must have been shot, because this guy was too large and too fit to have been overcome any other way.

Rudyard Creek. She pondered. She felt as if she knew that peculiar name. But names slid away from her these days. She was in six card groups, each playing twice monthly, and prior to each game, she'd review the membership list and mutter to herself, "Donna, Karen, Janice, Barbie, Suzie, Prudence, Colleen." It often worked, and if not, she would cry, "Hiiiiii! Darling, how are you? Love your handbag!" and wait for somebody else to call the girlfriend by name. The worst moment was if you were keeping score and had to list the names and you couldn't remember with whom you were playing. That's why most people labeled two columns "We" and "They" instead of attempting names. Except for the people who wrote "Us" and "Them."

A few days later, the name popped up in Veronica's thoughts. One of the handicaps of age was forgetting, but one of the obscure pleasures was that memory often returned with a sort of explosion. *Wham! Here's your memory!*

She had heard the name Rudyard Creek at the Mountain School, an institution she had never forgiven; that cold, hard place where she had to survive until her baby was taken from her, and she never even knew if it was a boy or a girl. That place where she herself had delivered the baby of another girl, a tiny Betty Boop of a kid who gritted her teeth and went through hours of labor without a sound, all night long in a grim, open dorm. She even remembered the girl's name. Clementine. It had been a joke to the rest of them. "Your parents actually named you that?" they teased, singing, "'Oh my darling, oh my darling, oh my darling, Clementine, thou art lost and gone forever, dreadful sorry, Clementine!'" But the girl cried, "Stop it! Don't sing that. He sang that when he raped me."

You didn't use the word *rape* then, even if it happened to you. Only Maureen made the same claim. Veronica had not thought of

Maureen in all these years. The rest of the girls had been in love or lust or, in one case, hadn't known the anatomy and physiology of sex and claimed literally not to have understood what her boyfriend was doing down there. Veronica remembered now how tidily Clementine had been pregnant: as if she'd tucked a basketball under her dress, while some of the girls just looked obese, a rarity in those days, a condition that required classmates to sing, "Fatty, fatty, *two* by four, couldn't get *through* the door."

The wayward girls had surrounded Clementine, demanding details. "What happened?" "Who was he?" "Did your parents know?" "What was his name?"

Even then, girls did not name their attackers. It would have been rude. But Clementine had. "Rudyard Creek," she said. "He was the basketball coach."

They didn't believe it. "Nobody's named Rudyard Creek. You made that up."

And now up leaped the memory of Veronica herself rifling through the adoptive mother's handbag, getting the real name and address so that the brave little mother could trace them later. I wouldn't be that daring now, she thought. Back then, I didn't care. So what if they caught me? The worst had already happened.

Veronica couldn't remember either the fake name or the real name of the adopting parents, and she couldn't come up with Clementine's last name either, but she called the police in Connecticut because she wanted them to know that the dead man had not been a good guy.

There was no phone number in the article, so Veronica Googled the police department and called.

"The cold case…" said a voice slowly, as if barely able to bring it to mind. "Let me connect you with a detective."

Veronica already had no use for these people. You should answer the phone in a snappy, alert way, especially if you were the police.

A man identified himself as a detective. "How can I help you?"

Veronica was suddenly inarticulate. She had not planned how to tell Clementine's story, and of course she couldn't use Clementine's name, and for that matter, she couldn't name the institution because in this day of descendants madly investigating their backgrounds, she wasn't going to give *that* out, and she heard herself blurt, "I once knew a woman who was raped by that man and had his child."

"Thanks," said the detective, who didn't sound even mildly interested. "You're the second woman to let us know about this kind of thing. Can you give me the name of the woman who got pregnant?"

This kind of thing? thought Veronica. I call it rape, but the detective refers to it as *this kind of thing*? He calls her *the woman* and not *the victim*? He says "who got pregnant," as if she failed to use proper birth-control methods, instead of got slammed to the floor by a rapist?

It dawned on Veronica that Clementine might just be the killer.

I'm dreadful sorry, Clementine. Shouldn't have made this call. But at least I didn't give you away. "I forget," she said sharply. "Just keep in mind that Rudyard Creek was a violent man who rightly met a violent end."

CAROLINE B. COONEY

In Barbara's house in Massachusetts, the television was on very loud because everyone watching had some degree of deafness. Barbara never watched true-crime shows. There was something about the bad acting and poor lighting used in re-creations that frightened her. But her husband was home, her brother and sister-in-law were visiting, and they all wanted to see *Homicide Hunter*. Barbara prepared snacks, which for these three was a simple task. They liked chips— four kinds—and dips—two kinds. She cleaned the kitchen, walking back and forth to replenish the dip, and did not glance at the show.

The family talked during commercials. They wrapped up a granddaughter's gymnastics tournament, a grandson's eccentric upcoming wedding—everybody was thrilled that he was getting married at all, since every other young person they knew just lived together—a terrifying death in a Midwest flood, and the annoying increase in local traffic.

Barbara's brother-in-law said, "Craziest thing. Saw it online. Some police force in Old Lyme, Connecticut, is opening up a *fifty*-year-old murder. Can you believe that? Your best chance for solving a murder is the first forty-eight hours, and how many hours since this crime? Fifty years times 365 days times twenty-four hours."

"Everybody involved in that whole crime is probably dead by now anyway," said Barbara's husband. "Or in assisted living."

"On dialysis."

"Having a second hip replacement to replace the first hip replacement."

"They just tried a ninety-four-year-old concentration camp guard," said her brother-in-law, "and found him guilty."

"That's 438,000 hours," reported her husband, who had been clicking his cell phone calculator.

In the kitchen, Barbara's flesh shivered.

A fifty-year-old unsolved Old Lyme murder.

How many could there be?

Barbara Googled Rudyard Creek.

TWENTY

Boro didn't believe that this woman had ever been in witness protection, but the fact was, the stupid nephew had also thought that. Could there be a grain of truth in it? Pronounced the way everybody said it, Spesante sounded like a possible mob name.

The woman claimed to have been connected before. She could be connected now. And Boro was still missing his cash. He could reasonably assume that it had been in the third villa along with his glass. He could reasonably assume that Wilson Spesante had been killed because of that money.

Wilson was known to Boro as Pinkman. The guy bore no resemblance to the character on *Breaking Bad*, but it was the dude's favorite old TV show, and he had liked thinking of himself as somebody who could cook meth, kill people in clever ways, and escape all enemies.

But in fact, Pinkman was just a runner. Boro had had long, stoned conversations with Pinkman when he dropped into the studio. Dropping into somebody else's workshop was what lampworkers did, so there was always somebody around who wanted to share dope and talk and maybe even make something.

Pinkman's life had not been as much fun as he wanted it to be—driving endlessly cross-country in a boring car because his supplier felt that a white Accord looked pretty much like a white anything else and therefore was unidentifiable; stopping at midlevel motel chains—identical Courtyards, Hampton Inns, Hilton Gardens, and DoubleTrees; staring sadly at the pathetic free breakfasts. It was impossible to date girls because he was always on the road, endlessly ferrying ganja oil and oxycodone from the West to sell in the East for an outstanding profit.

"My parents want me to earn a living," he had said glumly. Without a doubt, Pinkman was earning plenty doing what he was doing, so that was code for "get a real job."

Pinkman hadn't wanted to *earn* a living, of course. He wanted to *have* a living. He must have figured: hit Boro's studio, take the cash, and be free from any work at all.

Boro wondered if Pinkman's parents were this Marcia and Roy, which meant it was a two-generation act they had going. Probably not, because such parents would be just fine with the way Pinkman was earning a living. Had assigned him the driving, for that matter. Was Dom his grandfather? Were they all related?

And an old babe in her seventies, who was not only willing to aid and abet Boro, but also placidly ignoring a murder next door? Who could calmly convince a sheriff in a murder investigation to let her drive off for cards? Could she have killed Wilson Spesante?

Pinkman was a big guy, but he was slovenly, slow, and bored. A gun didn't care about size anyway.

When you're old, you need lots of money to pay doctors and go on cruises and stuff. And when you're old, you have cover; you're invisible. And when you're also small, like this old lady, they wouldn't believe you could carry the garbage out, let alone kill Pinkman. But if she'd shot him when the two of them were in the golf cart, she couldn't miss and it didn't take strength.

The third villa had not had a security system, maybe not surprising in a trap house; you didn't want some professional company showing up to inspect your property. The two video cams had been disabled, but nothing would have recorded the murder because Boro had not found a camera in the middle garage.

The old lady did not have one of those little signs in her yard or window proclaiming that her property was monitored by a professional firm. Was this because drug dealers handled their own security, thank you?

Probably Dominic Spesante had killed Wilson, but the fact was that the old woman had a whole other life out there, and not one person in her crowd suspected it. And not only did her nephew have no idea where his aunt actually lived, but he hadn't even noticed until now that he didn't know. The woman was a champ at evading people. Right now, she was showing a complete lack of fear, and her good planning suggested that she'd been around this block before.

Almost certainly Dom had the cash with him, but the old lady was a contender. Boro couldn't leave until he had ruled her out. If he didn't find money, he might find information. It would be stupid to run before he had explored every inch of her villa. That had not been possible because all the curtains were open, and cops could look right in. But the old lady had closed them.

Boro unfolded himself from her car, grabbed a pile of towels stacked on the dryer and a full brown-paper grocery bag marked *Goodwill* sitting on a shelf next to the washer, tossed them on the back-seat floor, covered them with the blanket, closed the car doors, and stepped behind the open door of Helen Stephens's bedroom.

She walked into the garage and said to the person she thought was in her car, "Okay, this is it. Sit tight." Boro heard the rumble and squeak of the garage door going up, the sound of the car engine turning over. A few moments later, the car was gone, and the garage door came slowly back down and sealed with a thud.

She wouldn't inspect the back seat until she had parked beside his rental car. If he didn't answer her remarks, she'd assume he was just rude. And when she realized that he hadn't come along and was still in her house, what would she do? Probably exactly what she'd told the sheriff she was planning: play cards. Because Boro wasn't the most important thing for this woman; acting normal in front of the law was the most important thing.

He started with the bedroom.

Billy Boone had not known he was adopted until the death of his mother when Billy was forty-five. He'd been helping with tax paperwork that had brought his father to tears because the other member of his partnership was gone forever. Dad fumbled and gave up, so Billy handled it, file after file, drawer after drawer, and came upon the adoption papers.

He had to read the documents several times to believe it.

His parents were not his parents. He felt as if he'd been hit in the jaw, had broken bones, would need surgery.

He fixed himself a drink, read it all again, and made himself a second drink. Then he sat down next to his lonely, depressed father and gently said, "Dad? Would you look at these? Would you tell me about it?"

Billy's father leafed through the documents, as stunned as Billy. "I forgot," he whispered. "I forgot we adopted you. You've always been mine."

It was the nicest thing his father could possibly have said. Billy's brief anger evaporated, and his love for his dad increased.

"I didn't want you to know," Dad kept saying.

"It's okay, Dad. I'm shocked, but I'll live with it. *You're* my father, and that's that."

Dad gave him the strangest wide-eyed look, as if that wasn't that, as if there were so much more. His mouth made funny shapes, and his hand trembled as he accepted the drink Billy fixed him. Billy figured that whatever more there was to the story, it was decades ago and irrelevant. They never referred to it again because they weren't men who confided.

Billy just wished that his dad didn't feel so lousy about it. But within a few years, Dad wasn't feeling lousy or happy about anything. Dementia set in, and Dad was just there, confused and anxious and vacant, with a habit of hanging onto furniture, peering around corners of rooms, tracing the shapes of picture frames, and above all, wandering out of the house. The third time the police had searched half the night and found Stan Boone miles from home, stumbling down the middle of a busy road, Billy located a memory-care facility, sort of a nursing home without the nurses.

When Billy's work took him to Charlotte, he moved his father too, finding another memory-care facility where his poor dad would never again know where his bedroom was and spend his remaining days in a low-level panic no pharmaceutical could soothe.

Billy didn't know how his own son and daughter—now both at Davidson, which meant they came home a lot of weekends—had found out about the adoption and was astonished and uncomfortable when the kids wanted him to find his "real" parents.

"My real mom died years ago," said Billy, trying to be polite, "and my real dad has dementia and I visit him every weekend."

"But, Dad," said his son, "don't you want to know? Don't you want to do the genealogy search and ask your biological mother what happened and why she gave you up and if she's suffered all these years and wept for you, and then we bring her back into the family and all have Christmas together?"

"No."

His kids begged him to watch a TV show whose purpose was to bring adopted adult children into the arms of their "real" parents.

"My real parents are the Boones, who were also your real grandparents," said Billy irritably.

"I love that show," offered Billy's wife. "I cry all the way through it. I think it's kind of cool that you were adopted, Bill. I'd like to know what the story is too."

Billy found himself watching a program of intertwined real-life soap operas in which a pretty but determined, sad but compassionate TV researcher moved with astonishing speed on the internet, picking up clues and getting results. He stared at middle-aged children and their elderly mothers and surprise half sisters and brothers, hugging and weeping and laughing and taking pictures and videos.

It made his skin crawl to think that he could have another entire family out there, leading their lives, which he would interrupt, popping out like some creepy child's puppet from a windup box. "I'm not interested," Billy repeated.

But his children were.

Billy struggled to understand the draw. In the end, he felt it wasn't new blood relatives they wanted. It was the momentary and meaningless "fame" of being on a TV show. But it wasn't fame. It was ten or fifteen minutes of selling your family's sad history to viewers, because all the stories were sad, with constant references to people who felt desperate and unmoored, who ached to be told by some woman they'd never met, "I really did love you, son. I had no choice. I'm so thrilled you're back in my life."

Billy bet there were plenty of cases where the biological mother said to the researcher, "Butt out." And then how would the grown-up child feel?

The following week featured such an episode. The "child" was a middle-aged man who wept when his birth mother didn't want to meet him. Billy felt a little sick at the idea that there could be a birth mother looking for him, and he would refuse, and she would sit alone somewhere while the tears ran down her cheeks. But he didn't want to know. He didn't want to meet.

Mack and Kelsey chose not to tell their father that they had already submitted saliva samples for DNA testing.

In the parking lot of the golf course, Clemmie stared down at the back-seat floor. No Boro. Just a stack of folded towels and the brown-paper grocery bag full of old purses, belts, and shoes destined for the Goodwill store. Boro had decided not to escape.

He wants his money, she thought. He thinks it could be in my house. While I'm gone, he'll search.

Clemmie had several hundred dollars hidden in a book on the third shelf up in the middle bookcase. She also had two fake books. Not the decorative kind with a hinged lid and pretend gold embossing. She had painstakingly used an X-Acto knife to cut hollows inside two real, very thick books, a Colleen McCullough and a Nelson DeMille. One book contained Clementine Lakefield and the other Clementine Murray.

Clemmie loved to buy books. She had four bookcases in the living room, each six feet high and thirty inches wide. There was another bookcase in her bedroom and a sixth in the tiny study. Her cookbooks filled two kitchen cabinets. Her Greek and Latin dictionaries were in a funny little rolling bookcase she had found years ago in an antique shop. She worried about the paperwork and the possibility that he would discover all of her lives, but Boro was looking for a cat carrier of cash. He was not going to page through a couple thousand books.

Her desk contained the life of Helen Stephens. Helen Stephens's retirement income from the years of teaching, social security income, and a few investments, mainly municipal bonds. Paid bills, checkbook, insurance papers. A file cabinet of lesson plans and master quiz sheets for Latin. She didn't want him there, but he couldn't hurt anything.

She doubted he could get into her laptop, which required a

password, and he probably couldn't guess *dear77Billy*, the sevens having no meaning except she had been required to include numbers and at least one capital letter. She had both cell phones with her, so he couldn't tap into them. She still used a big paper calendar, with lots of room on each month's squares to write the day's activities, but she did nothing that could be of interest to Borobasq. And she made no Sunday entries, although Sunday was the most important day of the week.

Clemmie was a church hopper from way back, and here in the South, there were churches everywhere: big, little, new, old, cathedrals, storefronts; churches with world-class pipe organs and churches with praise bands; churches whose sermons lasted fifty-five minutes and churches with ancient liturgies. There were Baptists and Catholics and Methodists and Presbyterians and Lutherans and Assembly of God and Episcopal, and all of these came in conservative and liberal varieties, and then of course there were the huge, several-thousand-member stand-alone churches, each started by a minister with a calling: Transformation, Elevation, Higher Ground. The noun churches, Clemmie called them. She liked the noun churches for their exuberance and the amazing spread of age and race in those crowds.

Sun City had a high rate of church attendance, and everybody discussed their churches and invited you to come. The big item was whether or not the congregation was friendly. Everybody insisted that theirs was the friendliest.

Even after all these years, Clemmie shrank from the intimacy that she desperately wanted. Church always had people to greet you and invite you to Bible study, their women's group, and their quilting society. They escorted you to coffee hour and wanted your street address so they could find out what members lived near you, and you could start a "small group." Small groups were the new big thing—fellowship, Bible study, and neighborhood all in one.

Clemmie practiced small-group avoidance. Church was about profound things: sin and sorrow, joy and hope. Clemmie knew the first two very well and the latter two not so well.

Once a month, she drove uptown to one of Charlotte's wealthiest and most beautiful neighborhoods, Myers Park, filled with magnificent old homes, towering trees, and grand churches. St. Saviour's featured a sublime choir, a great preacher, and impressive community outreach.

Some Sundays, she was blessed by seeing all four Boones: Billy and his wife and their college-age son and daughter, Mack and Kelsey. Both the children—Clemmie's grandchildren!—had graduated from Charlotte Latin School, so called because it had a very traditional curriculum for its nearly 1,500 students. How marvelous, how serendipitous that Billy would put his son and daughter into a school featuring the classics.

Mack and Kelsey were now both at Davidson College and often came home on weekends. Mack rarely posted on Facebook, but Kelsey posted on Facebook and Instagram on and off all day.

On her chosen Sunday, Clemmie would slide into a pew one row behind and across the aisle to the right, so she would have a partial view of her family but not sit close enough for any of them to come shake her hand during the peace.

Following the Boones to church seemed benign to her. But would it to Billy? Would it to her grandchildren, who didn't know she existed?

She forced herself to think about what Boro was doing.

He suspected her of being part of whatever Dom, Wilson, and the Coglands were doing.

What *were* they doing?

Selling drugs, he had said. She could not imagine Dom successfully selling anything. And he simply didn't leave the house enough. The only place he ever went was the shopping strip. Unless all those parking lots were actually roiling with drug transactions. Was Dom pocketing cash while junkies leaped back into their cars? While shoppers trundled in and out of the grocery store and women went in and out of the nail salon and people bought useless, expensive knick-knacks at the gift shop, had those very same people jotted "Meet Dom" on their to-do list? "Bring cash"?

Well, at least she knew what she had to do. Play cards, because that's what she had told the sheriff. She parked at the Sun City clubhouse, silenced her phones, walked in, swiped her Sun City membership card, and wondered how on earth she would focus enough to play.

Every table was full.

"Somebody else will show up, Helen!" called a friend. "Stake out a table and wait."

"Sit with us!" shrieked another girl. "You live next door to the murder! Come tell us everything, Helen!"

She was enveloped by card players who, for once, had something better to do than shuffle and deal. "So do we absolutely know that that guy Spencer killed his grandson?"

"Spesante," Clemmie corrected.

The questions came on top of each other. "Where's Joyce?" "How come you're not with the cops being interrogated?" "It's right next door to you, Helen. Do you want to stay over with me for a while?"

"Thank you, Karen, that's so thoughtful, but I've made arrangements."

"Did you see the body?"

"No."

They lost interest. "Let's play cards. Did we shuffle enough? Somebody deal."

How helpful that all the tables were full. Clemmie took five minutes in the ladies' room, closing herself in a stall and trying to think. She could drive to the airport and get out of town, but she had to behave reasonably, and at this juncture, flight was not reasonable. The sheriff himself had said he needed to talk to her later. If she vanished instead, he'd really want to talk to her.

She glanced at her family phone to see if Borobasq had called, but he hadn't. Was I thinking he'd update me? "Finished the closets. Headed to the attic."

On her Sun City phone were messages from Joyce, and since there was nobody else in the ladies' room to overhear, she played the first one from a few hours ago.

"Helen! Helen, Dom was murdered? I mean, I can't even believe it! Who would murder Dom? That's horrifying. That's so scary. I'm just sick. You can't stay there! Listen, you go to that wedding after all, that wedding of Peggy's down in the islands. Or at least spend the night at Betty Anne's! She said she asked you. And you have to call me back right away with the details. If I weren't so determined to keep my distance from Johnny, I'd drive right back. I mean, there you are with all the excitement, and I'm missing it."

Joyce's second voicemail had been recorded shortly after the first one. She must have heard from some of the other girls. "So it wasn't Dom. It was Wilson! I hardly ever even laid eyes on Wilson. The man would park in the driveway and sneak into Dom's, and the next thing you knew, the car was gone. Helen, you call me this minute and tell me everything! Listen, did your boy toy see anything interesting? Or was that Bentley?"

Clemmie drove home but could not get close to Blue Lilac because an amazing number of vehicles were now parked on both sides of Marigold. At the corner of Pink Camellia and Marigold was a locksmith's truck. Not the same company that had handled Joyce's change of locks. So already, people were afraid and beefing up their security.

Clemmie turned down Pink Camellia and parked in its little turnaround.

The villas on Pink Camellia backed onto Joyce's side of Blue Lilac. Between the units, Clemmie could see rescue and police vehicles, reporters and neighbors with dogs on leashes. Practically every one of them was filming on various devices, or texting or calling on cell phones.

She walked over the crunchy grass to Blue Lilac and stood behind a crowd of strangers who were entertained by the hope of seeing something. Anything.

The locksmith was drilling Joyce's front door! Johnny was standing there supervising. How had Johnny coaxed the locksmith to do it? Didn't Johnny have to prove by a driver's license, at least, that it was his house? Wouldn't Johnny's license have the address of his own home on the other side of Sun City? On the other hand, who would suspect anything when the police were literally standing there?

She rather admired Johnny's decision to swipe Joyce's house back. Clemmie had a lot of gall herself, having misrepresented practically everything over the decades, and many a night she had lain awake questioning her actions. She didn't picture Johnny losing sleep over it.

In a normal situation, Clemmie would have telephoned Joyce: "Johnny is getting inside after all! What do you want me to do?" But she was too distraught to have normal thoughts, and anyway, there was always the possibility that he *had* talked to Joyce, and they had reconciled, and Joyce had been exaggerating about the checking account.

Clemmie thought of Dom on the lam. An interesting word, not from Latin or Greek. I've been on the lam for most of my adult life, she thought.

She remembered Rudyard Creek singing to her. "Thou art lost and gone forever, dreadful sorry, Clementine."

She sometimes thought that Rudyard Creek had won, because Clementine Lakefield was indeed lost and gone forever. She was left with her shell, and the name Helen, which also belonged to someone lost and gone forever.

TWENTY-ONE

When Clemmie felt safe enough to return to the diner, she found that they had kindly held her coat for her. But Rudyard Creek had not put her purse and scarf back in her car, and of course he had kept the locket. It made her ill to think of her rapist collecting souvenirs of her.

And then he telephoned.

"How did you get this number?" she whispered.

"I asked your mommy. I told Mommy I was going to pass through Ohio and thought I'd look you up. Your parents are very trusting, you know." Gleefully, Rudyard Creek explained what he was up to. Afterward, Clemmie wondered why. Perhaps he thought that a demigod such as himself should have admirers, that now Clemmie would realize he was clever enough to do anything, and she would stop obstructing him.

He had gotten Pete to ask their parents where Clemmie had had her baby. The Mountain School had disbanded only a few years after Clemmie was there, because society had changed at warp speed. Girls no longer fled hometowns when they were pregnant. They got abortions or stayed home and kept their babies. Overnight, people eager to adopt had almost nowhere to go. Overnight, women faced with a pregnancy out of wedlock had choices. Overnight, people didn't even care about wedlock anymore. The whole idea of entering into something with the word *lock* was passé, because now marriage was known to be useful only as long as it was useful. Not that "lock" was the actual meaning of the second syllable.

But with the school shut down, how to get at its records? Rudyard Creek's method was simple and efficient. He located the former matron and wined and dined her. "We had a brief affair," said Rudyard Creek, chuckling. "I took a photograph or two. She dug out your file, because she absolutely understands that I am the right father for our baby. Our son, Miss Clementine, was adopted by Stanley and Marjorie Boone. And I even have his baby picture, nicely tucked into a little gold locket."

Sure that Clemmie had gone to college in Ohio only to follow his baby, he had hired a private detective out of Columbus. Back then, you could dial 0, get the operator, and say, "May I please have the number for Stan Boone in Columbus?" and the operator would say, "I have two Stan Boones in the area, one in Victorian Village and the other in Upper Arlington." The Boones in Arlington were

not the right ones, and other Boone number was no longer in service. The detective had no success finding where they had gone,
but Rudyard Creek reasoned that since they had adopted his son in
Connecticut, they had Connecticut connections. If the reason for
vanishing to Ohio had been to hide the adoption, perhaps they had
now safely returned because nobody would guess that their little boy
was not in fact their own.

So he hired a second private detective in Connecticut who
simply called Information for every single town in the state, looking
for a phone number for Stanley Boone. It took the detective only
two hours to get the number. The operator would not give him the
corresponding address, so he went to the library, found the correct
local phone book in their extensive collection—phone books were
a big library resource in those days—and there was Stan Boone's
address in East Lyme.

"I'm off to get me a son," said Rudyard Creek. "I have my locket
for proof, you see. The birth mother gave it to me."

Clemmie hung up, waited for the dial tone, and called the operator herself. "May I please have the number for Stanley Boone in East
Lyme, Connecticut?"

Stan Boone was always glad afterward that he had been the one to
answer the phone, that his wife was at a PTA meeting while he was
home with a sound-asleep Billy. He didn't know how his wife would

have reacted. He himself was caught so off guard that he just stood there in the little front hall next to the little telephone table, clinging to the heavy receiver.

"Please don't hang up on me, Mr. Boone. This is the girl who is the biological mother of your little boy. Something terrible is happening. I have to tell you what it is, so you can keep Billy safe."

A wave of fury and fear ripped through Stan. How could she know who he was? How could she know his phone number? The adoption had been private! Absolutely no one knew their son was adopted! Not even Stan's own parents!

Was this girl going to try to ruin the adoption? There had been such a case, a well-publicized nightmare, in which a wicked, criminal young woman attempted to snatch back the child she insisted was hers. A horrible, vicious act. Once adoption was complete, the new parents were the parents. Period. Stan would never let this female near his son.

"The biological father is a terrible man," said the girl. "Truly, I didn't let him touch me. He was so much stronger. I couldn't stop him."

Mr. Boone was skeptical. It was his view that a girl had to yield or the act could not happen, but he let her talk. He needed to know how to prevent whatever plan she had.

"At the Mountain School, the day you and your wife came for my little son—"

Your son! thought Stan, outraged.

"—one of my friends went into your wife's purse and got your real name from her driver's license. Later, I traced you to Ohio, and I managed to take a photograph of Billy, which I kept in a locket. I kissed it every morning."

He was nauseated. This little slut had his son's picture in her locket? He tried to remember what she looked like, this girl who had had the nerve to lie there—on the cot where she'd given birth in the night, not even at a hospital, which certainly proved her lack of fitness to be a parent—and actually interrogate the Boones. Make sure they'd be good parents! When *she* was the sinner.

"He found me. The man. The father. He was a high school basketball coach, and my brother, who played on a team he coached, told him I'd been sent away to have a baby. I never told anybody who the father was, but he believes he can establish it through the locket, which he stole from me."

So you kept seeing him, thought Stan. So much for your rape story.

"He has a wife now, and they can't have a baby of their own, and he knows I had a baby, he knows he is the father, and he wants the baby. Your baby."

The *father* was coming forward? That was extraordinary. Men did not acknowledge bastards, or if they did, it was with snickering pride. But a man claiming that fatherhood had been denied him by this woman? That man now wanted his little son? The Boones were to recognize the folly of their adoption and yield to the true love of true fatherhood?

Stan had a vision of courts and kidnaps, attorneys and reporters and cameras, his dear little boy and wife exposed to the world. It could actually work for the father because it was so unusual. If the man played his cards right, the court might be sufficiently sympathetic to order Stan to give up his son.

"He follows me," said the girl. "Wherever I go, however I hide. He's a monster. No matter what he says, don't let him have Billy! Do not let him *near* Billy."

Stan Boone took control. "How could he establish that he's the father? If in fact he is? We were told how you were the kind of girls who would go all the way with absolutely anybody. You have no morals." Mr. Boone did not feel bad about stating the truth. The hysterical girl on the phone had to face up to herself.

She said quietly, "The important thing for you is that *he* believes himself to be the father. He wants that child, and he will stop at nothing. You must protect Billy."

Stan stood tethered to the telephone by its cord, his skin crawling, but not because of the father; because of this woman who had endlessly encouraged the man, tempting him at every turn.

Do we have to move again? But we're back near our families, back where we grew up. Billy plays at the same beach where I swam as a boy. He romps by the same creek, and before I can blink, he'll be old enough to play Little League.

Stan disconnected, relieved to hear a dial tone instead of the thin, quavery voice of that depraved woman. He couldn't bring himself to discuss the threat with his innocent wife, so happy in her family and her home.

One week later, a man much taller and stronger than Stan, much broader and more muscular, dropped into his office, lowered himself into a chair, smiled a big, toothy smile, and said, "I'm here for my son."

I'll kill you first, thought Stan Boone.

TWENTY-TWO

Johnny was standing well back in Joyce's kitchen, assuming he was invisible, studying his narrow view of street and action.

He'd been buying pot from Wilson for two years. They'd separately drive down to the softball fields, where they and their golf carts blended into the many golf carts of practicing teams, pickleball players, horseshoe club, and gardeners working on their raised beds behind the rabbit-proof fence. Johnny would saunter down the dirt path through the meadows to the Catawba River, surrounded by high grass that Joyce assured him was full of ticks and he'd get Lyme disease. Wilson, having come in Dom's golf cart, would meet Johnny behind a thicket of wild roses at the edge of the river where they had tucked a couple of folding aluminum chairs. Weed was a social drug. Who wanted to smoke alone?

River access was possible, but thick vines and the strong possibility of snakes weren't a draw. They never even encountered a birder or a walker. Wilson was a babbler, which gave him an unfortunate resemblance to Joyce, but Johnny was peacefully high and didn't care what Wilson had to say. Now and then Wilson referred to cash: piles of cash, shoeboxes of cash.

Joyce was a great buyer of shoes, which she kept in their boxes, entirely covering one wall of her walk-in closet. Johnny couldn't see the point. Was Joyce worried her shoes would get dusty? Johnny would listen to Wilson and vaguely wonder how much cash a shoebox would hold. Depended whether it was one-dollar bills or hundred-dollar bills.

Joyce knew nothing about his return to pot and adolescence, and he didn't want her to know. He liked shutting her out. She had become a little too grabby of his life anyway.

When Helen told him that Joyce had changed the locks on the house, he'd been angry, scared, and kind of impressed. He had thoroughly enjoyed taking little bits from Joyce's checking account. He had no expectation of getting caught because Joyce was careless, but she had caught on. He didn't know what to think of Joyce taking off for Galveston, but it would certainly be easier to clean up her garage without her around. Having cops a few yards away was not good, but he'd even chatted with the sheriff about changing the locks, using the old "senior moment" explanation, and probably nobody knew more about senior moments than the sheriff's department, endlessly rescuing confused elderly people.

Joyce had emailed, explaining that she'd removed every trace of him from her house and thrown it on the floor of his own garage. Which meant that his gun, which he kept in a sack in a work boot— not because that was sensible, but because he liked the act of tucking it there—was not here. Probably just as well.

In her frenzy, Joyce had not gotten to the garage. She probably hadn't even thought of the garage. Since he did all Joyce's home maintenance and upkeep, she probably assumed that the jars, boxes, and containers were full of picture-hanging necessities, gutter-cleaning tools, sets of drill bits, vacuum cleaner bags, and stepladders. In fact, Wilson was skimming and had asked Johnny to store marijuana oil and oxycodone for him. It took little space and had no odor, and what better place than a wall of overflowing garage shelving?

Johnny didn't know how to sell what he had, or to whom he could sell it, but right now he needed to move it where the police wouldn't poke around, and definitely where Joyce wouldn't.

Betty Anne had already called Joyce with the details of the murder, which he knew from Joyce's second email. Joyce was gossip central. It was possible that she would turn around and come right back, irked at missing something so exciting, and when she found *herself* locked out instead of him… Whoa boy, that would be a serious scene. He didn't want that to happen with Joyce's garage door up and the jars awaiting inspection by a sheriff a few paces away.

The cops would be aware by now that the third unit across the street from Joyce and Johnny was a little strange. Would they know instantly what was going on? What would they find? Or were the cops still waiting for a warrant and hadn't even gotten into the third villa? Or would they just see weird old people living weird old lives and doing weird old things, including snuffing out the only youthful visitor?

No, they'd figure out the drug angle, and they would make the reasonable guess that Wilson had taken more than his share and paid the price, shot by Dom. The proof was that Dom had vanished, although that was a puzzle since Dom had no vanishing capacity as far as Johnny knew. Walking was a rare activity for Dom. Had Dom tottered from his house to the gate and over the little rise into the parking lots where presumably Wilson's car sat? Could Dom have driven that car to the airport? Left it in long-term parking and flown away?

If Dom had managed that, one thing was for sure: he wasn't carrying much. He couldn't balance or drag a suitcase of cash.

But the Coglands were probably part of this and had whisked Dom away. Unless they were Wilson's parents, in which case they would have whisked Dom into a grave someplace else. But nobody had mentioned seeing the Coglands recently.

Once when they were both stoned, Wilson had told Johnny that he had a partner in the pod. Duh, Johnny had thought. Whatever you're doing, it includes Dom and the Coglands. But he thought now, Could it possibly include Helen Stephens? She had the key to Dom's, which meant she could come and go to the Coglands as well.

Prissy, churchy, never-married old Helen, who didn't smoke,

drink, buy lottery tickets, swear, or even use vulgarities. When she was really stirred up, she might say, "Goodness!" That she and Joyce were best friends was almost comical. The only thing they had in common was proximity.

What could Helen's role be? Did she keep the books? Did dealers ever keep books? Did Helen even know what drugs were? The woman taught Latin. By definition, she was out of the loop. Any loop.

And yet it wouldn't surprise Johnny if Helen also had a concealed-carry license. A little old thing like her was just the candidate. More than a third of Sun City households had guns, a statistic gleaned from the number of licenses issued. Nobody would expect to be shot by Helen. Nobody would be afraid of her. And Wilson was a slow kind of guy. Slow to think, slow to move.

Would they suspect Helen of popping Wilson? Did Johnny himself suspect her?

Johnny could not imagine her dealing or delivering because she was so tiny a third grader could overwhelm her. But he could readily see her banking. She might be the money launderer in the bunch. In fact, how did Johnny know she really taught Latin? Talk about a cover story. Those days she was supposed to be teaching, she could be driving all over the state depositing $500 here and there in various accounts, or whatever you did to launder money, a complete unknown to Johnny who instantly spent anything that came toward his wallet, and a lot more besides.

Without a doubt, Helen Stephens needed money. A spinster in her seventies still working? Teaching, of all things. The world's worst profession—struggling with stupid, swearing teenagers and still commuting, coming up with lesson plans, arguing with helicopter parents. She had to dream of actual retirement.

The sheriff had let her drive away, so he didn't suspect her of anything, but then *competence* was probably not the guy's middle name. Certainly *speed* wasn't the guy's middle name.

Johnny shrugged and got to work. As in so many Sun City garages, one wall was lined with storage shelving up to the ceiling, while high on the back wall hung more shelves under which the front end of the car was tucked. Joyce had changed the garage door code so that the clicker on his visor wouldn't open it, but the wall control on the inside functioned no matter what the code was. Opening the garage door by the button at the utility-room door, Johnny walked outside to his car and drove into the slot where Joyce's car usually went. He needed to look casual, so he got slowly out of the driver's seat, slowly circled the car to the utility-room door, and pressed the wall control again. When the door was down, he closed the blinds on the single garage window and flicked on the overhead lights.

He was pretty sure he had five stashes, and to his relief, he located all five. He put them in his trunk, surrounding and covering them with miscellaneous tools, cans of paint and stain, boxes of sandpaper, unopened varieties of screws, and loose piles of batteries, then rested some furnace filters on top and rolled up a few extension cords and dropped them alongside, giving it the messy, settled look of a trunk that always held this stuff.

A thunderstorm was boiling up, a frequent occurrence on hot Carolina summer days, but all month long, the storms had bypassed Sun City. They desperately needed rain. Grass was now at the crunch level of potato chips. The black blotch in the distance was turning purple, and distant thunder boomed. It might actually rain.

———————

Last summer, when Joyce was off doing whatever, Johnny had been sitting on the little front porch, oppressed by the relentless sun. He wasn't in the mood for anything. Boredom lay as heavy as the heat.

Wilson's car sat in Dom's driveway. Marcia and Roy Cogland showed up, or at least a car arrived and the garage doors went up and down; he couldn't see through the tinted windows to identify the driver or passenger. Marcia and Roy stayed in their home barely ten minutes and then drove away.

Johnny thought of shoeboxes and cash.

A few minutes later, Wilson drove away. Almost immediately after Wilson's departure, Dom's garage door started to rise. Dom had never hired anybody to lubricate the hinges and pivot points and tracks, so his door lurched and screamed when it moved. One of these days, it would stop functioning altogether.

As always, even before the golf cart was clear of the garage, Dom lifted a clicker and the door began to lower again. Johnny walked over. Dom set his garage-door device down in the cup holder, backed into the street, swung a U-ey, and lined up the driver's side of his golf cart with the mailbox. Nobody got mail anymore that mattered, just glossy folders about Rhine River cruises, but getting the mail probably qualified as an adventure for Dom.

Dom, having not a single social grace, paid no attention to Johnny. As Dom aligned himself with his mailbox, Johnny swept back the cart's plastic wall, which was not zipped but just sagging open, and sat down on the passenger side of the front bench. "My man," he said to Dom. "Getting your fresh air?"

Dom looked incredulously at the trespassing body on his bench, said nothing, and turned his face toward the mailbox. Johnny had planned to snitch the cup-holder device, but now he saw that there was a second garage-door device on the visor. It seemed seriously stupid to keep your spare in the same place as your original. "I'm heading out to Home Depot for some supplies, Dom," he said loudly, because Dom was deaf. "You wanna come? You got any errands you need to do?"

Dom squinted into the newspaper tube.

Johnny removed the visor device and pocketed it.

Dom came up with flyers for gutter cleaning and better Medicare coverage. "No," he said. "I gotta pick up barbecue." He glared until Johnny slid off the bench.

"Hey, zip it up for me," Dom ordered, and as soon as Johnny had closed him up, Dom drove off to the gate that led to the shopping strip.

Everybody in Sun City, or at least on Blue Lilac, had expensive drapes, curtains, plantation shutters, or shades, all closed against the sun. Blind rectangles stared at the little street. Nobody but Johnny was outside in the heat. Was he up for a tiny, risky adventure?

He pressed the stolen garage-door opener. Picking up barbecue was probably a ten-minute errand, but ten minutes was plenty. He felt a thrill of excitement at the prospect of slipping into Dom's and hunting for shoeboxes filled with cash.

But the garage door that opened was not Dom's. It was the Coglands'.

Johnny walked directly into the Cogland garage and clicked the device to close it behind him. Inside, the villa was creepily empty and creepily clean, like a model home without even the wrought-iron wall decor. Johnny found nothing. No food, no DVDs, no clothes, no drugs, no shoeboxes, no money.

He studied the windows on the side wall of the living room. Every Sun City window was double hung, featuring two very small, slim tabs that locked and unlocked to the left and right respectively. It was hard to tell whether a window was locked except by testing it, because as long as both tabs faced the same direction, everything looked fine. Even when they didn't face the same direction, everything looked fine, because they were so unobtrusive.

Johnny unlocked the window farthest from the sofa—probably nobody ever sat there to cast a suspicious eye on window locks. He pulled the glass up, released the screen latches, tipped the screen into the grass, and eased out the window. Then he closed the window from the outside and carried the screen home. Nobody ever used their screens anyhow because the pollen from the pines was so heavy you choked on it if you opened your windows. If the Coglands were only here ten minutes at a time, they weren't noticing whether a screen was gone. But Johnny wasn't sure that the Coglands even existed. He had been paying insufficient attention to Wilson during their riverside hours, but he had a feeling the deliveries were from miscellaneous people.

The next day, Johnny caught Dom again, but this time Dom was fully zipped, and returning the filched garage-door opener to his visor was not possible. "Hey, man," Johnny said instead. "Found this in the gutter yesterday after you drove off. Pretty sure it's yours. Want to test it?"

Dom's eyes flickered to the visor. "Yeah, it's mine. Give it over."

And that was that for neighborly affection.

Johnny had been proud of the guts he'd shown getting in and out of the Cogland house, cleverly giving himself access for future trespass, but to his dismay, he didn't find that courage, or maybe stupidity, again. The plan to go back through that window in the middle of the night loomed large. He'd think about, and then he'd unthink about it. One insomniac night, he sauntered with his cigarette around the villas to his personal window but couldn't make himself climb in.

As time went on, he couldn't even remember what the plan had been. Had he seriously expected to find a shoebox of money he could carry off?

Yes.

But month after month, cowardice or wisdom kept him from doing anything.

Right now, it was imperative to get rid of the stuff in his trunk. If he got caught using pot, who cared anymore? Especially who cared whether a guy in his seventies inhaled? But storing opiates for a drug dealer—they'd care. He couldn't imagine how his children would react to his arrest. He'd never see the grandkids again, that was for sure. And prison was not a good retirement center. Johnny watched all those jail reality shows. He couldn't survive prison. They'd off him the first day.

Twenty-Three

Clemmie's silenced phones bristled with voice and text messages.

Her principal at Dexter River High had called. "Helen! We saw the news. I know you live on Blue Lilac. Are you all right? Do you need me? Mindy and I can drive right over. We have a guest room."

Clemmie began to cry.

There was a voice message from the mother of her favorite and best Latin student, Jimmy Mitchell, who had graduated in June and would attend Duke in the fall. "Miz Stephens, Jimmy called us from his summer job. It was on the news. A murder right on your street. He wants us to drive over and check on you. Let me know what you need. Anything, Miz Stephens. My husband can bring the car around right now."

There was a message from the band teacher, a delightful man who loved his job and his students, one of the few on the faculty who completely understood a person still teaching in her seventies because he was pretty close to that himself and never wanted to give up marching band. "Helen, a murderer?" said Marvin's voice. "Seriously? Hoping it's a couple who shouldn't have stayed married fifty years and nothing to do with you and no threat. Call me back and reassure me, or else call me back and I'm the cavalry."

Clemmie imagined a flotilla of Dexter River people arriving on Blue Lilac. But nobody was coming unless she requested it. She yearned to request it. But she had to get rid of Borobasq first. Or maybe she should forget about Borobasq and call Marvin back, asking him to pick her up at the clubhouse.

The phone rang in her hand. Clemmie said "Hello" before she remembered not to, and it was Joyce. "Helen, I've gotten calls from Betty Anne and Shirley and Lois and Edith! Are you all right? Why didn't you call me? I'm frantic! Are you safe?"

Lois and Edith were canasta friends, each of whom lived in a pod a mile or two away, so apparently every single person in Sun City knew what had happened here. "I'm all right, Joyce. Just shaken."

"Is it true? Dom killed Wilson?"

"I don't think they know that," said Clemmie, "but it is the neighborhood assumption. I mean, who else would?"

Joyce said, "I can't imagine what happened," and then proceeded to offer ludicrous theories of what might have. "I haven't even gotten as far as Columbia. I only got about fifty miles and then I stopped for something to eat and then I couldn't even eat. Me! Joyce! Unable to eat! I'm so rattled over Johnny, and now I'm so upset about Wilson. Maybe I should just come home and deal with things. Helen, was that dreamboat your nephew?"

This was not a topic Clemmie could address. She had to distract her friend with something compelling. "Joyce, Johnny couldn't understand why he couldn't get into the house. He didn't realize you'd changed the locks. He thought they were broken or something, and when he couldn't reach you, he just took charge and acted. He called a locksmith himself. He's that kind of man, of course. I know you wanted him out of there, but he's back in."

Joyce was quiet for so long that Clemmie wondered if she'd lost the phone connection. She would never give up her beloved cell phones, but sometimes a person longed for a cord, that sturdy proof of connection. How did the voice travel when it didn't go down a wire? Everything in life was such a mystery now.

"Helen," whispered Joyce, "I'm scared that Johnny did it."

"Did what?" asked Clemmie, her mind on locks.

"Killed Wilson."

"*What?* Oh no, Joyce, it was surely Dom. I mean, why else would Dom have vanished? Dom probably didn't mean to do it, or maybe he thought that Wilson wouldn't actually die from a gunshot wound." Although Clemmie knew better. When you fired a gun at somebody, you did think they would die; that's why you fired it.

Dom had planned to kill Wilson, even if he planned only a split second in advance.

Her eyes landed on the sweet front porches all around, their little decorations and flags and planters. Deceptive advertising, she thought. This has turned out to be one scary neighborhood.

"Johnny has insomnia," said Joyce, apropos of nothing. "He also smokes, although I pretend not to know. Sometimes he circles the block at one or two in the morning, having a smoke. Sometimes it isn't tobacco. Sometimes it's pot, which works better for insomnia anyway."

Wilson and Borobasq and Roy and Marcia and Dom—they were all linked, and they were linked by drugs. Drugs producing enough cash to make Borobasq fly across the continent for it. And now Johnny.

Clemmie herself needed love, not money. Her small pension, her small social security check, her parents' small legacy, and the small salary from part-time teaching—these comfortably paid the bills. Clemmie had no travel bug; she didn't need cruises and tours; she had no bucket list; she didn't care about fine watches or high fashion or famous wines or great cars. If she suddenly had access to a pile of cash, she would have no mental shopping list. It seemed to her that at their age—Sun City ages—people would be past greed. They surely knew by now that possessions were fun, but it was health that mattered; that bank accounts were necessary, but the attention of grandchildren was better.

But Wilson was young, and young people knew nothing of these truths. And Dom was locked into an isolated, dreary life, and perhaps sheer frustration had made him pull a trigger.

"Wilson was Johnny's supplier," said Joyce. "I think Johnny might have killed him for the cash. There's a lot of cash in drugs. It's all cash, actually. And a man who would steal from his girlfriend's checking account... What else would that kind of man do?" she asked, as if it were not rhetorical but perfectly likely.

This was the man Joyce lived with! Ate and slept and bowled and joked with! How casually she tossed out the theory that he was also a killer.

Clemmie didn't believe Johnny would steal, and she certainly did not believe that he would kill, although she could believe Johnny was smoking a little dope now and then, because why would Joyce make that up? On the other hand, Clemmie's entire life was made up, so who was she to cavil at the idea of somebody else telling a fib? "But why would Johnny shoot anybody to start with, Joyce? And where would he get a gun?"

"Oh please, Helen, don't be childish. We have guns. Everybody has guns."

Everybody? Girls with whom they played cards or stood next to in line dancing or made such fine pottery? Women who did water aerobics and beading and garden club? They all had guns?

"We like to go to the shooting range now and then," said Joyce in a warm, remembering voice, as if she had not just referred to

BEFORE SHE WAS HELEN

Johnny as a killer. "There's an excellent one down near that great furniture store, the one where I got my new sofas, the ones that look so beachy. It's a very relaxing hobby," she added, presumably meaning the shooting range, not the sofas.

Clemmie wasn't against guns, knowing firsthand that they could indeed achieve a desired end, but she hadn't had a picture in her mind of Joyce and Johnny going to a shooting range for relaxation.

"We both have concealed-carry licenses," added Joyce. "Tons of people here do."

Concealed carry? That controversial thing where the gun owner kept a handgun in a holster on his ankle or strapped under his arm? Joyce?

Clemmie didn't believe it. Joyce was chunky. She favored knit tops that clung to every roll of fat. She was not hiding holsters on the top half of her body. She favored pants that should have been discarded years ago and replaced with a larger size, so she was not hiding holsters on the bottom half of her body either. If Joyce carried a gun, she carried it in her purse.

And immediately, Clemmie believed that. She occasionally shifted Joyce's purse out of the way while they sat together on the golf-cart bench. Joyce's purse was remarkably heavy. Clemmie had attributed it to the weight of iPad, iPhone, water bottle, a choice of snacks, and an amazing number of keys.

Down at the bottom of all that clutter was a gun?

Was it rational to carry a handgun in your bag? Because then it was not actually on your person. When you set the bag down, it could be whisked away or impossible to get at. The weapon could get lost at the bottom and you'd have to dig for it, handing your victim your tissue pack, your devices, your charger, until you finally hit bottom.

As for Johnny, Clemmie wasn't sure she had ever seen him in shorts, even in the hottest weather. He wore long trousers, usually khakis, at all times, so he might actually have an ankle holster. Where in Sun City would he wear this? At horseshoes? At a '50s dance? At the pod meetings?

Clemmie had her own concealed carry: a slender folding knife on her key ring. It had taken a lot of shopping to find one she could actually open, with her weak fingers and short nails. This one didn't have the little blade slot requiring you to pry up the blade with your fingernail. It had a tiny button to press and then the blade flashed out. The blade was two inches long, and what she could do with this, she didn't know. Certainly when Rudyard Creek had had her in his grip, she couldn't have reached or used a knife. But she'd had it for decades now, and once in a while she tested it to make sure it hadn't rusted shut or something. It seemed so innocent compared to a gun. You could peel and core an apple with your knife. A gun had more limited application.

"Sometimes when Johnny went out at two in the morning," said Joyce, "I'd get up to see what he was doing. One minute he'd be circling the flower island in the middle of Blue Lilac, and the next minute he'd vanish. Where did he go? At one point I thought he and that Marcia Cogland were having an affair, but that was impossible because the Coglands were never there. So where did he vanish *to*?"

Clemmie envisioned Marcia and Roy and Dom and Johnny getting together at two in the morning, going through the illegal door, and gathering in a villa with no food and no comfortable chairs so they could share marijuana in the dark.

Nobody cared anymore! Just sit on your patio and smoke whatever you felt like!

"I'm coming back home," said Joyce decisively. "Sit tight, Helen. You and I will manage this together." She disconnected.

This was not good news.

Clemmie had to be rid of Borobasq because if Joyce told the sheriff about the dreamboat in Clemmie's car, and if the sheriff came over, and if Borobasq were there in her house, the first thing he would do would be to expose her other name and life. She still had a shot at keeping herself intact. If she gave Borobasq another chance to escape, surely he'd jump at it.

Police car lights whirled. Neighbors came and went. The Carolina blue sky was suddenly half clouds—beautiful clouds layered in pearl gray and white and alabaster, the kind Clemmie tried to paint in watercolor and rarely got right. In the distance, the clouds had blackened and looked as if they might actually contain water and it might actually rain.

Joyce liked to exaggerate. Her stories were often half fiction, although wholly enjoyable. She might not even have gone the fifty miles she cited. She might be just down the road scarfing down a bag of Fritos, torn between keeping Johnny and throwing him out. Joyce enjoyed having a man. She strutted in Johnny's company, making sure that the world knew that she had more value than a single woman.

But Joyce was making up the part about Johnny being the possible killer, a theory probably advanced from a need to be involved. Unless when Clemmie and Johnny had checked Dom's house, he had trotted across the street to make sure that she, Helen Stephens, would not enter the garage. Unless he had already known about the dead body in the garage because he had caused it to be dead.

Ridiculous. Dom had killed Wilson and run. Period.

Clemmie threaded through the crowd and crossed Blue Lilac to her own sidewalk.

"Miz Stephens?" called somebody.

"Helen?"

"Ma'am?"

Handsome young people were advancing on her, stretching out their microphones like teeny metal dogs on leashes, using their wide, toothy smiles like entrance fees. "Helen, can we just chat a minute?"

"How does it feel to live next door to a murder?"

"Did you identify the body? How did that feel?"

Clemmie flung herself onto her porch, unlocked her door, stepped in, and slammed it behind her.

The air-conditioning was frigid. She wondered why she wasn't sick all the time, going back and forth from glaciers to tropics.

She was almost weeping from that tiny moment of exposure. How would she deal with real exposure? You lead two lives? You faked your whole existence? You stole a dead child's identity? There is no Helen?

Boro emerged from the laundry room. "Okay, you don't have my money," he said. The pitch of his voice was slightly higher than it had been. He was blinking too much. Anxiety was taking over or he was on something, or both. "Here are the keys to the rental car," he said. "Drive it to Wendy's, over there in that strip mall. I'll get out tonight after the police have gone."

"No. You have to get out now. My neighbor who brought over those groceries saw you in the passenger seat when we first drove in. She was headed out of town, so I didn't worry about it, but what with all the excitement, she's coming back. She'll tell the sheriff. You have to be gone. I'll give you my camera. You take that and this notebook and a sharp pencil. You'll look like one of the media people. You'll blend right in. Your need of a shave is very trendy. Walk right out the sliders and around the house and stand with all those reporters and video people, but then just keep going. It's not far to the golf-course parking lot. Probably a quarter mile. Five minutes."

"No. Get the rental car. Tonight I'm going back into the neighbors' houses once the cops have gone."

"They'll have locked the villas up."

"You have a key," he said. "I'll use that. Go get my car."

"I'm not getting in your vehicle. Get it yourself."

"Then I'm letting the sheriff know who you are."

She was sick of this spoiled, entitled, overly handsome brat. She gave him her Latin teacher's look. *Again today you are not prepared to conjugate the irregular verb you were assigned?* "I'm not afraid of the sheriff. You're the one who's afraid of the sheriff."

Borobasq took the Swiss Army knife out of his pocket, opened the blade, not the screwdriver, and rotated his wrist so the knife would glint. He smiled at it, as if it were his pet Yorkie. "Nobody's gonna come looking for you," he said to Clemmie without looking away from his knife. "You'll lie here dead even longer than Wilson did." He took hold of her wrist, tightening his fingers until it hurt, and the old panic swept over her, scalp to toes, and her eyes fogged. Borobasq smirked, and Clemmie realized that this actually *was* her first rodeo, because Borobasq was no lazy Latin student. He wasn't Rudyard Creek either. He wasn't looking for entertainment. He was looking for his money.

"We're doing things my way," he whispered.

Rudyard Creek had said that. Just before he was killed. *We're doing things my way.*

He had smiled, leaning his hips casually back against the picnic table, steepling his fingers. It had never occurred to him to be afraid.

TWENTY-FOUR

Joyce had now talked to Betty Anne, Shirley, Elaine, Linda, Joan, and Eileen. Actually, they'd done all the talking. They were bursting with excitement. Nobody knew the dead man, and Dom, who had killed him, was just a rude, smelly, rarely seen hermit. Not one of her girlfriends addressed the actual physical horror of Wilson's death: a young man's body penetrated by a metal cylinder that exploded inside him. Nobody seemed particularly interested that a young man's life was over. They were interested in the excitement surrounding it.

Joyce had a fondness for novels set in ancient Greece and Rome, and this situation seemed rather like a Roman amphitheater. Her girlfriends were the masses screaming in the Colosseum, getting their jollies from violent death. Or, less hideously, it was just television for them, no different from a show about cops, CSI, chases, drugs, and autopsies.

How lucky Helen was to be so sturdy and rational. All those years of living alone had given her such strength. Joyce couldn't bear living alone and was halfway ready to let Johnny stay anyway. Maybe take a cue from Helen, who never watched violent television or even violent news. Surely a person was happier in a state of ignorance.

Shirley called again. "The police want to talk to you, Joyce."

"Me?"

"They're talking to everybody. They're hoping you know the make of Wilson's car since you live directly across the street. Johnny couldn't identify it. I would have thought that Johnny was more into cars than that, but he just stood there and said, 'Well, it was white.'"

Joyce felt a quiver. Johnny would never say that. He would know the make, the year, the name of the color (certainly not *white*—more likely a paint was called *ivory* or *winter*), and engine specifications.

Shirley went on. "We think the police think that Dom made his getaway in Wilson's car. You know what else? People are saying that the Cogland villa was a trap house!"

"What's that?" Joyce asked, as if she'd never watched hundreds of cop shows.

"A way station for dealing drugs. Right on your street. Kitty-corner across from you! And two doors down from poor Helen, who is totally falling apart. She forgot to wear her wig. She looked awful," said Shirley smugly.

Joyce wanted to say, *So do you, dying your hair that pathetic color and then too stingy and lazy to touch it up often enough, so you're always a two-tone failure.*

"Have you seen people coming and going from that third villa that shouldn't be?" asked Shirley.

"Nobody comes and goes at all. And how would I know what car Wilson drove? I can barely tell a four-door from a two-door."

"They're fingerprinting the villas," said Shirley. "Well, we think they are. I mean, we can't see anything, but we're making educated guesses, and what we know from a guy on the landscape crew is that one of the windows in the Cogland unit was left unlocked, and the screen was gone. The police were taking photographs of it. Furthermore, when the police got there, they found out that the Coglands' slider had been left unlocked. So maybe people came and went all the time by the side and the back, Joyce, which you wouldn't have been able to see from your house. In fact, hardly anybody can see anything about that villa from any house. I am absolutely stunned and horrified," said Shirley happily. "So, so glad that I live over on White Lily," she added, implying that the better sort of residents had wisely chosen a different cul-de-sac.

Joyce's thoughts began flying out of her, meaningless crazed thoughts, as if she'd suddenly taken a new prescription or tried LSD. She could not think what to do next—what her obligations were, what her choices were.

When she moved away from Ohio, Barbara did not give Clemmie her phone number or address because it seemed to her that their rapist had supernatural powers and would inhale the information from Clemmie's correspondence, but after reading Clemmie's latest and frantic letter sent in care of her parents, Barbara called her old roommate. Clemmie told her every detail of the nightmare of Rudyard Creek wanting to seize Billy, of Stan Boone's contempt for Clemmie and his refusal to take the threat to Billy seriously.

"I need your help," said Clemmie. "I need to prove that Rudyard Creek is a rapist. Then he'll never be allowed to disrupt an adoption. I want you to go to the police with me and testify with me."

Barbara literally screamed. "Never! *Never!* Clemmie, we didn't go to the police then, and we're not going now. You can't claim later that somebody hurt you when you have no proof and you didn't have proof then and you never said so at the time and there are no witnesses. I want my life intact. Leave this alone. You warned the Boones. They have to handle it. But there won't be anything to handle! Nothing can happen. They legally adopted Billy. He is their son, and he has been all this time, Clemmie. Nobody can undo an adoption!"

"I've heard of it happening."

"It's a myth. Like alligators in sewers," Barbara snapped.

Clemmie said nothing.

"Okay, so that was a ridiculous comparison. But he cannot get

Billy. Any court would stand by the adoptive parents. How could he prove he's the father? The only thing he could do, and he'd love it, is drag you through the mud. If his demands went to a trial, or even a discussion, it would be hideous for you. Imagine Rudyard Creek with that terrible grin, that mockery. He'd enjoy himself, you'd be worse off, and Billy would learn the name of his biological father. Over the years he'd wonder about it, and later on in life, Billy might want to get to know him. 'My real dad,' he might say eagerly. Never let Billy know there is such a person, Clemmie!"

Stan Boone's first inclination had been to go to the police. Thanks to Rotary, he was acquainted with the chief of police. But nothing good could come of revealing an adoption. His wife had never wanted friends and family to know that sleazy fact.

Stan Boone telephoned the high school where the fellow had supposedly coached when he supposedly raped the mother, and the school secretary said, "Why, yes, he was a coach here for four or five years, very successful, but he moved on. I think maybe New York State somewhere."

In the public library, Stan found the specialized storage of microfilm for Connecticut newspapers. He scrolled through the sports sections during basketball season the year of his son's birth and easily found photographs of the huge, grinning man who had invaded his office, standing there with his winning team.

Stan could imagine the man literally snatching Billy from Stan's grip and driving away. Stan would charge Rudyard Creek with kidnapping, but what if it turned out to be a finders-keepers situation, that possession was nine-tenths of the law, especially if the man could prove fatherhood? But how could he do that? He'd have to use the birth mother, obviously an unpleasant, sneaky person, probably looking for some payoff. And what if then the birth mother insisted that *she* should have her son? What if they got involved in a three-way fight? Neither he nor his wife could bear the publicity of that. And dear good, funny Billy, whom he adored, would be destroyed.

Clemmie had given Stan Boone her home phone number, although she had not told him either of her names. When she heard Mr. Boone's voice over the telephone wire, she thought that Rudyard Creek had already grabbed Billy. She choked back sobs.

"He called me again. He wants to meet Billy."

She sagged with relief. Billy was still safe. "He's dangerous," she said. "You cannot bring Billy into his presence."

"I believe he'd take money instead," said Mr. Boone.

That was delusional. She said carefully, "My instinct is that money is irrelevant. He wants a son. You cannot deal with him. You have to dismiss him for good. Maybe tell him you've talked to the birth mother, and she says the father is somebody else."

"So you did sleep around," said Mr. Boone distastefully.

The defamation of her character was already here, beginning with the one man who should be her ally. "When and where does he want to meet?" she asked, wondering about the expression *sleep around*. The last thing a violent rape included was sleep.

"A highway picnic area in Old Lyme," said Stan. "I'm to bring Billy."

She had grown up on the shoreline. She knew exactly the place Rudyard Creek had chosen. It was on a main road, but far more isolated than it looked. "This is about winning, Mr. Boone. Not having a son of his own makes him a loser. But asking you to meet clandestinely in a picnic area is crazy. The reasonable method to regain a child is through lawyers and courts. Face-to-face sneering and snatching is insane. It could go wrong a dozen ways."

"I agree. That's why I think he'd take money. I think he's angling for money. I've cashed out everything I can."

"No. You could never give him enough. It's Billy he wants."

"I have to end this. I agreed to meet. He has a three-day weekend coming up. That Friday is a teacher's workday at his high school, but he'll skip the sessions and drive down here instead."

"What does your wife think?" Clemmie asked.

"She doesn't know. She will never know. My job is to protect her and protect Billy. I'll kill the man if I have to."

Clemmie was in Akron. She could take sick days and also get there. Why would I do that? she asked herself. Isn't this between these two men? Do I have a stake here?

But she had the largest stake of all, really. It was her son.

She called Barbara again because there was no one else to call. She had to run her chaotic thoughts past somebody.

"I haven't thought about anything else in days," said Barbara. "Stan Boone is right that somebody somehow has to stop this man. But there's no point in you and me going to the authorities, trying to present our case to the police. The only person who could go to the police is Stan Boone, and that's what he ought to do, but he'd rather give all the money he has to a vicious rapist bully than admit that his little boy is adopted. I don't know why it's so awful to have an adoption. Why can't he just say so?"

"Because the child's blood is suspect," said Clemmie drearily. "And in this case, it's true. This little boy is half Rudyard Creek."

They contemplated the awfulness of that. Clemmie prayed that in the argument of nature versus nurture, the nurture of the Boones would triumph over the nature of Rudyard Creek in Billy.

Barbara drew a deep breath. "Maybe, just maybe, if both you and I go to that picnic area and face Rudyard Creek down, collectively we can shame him."

"Oh, Barbara! Would you go with me? Would you really do that?"

"I might. I'm thinking."

They talked a long time, squared their shoulders, and made their plans.

They felt brave and proud. It did not occur to them that Rudyard

Creek would also be proud, seeing his trophies all dressed up to meet him again, and that he would also find it hysterically funny: these two tiny women seriously thinking they could prevent him, Rudyard Creek, from getting what he wanted.

In Sun City, the thunderstorm broke.

Clemmie had always loved that idiom, reminiscent of some ancient god lifting his hammer to smash the clouds. The sky was so dark that the streetlamps came on. After a huge thunderclap came welcome sheets of water: the blinding monsoon that usually lasted only minutes but was frightening in its power. It would run off the baked clay soil and flood low-lying areas and probably end before it saved the grass and the gardens.

Clemmie stood in her open front door, unwilling to launch.

People hunched, as if that would keep their hair dry, and scurried to cars and houses. They tapped the Weather Center on their smartphones and checked out the radar. There were the usual tornado warnings. Some areas were experiencing hail.

Clemmie opened her umbrella and struggled through the downpour to her car on Pink Camellia.

She could go to Costa Rica, but she didn't want to go to Peggy's wedding, and she certainly didn't want the sheriff wondering why she was fleeing the country.

She could go to Florida under her birth name, Murray, and live in her own condo, and she didn't think anybody could find her, but Borobasq had found her here. Of course, Bentley had given him the tools. Bentley didn't even know she had a birth name because he assumed it was Lakefield. Becoming a Murray again was possible but ridiculous. And what would she do in Florida, really? And for how long?

She found the courage to look at her finger, which she hadn't examined even when it happened. The dishrag she'd wrapped around the wound was blood-soaked. It hurt so much. He had sliced vertically through the pad of her index finger, exposing the bone. She could go to the urgent care clinic for stitches and say, "I was careless with a knife," and they'd stitch it up.

It didn't seem to Clemmie that cutting her achieved anything. Borobasq was relying on her fear of getting hurt to make her obey. But wouldn't fear of getting hurt again make her disobey? He'd ordered her to bring his car around, but why would she do that now that she was safely out of the house? Did he think keeping her two selves secret was so crucial that she'd drive right back into his clutches?

Perhaps the point of slicing her finger was that he enjoyed it. Rather like rape, she thought. And in fact, Borobasq had a lot in common with Rudyard Creek. He too was a very handsome man bigger than her, choosing a diminutive victim who could never fight back.

Tell that sweet sheriff everything, she said to herself.

But there was never going to be a time when Clemmie would tell a policeman anything, let alone everything.

Clemmie turned on her car, and the air-conditioning was a blessing.

In fact, she thought, he's the one who is trapped. I have his car keys. He could walk out; he can get himself to the airport and fly away. But that abandoned rental car will come back to haunt him eventually. Or not. He probably doesn't do anything under his real name, any more than I do. Or Dom does.

She put the car in gear and crept up Pink Camellia.

Oh! How her finger hurt. It was like being knifed again with every pulse beat.

———————

In Joyce's kitchen, Johnny took the spare key to Helen's house that Joyce kept in case of an emergency. It was on a thin, red velvet cord, and along with the key was an identifying paper tag in an aluminum circle the size of a soda-pop top. *Helen*, it said in Joyce's tiny script.

Johnny loved weather and was always secretly hoping for a tornado to live through. He watched the street. Apparently the wind was angled because the police huddled in Dom's garage now lowered the garage door to protect the crime scene. The cops could no longer see the street. The cul-de-sac previously packed with spectators was empty.

Johnny Marsh crossed the street, unlocked Helen Stephens's front door, and let himself in.

Since Boro was looking for a suitcase of cash, the Latin teacher's house had been easier to search than if he'd been looking for, say, a handful of diamonds.

He had flipped through the pages of a couple of books, but the most she could hide in one book was a hundred-dollar bill, and he wanted hundreds of hundred-dollar bills.

He pulled down the stairs to the attic, which were in her walk-in closet and obviously not used often because he had to shift a chest of drawers to lower the stairs. The temperature in the attic had to be a 120. There was no flooring, and nowhere to hide or even set anything down, and she hadn't put so much as a cardboard box of Christmas decorations up there.

There was no basement.

He had unzipped the suitcases in her storage closet. Empty.

He removed a pile of neatly folded sheets in her linen closet. Nothing behind them.

He found the box of Christmas ornaments, untaped it, and then untaped the box labeled "woolens." They were what they said.

Her tiny office was strictly school stuff. She really did still teach, and it really was Latin. The file drawers held nothing but lesson plans, ancient-world battle maps, and master sheets for photocopying.

He'd passed on her little exit plan so he could find the money, and she didn't have it. He got angrier by the moment, like an expanding graph, his sides spreading outward and his heart beating faster. Then she came back, all tough and sure of herself, so he put a stop to that. Now she'd bring his rental car to the parking lot behind the gate. The code for the gate, obviously designed for pathetic old people who couldn't remember anything, was 1234.

He had a few moments before he had to escape out the back. He wasn't worried about walking around. He liked her TV reporter idea.

He Googled "Wilson Spesante" and turned up nothing. He did a Facebook search because Wilson was the right age for Facebook, and a very interesting thing happened.

Normally, he hated a computer program that decided to spell words for him. But this was thought-provoking. Facebook found nobody named Spesante and instead presented Pesante for his consideration. There were only a hundred or so people with the last name Pesante, and there was no Wilson among them. But there was a couple named Marnie and Ray. Names that sounded a lot like Marsha and Roy.

Were these the occupants of the third villa?

Was Wilson maybe their kid or grandkid?

He couldn't see anything on that Pesante page unless they friended him, and if they were who he thought they were, they weren't going to.

He was startled by a boom and a tremble right down to the villa's foundation. Just a thunderstorm. The media crowd was leaping into vehicles. People didn't like getting wet. They didn't like it so much that Boro thought fear of water from the sky must be some primitive instinct like hunger. They adopted similar postures, hunched like apes, pulling their shoulders up as if this would keep them dry or ward off some dreadful fate.

Even the police had withdrawn.

Thunderstorms moved quickly, so he had to take advantage and leave now.

He had just opened her slider to go out the back when a key turned the front-door lock of Helen Stephens's home.

———————————

The woman in the cubicle next to Bentley stood up and rested her chin on the divider. "Doesn't your aunt live in Sun City in Charlotte?"

"Yes," said Bent. He couldn't imagine when he would ever have mentioned that.

"They've had a murder. Can you picture that? You're eighty years old, doddering around playing dominoes, and you murder somebody over it?"

Bent was shocked, which itself was shocking, since his primary goal in life was to be unshockable. Had Aunt Clemmie bumped into the drug dealer after all, thanks to him, and gotten killed?

"It's a breaking news banner on the *Charlotte Observer* newspaper site. I used to live there, so I have the app, and every day I spend about twelve seconds reading the headlines." She giggled, consigning Charlotte to its twelve-second slot in her life, and handed over her phone.

Bent clicked to the article, written minutes ago by no fewer than three reporters on the scene. It could not possibly be that newsworthy. Plus, the murder was actually in another state from Charlotte. But when the reporters described Sun City as a "largely white, wealthy, gated enclave where no one would ever expect such a thing," Bentley figured that was the fun part for the reporters, who relished the chance to be snide.

The murder had taken place on Blue Lilac Lane. Were lilacs ever blue? Weren't they lilac? Wasn't that, like, the point?

Bentley's heart rate doubled. Had the internet posts been right? Had Aunt Clemmie gotten between a drug dealer and his money, and he, Bentley, was responsible?

But to his immense relief, the murder victim was male.

Bentley said, "Wow. That's awful. I'll call and check on my aunt. But there are thousands of people there. She probably doesn't even know about it yet."

His colleague laughed. "Probably playing Rummikub or Scrabble."

Bent texted Aunt Clemmie. Just found out about the murder on Blue Lilac Lane. You live there? Did the drug dealer come to collect his stuff? Listen. I know you went someplace else, but let me know you're okay. I'm really seriously worried. And then go to Costa Rica. Mom will pay for the hotel.

Bent felt good giving these instructions. He was a natural-born leader. The problem was, Aunt Clemmie was not a natural-born follower.

The rain pounded so hard that Clemmie could not see out the front windshield, even with the wipers flapping on high. She swung her gaze to the side for relief from the violent cascade of water and found herself with a view between the units on Pink Camellia over to Blue Lilac. There was her own front door, her own little canvas chair, and her Knock Out roses edging the porch. The sight made her feel weirdly exposed, as if the whole time she'd been living here, Pink Camellians had been checking her out, noting her comings and her goings, keeping a log.

Johnny Marsh strode up her little steps, put a key into her lock, turned her doorknob, and walked right into her house.

Johnny knows Borobasq? Borobasq's expecting him? I have not only a drug dealer who likes to use a knife in my house, but also a neighbor twice my size with a key?

Could Joyce's guess be correct? Could Johnny have stolen Boro's cash and ended up killing Wilson in the process? And was that cash now in Joyce's house? Was that why Johnny had to break back in?

But why go into *my* house? To let Borobasq know where the money is? To normalize their relations? The way North Korea normalizes relationships maybe? Killing each other?

She had seldom felt so elderly. Thoughts lay separately, refusing to coalesce.

Bentley texted. Young people thought a text accomplished something. For them, communication was everything. Action was, like, whatever. He undoubtedly felt that he'd hit the ball into her court and now he was out of the game.

Clemmie sent her usual untruthful answer that all was well and he must not worry, and he texted back a single letter. K. She Googled and found out that *K* meant you were too lazy to type *OK*.

Joyce called yet again and Clemmie answered, because although it could only be more trouble, it was probably immediate.

"Helen," said Joyce firmly, as if forestalling argument, "I turned around. You cannot be there on your own. I'm your best friend, and I need to be there for you. You'll stay at my house so that we have each other. I don't know what we'll do about Johnny and the locks. I guess change them a third time." She giggled, but Clemmie did not. I can't let Joyce go back into her house, she thought. Somehow, Borobasq and Johnny are in cahoots.

If Johnny killed Wilson, though, why was Dom the one to run? Was Dom's background so tricky that running was his only choice?

Joyce was still talking. Babbling, really. A flow of run-on sentences Clemmie could barely follow. *Friends*, Joyce was saying, *had to stick together*. If Clemmie's guesses were even partly true, Joyce was going to need every friend she had. Clemmie said, "Call me when you're close, Joyce, and we'll figure out where to meet, because we shouldn't meet at your house."

"Exactly. Because whether the killer is Johnny or Dom or some stranger off the highway, it's bad."

Some stranger off the highway sounded like country song lyrics. Clemmie had an image of fifty years ago in a highway picnic area. Too many players in that murder too. Because who had actually killed Rudyard Creek? It was still hard to decide.

Joyce half sang, "Heavy traffic. Bye for now, Helen."

"Bye, Joyce," she whispered, but Joyce was already gone. The phone rang in her hand, and it was the sheriff. Stress, thought Clemmie. Doctors are always telling you not to have stress in your life. How is that done, exactly? It's not as if stress is a possession, and you could just shelve it, or not buy more of it. It arrives under its own power. "Hello?"

"Miz Stephens?" said the sheriff. "You okay?"

"No. I'm not. It's so upsetting."

"You home?"

"No. I don't want to be home. Too close to it all."

"Want to meet me at Wendy's? It's just behind the villas," he said as if she had not figured that out in her years of living in those villas.

"Wendy's is good," said Clemmie because she had no choice.

"Ten minutes?"

"Twenty," she bargained, because she had to deal with the rental car and then go to the pharmacy and buy extra-large Band-Aids for her cut. She could fix her finger in the restroom at the pharmacy.

What could the sheriff want to talk to her about, except details she didn't want to give? She felt as if her execution was coming up.

She thought of Rudyard Creek.

Had his death been an execution?

And if so, who had done it?

TWENTY-FIVE

Clemmie parked next to the rental car. She polished the key fob to get rid of prints, using the hem of her blouse and the hand that was not seeping blood. Using her blouse as gloves, she opened the door, set the keys on the floor of the driver's seat, and nudged the door shut with her elbow. The car didn't honk a warning about keys left inside, probably because she hadn't tried to lock it.

She got back in her own car and drove to the strip mall—past the gift shop, UPS, grocery store, and nail salon—and parked at the pharmacy. The rain had not slackened. She opened her umbrella and went into the pharmacy, where she bought a box of large Band-Aids and a disposable cell phone. In their restroom, she washed her finger with the slippery soap from the dispenser, dried it under the high-power hot air, wrapped it tightly in a Band-Aid, and then added a second Band-Aid and a third. Her finger looked like a biscuit. If the sheriff asked, she'd say she cut herself slicing a bagel.

She usually had a hard time opening sealed packages, and invariably, instructions themselves were impenetrable. This time, the cell phone package opened easily but posed an immediate problem: the little phone had to be charged.

She couldn't go home to accomplish that because the sheriff was expecting her at Wendy's. She drove a few hundred yards to Wendy's, went inside, and found a seat with a charging plug.

How long did it take to charge a phone for the first time anyway?

Clemmie fidgeted, staring out Wendy's large windows at the rain.

Johnny Marsh stood on the welcome mat on the shiny hardwood in Helen's tiny foyer, dripping wet from the rainstorm. What had possessed him to come here? Was he really thinking of searching her place? Aside from how ridiculous that was, he'd leave traces everywhere. And where was he going to look, anyway? And for what?

He felt embarrassed and pathetic.

But in fact he hadn't come to find money. He just wanted stuff to happen. Everybody else seemed content with their Sun City lives: their little schedules of bocce and golf, poker and horseshoes, cruises to Aruba and bus trips to Dollywood, babysitting grandchildren and endless dinners out because none of the wives liked to cook anymore. They'd been cooking for half a century, and they were done.

At his age, Johnny had had to face the fact that the conventional, careful life he'd led so long was going to be the only life he led. Okay, so he'd had some affairs during his marriage, and he was having one now. But those weren't adventures. They were routine. He'd never done a thing that stood out, nothing crazy or wild or memorable. He would die in a year or a decade, and he was possessed by regret: *I didn't live hard enough. I didn't dare. I didn't risk.*

It had been a stupefying shock to see the dead body of Wilson in the golf cart. His first thought had been for himself. Get away from what had to be a drug war of some kind. Get Wilson's stuff out of his garage. Make sure Helen sensed nothing; make sure Joyce sensed nothing either. By now, he was mostly shocked that he had not called 911. Even though it had been hideously clear that Wilson was beyond help, the poor man had deserved better than being abandoned to rot.

Johnny's guilt flared up. Ignoring the dead? Sneaking into yet another house? What was he thinking?

What had he been thinking when he'd siphoned off Joyce's money? It was just a game, like weed with Wilson, something to do.

Johnny had known that sooner or later, Joyce would figure out that money was escaping from her ridiculously endowed checking account, and she'd know who was doing it. Joyce would not rat him out. She cared as much for her public and family persona as he did. More, probably. She wasn't going to the police.

He had a perfectly good house to live in. Sometimes he did live there. But he hated living alone. It made him tired to think of finding another girlfriend.

Joyce had been fun while she lasted. A fine cook on the infrequent occasions she bothered. Good company. Somewhat willing in bed, although Johnny was usually past it unless he started using Viagra. Joyce seemed fine with cuddling, and Johnny wondered if this was Nature's plan: all the guys run out of steam, and all the girls get over it.

Except for the light coming in the top half of the front door, Helen's house was dark, all drapes closed, no lamps lit. You couldn't tell that the walls were gold and the paintings bright. It was a cave.

Johnny held his breath to calm himself, and in that silence, he heard somebody else breathe.

He froze.

There was another indrawn breath, purposefully loud, like conversation.

It could not be Helen. She'd driven away.

He turned slowly, as if turning fast would make it worse.

───────────

Clemmie sat in Wendy's, gazing across a long, thin grass island and an access road. Joyce was driving into the grocery-store lot! Joyce was already back? Surely when they had spoken, Joyce had not been nearby. Had she even gone anywhere to start with? Had she been lurking around here, waiting to see Johnny's reaction or something?

But Joyce would not have emptied her fridge just for verisimilitude. She had intended to be gone. The threat of Johnny getting back into the house or the excitement of a murder or perhaps even the rescue of Helen herself had caused Joyce to turn around. How efficient and also terrifying of Joyce to think of buying groceries prior to facing down a chiseling boyfriend she suspected of committing murder.

When a man sat down at Clemmie's table, she actually let out a tiny scream.

"I'm so sorry," said the sheriff. "I didn't mean to startle you, Miz Stephens." He was smiling his sweet smile.

"I didn't see your vehicle," she whispered. He wouldn't necessarily know that the charging phone was hers because it was sitting on a ledge, plugged into a row of outlets. But even if he realized it was hers, he wouldn't give it a thought. Charging phones was as reasonable as ordering a coffee. And although most people had smartphones, quite a few in her generation had stayed with simple clamshell phones. Unless he had seen her own smartphones. Had she taken them out when he was in her living room? Why couldn't she ever remember anything useful?

"You didn't see my squad car because I walked over," he said.

"It's just that I'm still so upset."

"Of course you are, and I didn't help, sneaking up on you. I thought you were expecting me." He wore a thin rain jacket, but his hair was soaked, and probably his trousers and shoes. Inside Wendy's fierce air-conditioning, his hair would dry in a moment, but maybe not his feet. Her own damp feet were so cold they hurt.

"Coffee? Frosty?" he asked.

"How thoughtful of you! Frosty, please. Chocolate." She hadn't had one in years, and when he came back and she licked the edges, the thick, foamy richness was so comforting she wondered why she didn't have these all the time, all day long. Clemmie's tears leaked out. She had used up all her tissues on her bloody finger, so she took a napkin from the stack the sheriff had brought.

"You're too upset to be on your own," said the sheriff. "How about I go back into your house with you, so we'll both know you're safe, while you fill an overnight bag to stay with friends or maybe drive up to Ballantyne and stay in a hotel?"

He was either a southern gentleman eager to comfort her, or a cop who wanted to get into her house and look around, because in order to prove to Clemmie that her house was empty and safe, he'd want to check every room, closet, and, of course, the garage.

The house where Borobasq was, where Johnny had simply walked in.

Borobasq couldn't have killed Wilson.

Johnny could have.

She thought of Johnny's concealed carry. To shoot Wilson in that golf cart, he would have to bend down, undo whatever holster was strapped to his ankle, withdraw the weapon, undo whatever kind of safety lock it had, sit back up, point it, and shoot. Wilson would be laughing. He'd already have disarmed Johnny or shoved him out of the cart.

Clemmie couldn't see Johnny shooting his neighbor in order to grab Borobasq's money. You got a gun license for protection, not assault. And what if he got caught? At their age, what people wanted most was to preserve their good health, but second, she believed, to preserve their record as a good citizen and family man.

Would you kill to stop somebody from telling on you? To stop Wilson from announcing that you used marijuana? But these were drug dealers. Who would they tell? They weren't going to call up the sheriff.

Maybe if you were terrified and couldn't think straight and felt cornered, maybe then you'd shoot. Perhaps it had been self-defense in a tragic, indefensible way: the killer defending his reputation.

But if Johnny had no reason to shoot Wilson, Dom had even less. Wilson was his lifeline. Wilson took him to his doctors, whose records probably contained Wilson's address and phone numbers because he was probably the next of kin. The sheriff would think of that. He probably already had the files. Unless you needed a court order. You probably did.

She thought of him as "the sheriff," but she knew his name perfectly well: Bay Bennett. He had fully merged with his occupation. Which meant he was a danger to her, not an ally.

Joyce and I cannot stay in her house because she can't get in, Clemmie thought. I don't want her to ask Johnny for a key because Johnny and Borobasq are some kind of team.

Clemmie couldn't get a handle on it. Johnny was not evil, just annoying. Unless that was how evil originated: somebody being annoying, somebody else overreacting.

Across the parking lot, Clemmie saw Joyce take up a peculiar and uncomfortable position. She appeared to be on her knees in the back seat, leaning over and shoving stuff around in the hatchback. If it weren't for the pounding rain, she'd have stood on the pavement with the hatchback open, and it would have been much easier.

"Friends have invited me to stay with them," Clemmie told the sheriff, realizing that she had forgotten to text the Dexter River friends back. Three offers. She'd take Marvin up on his. He was such a good man.

Against her will, she had the eternal thought, *Is he married? Is he the one? Will we fall in love?*

Her finger throbbed. Why hadn't she bought Tylenol while she was in the drugstore?

She rejected scenarios involving Johnny. It was Dom who had killed Wilson, some sad family thing, some internal feud or disaster—probably, but not necessarily, over Borobasq's money. It was difficult to use cash even for small purchases now, let alone big ones. It wasn't going to be easy for Dom to support himself on hundred-dollar bills.

"Now, Miz Stephens, the murder took place right inside Dominic Spesante's golf cart, which was in his garage, so Dom is the likely shooter, is that correct?"

Something about the sheriff's inflection told her that he was not making small talk, that this was a gently worded interrogation. "I've completely fallen apart," she said, which was true; she felt as if her head and thoughts had floated somewhere out of sight. "It's because I got caught earlier without my wig. I can't think if I don't have hair."

He was smiling. "I can imagine that. But you do have hair right now. Lovely reddish-brown hair with big curls. You look good."

"I can't possibly look good. I've been crying for a long time. At least, it feels like a long time. I'm so worried about Dom. I'm so sorry about poor Wilson. He was so young. Somewhere he has a mother and father who will be devastated."

Joyce was getting out of her car now, inserting her huge golf umbrella into the air, standing up under its dry cover.

"We haven't been able to trace the Spesantes," said the sheriff.

But then Joyce didn't go to the grocery store after all. She walked toward the gate, head and shoulders hidden by the umbrella. Perhaps Shirley or Betty Anne had instructed her to park here, because knowing Joyce, she had a running conversation with every woman in the pod, all of whom were better talkers and gossipers than Helen, and her girlfriends had explained that it was too congested to drive down Blue Lilac right now.

"You're the only person upset about Dom," he said.

Clemmie's eyes blurred and ran over. "He wasn't a nice man. But I don't want anybody to have killed anybody. It lasts forever, you know. Death." Although fifty years ago she hadn't minded that somebody killed somebody. She just hadn't wanted anyone to get caught. She still didn't.

He stirred his coffee, which he hadn't touched. It was just an activity. "I deal with a fair number of murders," he said. "Most killers are people who didn't stop to think. There's no plan, like in a movie or a TV series. They get furious or scared, and they lash out. They finish killing, and then what? What to do about the body? What to clean up? What to hide? What to say? Where to go? I've never come across a killing where the killer was ready for the aftermath. It's very scary to take a life, and when they see what they've done, they drive aimlessly around or head home or get drunk. Heading home is the number-one choice. They didn't plan ahead of the murder, and they can't plan after it. Even if home is the least safe place, they feel safe there. Stuff happens, they trip on themselves, we find them."

He was using the currently acceptable *they* in order not to say *he* or *she*. Never be gender-specific.

Is the sheriff being pronoun careful because he thinks *I* did it? she wondered. Does he look at me and see a possible killer of Wilson? Or do I give off vibrations of a killing fifty years ago?

Joyce took a detour around a parking-lot puddle. She obviously didn't want to ruin her good sandals. Clemmie was touched. Even with a murder to consider, Joyce remembered her shoes.

"So I'm told that your neighbor Joyce likes to keep an eye on things. Can you give her a ring, and I'll talk to her for a moment on your phone?"

Clemmie was not that far gone. The sheriff already had Joyce's cell number because he had called Joyce already, and she didn't pick up. Either he thought she would pick up if the caller ID said Helen Stephens, or he wanted to get his hands on Clemmie's cell.

"Joyce is on her way to Galveston," she said. It wasn't really a lie, because Joyce had told her that this morning.

"What's up with those two? They've each changed the locks today."

So somebody had told him that Joyce had had the locks changed early in the morning, and then he'd seen for himself when Johnny changed the locks an hour ago. Or was it many hours ago? Or just a minute? What a worthless witness she would make. "It's almost comical, isn't it? I suppose everybody in Sun City is slightly comical, when senior moments pile up."

He didn't disagree. "Would you give Joyce a call for me though?"

Joyce disappeared through the gate.

One-handedly, her bandaged hand in her lap, Clemmie set her Sun City phone on the table, clicked it open, clicked contacts, scrolled to Joyce, clicked again, and held it against her ear.

"Helen," said Joyce immediately, "are you okay?"

"Hi, Joyce. I'm fine, but I'm over at Wendy's with the sheriff, who is hoping to talk to you."

"I'm in traffic, honey. Bye for now."

Talking with a sheriff was not on Clemmie's preferred list either, but surely Joyce had come back so she could get in on the action.

Surely she'd rather hustle back here and talk about the dreamboat in Clemmie's car than go home—a home she knew she couldn't get into because Clemmie had explained that the locks were changed.

Clemmie thought of Johnny in her own house, cozied up with her home invader. Did Joyce have a part in that? It was inconceivable.

The sheriff asked more questions but Clemmie couldn't listen, let alone answer. He got a phone call of his own and frowned and looked gleeful at the same time. "I have to get back. Want me to walk you home?"

Clemmie was desperate for him to leave her alone. "You're so kind. I'll just sit here for a bit and finish the Frosty you were so thoughtful to buy for me."

TWENTY-SIX

After Rudyard Creek's death, Clemmie came home often to visit her parents and her brother and sister-in-law. Soon there was a little niece, Peggy, to adore. Clemmie yearned to see Billy, but she and Stan had promised never to cross each other's path again. When she broke that promise a few years later and drove to their house in the hope of glimpsing Billy, they had moved, and she did not have the heart to try to find them yet again.

The wise choice at that point was to go back to being Clementine Lakefield, ending her difficult double life, because the murder of her stalker had ended the reason for stealing Helen's name. Clemmie would reenter Ohio State, finish up her credits, and get a degree after all.

But the world had lost interest in Latin. Schools all across the nation were dropping it from the curriculum. By the time she completed that degree—which would take at least one year because she had no teaching history as Clementine Lakefield and would have to student teach—she very probably could not get a Latin job at all.

So she remained Helen Stephens in Ohio.

It wasn't until Facebook was invented that Clemmie found her family again. Very early, when people barely knew what Facebook was, her students coaxed Miss Stephens to get a Facebook page. She posted nothing and never put up a photograph, but the kids showed her how to friend others. She typed in William Ames Boone, and there was her grown son with nice photographs of himself, his wife, and their children. He carefully listed his old high school, college, current employer, and town of residence.

He accepted her friend request, apparently not even wondering who she was. That wouldn't happen now, but when Facebook began, people weren't fearful about lost privacy. They just got a kick out of their high friend numbers.

William A. Boone lost his enthusiasm early on and rarely posted, but his two children, whom she also friended, posted all the time. She discovered Instagram and followed them there too. She learned a stunning amount about her family from Kelsey and Mack's photographs, videos, and captions, and when the family moved to Charlotte, Clemmie retired immediately and moved just south of Charlotte to the warm, friendly enclosure that was Sun City.

She imagined the Boones discovering that this creepy woman

had been a "friend" on Facebook for years, had stared at them from church pews, even once followed them into a restaurant, because the children posted virtually everything. She even knew what they ordered when they ate out because Kelsey liked to put photographs of her dinner plate on Instagram.

When the sheriff had also passed through the Sun City gate, Clemmie left Wendy's with her new phone. It was still so hot outside. Under her umbrella, she headed for her car.

It's Saturday, she thought. Tomorrow is church.

People liked the same row every week, so Clemmie always knew which pew at St. Saviour's the Boone family would take. Clemmie thought about sitting directly behind them, because then her actual son, her Billy, would turn and smile and shake her hand and say, "Peace be with you," and maybe at last Clemmie would actually find peace.

No, she thought sadly. The way to find peace is to stop this. Never go to that church again. Stop following Kelsey and Mack on Facebook and Instagram.

Stop.

Her teary eyes landed on Joyce's small, sporty lime-green car. She noticed now that the hatchback was full of flowers. Why would a person leaving for Texas, sufficiently careful to empty her refrigerator, buy armloads of fresh flowers?

Clemmie walked over to Joyce's car.

She definitely needed cataract surgery because it was just

Joyce's matched luggage, bought new for their last cruise. Two were Vera Bradley with those recognizable bright flowers on black backgrounds—and how she could possibly have thought they were real, she didn't know. A third was a bright-pink hard-sided case, probably not Vera Bradley; and a fourth, barely visible, crushed by everything else, was a small, worn navy-blue duffel bag, the sort of thing Johnny might own, but Joyce would take straight to Goodwill, if not the garbage.

Clemmie hurried over the rain-slick asphalt to the Sun City gate and tapped in the code. In its slow-motion way, the pedestrian gate opened for the third time in maybe five minutes, and Clemmie went down the tiny hill, expecting to see Joyce fighting her front-door lock. But it was the sheriff's back she saw going in Dom's front door, and there in Joyce's driveway sat Johnny's white Avalon. The garage door was up. Joyce must have gotten in by bringing the remote control from her own car. Clemmie walked through the garage and, amazingly, on this day of murder, Joyce had not locked the utility-room door behind her, so Clemmie went on in, calling, "Yoo-hoo!"

"I'm in the bathroom!"

Joyce had plopped her handbag down on the kitchen counter. It was a sweet robin's-egg-blue patent-leather bag, shaped like a small A-frame, with a fragile handle. It wasn't even half the size of her usual choice of handbag. The little purse definitely did not contain Joyce's Kindle, which she was never without, or Joyce's—

—gun, thought Clemmie. Joyce does not have her gun.

A woman sufficiently concerned about protection to have a concealed-carry license would take her gun when traveling several hundred miles. Maybe Joyce had left it in her car, under the seat. But Joyce knew now about the murder on her street. Wasn't this the proper time to be armed? Or could she have forgotten to pack her gun when she set out for Texas? After all, nobody had known about the murder when Joyce drove away. She had been in a tizzy over Johnny and perhaps not thinking straight.

But when you changed purses, you dumped everything out on the bed and transferred it. You would notice a revolver, or whatever weapon Joyce owned, lying on the bedspread. You wouldn't forget it.

The toilet flushed.

Clemmie opened the large, shallow kitchen drawer where Joyce and Johnny kept small miscellany: ChapStick, paper clips, Magic Markers, clip-on sunglasses, business cards from people who washed windows, a measuring tape. She removed Joyce's spare car keys and hurried back through the garage, across Blue Lilac Lane, through the gate, and over the parking lots. The rain was helpful; people, including police people, were inside largely viewless villas. She got into her own car and drove around Wendy's parking lot to park alongside Joyce's car.

She got out in the rain, not bothering with the umbrella, and her chestnut wig shed water in its polyester way. With Joyce's key, Clemmie popped the hatch. Joyce was tall and strong and could move anything and reach anything easily. For Clemmie it was a struggle to get the three suitcases out of the way. In the end she had to drag out the duffel bag by climbing in the back seat, just as Joyce had. She hauled the duffel into the rear bench and unzipped the single, fat top zipper.

Bundled hundred-dollar bills.

Clemmie rocked the duffel back and forth so that the bundles shifted. There was nothing inside it but money. The bag weighed much more than she expected it to, which meant it was worth more than she had guessed. She heaved the duffel onto her front seat and relocked the green car. She didn't look around to see if she had witnesses. If you looked as if you knew what you were doing, everybody assumed you knew what you were doing. And besides, in a grocery-store lot, everybody was carrying and moving bags.

Life is full of choices. Clemmie had made many bad ones. She wished she could have a lot more time to think through her next choice. She needed days or weeks, not minutes. What did she want most right now? She wanted Borobasq out of her life. How could she do that? Give him the money he came for.

She drove back into Sun City, turned into the golf-course parking lot, pulled up next to the unlocked rental car, transferred the duffel bag onto the floor of the front passenger seat, and sat back in her own car, her own safe, tiny space, with its automatic locks. She was weeping now. The air-conditioning chilled her right down to the bone.

She took refuge, as a person did these days, in her cell phone.

Googling filled one's mind and used one's hand. It felt as if one were accomplishing something. The weight of a million dollars in hundred-dollar bills, the internet informed her, was twenty-two pounds.

Clemmie usually bought a five-pound bag of sugar. The duffel bag was definitely three of those, and it might be four, which certainly explained Borobasq's zeal in searching for it. It didn't explain how Wilson had shoplifted a million dollars, but this was not Clemmie's problem. Nor was it Wilson's now, for that matter.

As for how it came into Joyce's possession, Clemmie would think about that in a minute. She checked Borobasq's cell phone number in her family phone but used the burner phone to text him. The new phone used the relatively antique method of getting the alphabet from multitapping numbers, but eventually she achieved the message she wanted. Cash in front seat of rental car.

She sent it, pleased with the anonymity because anybody could have sent this—Dom or those Cogland people or Joyce or Johnny—but as it made the little *whoosh* sound of delivery, she realized that she was the only one on that list who knew about the rental car. Borobasq would absolutely know the message was from Clemmie. She wasn't crafty after all. She was just an old woman staggering around the way the sheriff had described, aimlessly rushing here and there, trying to find a safe place.

She prayed Borobasq would act immediately.

She drove down Marigold and this time turned into White Lily and parked facing out at the back of the cul-de-sac. Unless he walked out the gate into the shopping center and hiked all the way around, which was a mile or more, Borobasq had to cross the street or the yards in front of her.

Now, on her real cell phone, she looked up the number of his airport rental-car agency and then called them on the disposable phone. "Your rental, about to be returned, Virginia plates, dark-red sedan, is full of drugs and drug money. Call the police." She hung up before the person replied. She did another Google search, made another call, and gave a similar message to airport security.

The disposable phone had outlived its usefulness, if indeed it had ever been useful, if indeed she had achieved anything except complexity. She would get rid of it and its amazing amount of wrapping material as soon as she saw Borobasq on the way to his car.

———————

Johnny could barely see in the darkened rooms of Helen Stephens's villa, but standing there was a young man with stylish sunglasses tight to his cheeks, a cap pulled low, and a black jacket. He looked like somebody out of a film. He said nothing. He was motionless.

Was he a cop? A drug dealer? A murderer?

"Hey," said Johnny, trying to sound relaxed. "I live across the street. I'm checking on Helen." He tried to smile. His lips wouldn't go there.

"How come you didn't ring the bell? Or knock?" The voice was soft. Like something that could suffocate Johnny.

"We're all very close friends. We go in and out of each other's houses all the time."

"You didn't think it would scare her? Somebody just coming and walking around? When there's been a murder next door?"

"I wasn't thinking." Johnny spread his hands in a kind of shrug and took a step toward the front door.

The man blocked him. He wasn't as big as Johnny, but he had the wiry strength of youth—strength Johnny no longer had even on a good day, and this wasn't one. He felt the jealousy of youth that sometimes assaulted him. And he felt stupid. All these years of hunting and shooting, and he was without protection. It sat in a boot on the floor of a garage.

I couldn't use it anyway, he thought. Guy's probably an undercover cop.

"You knew she wasn't home, or you'd have called out once you opened the door."

"You're right," said Johnny, coming up with a brilliant idea. "I saw somebody moving around in here, but the house should have been empty. What are *you* doing here?"

"The cops are on the other side of this wall. Why didn't you have them check out the movement in this house?"

"I get confused. I'm on a lot of medications, you know. Early-onset Alzheimer's. You take Aricept. It makes you cuckoo." He wasn't taking Aricept and didn't have memory problems, so now he'd told yet more lies he would have to deal with later, and then it occurred to him that he probably *did* have early-onset Alzheimer's, because what else would make him cross the street in the middle of a murder investigation and creep into the neighbor's house?

"You're a dealer," said the young man. "You and Wilson and Dom and Helen."

Johnny's instincts had been correct. Helen was the key. Amazing. "Nah. Not me. All I did was keep Wilson's stash for him. I've moved it to my car. You can have it." Once we're out in the street, he thought, I'll yell for the cops. Actually, they'll be on the street too. No, they won't because of the rain.

Johnny edged closer to the door. The guy won't hurt me, he told himself. He can't because he's right; there are cops on the other side of the wall. Johnny took another step, caught his wet shoe on the edge of the welcome mat, and staggered.

All advice to seniors and their long-term health stressed that you should never have throw rugs because falling was your worst enemy, and throw rugs were a frequent cause. Johnny had never fallen. He was proud of his balance and his ability to play softball, so this fall happened now, he supposed, from too much to think about. He put out his hands to catch himself and fell against the legs of the home invader.

———————

Everyone around here was ancient and pathetic, completely past it, but the dude lunged at him and Boro didn't give it a thought. He slashed as he jumped back. The blade cut across the old guy's arm and chest, opening the flesh of the forearm and thinly slicing the breasts of old age.

Shocked by the wound, the old guy swung his arm up, flinging an arc of blood droplets across the tiny hall and onto Boro's clothing and the wall.

Boro knew instantly that slashing this dude was the worst mistake he'd ever made. There was no walking away from all this blood. Boro had just escalated himself into a serious corner. The cops next door weren't simply floundering; they were so confused they were wandering up and down the block on the off chance they'd stumble onto something. Stumble into this unit, and they would have something.

This guy didn't have Boro's money. If he'd had it, he would've stayed home and counted it. He was here to search the Latin teacher's place, thinking *she* had it. But she didn't. Neither did villas two and three.

Boro should have taken the opportunities the old lady gave him—her car, the reporter trick, the back gate—but no, he had to get cute and keep searching for cash that had undoubtedly gone with that guy Dom. And this guy, bleeding all over the place, he knew enough about the money to hunt for it. So he was part of this. Boro couldn't come to grips with the fact that four of the nine villas on Blue Lilac Lane were in on this. It was practically a cartel.

Boro removed the guy's cell phone from one of his pockets and a fat ring of keys from another. The guy had an amazing number of keys. What—was he prepared to enter every house in the cul-de-sac?

The guy was hugging himself to stop the bleeding, but blood slid steadily out of the wounds. From his knees, like an animal sacrifice with its throat cut, except it was his chest, he looked up at Boro. "I take blood thinners," he said wildly. "It won't clot! Hand me a towel or something. Call an ambulance."

TWENTY-SEVEN

I knew Wilson traded drugs, thought Johnny. I knew it was a dangerous world, and instead of running away and slamming the door on it, I was all happy and excited to be close to crime. But this is what crime really is.

It seemed so unlikely, here in Helen Stephens's tasteful little house, that he was cut and bleeding and on his knees before Dom's killer.

"Which house do you live in?" the man said, as if it were a crime to live in a house at all.

Johnny couldn't point because he was gripping his wounds tightly. He straightened his back so he could see out the glass top of Helen's door and nodded his head toward Joyce's, and was immediately confused. The garage door was open. Hadn't he closed it?

Hadn't he been working in there, moving his stash with the door down? Hadn't he then come out the front door when he walked over here? He hadn't come out the garage and left the door up, had he? His Avalon, with Wilson's stash in the trunk, still sat in the drive. Had he locked his car? Of course he couldn't remember that either.

"Anybody live with you?"

"My wife," he said, which was easier than explaining his relationship to Joyce. Which was over anyway.

A squad car with a SHERIFF decal in foot-high letters across the entire side moved slowly through their slot of vision. Johnny didn't know whether to feel safer or deader with the sheriff gone.

And then, amazingly, Joyce opened the interior door at the back of the garage and looked out at the street. "She's home," said Johnny, astonished. How could she be home? Where was her car? Why wasn't she south of Columbia by now? Or even in Atlanta?

She'd sent Johnny two texts. One about the checkbook, full of fury and her decision to kick him out; one a bit later about going to Galveston to stay with her sister until she had calmed down. But she was right here. Had she been home when he'd cleaned out the garage? Had she watched from some spy position he couldn't think of?

"Why wouldn't your wife be home?" asked the man.

"She went to Galveston. I mean, I thought she did."

"And?"

Johnny flailed. It felt as if he needed to protect Joyce. But from what? What could Joyce's decisions possibly mean to this guy, this killer of Wilson?

Johnny held the lips of the wound in his forearm, trying to seal the blood in. "She decided to visit her sister," he said, and it came out in a whisper, as if he were already too weak to talk normally. "But here she is after all. I guess she knew I'd miss her, or she figured Helen would need her, what with a murder next door."

His knees hurt. He was going to have trouble getting up, if indeed he was allowed to get up. But no matter the outcome here, Johnny was ruined. He almost hoped the guy would slash him again. Then he'd be the victim, guilty of nothing, and if they found him guilty of something, he'd be too dead to suffer from shame and prison.

The man jabbed his knife in Johnny's face. Johnny was afraid he was going to shit in his pants.

"When did she decide to drive away?" the man asked intensely—as if it mattered, as if Joyce had anything to do with anything.

"Um. Last night, I guess. I got her email, um, I think this morning."

"She didn't talk to you about it?"

"No."

"That's her car? The white Avalon?"

"No, that's my car. I don't see her car."

"Where would hers be?"

Joyce hated exercise. She never walked a step if she could avoid it. She yearned for the day she could have a handicapped sticker and park adjacent to stores. But she had walked from somewhere. Shirley's or Betty Anne's? "Maybe she had to park around the corner, like everybody else."

Together they stared across the street, through the rain, at the empty garage; at Joyce, chunky and oddly aggressive-looking, stomping back into the house and shutting the door behind her, but leaving the garage itself open.

She's not worried about anything, thought Johnny, or she'd lower the garage door for extra protection. She knows I'm here because my car is. She left that garage open because she's expecting me. She's ready to talk about checkbooks. She's ready to make peace, or she's ready to kill me.

"But suddenly, last night, she needed to drive to Texas," said the man slowly. He gave this serious consideration and then said, "Listen up. I'm Jason. Jason the reporter. You're giving me an interview. We're going to sit in your living room with your wife and chat."

Johnny could think of no reason whatsoever that this man would want to fake an interview with Joyce, who, now that he considered it, had come home because an across-the-street murder was too exciting to miss. He wondered if his own death would be exciting. Probably not. It would just be stupid.

Johnny heard the faint pulse of the man's cell phone vibrating. The man glanced at it, frowned, half laughed, and then looked thoughtful. This is it, thought Johnny. This is when he offs me because he's got places to go, people to see, and I'm in his way.

The man stepped into Helen's kitchen, removed the crisply ironed dish towel hanging neatly on the crosswise handle of Helen's oven, and handed it to Johnny, who had a hard time letting go of the arm wound and a harder time trying to wrap it. The slice was sideways across his forearm and not deep; it just needed some stitches. The problem was not the wound; it was that it wouldn't clot without—without what? Did they give you some kind of antidote for Coumadin? Or did they hook you up with blood donations so it poured into you faster than it poured out of you?

Johnny got the edges of the tea towel in his fist and pulled them tight, pressing the wound edges together. There was no way to solve the slice across his chest, which wasn't serious. Mostly the fabric of his shirt was sliced, but in one place, where he'd gotten fat and sloppy and all but had boobs, the knife had caught the flesh. If he weren't on blood thinners, he'd probably be okay with extra-large Band-Aids.

How had this guy gotten in here? Maybe Helen had given a key to Dom, even though she said she hadn't, and what if Dom and this guy routinely slid into Helen's house? With her knowledge? Or not?

He had a vision of Helen sleeping in peace, not knowing that a mobster with a knife came and went from her home.

When Johnny had trotted over here, ten minutes or a lifetime ago, he had thought that she was part of it. That was why he came—to find the money she had. But kneeling here, he could not imagine Helen associating with this guy and certainly not with Dom. If nothing else, drug dealers didn't fold, let alone iron, their tea towels. They didn't *own* tea towels.

He thought, If this guy killed Wilson, where's Dom? Is he dead too? Is there a second body? Is that what is keeping the police busy? Dealing with another murder in another place?

The man in Helen's house had somehow become a different person and now held a notebook, pencil, and iPad, while a camera hung jauntily around his neck. He had tilted the sunglasses up high on his forehead. He not only looked normal, he looked handsome. And young. Twenty, twenty-five. How old had Wilson been? Wilson's layers of fat had obscured his age, but Johnny thought he'd probably been about twenty-five too.

There was no sign of the knife.

"Get up," said the boy.

Johnny had to let go of his dish towel and sort of crawl himself up the wall until he was standing. He left bloody handprints on the paint.

"Open the door," said the boy.

Johnny opened Helen's front door. I can't bring him into my home, he thought. Joyce is there. I'll stop in the middle of the street. Yell for help. There must still be cops at Dom's.

He cinched the tea towel around his arm again. He was dripping blood, but it would leave no trace on the pavement. The rain would wash it away. Although the rain was slackening. Large patches of sky were suddenly blue. The storm was going to end in a minute, and everybody would come out. The police would save him. Johnny would explain that he had gone into Helen's house planning to rescue her.

The guy took Johnny's elbow, which was a good idea because Johnny felt as if he could pass out, and they stepped over a gutter running with water like a tiny creek.

With the tip of the knife pressing into his skin, which was thin from years of too much sun, Johnny forgot about stopping in the middle of the street. The boy took him up to the Avalon and said softly, "You're driving." He opened the door, and Johnny dropped into the driver's seat, thinking, Oh, thank God, we're not going into the house. Joyce is safe.

The boy moved into the passenger seat with the speed of youth and said, "Turn the car on. Get out of here."

Johnny pressed the Start button and the engine caught, because the boy had Johnny's key fob in his possession, and proximity was all it required. It didn't know it was in the hands of a kidnapper. Johnny backed out of the driveway, maneuvered around parked vehicles, the steering wheel sliding in his bloody grip.

"We're going to the airport," said the boy. "You're going to drop me off, and you can head to a doctor."

Johnny was going to live through this? Come on. The guy couldn't trust him not to go to the airport police before he went for medical help. I'm going to be dead, thought Johnny, unless I think of a way to avoid it, and right now I'm so scared, I'm dumb as a rock.

He drove past a media van, people already emerging as the rain petered out, and past parked cars full of gawkers, also opening their doors, and even a sheriff's car, but nobody got out of that, and then they were beyond the press of vehicles and the boy said, "Turn into the golf club."

He directed Johnny to a space next to a plain maroon sedan and gave Johnny a captivating smile. "My money is in that car. We're going to split it, my man. I'm going to buy you off." He leaned over, turned off the Avalon, and got out.

Johnny considered restarting the car, which he could do, because even in the boy's pocket, the fob was close enough. But he couldn't drive forward because there was another car in front of him, and if he tried to back up, the open passenger door would hit the sedan. Johnny could not make plans with blood oozing out of him. His mental measurement was that he hadn't actually lost much. Not a cup, say. If you donated blood, didn't they take a cup? A pint? How big was a pint? But all you needed afterward was a cookie and a glass of orange juice. Losing a cup of blood was not death.

The boy hoisted a duffel bag out of the maroon car and was back in the Avalon in a moment, tossing the duffel bag on the center console between himself and Johnny. "Open it," he ordered.

Johnny let go of the steering wheel and the dish towel.

"First wipe your hand on your khakis."

Johnny cleaned blood off his right hand, although certainly not all of it. The zipper was fat, and its ends met in the middle. He gripped one tab and unzipped toward himself, and there, piled and stacked, were hundred-dollar bills. His jaw dropped. He occasionally got hundreds when he cashed a check, but he didn't like hundreds. He didn't even like fifties that much. Twenties were more service-able, and anyway, he generally used a card.

"Pick up the top one," said the boy.

Johnny picked it up.

"I need to know it isn't torn newspaper in the middle of the stack," said the boy. "Shuffle it."

Johnny shuffled. It was $100 bills all the way through. Wow.

Whose money was this? Was it Dom's? Wilson's? What was it doing in this car? How much was it altogether? He couldn't multiply intelligently.

He looked at the knife guy for clues. What was going on here?

What was going on was that Knife Boy had taken a video of Johnny on his cell phone. He held it up and played it. There was Johnny, eagerly unzipping the duffel, feeling among the packages, removing one, shuf-fling it, nodding, holding it up like a trophy. Even smiling a little.

"So," said the boy, "this will convict you. You get to keep that cash, but remember, I can send you to prison whenever I'm in the mood. Get out of here. We're going to the airport."

Johnny drove north on Route 521.

Red lights, green lights, merging onto I-485. Interstate traffic was thick and slow. After I drop him off, thought Johnny, I'll go to an urgent care up on that side of town.

They'd give him whatever meds he needed and stitch up the slit on his arm, and he'd say he'd been fooling around with a hunting knife and playacting or something and been stupid or whatever.

He'd drive to his own house and then...

No, first get rid of the drugs in one trash can after another in various fast-food locations. Then drive home.

Or, when I drop Knife Boy off, I can go to the police. I'll say I got kidnapped by a murderer. He had a knife. He made me take this money.

But when the murderer was caught—because on a plane, that would be a cinch; they'd be waiting wherever he landed—Knife Boy would play the video. "Johnny was part of it," he would say, and that video would prove him right by showing gloating coconspirator Johnny with his cash and Wilson's stash, each container covered with Johnny's fingerprints.

Twenty-Eight

Barbara Farmer brought her gun.

Originally, she had it in her purse, but she decided it would be hard to reach and she might fumble. She transferred it to the pocket of her pants where it didn't really fit and was uncomfortable, so she shoved it into the waistband, taut against her shirt. The fad of wearing an untucked shirt had not yet begun, and it never occurred to Barbara to pull out the shirttail, so the gun was exposed. She wore a cardigan to hide it. She was sick with anxiety. It was fine to be armed at a shooting range or when hunting. It was not fine when going to talk with a human being.

Would she really shoot him?

Was she not a civilized person who wanted a trial and a jury and a legal outcome?

She patted the gun for courage, appalled to find herself excited in a hot, dark, shuddery way. Was this how Rudyard Creek felt just before he attacked a victim?

It was late afternoon when Barbara and Clemmie and Rudyard Creek came together at the little picnic area off the two-lane shore-line route. The shadows at this time of year were long and soft, ready to lie down and become night. The sun sank and dusk came on and Rudyard Creek was laughing.

It was what Barbara remembered best: that he was laughing at them. Enjoying himself. It had the strange, disjointed feel of a party with guests and jokes.

And then, so quickly that neither girl was prepared, Rudyard Creek attacked Clemmie, ripping her clothing with a violence that made both girls scream. They had underestimated their enemy. Clemmie was utterly helpless on this night when the girls had planned for strength and success.

Barbara hadn't realized how frightened she would be of her own gun when it was human flesh she was shooting at. Her hands shook. She couldn't even aim at Rudyard Creek because he was wrapped around Clemmie.

Clemmie took the only defensive route open to her, dropping down, hoping the weight of her body would at least partially remove her from Rudyard Creek's grip. When Clemmie sagged backward, Barbara had a clear sight of his chest, and she fired.

She missed entirely.

She actually looked back down at her gun to see why it had missed, and Rudyard Creek, still grinning, abandoned Clemmie for Barbara.

Years later, Barbara would read that fifty percent of armed combat within six feet missed a fatal shot. Half! Seventy percent of armed combat within twenty-five feet missed altogether. Being good in target practice had little to do with being accurate in real life.

Rudyard Creek didn't want to be shot on her second try. He jumped left and swerved, an athlete executing a play on a basketball court. She didn't know where to aim. He was grinning like a jack-o'-lantern, his teeth too big, his smile all excited. Like *she* was the victim, not him.

She got off a second shot, and it hit him but didn't stop him, and he was upon her.

All that practice, she thought, and it had nothing to do with reality.

But reality changed so fast. Stan Boone came up behind Rudyard Creek and whacked him in the skull with the wooden-handled, cast-iron grid off a charcoal grill.

Barbara actually heard the cranium crack.

Horrified by what he had done, Stan hurled the grid into the darkness.

They stood over Rudyard Creek—Barbara, Stan, and Clemmie—as the moon went behind clouds and the stars failed. Barbara was weeping, Stan was muttering, Clemmie was panting, and unconscious Rudyard Creek was bleeding from the gunshot wound and the smashed head.

They could synchronize their stories and sell the death of Rudyard Creek as self-defense. Which it was.

But Stan was desperate to stay uninvolved. He didn't want his son to know how horrible his natural father had been nor how violent his adopted father could get. And there was a strong chance that the law would not consider them innocent; that the law would decide this was a conspiracy, and all three were guilty of murder.

Barbara didn't want her family or her as-yet-unknown future husband and children to know she'd been raped at all, let alone that she had shot a man.

In the rushing dark, the man on the ground was barely visible even to the three hovering over him. He was nothing but a mound among picnic tables. A rock, perhaps, or a shrub. No one would see him 'til morning, and maybe not then, because who would come to a picnic area at breakfast?

"You two go," said Clemmie. "I'll clean up."

Was Rudyard Creek's chest still moving?

Barbara whispered, "There will be fingerprints."

"Only on your gun," said Clemmie. "Take it with you. Get rid of it in some other state, some other time. As for the grill, I'll find it and get rid of it, Mr. Boone. Go! If you're found here, Rudyard Creek can destroy you even though he's dead."

Barbara was shaking. "But...but what will happen to you?"

"Nothing. Nobody knows I ever had anything to do with this man. Go, Barbara. Now. Any moment, another car could drive up."

Barbara fled.

Stan Boone didn't. "You are so brave," he told Clemmie. "I'm ashamed of how I acted toward you. I apologize."

Clemmie had no time for this. She herded him toward the little lane. "Drive away. You owe it to your son and mine to get out of here."

"I can't let you pay for this."

"Nobody will pay for it. I'll get the grill and be out of here in half a minute. Your job is to bring up my son."

He trotted down the gravel lane, headed for wherever he had hidden his car.

Rudyard Creek made a tiny sound. He was still alive.

Clemmie was now many paces away. She could barely make him out, let alone some small, dark grid with a small wooden handle. She swept the soles of her shoes over the grass, crossing back and forth, but she didn't turn up the grill. She got on her hands and knees and crept under the picnic table and crawled in circles. Nothing.

She pictured the melee and the four combatants attacking, throwing, shifting, hurling. She walked in wider circles, sliding her shoes in the grass and gravel. She bumped into the coach's car and pushed herself away.

The moon came out, and its silvery, cold light cast faint, unhelpful shadows. Any minute now, a necking couple, a police car on a routine drive, or a sleepy driver needing to doze might appear. The grill could be fifty feet away in the woods. The police will find it, thought Clemmie, but I won't.

She told herself that Stan's fingerprints would not stick to wood or greasy, caked metal, because for sure, nobody had ever scrubbed the grids in these barbecues.

Clemmie did not touch Rudyard Creek. She did not take his pulse. She did not choose to run to her car, drive to a pay phone and call the operator, requesting an ambulance. When she was quite sure that the coach's breathing had ended, she hiked to her rental car, ducking into the trees and weeds at the side of the road when cars went by. She had parked at a grimy, closed-for-the-night car-repair shop where one more car just blended in. She had a room in a motel several towns north, halfway to the airport, the kind of motel where you didn't go past the night clerk to reach your room but parked in front of it. She had used the credit card of Helen Stephens. There was no trace of Clementine Lakefield in Connecticut.

Over the coming years, when her niece was in elementary school, Peggy's favorite board game was Clue. Peggy never tired of Clue. Was the murderer Colonel Mustard or Professor Plum? Was it in the library or the billiard room? Was it with the rope or the candlestick?

Clemmie, playing with Peggy, would remember the silvery light and the body in the dark under the trees.

What had been the murder weapon? The grill or the bullet?

Who had committed the murder?

The woman with the gun?

The father with the grill?

Or Clemmie, who waited for him to die?

Clemmie sat in her car on White Lily, engine running and air-conditioning on high, watching between houses, keeping an eye on all grass and sidewalks. She didn't watch cars because Borobasq didn't have one, but now she glimpsed Johnny driving his Avalon out of the pod.

He had a passenger. It had to be Borobasq. Or no, actually, it could be Joyce. It could be all three of them!

How incredible that Johnny—big, blustery horseshoes-and-poker-playing Johnny—was partners with Dom and Wilson and the Coglands. But it was more incredible that the money had been in Joyce's car.

When Joyce had seen a duffel bag she had not packed in the back of her car, she would have looked inside. Had she looked inside for the first time when she parked at the grocery store a little while ago? Whether or not she'd known already what was in it, she certainly knew now. And what about Dom? Was Dom dictating this action? It was impossible to imagine Dom in charge of anything, let alone Joyce.

So...Texas. Was it about sisters? Or about taking cash to safety? And if it was either of those, why come back?

Clemmie thought about Dom's smelly, messy, sorry old place. It had not been kept or swept clean like the Coglands'. Dom didn't care that his fingerprints smeared every switch plate and counter. He had not paused to take his toothbrush or cell phone charger.

He had left in a great hurry or been taken in a hurry, but he had not left with the money. So what was the rush? It could only be that having killed Wilson, Dom decided to go while the going was good.

Johnny and Joyce had something to do with the money, but they had nothing to do with Wilson's death. And in any event, they were gone, because Borobasq had gotten Clemmie's message about the cash in the rental car and had taken his partners to collect it.

The rainstorm ended abruptly, as if the weather gods had gotten bored and slammed the door. The sun was glaring, the puddles were steaming, and the sky was Carolina blue. At warp speed, reporters reappeared, neighbors trotted out, gawkers returned. Deliveries were completed, and plumbers and cable-TV repairmen showed up for their appointments. Dog walkers emerged. The landscape crew moved on to the next pod.

Clemmie wanted to get rid of Joyce's spare key and the burner phone. She wanted to go to the doctor. Her finger hurt so much that she yearned for stitches to hold the edges together. *Please, please, shove a needle through my skin.*

She put the family smartphone and the Sun City smartphone into her purse, leaving the burner phone and Joyce's spare car keys in her skirt pockets. She had no plan. She leaned against the car window and looked straight into long nostrils and a fat chin. Clemmie screamed.

Betty Anne was laughing and knocking on the car window, and Clemmie pressed a button and it rolled down. The heat was horrible, as if her skin were being ironed.

"I really caught you by surprise, Helen," Betty Anne said proudly. She held out a plastic-wrapped coffee cake on a big, heavy-duty paper plate. "My famous plum cake. It's my ticket into Joyce's. Nobody stops a woman offering a fresh-out-of-the-oven coffee cake. Especially not Joyce. She loves it when I host canasta because she can't get enough of my baking. Come on. Shirley and I are going over to get all the details. I saw Joyce come back, I saw Johnny drive off. He's been monitoring the situation, which means that Joyce will know everything."

Clemmie was still hoping that her dear friend did not in fact know everything, that Joyce was somehow a bystander. "Today of all days, Betty Anne, you paused to turn on your stove and bake?"

"I always keep desserts in my freezer. It's so hot out, the cake will defrost during the walk over. Come on."

"I think you should let the sheriff handle things."

"He drove away," said Shirley dismissively, "which seems to be the main skill of this police force." She opened the car door to make Clemmie get out.

"Don't let's go," said Clemmie. "They've had some sort of

altercation, which is why they both changed the locks. Let them sort it out."

Shirley beamed. "We want the details on that too."

The house would be locked because they had all left. On the other hand, if Joyce was still home, then she wasn't part of a triumvirate of drug thieves, and Clemmie could sneak the car keys back while Betty Anne and Shirley grilled Joyce. I'll put her keys back, make my excuses, head home, lock my doors, and it'll be over, whatever it is, and I can think about cold cases and my old life, my real life, my future life. How much will be destroyed, and how much does any of it matter? How many terrible mistakes have I made here, and what will my prison sentence be?

Or take a nap.

Clemmie turned off her car, took the keys out of the ignition, dropped them in her pocket along with the burner phone and Joyce's keys, and lurched out of the front seat. It was difficult for a short person to purchase a vehicle that actually worked in her favor. Leaving her bag in the car, she locked up carefully, as if locking a car had any impact at this juncture. Betty Anne and Shirley led the way through yards and circled to Joyce's front yard. Her garage door was still open, so Betty Anne walked past the Panthers golf cart, knocked on the interior door, and opened it without waiting a beat. "Joyce! It's me. I baked a plum cake! Let's have coffee, and we'll tell you everything, and you'll tell us everything."

Betty Anne and Shirley plopped down on the fat pink plaid cushions tied with pink laces to the spindles of the maple chairs in the breakfast nook.

Joyce looked confused, as if she had never met any of them before.

"I'll make coffee," said Shirley, because they all knew where everybody's everything was. Joyce used a Mr. Coffee and kept the coffee and sugar in unevenly glazed lidded jars she had made in pottery. Shirley prepared a full pot while Betty Anne set the coffee cake out and found dessert forks. Joyce handed out pretty paper dessert plates with red geraniums and green leaves.

"Napkins," Betty Anne reminded Joyce.

Joyce opened the narrow pantry door with its little floor-to-ceiling shelves. She located a pack of matching cocktail napkins, set them on the little round table, and sat down heavily, her back to Clemmie. Betty Anne plumped down next to Joyce, and Shirley opposite.

"Have you kicked Johnny out?" asked Shirley, going for the gold.

Clemmie drifted behind the kitchen peninsula, opened the drawer, and silently set the keys inside. As for sitting, the only remaining empty chair at the table was in the corner, where Clemmie would be trapped by the bodies of three fat friends. She couldn't sit there. She couldn't sit anywhere. She wanted to be out of here.

She remembered the sheriff saying that people who killed fell into aimless panic. I didn't kill Wilson, she thought, but I am panicking.

After the murder of Rudyard Creek, though, if she or Barbara or Stan had panicked, no one ever knew about it. In Akron the following week, her mother's weekly letter arrived, enclosing a lengthy newspaper clipping about the murder. "Imagine!" wrote Mama. "I didn't keep up with his wife. But I've written a condolence note. You'll want to write one too. You were always glad to see Coach when he visited." She appended the widow's street address.

Clemmie's mother mailed follow-up articles, but there weren't many. It was the '60s now, and society was beginning to fall apart. Protests had begun against segregation, Vietnam, the Establishment, restrictive clothing, the army, ROTC, hairstyles, old-fashioned sexual mores, and the role of women. College students everywhere were rocking the boat and, in some cases, sinking it. Interest in the death of some high school coach was minimal, especially since there had been few clues to start with and no additional information ever showed up.

When Joyce declined to discuss Johnny, Shirley moved on. "Have you talked to the sheriff yet? I swear these people have no idea what they are doing. We're in danger here, and they're just smiling and nodding and asking if we knew Dom."

Betty Anne cut the coffee cake and shifted squares onto plates.

"Just a little tiny piece," said Shirley severely. "I'm still on my diet."

———

Betty Anne's famous plum cake called for fresh plums, which were hard to find, and Joyce suspected that this was a canned plum cake, but who cared? It was so comforting to be surrounded by giggling, gossipy friends. It gave her hope.

Helen had finally been induced to sit, but she was struggling with her fork.

"What happened to your finger?" Joyce asked, looking at the fat wad of Band-Aids.

"I slit it on a can lid. You stand there telling yourself to be careful, and then you aren't careful."

The girls all told not-careful stories.

Shirley stood up, squeezed behind Joyce into the kitchen, and opened the lower cabinet door behind which Joyce's garbage can sat. It was full. Shirley dropped in her crushed napkin and paper plate, yanked the red plastic ribbons to close up the trash bag, and pulled it out. Joyce, feeling she could not accomplish one more thing in this lifetime, was relieved to have somebody else take the garbage out.

Shirley walked to the utility room and opened the garage door so she could throw the full bag into the trash barrel in the garage. "Where's your car, anyway, Joyce?" she asked, coming back.

"You all texted me that nobody could drive in or out of the pod, so I didn't try. I parked over near the grocery."

Shirley hooted. "You walked from the grocery? You?"

"I know, right? Me, walk?"

"Do you think you'll head back to Galveston later?" asked Betty Anne.

"Not immediately. Helen and I will stay at a hotel tonight. Maybe Ballantyne Resort. What do you think, Helen? A fine hotel, room-service dinner, and good company. Doesn't that sound wonderful?"

Her best friend shook her head. "Thank you, Joyce, but the sweetest thing happened. Friends at Dexter River offered to let me stay with them."

Helen was letting her down at a time like this? Joyce could not bear to be alone tonight. She would talk Helen into it. They'd have a good time.

A cell phone began ringing, a patter of electronic notes unknown to Joyce. This was puzzling because the girls certainly knew each other's ringtones. Everyone looked back and forth, startled, and Helen stared down and twitched, as if some little creature had jumped into her lap.

Shirley said, "You changed your ringtone?"

Helen looked as confused as if they had all started speaking Mandarin. Helen, the most articulate person Joyce knew.

"Turn it off," said Betty Anne irritably.

The phone stopped, having rung four or five times while Helen did nothing but sag, her whole face and spine getting old while Joyce watched.

"That's what it is to be a Latin teacher," said Shirley. "You live in ancient times. You can't even turn your phone off."

"What's amazing is that she figured out how to change her ringtone," said Betty Anne.

Joyce was feeling pretty old and saggy herself. "Thanks for the cake and the company," she said, standing up. "Here, Betty Anne, you keep the leftovers for next time. I'm already packed; my stuff is in my car. Helen just has to get a few overnight things, and we're headed out."

"So much for Dexter River," Shirley called to Clemmie, giggling.

Clemmie was still praying that Joyce was not in the loop, that only Johnny and Borobasq were. But she couldn't test her hope, couldn't risk getting into Joyce's car and driving off with her. She had been so stupid to come along with Shirley and Betty Anne. She must leave with them, must leave Joyce behind. Now she was stuck in her corner of the breakfast room while Joyce swept the other two girls to the garage door. Clemmie shifted chairs out of the way, but by the time she caught up, Betty Anne and Shirley were walking out of the garage and Joyce's large hips blocked Clemmie's exit.

"Joyce," she said, hardly able to get the syllables out, unable to discern why she was so frightened. "I'm expecting my Dexter River friends any minute. I have to head on out. We'll talk later, okay?"

Joyce turned and looked down at Clemmie, who saw again

how small she was compared to her friend. It was not a reassuring contrast. Keep bluffing, she told herself. "Joyce, I really have to go. Thank you for the coffee." Clemmie stepped forward where there really wasn't space, expecting Joyce to yield and let her by, but Joyce did not. She was frowning, looking down at Clemmie's skirt pocket, where the bulge of the $19.99 phone was much smaller than Clemmie's iPhone.

Joyce did an extraordinary thing. She stuck her hand into Clemmie's pocket to get it.

The little black phone lay in her huge palm like a toy. "What's this for?"

"I'm experimenting," said Clemmie. "Finding ways to save, you know. I haven't even learned how to silence it yet. That's why I was so hopeless a minute ago." She tried again to edge past.

Joyce flipped the top open. "Your caller left a message," she said slowly.

"Thank you," said Clemmie, holding out her hand to take the phone, but Joyce ignored her. With her long, hard thumbnail, painted this week a glorious vermilion with a tiny silver design, Joyce tapped to play the message. Clemmie recognized Borobasq's voice on the first syllable. His smug voice said, "Thanks for the money." Clemmie stepped backward, turned, and ran for the front door as Borobasq laughed his mocking laugh.

The front door was locked. She swung the latch around and grabbed the doorknob, but Joyce caught up, closing long, thick fingers on Clemmie's wrist. She could no more escape Joyce's grasp than she could have escaped Rudyard Creek's.

She remembered the highway picnic area, how Rudyard Creek hadn't known enough to be afraid, how he was laughing right up to the first gunshot. He even laughed after that first gunshot because it missed. He was too busy with two small women to consider that there might be a third person and a different weapon behind him.

But here on Blue Lilac Lane, Clemmie had had plenty of chances to drive away, stay away, get help, or tell the truth. I didn't take them, she thought. I wanted Joyce to be my friend. I wanted it all to work out. I could have told Shirley and Betty Anne to go without me, but no, I pretended I was just one of the girls and Joyce was just one of the girls and we were just block buddies having plum cake. But I knew we weren't. I knew I had gotten between Joyce and her money.

Oh, Joyce! What have you and Johnny done?

Joyce shifted the phone in her free hand and clicked again. Clemmie knew what the click had to be: Joyce was checking texts. Clemmie had sent only one. "'Cash in front seat of rental car,'" Joyce read out loud. She flung the phone across the room. It whacked into the wall and fell to the polished hardwood floor. Grabbing both of Clemmie's shoulders, Joyce shoved her all the way from the front door to the high counter that divided the living room from the kitchen, and when Clemmie could stumble backward no more, Joyce battered her against the counter rim. "You were my friend!" she screamed. "I trusted you!"

Friend. Trust. Such beautiful words. I'm not a friend after all, Clemmie thought, and who would ever trust me? I'm all lies and stories.

She stopped resisting and tried to drop to the floor, but Clemmie's weight meant nothing to Joyce, who was screaming solidly now. There was no Joyce left, just rage expanding like gas. Clemmie's spine would break with the next slam against the counter.

Clemmie swung to her left and swung to her right and achieved little. Joyce slammed her again into the countertop, and now Clemmie also was screaming. Joyce was shaking her by the arms and in a moment would pull Clemmie's arms out of their sockets.

Arms could be fixed, but if Joyce's hands moved upward, they would close around her throat.

Clemmie stretched her fingers into the other pocket and closed around her key chain. She opened her own concealed carry, the two-inch knife, and stabbed Joyce in the only place she could reach: the roll of fat around her belly.

Joyce was screaming already; she couldn't scream any louder. Her grip slackened. Her screams ended. She stared down. Blood was spurting out of the wound. "You cut me," she whispered. She was genuinely shocked. "You took a knife and cut me!" Joyce flung Clemmie away from her to tend to her wound, and Clemmie hit the floor. She wasn't sure she could ever get up. Or wanted to.

I knifed my best friend, she thought.

TWENTY-NINE

Joyce leaned on the kitchen counter, sobbing.

Clemmie was lying on the floor, half hidden by the breakfast bar, and sobbing. She managed to reach the burner phone Joyce had hurled against the wall and stuff it back in her pocket.

Joyce's polyester knit top absorbed no blood. She snatched up a heavy, woven cotton Panthers' dish towel and pressed it hard into her stomach. "How could you hurt me, Helen?" she asked, her voice trembling, as if she had no memory of bashing Clemmie against a bone-breaking granite shelf.

The utility-room door from the garage was flung open. It slammed against the washing machine. "Helen!" yelled a man. "Helen, are you here?" Feet pounded toward the kitchen.

Was it the sheriff? Clemmie prayed it was the sheriff. But he wouldn't call her Helen. He'd say Miz Stephens. Clemmie couldn't move. She huddled on the floor, splinting herself against the pain.

"Who are you?" asked Joyce, her voice dazed, her fury gone.

"Friend of Helen's," said Dexter River's band teacher. "Are you all right, ma'am? Something terrible has happened. There's blood on Helen's sidewalk. It crosses the street and ends in your driveway. Is Helen here? Do you know where Helen is?"

"Marvin," whispered Clemmie. "I'm over here." Whose blood could possibly be in the street? Her finger was certainly not the source.

Marvin knelt beside her, and his hands closed around her ribs, lifting her to a sitting position. "Where are you hurt? Talk to me, Helen."

Police poured through the same garage door.

"I called 911," he said to both women, as if apologizing for over-reacting. "I knew the police were right here because their cars are, but I couldn't see anybody, and in here somebody was screaming. Was it you screaming, Helen? Tell me what's happening." He lifted Helen to her feet, dusted her off, and kissed her.

It was a kiss of relief. An "Oh, thank God it isn't *her* blood all over the street" kiss.

How long had it been since anybody had kissed Clementine Lakefield? She rested her head against his chest and felt his warmth and thought, *He drove all the way here to rescue me. Oh, Marvin.*

Police literally filled the room. They wore khaki pants and

brown shirts except for the ones with gray pants and pale shirts. They all wore those amazing belts, loaded with weapons and phones and Tasers and who knew what.

Marvin rocked her. "It's okay," he whispered. "It's all okay now." Marvin wasn't a tall man, maybe five seven or eight, but to Clemmie, he was a giant of concern and protection.

"Don't touch me," said Joyce tearfully, trying to shoo the police out of her house. "You get out of here."

Marvin walked Clemmie over to the huge sofa that was really two attached recliners with cup holders and flip trays, like first-class plane seats. He sat down and arranged Clemmie on his lap. Clemmie thought, I'm bald again. Where's my wig? Probably came off with all that shaking. Probably on the floor somewhere. Nobody at school has ever seen me bald. And it has to be Marvin who does.

The sheriff spoke in his honey-sweet voice. "Joyce Tower Biggs, you have the right to remain silent. Anything you say can and will be used against you in a court of law." In his lovely drawl, the words sounded rather neighborly.

"Stop it," said Joyce. "You just stop it. I have nothing to do with anything." Her voice was raw from all the screaming at Clemmie.

"You have the right to speak to an attorney," said the sheriff gently, "and to have an attorney present during the questioning."

They'll question me too, Clemmie realized. No matter what, I'll be swept up in this. My lives will be thrown into the questioning and examined.

And what would happen at the airport to Borobasq and Johnny? Even if Borobasq didn't tell the police her two names, they'd have his cell phone and his records calling her and her texts to him. She wasn't in as deep as Joyce. She had the proof of her slashed finger that Borobasq had used his knife to force her to obey, but she also had the tree dragon in her front seat.

She imagined Peggy at her wedding in the islands, saying, "My boring, never-had-a-life aunt! Mixed up in drug dealing and murders! I hope she gets a light sentence."

The sheriff went on in the same kindly voice. "We have a clear video, Miz Biggs. The countryside of South Carolina may look empty to an urban eye, but it hardly ever is. There was a fisherman on the bank of that creek where you stopped your car."

Clemmie was puzzled. What could have been filmed at some creek in the country that mattered? Joyce never drove in the country because she believed that the movie *Deliverance* was the truth about the rural South, and she expected homicidal maniacs to pop out of rural woods.

And maybe one did, thought Clemmie.

Joyce had backed against the counter where she had been bashing Clemmie. Both hands were gripping the towel, pressing it against herself. It was an odd posture, but Clemmie didn't think the police could analyze it as wound protection. Joyce just looked crazy, which possibly she was at this moment. Wasn't Joyce normally a sane and funny woman? Great company? A good card player? A fine cook when she put her mind to it? A good shopper and a good driver? And, in fact, a good friend?

"The video," said the sheriff, "records the actual minute in which it was taken this morning, when you were throwing your gun into the creek on your way to Galveston."

So that was where Joyce's concealed carry had gone. It should have been lost and gone forever in some remote stream. But it hadn't been remote, and it wasn't lost. When everybody on Blue Lilac thought the police were doing nothing, they were wading in a creek, retrieving a murder weapon.

Joyce.

Murder weapon.

Clemmie wept against Marvin's shirt. It isn't true, she told herself. Joyce didn't kill Wilson. I absolutely don't believe she would do that.

She remembered the sheriff stirring his coffee at Wendy's. *They drive aimlessly or head home or get drunk. Heading home is the number-one choice. They didn't plan ahead of the murder, and they can't plan now because they can't think. Even if home is the least safe place, they feel safest there.*

"We retrieved the gun," said the sheriff.

Joyce dropped the towel and pressed bloody hands against her cheeks.. "Johnny did it," she whispered. "I love him. I had to cover for him."

Clemmie was too exhausted to make the various pieces of this nightmare add up. What about the lock changes and the glass? What about Dom? What about the Coglands? How could Johnny know Borobasq when Borobasq didn't know Sun City?

But safe in the warmth of Marvin Candler's arms, Clemmie realized that she did not have to add anything up. The police would do that.

———————

Joyce could not breathe very well. The air kept seeping out of her, like the blood she could feel but hadn't let the police see.

How interesting that she had a right to stay silent. She had no experience with silence, a thing in which she never participated.

She had deduced months ago that Wilson was the source of Johnny's marijuana. She had half wondered if Wilson was a drug runner, although it seemed comical—running drugs through a retirement community. She didn't know what to do about it, and she didn't really care. If Johnny wanted to smoke dope, whatever.

The other day, she had seen Wilson walk through the parking gate and onto Blue Lilac. His car was not parked in Dom's drive. He proceeded to open Dom's garage door with a clicker in his hand. In his other hand, he carried a gym bag. It seemed odd that he would enter from the garage instead of the front door and even odder that he hadn't parked in the driveway, but apparently had left his car in the grocery store parking lot. Just before the garage door closed behind him, Wilson passed through an interior door she had never noticed. He wasn't going into Dom's. He was going into the Cogland place through Dom's garage. It was so bizarre that Joyce couldn't think it through.

A few minutes later, Dom's garage door went up again, and both Wilson and Dom headed out in Dom's golf cart. Wilson did not have the duffel bag.

Joyce knew about the open window in the Cogland living room because the screen leaned against the wall in her garage where Johnny had put it. She hadn't asked him about it. Now, Dom and Wilson having disappeared through the gate, she walked around the third villa, confident that nobody would see her.

A duffel bag was for clothing, but Wilson never stayed long enough to need a change of clothing. What else might a drug dealer put in a duffel bag?

Joyce lifted the Coglands' living-room window, hunched down, and carefully eased herself inside. How creepy the place was. How sparse and unoccupied and weirdly clean, as if Swiffering was all that ever happened here. The duffel bag lay on the kitchen counter. She unzipped it, expecting drugs, and she only knew what that might look like from TV shows, but the bag was filled with hundred-dollar bills. Filled solid. Packed.

Joyce didn't give taking that bag any more thought than if she'd been dealing a hand of canasta. She went back out the window with it and home again. I have a million dollars, she thought, giggling. Cash dollars. Like some amazing across-the-street lottery.

She loved that she had done it, seized his old drug money. And nobody would ever know. She'd become a millionaire through a window. It was the craziest adventure or secret she'd ever had. *I'm a millionaire!* she kept thinking, giggling to herself, wishing she could tell Helen.

Johnny had gone out to join a late-afternoon poker game and wouldn't be home for hours. Joyce thought about watching TV, but she was too excited to do anything except think about her million dollars. She tucked the duffel bag in the back of her closet, which made her giggle even more.

When there was a knock on the front door, she opened it without thinking, and there stood Wilson, who gave her a charming smile, which she would never have thought he possessed. "Hey, listen, Joyce. I need help picking out a present at the gift shop. Wanna come? I need a shopper buddy with style."

Joyce loved shopping, and she especially loved a shopping mission. The gift shop in the strip behind the gate was packed with delightful stuff, jewelry and topiary and clocks made of picket-fence pieces. "I'd love to," said Joyce, happy to be recognized as a shopper, never once considering that something else might be going on, not a flicker of worry about the man whose money she had taken. She got her purse, and together they walked over to Dom's garage and got in Dom's golf cart.

But instead of backing out of the garage, Wilson said, "You know, Joyce, I need my money back."

She gasped. How could he possibly know? He hadn't been home. Nobody had been home. There were no witnesses. "What are you talking about, Wilson?"

"Joyce, Joyce. I have a hidden camera in the third unit. You went in through a window. A window you must have used before," said Wilson, "because you left it open, and I'm a jerk for not checking or noticing, but now I know." He held out a tiny metal thing. It wasn't a camera, but maybe the important digital part of a camera. Was it called a flash drive? A thumb drive?

A huge, blinding fear of exposure closed in on Joyce. A video of her trespassing through a window. Taking somebody else's money. Her children would find out. Her ex. Her grandchildren. Johnny's puny thefts of a hundred here and there would be as nothing.

How would her children react if she got arrested for stealing? Would they stand by her? Would they even come?

It didn't dawn on her until the next day that Wilson couldn't have shown the video to anybody, let alone the police. What would he say to the cops? *She's stealing my drug money!*

All she could think of was that little video. If she had that, nobody could prove anything. She just had to get it away from him. Easy peasy. She'd give him back his cash, but he'd have to give her the video first. "I'm sorry," she said, letting herself weep, although she was not a woman who shed tears. "I was greedy. Let's go back to the house, and I'll get the duffel for you. I didn't take anything out of it. It's all there."

"First we need to talk. When did you start using that window?" He put the little metal piece in his shirt pocket, and she realized he would never give it to her. He'd take his money back, and he'd also forever have proof of what she'd done.

"Please put the garage door down," she said. "I'm afraid Helen or somebody will see us."

"It's the video you need to worry about, not them," said Wilson. "I laughed the whole time I watched it. You could hardly fit, you're so fat. As for getting back out with the duffel bag, you can't figure out how to manage it. You try one fat leg and then the other, and finally you throw the bag onto the grass ahead of you and squish yourself out like a balloon." He was enjoying himself. He said, "Videos, they're such great proof. Plus they show a person as she actually is, Joyce. Greedy, obese, and uncoordinated!"

He took the garage-door remote control out of the cup holder jutting from the dash and brought the door down just as she had requested, and Joyce reached into her handbag, closed her fingers around her gun, lifted it, and shot.

She didn't aim. She didn't choose an angle. She just did it. She got him low in the gut. He wasn't dead. He didn't even look deadish. He just had a hole. He stared at it and then at her, and she shot him again, farther up, and that was that.

The racket of the closing garage door probably hid the sound of the first gunshot, but maybe not the second. But it was Dom's garage, and Dom was too deaf to hear anything anyway. He probably had his television on so loud he couldn't have heard a machine gun.

Wilson began to tip over. Joyce retrieved the video thing from his pocket and just managed to get out of the golf cart before he went down in a twisted huddle, headfirst onto the floor of the passenger side. The unzipped plastic walls closed around him, and he was invisible.

I touched things, she thought, putting the thumb drive into her purse with the gun. Left fingerprints. But I'm a neighbor. Of course I've touched Dom's golf cart. Dom will be blamed for this. It's his family, it's his problem. He's probably dealt with this kind of thing before.

She hurried into the Cogland villa and out their window, trying not to admit that she really was obese and ungraceful, and then somehow she was home again. The duffel bag was safe at the back of her closet. Johnny never touched her physical things, just her checking account. He couldn't care less what she had stored in her closets. He'd never dig around.

Back in her kitchen, her street view directly facing Dom's closed garage door, Joyce began to tremble. *There's a body there*, she thought. *I killed a man.*

Shock inched into her, like one of those diseases on that mesmerizing, nauseating show, *Monsters Inside Me*. But the monster inside Joyce was not a tropical parasite. It was Joyce herself.

It was self-defense, she thought loudly, as if making a statement to the public. What choice did I have?

She considered calling the police. "I had to do it. He was attacking me. He wanted me to drive somewhere scary. Down to the river. He would have killed me and thrown me in."

But how to explain the duffel bag of cash in her closet?

Wilson is dead, she thought. *I killed him.*

Shivers of horror coursed through her. She rejected the idea that she would do a thing like that. She would never do a thing like that. She hadn't done it. This was some nightmare, some sort of stroke.

Her thoughts tumbled and her blood pressure soared, and as she stared at the scene of her crime, Dom's garage door went up yet again. She stared at the rising door in utter horror. Wilson was still alive? Had gotten back into the driver's seat? Was going to drive himself to urgent care? Or to the police?

But it was Dom driving. The cart was zipped now, but she could see no body on the garage floor, so Wilson must still be in the cart. Dead. With Dom driving! Dom backed onto the street and headed for the gate. He did not glance at Joyce's house.

If he knew I shot Wilson, he'd come over and shoot me, she thought. He doesn't know who did it. He probably thinks somebody in the Cogland house did it. I'm safe.

But Wilson had two holes in him. Holes Joyce had made.

She refused to believe it. But she had to do something. Cover things up. But how? Where was Dom going? What was he going to do with Wilson? She needed to know.

Joyce rarely walked anywhere, but she strode after Dom, tapped the code in the gate, and hurried into the parking lot. She was still holding her purse, afraid to set it down, afraid the used weapon would escape or something. She didn't see how she'd ever be able to use this purse again.

Most parking was delineated by little grassy intervals, separating doctors' offices from the bank and so forth. But there was one rather large parking lot nearby without a store or offices. It was just there waiting for buildings to be put up, which would happen soon. Growth here was manic: woods on Monday, scraped red clay on Tuesday, buildings on Wednesday.

Dom drove over to a white sedan that looked exactly like any other white sedan, got out of the golf cart, zipped up the driver side, and drove away in the sedan. He wasn't going to the police or the doctor. He didn't even care about the body. He had just needed transportation to what must be Wilson's car.

Joyce had a brilliant thought. Let the body molder inside Dom's garage, because Dom might never return. Certainly *she* would never come back if people were shooting her relatives. And when the body was found—who knew when, maybe never, because who ever went into that house?—she'd have gotten rid of her gun...and so what if her fingerprints were on the cart? She was their neighbor. Of course she sat there now and then. Much better to hide Wilson inside Dom's than for him to be found late tonight by some sheriff's department guy checking an abandoned golf cart.

If only she had left the cart and body there. The police would have gone after Dom, who had so visibly fled, even taking off in the car of the dead man.

But no. Joyce had unzipped the driver side, wedged herself next to the body, pretending it wasn't one, pretending she hadn't created it. She turned the little key still sitting in the ignition and drove right back to Blue Lilac, expecting to zip into Dom's garage and abandon the body and use her trusty window again.

However, a UPS truck idled on one side of Dom's driveway and a cable company truck on the other side, the drivers behind their wheels, looking down at their electronic record notations. She should have bluffed, should have driven in anyway, opening the door with Dom's clicker. It was too normal an activity for either man to look up. But she panicked, dug into her bag, feeling the horrible gun that had done such a horrible thing, found the remote, and opened her own garage door. Her own car sat in the drive because she'd been too lazy to put it away earlier, so there was room next to the Panthers golf cart for a dead man.

But now she had the problem of Johnny, who would leave his Avalon in the drive but come in through the garage. He mustn't find out what was in there. She paced and panted and finally had a plan. When he finally turned into Blue Lilac, Joyce came out the front door and called, "I could hardly wait for you get home! I want to have an ice cream sundae. I heated the chocolate sauce already."

Johnny loved chocolate sundaes.

He joined her on the porch, and they went in the front door, which they never did, but he didn't see anything odd about it. Joyce followed up the ice cream with a lot of cuddling and telling Johnny how wonderful he was, in spite of the fact that she had already arranged for a locksmith to come the following morning and change the locks so she could kick him out.

Maddeningly, he wouldn't go to sleep that night because there was a late movie he wanted to see, so the TV in their bedroom was on forever, and she was the one who fell asleep.

In the morning, while she busied herself blocking the utility room, he left for horseshoes through the front door. Now. How to get the golf cart safely back into Dom's garage?

She and Helen were going to play cards. Joyce phoned Helen with a five-minute warning, but Helen was a ten-minute girl and, furthermore, Joyce could see the light in her bathroom, which Helen always put on when she entered and always turned off when she left. Living so close to one's neighbors presented too much information, but today it was welcome.

When Clemmie's bathroom light went on, Joyce drove Dom's golf cart into his garage, got out, and was halfway back across the street before the slow-moving door had fully lowered again. Then she drove her own golf cart over to get Helen, feeling giddy and successful. How shapely her plan was, how well executed.

Executed, thought Joyce now in her kitchen, as the khaki-and-brown police uniforms blurred and shifted in front of her.

What states had death penalties? Did South Carolina? Would they execute her? They had the video, and they had the gun. There was no way around those two things. They didn't have the thumb drive. She'd tossed it in the woods.

There was no proof of her theft.

Except, of course, the cash.

Which somebody had taken. Somebody associated with Helen. Somebody who had left a message on Helen's burner phone. Who had burner phones? Drug dealers. *Helen?*

How had Helen gotten to the duffel bag? Had Joyce forgotten to lock her car? It happened a lot these days. Joyce was never entirely sure five minutes later if she had locked or closed anything.

Was it the handsome passenger? The boy toy? Or was that boy Helen's great-nephew? Or perhaps the dreamboat had been Dom Junior or the son of Dom Junior.

Now in the midst of all these uniforms using up all the oxygen, Joyce thought, I shouldn't have killed Wilson. I should have laughed at him. I actually had the upper hand because I had the money.

She had an awful feeling that she would never laugh again, and yet even as she thought it, laughter bubbled up in her, a sort of champagne toast to her own unthinking murderous action.

There were not going to be do-overs. She had taken a man's life. That was now the sum total of her own existence: taking somebody else's away.

She had come back home because the drive to Galveston was

too much; everything was too much; she wanted her own kitchen and her own bedroom and her own doors, locked against whatever was coming next.

But the police had surrounded her, right here in her own house, with the slit in her body where her best friend had stabbed her.

Traffic on I-485 was heavy and slow. Johnny's arm oozed. His chest oozed. His lap was bloody.

The guy doesn't have a gun, thought Johnny. He has a knife. He's telling me that I'm safe, but I'm not. He used the knife once; he'll use it again.

And even if he lets me go, and I drive to some urgent care place, the computer will turn up all my previous medical records. I can't get stitched up anonymously. My cuts are public knowledge.

He killed Wilson. There's nobody else who could have done it. Well, Dom—but I think Dom just ran. Not literally, since Dom could hardly even drag one foot ahead of the other. But somehow, Dom got out of Sun City for good.

And me, what am I going to do for good?

Run around with a little package of dollars?

He has to kill me. It won't bother him. No matter what he says, he's not giving away any of his money. He needs my car to get to the airport. He doesn't need me.

The traffic in their center lane was down to about ten miles an hour, the left lane going about twenty and now the far-right lane stopped altogether.

Johnny couldn't call 911 because Knife Boy had his cell phone.

But every single car up and down I-485 still did have their cell phones.

Johnny stopped driving and opened the door. Knife Boy reached for him, but the front seats were wide and the duffel lay between them. Johnny heaved himself into traffic. The left lane honked wildly at him. The Avalon continued to move forward and hit the car ahead of them, and Johnny stood covered in blood, waving his arms.

———————

The police were like gnats, swarming. Joyce kept brushing them away.

Her life wavered in front of her and behind her. She tried to think what she stood for, what her life meant, why she had lived at all, and whether she should live any longer.

It seemed to Joyce that hours had gone by, with the police waiting and the little house on its way to being somebody else's, some buyer she would never meet, all her precious accessories trucked to the secondhand store. She stared at her breakfast table. She wouldn't get to replace the pink plaid cushions with the autumn set and its red apples, or the Christmas set with the reindeer.

She didn't make a decision about what to say next. It just happened. "Johnny had nothing to do with it. I shot Wilson."

THIRTY

Clemmie's plane arrived in Costa Rica. Peggy was there, waving. "Aunt Clemmie!" shrieked her niece, beaming. "This is Arch, my darling Arch. Arch and I placed bets on whether you'd come, you know, and I said, 'She'll come, Arch. She loves me.'"

Arch seemed closer to Clemmie's age than Peggy's, but he was smiling proudly at his bride-to-be, and Clemmie thought, Peggy has been loved four times. And I haven't been loved once. Her eyes prickled with tears.

Arch said, "It's tiring to fly these days, isn't it? But it's not a bad drive to the resort, and then you can soak up the sun and get ready to party."

"I've never really learned how to party."

"It's time," said Arch, smiling down at her.

They sat together in a large comfortable van while a chauffeur took them to the resort Peggy had chosen.

"Have you looked at your messages yet?" Peggy demanded.

"No. My phone is still in airline mode."

"Oh well, then, read on mine," said Peggy, and she thrust her phone into Clemmie's hand. It displayed a newspaper headline, of course, from Peggy scrolling the internet, latching onto things. The headline was about Rudyard Creek.

Clemmie thought her heart would stop.

Marvin had brought Clemmie to his house and installed her in his guest room while Jimmy's parents brought casseroles and salad and the principal and his wife brought ice cream. Marvin said, "Just stay here with me for a while. You need a break from Blue Lilac Lane, and I'd love the company," and they all played cards to distract Helen, and it was a distraction because six was a difficult number for cards, and she had to concentrate, and Marvin patted her hand.

It gave her hope. Not that Marvin would be the love of her life, that at the very last minute, she would suddenly find true love, but that she had good friends, people who cared, and she was safe—both of her selves were safe—from exposure. Because the police were (so far) too busy dealing with Joyce and Borobasq to go after Johnny or Clemmie. It seemed that in her case, age and fragility saved her from responsibility; they found it quite reasonable that she'd done everything Borobasq told her to. Johnny, poor man, had explained that he'd crossed the street because he saw somebody in

Clemmie's house and was trying to be a hero and instead got slashed by Borobasq. But he was a hero in the end, stopping traffic in the middle of the interstate.

Clemmie was fairly sure that more details about herself would emerge; the whole glass thing would be revealed, and her trespass would come up and Bentley's post, but she didn't think much would come of it.

And now, from Connecticut, total exposure had arrived. The cold case was about to get hot. "I don't think I can read it," she said, utterly worn out by the whole nightmare of it.

"Small print," agreed Arch. He took the phone, stroked the screen surface, and the print enlarged. Clemmie was awed. Does my phone do that? Could I have been increasing type size all this time?

Even with the type size increased, Clemmie didn't take the phone, so Arch read out loud. She was familiar with everything he read until he came to the sentence, "'Police revealed that their investigation involved Rudyard Creek's DNA and blood type.'"

Clemmie braced herself.

"'Rudyard Creek,'" read Arch, "'had been a suspect in two rapes more than fifty years ago. One of these rapes culminated in the death of the victim. It was that case which was reopened, and police are not releasing the name of the victim, even half a century later. The former basketball coach had always been the primary suspect in the rape-murder, but there was insufficient proof. When Rudyard Creek was killed, the rape-murder investigation shut down because the police couldn't go after a dead man. But the sister of that victim, now in her seventies, having seen on television the efficacy of DNA evidence which was not meaningful at the time of the old murder, requested that the case be reopened. Amazingly, evidence seized at the site of Rudyard Creek's own murder was still in storage, as was evidence from the unnamed rape-murder victim. DNA was conclusive. Rudyard Creek was the rapist of that long-dead teenage girl and, therefore, presumably her murderer as well.'"

Clemmie's mind went to Dom, whom she had located rather easily. Back when she rescued Dom's envelope from the grass, she had read not just the name Sal Pesante, but also Sal Pesante's address. It took only a minute on the computer to find that Sal Pesante had a landline. On the burner phone she had not had the time or solitude to discard, Clemmie called the number and asked to speak to Dom. "Sure. Just a minute," said a woman, and Clemmie hung up. She had nothing to say to Dom; she just wanted to know that he had made it out.

She thought of Joyce, who had done a terrible, irretrievable thing for no reason. Of the sheriff, who told her that all the murders he dealt with could be described that way.

She thought of Marvin.

"'Asked whether they now intend to pursue the murder of Creek himself,'" Arch read, "'police replied that they have nothing to work with and never had. No fingerprints, no weapons, no nothing.'"

"So that's that," said Peggy. "Let me show you my gown, Aunt Clemmie."

In Charlotte, Kelsey and Mack Boone tried to talk their father into taking a saliva sample for DNA research.

Billy Boone's initial horror had passed, replaced by a sort of gentleness. What if he did have a mother or a father out there wondering about him? Hoping to meet him. Hoping he'd done well and been happy.

Was there a moral obligation to step up and open the door? Or a moral obligation not to?

He looked at his eager son and daughter and wife and wondered how they would react if some aged grandparent actually appeared? Some graying, tottering old woman who would stagger up at some staged place as cameras recorded the meeting?

But there would be no cameras; they were not doing this for a show.

There might not be tottering either, because Billy's birth mother was most likely only fifteen or twenty years older than he was.

There might be nobody out there at all.

There might be joy.

Billy looked at the family he loved so much and was so lucky to have. He owed a debt to that biological mother. He thought about the possibility of a parent he might get to know and also love, and he nodded.

DON'T MISS THE NEXT GRIPPING MYSTERY FROM CAROLINE B. COONEY

Freddy rode his bike instead of taking his grandmother's old Avalon or his grandfather's old pickup. He raced happily up narrow back roads wrapped in old stone walls and took the sharp curves at high speed. For nine miles, orange and red leaves drifted down on his shoulders and spun under the tires. Great trip. The destination— not so much. He was headed to Middletown Memory Care, an institution that was not in fact caring for memories. They were caring for people who had once had memories and would never find them again.

In a vehicle, he'd arrive at MMC from Route 9, but bikes weren't allowed on the divided highway. He ended up west of MMC in a neighborhood of tiny old houses, cramped lots, and street parking on short one-way roads. The houses favored fencing, and there were chain link and white picket, bamboo and cast iron—everybody safely tucked into their little kingdom. Each garage was a separate little building in the backyard. Freddy entertained himself by planning how to convert the garages into glassblowing studios.

Ahead of him was a four-way stop. Freddy was pretty casual about stop signs, on the theory that they didn't apply to bikes, but he did slow down.

Coming from the right, braking for the stop sign, was a white Toyota Corolla. The driver's window was down and his elbow halfway out of the car. He was looking straight ahead and had not glanced in Freddy's direction.

The profile was unmistakable.

It was Doc.

Doc?

He was supposed to be in Vegas. What was he doing in a plain little city in Connecticut?

He's not going to kneecap me, Freddy told himself. It's not as if I owe money. I just push paper.

Still.

Freddy swerved into the first driveway on his right, hoping for a fence-free escape route. The house sat close to the street, and almost immediately, it protected him from view. There was fencing, but just six-foot chain link to keep a dog in. The dog raced back and forth, barking. Freddy rode between shrubs into the yard directly behind.

Here, a vegetable garden was fenced but not the driveway, so he zipped down it and came safely out on the parallel street.

He turned left to emerge behind the Toyota and get a second look at the driver.

The intersection was empty.

Either Freddy had conjured Doc out of thin air or Doc had driven on.

Freddy zigzagged uphill to the low brick buildings of MMC. He locked his bike behind the stinking dumpster and the row of massive, never-pruned rhododendrons, where it couldn't be seen from the road or the parking lot. He did this a lot because he liked alleys but now on the remote chance that Doc really was out there. Doc was not a guy you wanted in your life. He'd been in medical school years ago and got caught with marijuana in his book bag, back when possession was a crime and not a recreational puff. He ended up with a jail sentence instead of an MD.

Doc was furious and bitter every hour of every day. Society had screwed him because of a handful of dried-up flowers, turned him into a felon with a record because back, then the world didn't rank marijuana the same as coffee or cigarettes. Doc's hobby these days was mixed martial arts, a violent, full-combat sport popular in certain pipe circles. It had not siphoned off his anger.

Freddy went in through the employees' entrance, which was supposed to be locked. In good weather, though, they propped it open for fresh air, which was in short supply in a place that smelled

CAROLINE B. COONEY

of cleaning fluids and old bodies. He preferred to skip the front desk, because they liked you to sign in, and Freddy was opposed to any kind of regimentation.

Two aides were heading for the staff room.

"Hey, Grace," he said. "Hey, Mary Lou." Grace was short and squat, wore her hair in a crew cut, and today sported filigree earrings dangling to her shoulders. Mary Lou was slender and pretty but always smiled carefully, embarrassed by missing teeth. She was saving up for dental work. They both had circles under their eyes.

He told them how beautiful they were, because it boggled Freddy's mind that anybody would actually do this for a living, and the women *were* beautiful in his eyes, no matter how overweight or underweight, no matter how tired or bedraggled. They didn't yell at him for coming through the employees' entrance because he was the only young man who visited and they loved him for it.

Grace and Mary Lou were on break or they wouldn't be in this part of the building. Listen, if he worked here, Freddy would be "on break" the whole shift. He headed to the locked door that led to the residence wings and tapped in the code that opened the door.

He walked through the big common room full of aides, dining tables, sitting areas, visitors, and residents. He didn't see Mrs. Maple, who generally visited her aunt Polly the same time he was visiting Grandma. That was too bad, because Mrs. Maple was his first line of defense against the horror of dementia visits.

In Grandma's wing, Jade was working. She was a few years older than Freddy, and why she didn't get a restaurant job or a grocery-store job or anything at all except taking care of his incontinent grandmother, Freddy didn't know. He asked once and she was surprised. "I like this," she said and didn't seem to be lying.

"Hi, Jade," said Freddy.

"Miss Cordelia doin' well today," said Jade.

"Hey! Great news," said Freddy. Except that Grandma doing well simply meant she'd had lunch.

Freddy found his grandmother in her little room, where the single shelf held photographs of the husband she no longer remembered. Jade had dressed her with care in a pale-yellow sweater, a soft gray skirt, and a necklace of Freddy's glass beads that his ex-girlfriend, Cynthia, had strung together. The color range was apricot apple, using an early swirl technique that Freddy would execute a lot better if he were making it today.

"Hey, Grandma," said Freddy. He knelt down in front of her so she'd see who was talking.

Her face lit up, which meant she knew him, and Freddy felt his own face going happy. She said, "Arthur!" in that eager, breathy voice.

Freddy took her hand. It was frighteningly thin, toothpick bones draped in saggy skin. She no longer had any grip, so it was like a piece of paper resting inside his own callused, burned, hard palm. Right up until last week, his grandmother could remember his name, and then last week, she said, "Arthur, dear, did you have a good lunch?" Arthur was Grandma's son. Died in Vietnam, so long ago

Freddy couldn't even remember the decade, but Arthur's death was burned in Grandma's soul.

Freddy didn't mind being Arthur. At least she knew he was family.

The activity director scurried up. Heidi's amazing enthusiasm penetrated even the most comatose dementia patients. "Freddy! Yay! Marvelous to see you! We're playing ball! Let's you two join us!"

Playing ball when you were deep in dementia involved using a foam noodle, like for a swimming pool, as a bat. You whacked at a heavy-duty balloon, generally bright red, so that even a really vague person could spot it. Half the residents were too vague even for that and just sat there. Half really got into it, whapping the balloon across the room to another patient, who would not notice or else swing hard but miss. Heidi would cheer, "Go, Edna! Yes, Herbert! Thatta girl, Betty!"

Respectively, Edna, Herbert, and Betty had been a history teacher, a civil engineer, and a bank executive. What had Grandma been, exactly? She had never held a job, never had that thing called a career. The list of her achievements was homely: typing up the stencil for the church bulletin and running the mimeograph machine; chair of the church fair for decades, every year stitching up a couple dozen aprons to sell, each with pockets and bibs and matching pot holders. She'd been on the library board for half a century, writing the newsletter and running the summer reading clubs. She had played pinochle and euchre and cherished her perennial garden.

She didn't remember any of it.

"Thanks, Heidi," said Freddy, suppressing a shudder at the thought of dementia ball. "You're awesome, but I think we'll go for a spin." He pushed Grandma's wheelchair through the common room to the locked exit, tapped in the code, and out they went. At first, Grandma had asked about that code. "Where do you get it, Freddy?"

"I'll find out for you," Freddy would say. "Now let's put this scarf on because it's chilly. You look great in that scarf, Grandma." And they would be through the door and she would have forgotten about codes.

Middletown Memory Care was a lockup because a large fraction of its residents spent all day trying to leave. The deep anxiety that ruled so many dementia patients meant they wanted only one thing: out. They didn't know much, but they always knew this wasn't the life they used to lead.

A large fraction of families never took their loved one on a drive or out for dinner because they'd never be able to shovel them back in.

Freddy and Grandma arrived in the sunshine. Since his grandmother always forgot that the outside even existed, it thrilled her. "It's so nice out!" she cried.

Listen, it was nice to be outside Memory Care no matter what the weather was.

Freddy sucked in fresh, uncaged air and said hi to Kenneth Yardley, who was just arriving. Mr. Yardley visited his wife, Maude, a lot. He fed her lunch, brushed her teeth, put her down for a nap, read out loud to her. If Maude knew her husband was around, she didn't show it.

It's strange to love somebody who is not all there, which was Freddy's lot.

It's strange to love somebody who does not know you, which was true for a good percentage of MMC residents.

It is strangest of all to love somebody who will not know or care if you ever show up again, and that was Kenneth Yardley's situation.

Mr. Yardley gave Freddy a distracted, desperate smile. He fumbled around trying to find the doorknob. This was not a good sign, because the street door was normal. Freddy had a bad feeling Maude was going to get a roommate in here before long. He waited till Mr. Yardley found his way in and then pushed Grandma down the sidewalk to a gate in the big iron fence.

"I don't like him," said his grandmother. "He's a meany beany."

Freddy was startled. Grandma's lifelong rule was to like everybody, and if she didn't like the person, she certainly never said so out loud. "Mr. Yardley?" he asked.

"I don't know who he is," said Grandma, who did not recognize her own daily aides. "But that little girl? He's mean to her."

Freddy pondered this information. There were no little girls around here. Maude was the same size as Grandma, though: down to maybe a hundred pounds with a lot of white hair that was no longer possible to brush or comb but just did its weird electric-outlet thing. Maybe Maude looked like an elementary school child to a ninety-three-year-old. Or maybe Grandma had some other little girl in mind, was thinking of all the little girls she had known over nine decades.

"He's a good guy," said Freddy. "He comes most days."

"Who does?" asked his grandmother.

"Mr. Yardley."

"Is that a friend of yours, Arthur?"

Freddy decided not to pursue this conversation. He lifted the gate bolt, too high up and too stiff for a resident to manage, even if the resident escaped the unit. They followed a paved sidewalk that wound slowly downhill toward the same neighborhood he'd just ridden through.

Sometimes he pointed out dogs and bikes and flowers to his grandmother, and after much direction, she might actually spot them. She loved airplanes and cried out with pleasure if she followed his pointing finger and actually saw a little silver streak in the sky. Once, she confided to him, "It must really be bigger than that."

Now she asked, "Where is Alice?"

Alice was Freddy's mother. She'd been killed in an accident last year. "Alice is in France," Freddy lied. Grandma had attended her daughter's funeral, but she had forgotten. Freddy usually went with the France excuse, and because his mother had loved France, visiting some region every year, he could pretend it was true. He certainly wished it was true. "You lived in France once, Grandma."

Grandma was puzzled. Freddy didn't know if she couldn't remember taking her year abroad in France or couldn't remember France in general.

Now they were among the little old homes wrapped in

old-fashioned shrubs like lilac next to old-fashioned front porches. Freddy was currently camping in Grandma's house, which was seriously old-fashioned, like a history museum for a curator who was never coming back. He'd turned the entire lower level into a glass studio. Everything he was doing in his life was a trespass on his grandparents, but especially smoking weed in the room where his anti-alcohol, anti-tobacco, anti-swearing grandpa had watched baseball and worked on his model trains.

Grandma said in a panicky voice, "Arthur?"

He circled the chair and stooped beside her again. "It's me, Freddy," he said softly. "Everything's okay, Grandma."

He often made this ridiculous claim. Sometimes Grandma called him on it. "What's okay, Freddy?" she would ask, as if she expected a list, since certainly *she* didn't know of anything okay. But today his answer soothed her.

He picked up an especially bright-red leaf and gave it to her. She took it wonderingly, as if it held secrets.

There at the corner, maybe twenty or thirty yards away, sat the white Toyota Corolla, as if it had never moved but had been waiting patiently, knowing that Freddy, with his stoner brain and lousy short-term memory, would be back.

No, Freddy told himself, white sedans are generic. It's a different one. It can't be Doc. I need it not to be Doc.

It was going the opposite direction from before, so now the passenger side was closer to Freddy. The front-seat passenger rolled down his window and leaned out. He was young, probably not out of his teens, and skinny, with pale hair pulled into a ponytail dry as dead grass.

"Hey, Freddy," he shouted, his voice a playground taunt. *Gotcha!* Freddy had never seen him before.

The driver shoved the kid out of his way and thrust his immense torso toward the window. Doc.

Reading Group Guide

1. Dom and Clemmie aren't the only two characters that live double lives. Discuss the duality of the other characters in the book. Do you think that everyone has hidden identities? Outline the different ways that people can lead "secret lives."

2. Bentley's message to Boro on Instagram triggers the events of the book. What are your views on social media? Discuss the pros and the cons.

3. A lot of these characters are everyday but morally complex people. Did you find yourself sympathizing with any of them? What did you like about them?

4. How do you feel about Clemmie exploiting the death of a childhood friend? Is it justifiable?

5. How would you characterize the younger characters—like Harper and Bentley—in this book? Did you like them? How are they different from the older characters?

6. Johnny and Joyce both crave excitement in their quiet lives, which leads to some serious consequences. Have you ever felt this way? What did you do about it?

7. To protect her own secrets, Clemmie's main goal is to get Boro his money and help him escape—even though he's a violent drug-dealer. Do you think her motivation is selfish? How would you handle the situation?

8. If you discovered that someone close to you had a second identity, how would you react?

9. Carol-Lee was the only victim of Rudyard's who tried to report his crime, but her accusations were met with derision. Do you think she was right to speak up? Or do you agree with Barbara and Clemmie's strategy of running away from him?

10. When Clemmie is raped as a young woman, no one believes her, and when the accusations resurface in the present day, police officers don't take the matter seriously. How much do you think the ideas surrounding rape have changed?

11. How do you think the reunion between Clemmie and Billy goes? Do you think she should be entirely honest about her history? How do you think he would handle the information?

12. Clemmie seems to think that her age has protected her from any more suspicion. Do you agree? Will anyone discover her secret?

A Conversation
with the Author

What inspired you to write Clemmie's story?

It all started with her name. Names fascinate me. I've written several books (the Face on the Milk Carton series, for example) where a girl is not living under the name of her birth. In Janie's case, it was because of a complex kidnapping. But what if you're an adult who makes a careful choice to live as a different person? Why would you do that? Why would you keep it up year after year? And how? Would you become a different person once you wore a different name?

Up until now you've written mainly in the young adult genre. Why did you decide to make the switch to adult fiction?

I loved YA. I used to do school visits. It's a great way to see America—through its libraries and middle schools. But then one day I realized I'd written over seventy-five YA novels. It seemed like enough! I decided to make the switch to adult novels, and because I read mysteries by the armload, I wanted to write a mystery.

You write a lot of mystery and suspense, but what are you reading these days?

I read history, but that's slow for me; it can take a month or even two, reading here and there. Mysteries and thrillers I read at a pretty good clip. I prefer paper, but I also read ebooks. I buy new at bookstores, I buy used, I buy online, I go to two libraries—I am a book hound!

What pieces of your own life made it into the book?

I grew up in the 1950s. Those days seem as remote now as ancient Egypt or Greece. I wanted to include details that people younger than I have trouble believing. Clemmie's story is packed with those differences. And of course, a huge difference is how we react to children born out of wedlock. We don't use any of the old vocabulary. In those days, it was all about the sinful bad mother, and the father was hardly considered, unless they were forced to marry. As a young church organist, I did actually play the organ for a shotgun wedding, and I still remember both the pregnant bride and the skinny groom weeping as their grim parents escorted them to the altar.

The retirement community is a unique setting for such a dark plot—what made you want to use it as a backdrop for the narrative?

I moved from Connecticut, where many of my books are set, to South Carolina and a place called Sun City. I have had the most wonderful time here. But it's an unusual place, full of surprises, like the odd anonymity of nobody at all knowing a thing about your previous life. You can say everything or nothing. You can lead a life that is practically public property, what with your activities and neighbors and Facebook posts. But you can also lead a life invisible to everybody else, and I decided that Clemmie and her neighbors would do both of those things at the same time.

Did you do any research into real events that shaped the story?

Before She Was Helen is completely made up. I think the trick to writing fiction is to fall into your heroine's life so deeply that both you and the reader believe it must be true. *You* know it isn't true. But the reader feels you must have experienced all of this or you couldn't write about it. No. Only Clemmie went through what is described in these pages.

ACKNOWLEDGMENTS

With thanks to Kerry D'Agostino and Anna Michels. It's been a very exciting time!

ABOUT THE AUTHOR

Caroline B. Cooney is the bestselling author of more than ninety suspense, mystery, and romance novels for teenagers, which have sold over fifteen million copies and are published in several languages. *The Face on the Milk Carton* has sold over three million copies and was made into a television movie. Her books have won many state library awards and are on many book lists, such as the New York Public Library's annual teen picks. Caroline grew up in Old Greenwich, Connecticut, and spent most of her life on the shoreline of that state but is now in South Carolina near her family. She has three children and four grandchildren. She was a church organist for many years and accompanied the choirs at her children's schools.